Love, NASHVILLE

LOVE, NASHVILLE
THE MISSISSIPPI QUEEN TRILOGY

TRACY BROEMMER

Love Nashville

Mississippi Queen Trilogy, Book 1 by

Tracy Broemmer

Contemporary Romance

Published by Tracy Broemmer

Edited by Lexie Broemmer

Cover by Vanilla Lily Designs

In the spring of 2017, I participated in a friend's online book release party. Though that friend, who happens to be a fantastic writer, is not into country music, that little bit of time that day when I hung out with her and some awesome writers and readers inspired me to write a little story about a musician.

So Jennifer Ann, this one is for you.

CHAPTER 1

THE HEAVY OAK DOOR WHOOSHED CLOSED IN SLOW MOTION behind Leah Hague. She stood for a moment just inside the bar to let her eyes adjust to the atmospheric lighting. She had expected a dingy hole-in-the-wall honky tonk, but the interior of Left Fork was cozy and just trendy enough to make her hesitate. She wasn't here on business, unless you counted personal business, and her personal business at the moment required something dark and smoky and clientele too drunk to notice she was there to wallow. She wanted to be alone in a crowd, and she wanted cheap whiskey to burn her throat as she nursed the heartache for one more night.

She had *cried* this weekend.

Left Fork was a little too much like the Mississippi Queen. She couldn't lose herself here; she couldn't forget anything here if she felt too much at home. Her eyes did another sweep of the bar. She decided it wasn't as big as the Queen and then startled when she saw the inevitable stage at the back of the long, narrow building. She supposed every bar in Nashville had a stage and a star, or a wannabe at the very least, but until this moment, she hadn't paid a bit of attention to the music.

The guy on the stage was singing something about blame, but Leah dismissed him without so much as a second thought. She hadn't ever set foot in a bar in Nashville; she'd never been to Nashville before tonight, but she knew she was in the heart of Music City. She just didn't give a damn about the music or the dreams nursed or crushed here.

One more night of oblivion.

She had told herself this morning when she'd hit I-65 and headed north from Destin that she would drive halfway home, soak up one more night of whatever it took to forget what she needed to forget, and go on home. Mind on Kenzi and Joe as she drove, she had to blink back tears a few times early in the drive, but her eyes had been dry by the time she crossed the Alabama state line. She wasn't a woman to cry often, and she was sick of herself a half-hour down 65.

The guy on the stage—looked the same as any other country musician to Leah—finished a song to some paltry applause. Leah raised her eyebrows and kind of hoped that the lack of noise and excitement was due to the small crowd and not a lack of enthusiasm. Then again, she didn't care. She wasn't here to commiserate with some cowboy artist or anyone, for that matter. She wasn't here to make friends.

The whole trip had been an exorcism of sorts.

A failed exorcism, but then as much as she needed to drive the grief out, she didn't want to forget Kenzi and Joe.

"Dammit, Leah." She sighed and finally took a step into the tavern. A few people glanced at her as she made her way to the bar on her strappy navy heels. Her long legs ate up the distance quickly. She set her small navy bag down as she slid onto the stool at the end of the beautiful polished wooden bar.

She smoothed the fingers of her right hand over the shiny surface with a small hum of appreciation. They paid a pretty penny for the wood they had used to build the bar at the Queen, but she had to admit it was the main focus of their business, and as such, needed to be appealing. Like this one was. Maybe she should find something else. Surely, if she looked harder, she could find a gritty, dirty tavern where she might feel less at home and more comfortable to drown her sorrows.

The ones that would still be there in an hour or two when she slid off the barstool and made her way back into the late spring evening.

"What can I getcha?"

Leah lifted her eyes at the smoker's voice, surprised to find herself looking at a woman. Craggy-looking with severe crow's feet etched around her eyes and bushy graying brows, but definitely a woman. Her ample breasts tested the denim material that covered them, but not in a sexy way.

"Pearl."

"Excuse me?"

"Name's Pearl," the woman told her.

Leah nodded. She thought of Duncan, imagined what it would be like to walk into the Queen for the first time, belly up to the bar, and order a drink from Duncan. Hard to imagine, considering she'd known him forever. He was better-looking than Pearl, certainly, though not in any conventional way. Would he be friendly? she wondered. Well, of course he would be friendly. He was a bartender, after all. And a good guy. But would he introduce himself? Or was that a southern thing?

"I would hate to see you faced with a real tough decision," the woman muttered. Leah directed an embarrassed smirk at her, relieved to see the ghost of a smile on the woman's face.

"Jack and Coke." Leah curled her fingers into a fist and stared at the woman, inviting her to comment on her choice. Leah Hague was a wine drinker, head to toe, inside out and upside down. But she'd consumed enough Jack and Coke this weekend that she thought she might bleed amber rather than red.

The woman nodded. "Fair enough."

Leah watched her short fingers, crooked with arthritis, grab a whiskey tumbler and fill it, first with a cube of ice, a stingy shot of Jack, and then the Coke. The woman snatched a small straw and stuck it in the glass as she set the drink in front of Leah.

"Where ya from?"

Leah took a deep breath and picked the drink up to sip it. She wasn't up for talking, but she didn't want to be rude, either. Catch 22. Her parents had raised her and her sister to be courteous, hard to shrug off that upbringing even when she was so full of bitter heartache.

"Illinois," she answered simply. Pearl nodded as if Illinois was the most interesting place in North America, and then she folded her arms over her breasts and cleared her throat.

"Holler if you need something."

Leah nodded as Pearl wandered down the length of the bar. She wondered about back pain with breasts so big, even wondered why the woman hadn't had a reduction, and then she gave herself a mental shake. She set her drink down and rested her elbows on the bar.

The evening sun had been warm as she had walked the sidewalks and ducked into Left Fork. Now she shivered, thankful she had a lightweight blazer on over her cami and a bra with cups thick enough to hide her nipples, now stiff with the manufactured cold air.

The singer closed another song, and Leah was distantly aware of that same smattering of applause. But her mind was already gone, and her heart hurt again. She should call Joe. She hadn't talked to him in over a week, and she knew he would want to hear from her.

But she couldn't.

Maybe tomorrow. Maybe back at the Queen. Back to real life.

The guy started singing again, and even though Leah was not a country music fan, she recognized the song. Who didn't know the classic Conway Twitty song 'Hello, Darlin'?'" She ducked her head and rubbed her fingertips over the bridge of her nose. A headache was pushing its way behind her eyes, and the whiskey was a bad idea.

She picked the drink up and sipped again. She didn't love the taste of it. Duncan handled the hard liquor purchases. Now and then he involved the rest of them in a tasting, but Leah had never acquired the *taste* for it. Just the need to be numb.

Unfortunately, she had to drive tonight. She had picked her hotel for that reason. Far enough away from downtown that she couldn't walk, therefore she couldn't stagger out of here, bombed on her ass.

"Kitchen's open until nine," Pearl told her as she made her way back down the bar. Leah started to thank her, to let her know she wouldn't be ordering, but Pearl only slid a menu toward her across the bar and moseyed on to lean into a conversation several stools down.

Would the kids be out of school now? Leah huffed out a harsh breath and tucked her hair behind her ears. Would that make it easier for Joe? Someone around to talk to? Leah bit her lip and squeezed her eyes closed. Wasn't that part of the reason he'd packed up their lives and moved them all the way across the country?

But wouldn't it be harder, too? Adelynn and Liam were busy kids; neither drove yet, and they both played summer sports, and Joe was working now. Running Edison to daycare.

Edison.

Leah dragged her fingers back through her thick hair and picked up the glass again. With Edison still in her heart, sipping time was gone. She gulped a healthy swallow and then sniffled when her eyes and her nose burned. She wondered what she was supposed to do if she'd already hit the spot where the whiskey wasn't working anymore.

"Hey, darlin'."

She shivered, though she wasn't exactly cold now. Even that stingy shot of Jack was enough to warm her. The deep voice that had just been singing was now so close to her ear, she felt the warmth of his breath there on her skin. Just a little bit turned on now by that delicious voice and a whole lot irritated that her body would betray her that easily, Leah ignored the tingle in her fingertips and the little hum low in her stomach.

Because she wanted to look, she refused to turn her head in his direction. Good grief. Was she that hard up, so stressed that two words from some wannabe Nashville star could start her up? Instead, she picked up her drink and sipped again. Set the glass down with a steady hand, eyed the elegant white gold watch on her wrist—she'd been here all of seven minutes—and finally turned her head just a tiny bit to the left with the intention of telling Nashville she wasn't interested.

Deep, dark, emerald green eyes caught hers in what she meant to be a quick once over.

Damn. She was wrong.

This guy didn't look a thing like any other musician she had ever seen. And no, she wasn't often up close and personal with musicians of any sort. But she knew it just the same, because she'd never seen such a gorgeous man. Anywhere. Leah struggled to swallow as she tore her eyes from his intense, probing gaze. That hum in her stomach kicked up a notch as she took in the razor-sharp cheekbones, the thick dark eyebrows, and the thick dark hair that fell over Nashville's forehead and curled just a bit behind his ears and over the back of his neck.

The slate blue t-shirt he wore was stretched taut over broad shoulders, and his legs appeared to go on forever. Leah tried to swallow again, but her mouth was bone dry. Being that she was five ten, she liked tall men.

Not that she was looking for any man, tall or not.

He was smiling when she dragged her eyes back up over his denim-clad legs (She wondered briefly if he was wearing Wranglers. Was that a thing? Did cowboys wear Wrangler jeans?) and his chest (also broad, not that she was really measuring) and his face. It was the ego in the smile that brought her back to her senses and saved her.

Sex with a body like that would work a hell of a lot better than whiskey to clear her head. But she didn't have time for it. No time or desire to deal with that kind of arrogance.

Still, she couldn't deny that he was the most perfect-looking man she'd ever seen. Heart still beating at the base of her throat, she looked back at her tumbler and picked it up again. Sex with that body might work better than whiskey to clear her head, but whiskey would be the far better hangover to nurse on the remainder of her drive home tomorrow.

He watched her sip her drink. When she looked at him a second time, he toned the smile down some, and rather than ego, she noticed the scruff on his jaw and perfect white teeth, and something that looked like charm.

Really, Leah?

Maybe in the south charm was equivalent to ego.

She turned her barstool a fraction of an inch toward him and noticed with amusement when his eyes grew wider. Drink still in hand, she shook her head.

"I'm not gonna sleep with you, Nashville."

Surprised to sound in control when she was still telling herself she wasn't interested in finding out what the scruff on his face would feel like in that spot where her neck and shoulder met, she snorted softly when he sagged his shoulders in defeat and jokingly ducked his chin a bit.

"I would never assume such a thing, ma'am," he promised her.

Ma'am?

Did he really just call her ma'am?

"Right." She nodded as she raised her glass and tilted her head back. When she remembered she had finished the whiskey, she crunched a piece of ice and put the glass back on the bar.

"Can I buy you a drink?" he offered. Leah turned her barstool back square to the bar and rested her elbows on opposite sides of her drink. Yes, she needed another. No, she didn't want this guy to buy her anything. Any further involvement here would be a bad idea.

"What's your name?" He turned square on his seat and rested his arms on the bar, too. Only he laid his forearms long ways on the bar and folded one hand over the other. He looked at her, though, and Leah ignored the way his t-shirt molded those wide shoulders. Instead, she focused on his face, and it hit her again. That…charm.

He appeared friendly.

Were guys this drop-dead good-looking friendly?

When she didn't answer him, he arched his eyebrows and tilted his head.

"Leah." Her voice was gruff this time, and she had a flash of memory suddenly of Kenzi and Joe. Reminded that she wasn't here to make friends, that she wasn't here to have fun, she turned away from him again and stared straight ahead. The prerequisite mirror behind the bar hung low, and Leah was taller than most women, so unfortunately, she found herself staring at a woman who looked to be a good ten years older than her thirty. Maybe Nashville thought she was a cougar.

She almost laughed at that; but when she looked his way again and found him watching her, she changed her mind. He certainly wasn't jailbait. Wasn't ready for a midlife crisis, either, but he'd most definitely grown out of that young cute guy vibe.

Not that it mattered.

"What're you drinking, Leah?"

She wiggled a bit on her barstool when she felt another shiver niggling at the base of her spine. That voice. God, she would hear that voice saying her name in her dreams for nights to come.

"Jack and Coke," she answered, because she desperately needed another right now.

"Okay." Nashville nodded. Leah saw him lift a finger, and a few moments later, Pearl was standing across from them. "Pearl, Leah would like another Jack and Coke."

To her credit, the woman did look at Leah as she went through the same motions to make her another drink, as if checking to make sure she did want another.

"Getcha anything off the menu, hon?"

Leah's shoulders stiffened. She hated to be called hon. Hated when strangers did it, even if they thought they were being friendly. If she heard Duncan say something like that at the Queen, she'd sock him in the gut or stomp on his toes.

"No, thank you." She flashed Pearl a small, tight smile.

"You hungry, Trace?" The woman turned to Nashville, and her face completely rearranged itself into something sweet and almost pretty. Leah flicked her eyes from Pearl to Nashville and back to Pearl. Okay, so Nashville wasn't a kid, but Pearl looked old enough to be his grandmother.

Nashville grinned sheepishly and ducked his head.

"I'm always hungry, Pearl. You know that."

"Don't I know it?" Pearl agreed. "I'll have 'em start you a—"

The woman stopped talking when Nashville shook his head.

"No time," he told her. Pearl shot a quick glance at the stage and then looked back at him.

"Suit yourself."

He smiled as Pearl made her way back down the bar.

"Leah what?"

Leah laughed softly, but she only bit her lip and shook her head.

"Where are you from?"

Hoping that his comment to Pearl about no time meant that he had to get back to the stage any minute, Leah turned on the stool to face him.

"Why does it matter?"

Nashville hesitated, but he eventually turned sideways again to face her, and Leah's eyes were drawn down over his lean-looking torso and his long legs. When she looked at his face again, he shrugged and offered her a small smile.

"Guess it doesn't," he said quietly. "You're passing through?"

"Yes." She nodded. "Back on the road tomorrow."

The wince was almost unnoticeable, but disappointment settled over his face like a mask.

"Okay." He took a deep breath and stood, giving Leah a full view of his long, broad frame. "Well...I guess I can say I had the pleasure of buying the most beautiful woman in the world a drink in a Nashville bar called Left Fork."

Leah blinked at him, stunned by his words and even more so by his soft, sincere tone. Sure, he probably said that to every woman he bumped into in Left Fork and every other damned bar in Tennessee. But it took a certain kind of man to sound sincere, and that look in his eyes zapped her. Not in her belly. Not in any special spots. Right smack in the heart.

The one that had already broken over Kenzi and Joe and the kids.

Leah opened her mouth to say something—anything—but Nashville smiled again. Frozen in place, she watched him reach toward her, and when she realized he was going to touch her, she held her breath. Her heart thundered now in her chest, Kenzi and Joe be damned, and her eyelids fluttered closed as he brushed her hair off her shoulder.

"Safe travels, Leah."

The tenderness in his voice stroked her skin as she had assumed he was going to do with his fingers. Goosebumps broke out on her flesh, but when she opened her eyes again, Nashville was gone.

Her breath came back in a rush, and her cheeks flushed with warmth that had nothing at all to do with the whiskey in the glass she still held. Realizing her hand shook just a bit, she turned back to the bar and put the drink down.

"Trace has that effect on a lot of women," Pearl told her. Leah huffed out another hard breath and nodded, chin tucked to her chest.

Maybe she should have taken him up on his offer. If he had her this worked up just from brushing her hair off her shoulder, she wondered what he could do for her alone in a bed.

…Trace has that effect on a lot of women…

Pearl's words came back to her. Hammered her right between the eyes.

Of course he had that effect on a lot of women. She lifted her chin when he strummed his acoustic guitar again. She refused to look that way, but from the intimate sound of his voice, she wondered if he was leaning in closer to the microphone.

His voice, a bit softer now, sang about a woman and her beautiful body.

"Haven't seen one get to him like you, though."

Leah blinked at Pearl. She most certainly wasn't here to listen to the chronicles of Nashville's pickups.

If Kenzi were here right now, she would give Leah an earful about not climbing the barstool and riding the singing cowboy bareback.

"He never comes to the bar until his last set's over," Pearl announced. "And everyone's gone."

CHAPTER 2

WITH A HEAVY SIGH, TRACE DIXON TAPPED ONCE ON HIS guitar and then closed his right hand around the neck. Pearl moved behind the bar, cleaning and putting away the pilsners and tumblers and pint glasses that would be used again when Left Fork opened later in the evening. Angie and Kadie moved with purpose through the main room of the bar, Angie wiping down the tables and Kadie pushing a broom ruthlessly over the floor and under the tables.

"You done?" Angie called all the way from the front of the bar.

Trace, still sitting on the wooden stool on stage, simply nodded. He'd let her get away. The most beautiful woman he'd ever seen—hadn't been a line; he didn't work that way—had been in Left Fork earlier, and he'd let her get away.

"Turn on some real music, Pearl!" Angie hollered to the woman behind the bar. Trace chuckled softly when Pearl stood with her hands propped on her hips and shot the girl a fake mean look.

"Lemme guess." Pearl cocked her head to the side. "You want that ABC group?"

"It's AC/DC," Angie corrected her. Even from the back of the long, narrow room, Trace saw the smirk on Angie's face. Seemed like they did this same routine every night at closing time.

"That's noise," Pearl muttered. She shook her head, glanced at Trace, and shrugged. He stood and carried the guitar—he called this one, his favorite, Loretta—by the neck down off the stage and toward the bar. "Beer?"

"Water." He shook his head in response to Pearl as he slipped through the door to the back of the building. There would be a sandwich waiting for him when he went back out front. He wasn't sure what kind, but Pearl would have something ready for him.

The office was dark. Sampson was long gone. Pearl was capable of running the show, and often, Sampson left her to it anymore. Trace rested his guitar on the stand in the corner of the office and then moved back through the darkness to the hall. Chino, the bald and beefy security guy, would be out back checking things over. Time to close up and go home. Sleep off the small hours and be ready to come back later in the evening.

Tanner and the guys were in Seattle tonight, if he remembered correctly. Odds were he didn't remember correctly. It used to bother him. Used to be a sharp pain, like a knife twisting in his gut. Now, mostly, Tanner and the guys and...Shelly...more like arthritis that woke up now and then and made him uncomfortable.

The sounds of AC/DC pounded out in the main room of the bar. Trace winced and rolled his head on his neck. He liked them as much as the next guy, but at the moment, it was the last thing he wanted to hear.

Angie and Kadie were still working, both of them crooning along now to the music, when he approached the bar. Pearl set a glass of ice water next to his plated grilled chicken and fries. He eyed the sandwich wearily. Hunger had come and gone hours ago. Eating now would mean indigestion.

Under Pearl's watchful eye, he picked the sandwich up in both hands, bit off a big bite, and chewed slowly. He was still restless, and he was still thinking about her, but he was amused by the show Angie and Kadie put on. They were good girls. Angie had no interest in country music; she'd grown up in Michigan and moved down here when she was fifteen to live with her aunt and uncle. Blond, blue-eyed Kadie hailed from Kentucky, loved country, and had a beautiful voice. She'd been at Left Fork for not quite a year, bussing tables, waitressing, bartending now and then, and lately, Sampson had let her on stage a few times. She'd be a crowd favorite once she got over the nerves.

"What'd she say?" Trace asked Pearl around a mouthful of his sandwich.

Pearl tended to look tired and frumpy and a bit frazzled at the start of a shift, so Trace was never sure how tired she was by one in the morning. He used to ask, but he learned quickly that she took offense to that sort of question as if anyone in the bar would question her stamina or her desire to do her job.

"Who?"

Trace scooped a handful of fries up and looked at her sideways. At least thirty years his senior, if not more, Pearl Allen was one of his closest friends. She knew damned well whom he was talking about.

"The woman I was talking to. With the dark blond hair and the pretty eyes." He shrugged as if to ask *who else?*

"She's from Illinois." Pearl stood with the bar rag in hand as if she was all done cleaning except for the small spot on the bar where he was eating his early morning dinner.

"And?"

Pearl shook her head.

"Nothing?" he asked quietly. "Did she pay with a credit card?"

Pearl's harsh laughter made Trace cringe and shove his sandwich into his mouth again. Angie and Kadie both glanced at her and eyed the two of them curiously, but neither of them commented.

"You're—? You're serious?" Pearl raised her eyebrows.

"I am."

"She paid with cash. For both drinks, by the way," Pearl told him. Trace bit off a silent curse and shook his head. "And even if she had paid by credit card, I wouldn't let you look at the slip. That's stalking."

Appetite dead in the water, Trace tossed his napkin on the plate and pushed it away. Pearl snatched it immediately as if she worried he would change his mind and eat the rest, keeping them from locking up and heading home.

"She told me her name," he offered.

"Obviously not her last name," Pearl mumbled. Trace rolled his eyes when she shot him a quick look.

"Did she leave a glass slipper or anything?"

"Nope." Pearl shook her head. "She wasn't very talkative. Didn't want anything to eat. Insisted on paying for both drinks."

He pinched the bridge of his nose and then rested his elbow on the bar and his chin in his hand.

"Damn."

"Tanner had a show tonight." Pearl tossed the words out casually, but Trace didn't know why she was feeling him out. They had talked that whole damned story to death. There was nothing either of them could add to it, so there was nothing for Pearl to be sly about now.

"Seattle."

"Shelly still with him?"

Trace stared across the room at the door. His heart had just about exploded out of his chest when she walked in earlier. He had had women; he'd had a little bit of love and a little bit of heartache, and he'd had a hell of a lot of fun, and he'd had the last year or two to himself. But he'd never seen a woman as beautiful as Leah from Illinois.

When he saw from the corner of his eye that Pearl was watching him, he shook his head and shrugged dramatically.

"I dunno, Pearl," he mumbled. "Tanner and I don't have much to say to each other anymore, remember?"

To her credit, Pearl apparently decided to let it go. She carried his plate back through the swinging door to the kitchen. Trace heard the silverware clatter to the sink, and then he heard Pearl talking to the new dishwasher Sampson had hired.

He was too damned old for this. For the late nights. The later dinners. The lovestruck feeling he had all damned night after he'd seen Leah—possibly the prettiest women he'd ever seen—walk into Left Fork. He couldn't remember the last time he'd been tempted to walk off the stage and talk to a woman at the bar. Not to proposition her. Hell, he was way too damned old for that. And she had been far too classy to proposition for one night, anyway.

"Did she tell you where she's staying?" Pearl paraded through the swinging doors again, a stack of three cookies in hand. Trace groaned and rubbed his already aching stomach.

"What? No." He scowled at her as he reached for the cookies he didn't want or need. Took a big bite of one.

She had smelled good when he leaned in close to her to say hello. Maybe it had been too cheesy. Calling her darlin'. It had taken her a minute to look at him, but when she did, she had seemed amused. Hit him in the heart with her words not because he had been about to ask her for sex. But because she struck him as witty and fun, and her warm brown eyes had lit him up.

"She did seem a little…" Pearl rested her hands on the bar and narrowed her eyes in thought. Trace held his breath. If she said starstruck, he'd let it go.

"What?" he urged her when she still didn't go on. Chomped another cookie down. Cookies weren't on their menu, but they always had a jar full of something homemade for the help. Trace would blame Sampson and Pearl when he got too fat to haul his ass up on stage and sing.

"Out of breath," Pearl decided as her eyes met his. "When you walked away."

"Out of breath," he repeated. Well, people could be out of breath because of attraction and because they'd just run an eight-minute mile, too. "Not helpful."

"Sad," Pearl continued.

"Sad?" He groaned and sat back on the barstool. "You kidding me? Like I made her sad? For talking to her?"

"No." Pearl snorted softly and shook her head. "She wasn't

happy when she walked in here. *You* took her breath away."

Well, *that* was something. That was different than saying she seemed out of breath, wasn't it? Trace wanted to think he had taken her breath away. But if he didn't know anything more about her than her name—who knew if Leah was really her name, anyway—and that she was from Illinois, maybe, it didn't mean anything if he had.

Didn't matter that her fingers were bare, either. He'd looked before he sat down by her at the bar. Marriage and commitment were important to him. He would have walked right on by if she had a ring on her finger.

"You got time to practice that song with me tomorrow, Trace?"

Trace dragged his eyes from Pearl to look at Kadie as she pushed her broom toward her pile of dust and crumbs— Trace raised his eyebrows, was that shiny piece of foil a condom wrapper? Here?—in the middle of the floor. What the hell? Left Fork was a nice establishment. Not the kind of place you'd find a condom wrapper on the floor. Not even in the bathroom, especially not in the bar area.

His mind flashed him a picture of the woman who'd said her name was Leah. Those eyes. Her shiny pink lips. The legs that had gone on for a day and a half. Damn. He imagined those legs wrapped around his waist and the rest of her body pressed up against his.

"Trace?" Kadie moved closer to him. She punched his arm playfully. Trace cleared his throat and blinked away the mental image. He was a guy, and he liked sex as much as the next guy. But now wasn't the time to indulge in fantasies like that. Fantasies that weren't going to happen, because the odds of finding that one particular Leah in all of Illinois were slim to none.

"Sure, Kadie." He nodded. She grinned and gushed a thank you and then turned her attention back to her task. Trace finished the cookies and stood.

"What is that?" He walked closer to the pile of debris, eyes still on what appeared to be a condom wrapper. "Did we have somebody gettin' dirty in the corner?"

"What?" Kadie looked up at him.

Trace squatted down and pointed toward the wrapper.

"Eww." Kadie shivered. "That looks like…"

"Oh gross." Angie joined them. "Makes me wonder where the condom is."

"We might need to step up the security out here," Trace said quietly. Left Fork was a reputable place, and tourists often came in to grab a cold drink and escape the heat. Tourists meant children. He looked at the rest of the debris. Looked like a few business cards. Toothpick wrappers. A nickel, but he wasn't about to reach through the dust and crumbs to grab it.

"I feel like we're on a crime show," Kadie said with a giggle. She used the toe of her boot to nudge one of the business cards. "Hmm. Looks like…" She bent at the waist to read the card. Trace glanced at her, but he looked away quickly. Her scoop neck shirt hung low enough that he had a good view of her breasts, but he wasn't interested. Maybe she wasn't jailbait, but he'd never been into younger girls, wild or not.

"Roddy Pelman," Angie said from where she was standing. "Damn, Kadie, you need glasses."

"Roddy Pelman is our suspect." Kadie shrugged off Angie's comment.

"What's the crime?" Angie asked with a grin. "Tumbling someone to one of Trace's love songs? Slipping some chick the drumstick?"

"You're sick." He pointed his finger at her. Angie, more the type to intentionally flash him her boobs, laughed and went back to work on the tables. Kadie laughed softly as she straightened. Trace propped his hands on his knees and let his eyes roam over the pile of debris again. Two more business cards there. No idea why, he tapped them to turn them flat. Kandra Morrison. Leah Hague.

He stood slowly. Thinking it was about that time. He would go home and hit the medicine cabinet. Swallow some Tums. Remind himself to either eat around seven or eight tomorrow night—right around the time he had been talking to Leah, tonight—or not eat at all, and then crawl into bed and hope for at least a few hours of sleep.

Wait.

Leah.

Leah Hague.

"Wait!" He moved quickly and snatched that particular card from the pile.

Kadie and Angie watched him curiously, but he ignored them and studied the simple yet elegant dove grey card in his hand. The name and address in black ink in the top corner. Two black lines and then he assumed a place of business and title. And phone numbers.

Leah Hague. Adams Bay, Illinois. Mississippi Queen. Owner/Purchasing. 555-9100 or 555-7719.

CHAPTER 3

Leah tapped her fingers on her coffee mug, eyes on the desktop computer, though the letters blurred, and her mind was on other things. Not on babies or friends or heartaches and missed phone calls, but dark green eyes and dark hair and slate blue t-shirts that looked soft to the touch.

Definitely not what she should be thinking about now.

Leah groaned and pressed her fingers into her eye sockets. Why hadn't she just touched him? Just to see if his shirt was as soft as it looked? So what if her fingers had brushed over the skin of his arm in the process? There was no question about the muscle under his skin. Definitely there. But Leah wondered now how firm it was, if the skin over it was soft and warm.

"Jesus, Leah," she whispered. She pinched the bridge of her nose, squeezed her eyes closed tight like a little kid wishing away monsters, and then sat up and cleared her throat. Trained her eyes back on the big screen on the desk and read the first few words of the email from one of her wine distributors.

Joe had called her on the drive home. At least she assumed it was Joe. Heart in her throat, she'd stared at the number on her digital display in the car. The cold sweat had been instant and the stomachache nearly, and she had once again taken the coward's way out. She figured the call would go to voicemail, and she planned to check it when she stopped for a caffeine break or to run into the bathroom after consuming too much coffee and caffeine. There hadn't been a message, though, and Leah sat in her car, paralyzed with the ridiculous idea that maybe it had been Kenzi.

She knew better.

Of course, she knew better.

Even now, though, her heart hammered in her fingers and knees and her ears at the possibility that it had been Kenzi who called her. But that was crazy.

Wasn't it?

Leah drew in a deep breath through her nose and closed her eyes again. Man, she needed to pull herself together. She'd just driven to Florida and left Margo and Stevi to run things—over a weekend, no less—for exactly that reason. Now here she was back in the office and feeling (looking, too) as strung out as ever.

Thinking about Kenzi and Joe.

And dammit all, if that damned cowboy hadn't starred in her dreams last night. Not the night before. Not the night he'd joined her at the bar at Left Fork and called her darlin' and oozed charm all over her. Nope. She would have expected it then. Nope. She had slept a solid six hours the night she left the Nashville bar, driven home with her mind constantly roving from Kenzi and Joe, to the kids, back to Kenzi and Joe, and to Nashville. The cowboy, not the city.

She had walked into her own kitchen midafternoon, taken a long look around the spacious room lit by the late day sun, and doubled over, breathless with tears and anger. She had run; she had run all the way to Florida and come home to find that nothing had changed.

Nothing had changed.

Leah breathed in again, the deep cleansing kind of breath that her yoga instructor taught, and then counted to five as she exhaled.

"Nothing's going to change, Leah." Her whisper sounded gruff even to her own ears. She lifted her mug and took another big drink as someone knocked loudly on the closed office door. She didn't look that way as the door swung open.

"You look like hell."

Leah jumped and moaned over the coffee that sloshed over the rim of the cup. She used to have a favorite mug she used all the time. Lately, she was doing well to find one clean. Everyone else was doing his or her part to keep things running smoothly, but Leah was struggling, and every day she reached blindly for whichever mug was on the counter or in the sink and half the time, it had already been used.

She could be offended by her younger sister's comment, especially considering Stevi didn't even look at her when she paraded into the office. But she knew it was true—she'd knotted her hair on the back of her head, yanked on yoga pants and a t-shirt, and brushed her teeth before coming in this morning.

Leah watched Stevi pace around the room. Her sister was dressed similarly, though her yoga pants were hot pink, and she wore a form-fitting shirt that outlined her slim hips, tiny waist, and big boobs. Leah eyed her sister's figure and wondered for the million and first time how she was so petite and cute and peppy and Leah was…not.

Stevi, her hair—naturally a lighter blond than Leah's—pulled back in a tight ponytail, perched on the arm of the oversized leather couch across from the desk. As much as she loved her, it hurt to look at something so shiny and perky at the moment, so Leah let her eyes slide over the cognac-colored sofa and remembered the day the guys had moved it upstairs to the office.

If she remembered correctly, and she did because she was cursed with an excellent memory, there'd been a lot of cussing, a few pinched fingers, a fight between an elbow and the doorway (doorway won) and a lot of beer consumed when the moving was done.

"Demons out?" Stevi asked quietly.

Leah moved her eyes slowly over the sofa to Stevi's hands, folded in her lap as if in prayer. She let her gaze climb up over her torso. Lips pressed firmly together, Leah ran her tongue over her teeth. The taste of toothpaste was long gone, replaced by the black breakfast blend coffee she favored.

She felt it in her belly. That zap of guilt when her eyes met Stevi's. They wanted her to feel better. It had nothing to do with the Queen. Stevi, Duncan, Margo—even Jess— wanted her to feel better. They had all bent over backwards lately to be supportive. They had assured her they would be fine if she took off for the weekend—not that she doubted them.

The fact that she came home feeling just as heavy-hearted as when she left made her feel guilty. So guilty she didn't want to admit it. Instead, she answered Stevi with a half-hearted shrug and looked away. She opened her mouth, but she had nothing to say.

"Leah, it's okay."

Stevi's whisper was below the belt. Leah didn't cry much at all, but she had spent the weekend wallowing and those emotions were still raw. That whisper only scratched the surface, but it stung Leah, and it hurt.

She nodded.

"Um." She cleared her throat. "Dare Hollow is offering us cases of that cab at forty percent off."

From the corner of her eye, she saw Stevi roll her eyes. Didn't matter. She rolled her chair back just enough to shift on it and draw her leg up to sit on her foot. Set her cup down and rubbed her face with her fingertips.

"The limit is six. I think I'm gonna do it," she continued, even though Stevi had to hear the tremor in her voice.

"Okay."

She blinked at the screen on the desk.

"Anything exciting happen here?" She took a quick breath, irritated that it sounded more like a sniffle. She didn't want Stevi to think she was going to cry. Not here.

"Mmm." Stevi twisted around to pop her back. "Not really. We had a couple get engaged Saturday night." She twisted around the other way. Leah cringed when she heard her sister's bones pop.

"Seriously?" Leah grinned. Okay, that was kind of cool. "And that's not exciting?"

"They aren't local," Stevi said simply.

"Still." Leah flopped backwards in the chair and threw her arms wide. "That says a lot about our atmosphere. Tell me you guys got some pictures and stuff to use for social media."

"Already posted," Stevi answered as she stood and crossed the room to the window on the west wall. Leah squinted when she opened the blinds. The sun off the Mississippi late in the day was hell; morning sunshine was bad enough.

"That's neat." Leah pursed her lips.

"Duncan set 'em up with a free bottle of champagne."

"Oh." Leah nodded her approval. "Did he know about it before?"

"Nope. The couple had reservations. Came in about ten minutes early. Had dinner. I think they were drinking wine." Stevi looked back over her shoulder at Leah. "It was kind of early, but we were steady. The next thing you know, the guy was on his knee and he pulled out this diamond. God, it was so big, it looked like one of those old-fashioned doorknobs Grandma Hague used to have at her house."

Leah laughed softly. Stevi was exaggerating, but still, the diamond must have been a little obnoxious. Stevi was a little on the outrageous side, so the rock must have been something else for her to make that comment.

"And Berkley said *Stevi*."

"My ass." Leah winked at her. Stevi stuck her tongue out. Their cousin Margo's little girl was ten months old, and both Leah and Stevi had been trying to teach her to say their names. So far Berkley's favorite words included *no* and *da*, which, of course, Duncan was convinced was *Duncan*, not *dad*.

With the way Margo felt about Berkley's father, Leah figured she would be okay with her daughter learning to say *Duncan* before she did *dad*.

Stevi turned to Leah and sat on the window ledge. Leah cringed. She hated it when Stevi did that. They were three stories up, and a fall from that window would be a really ugly death.

"I have a date tonight," Stevi announced.

Leah swallowed the sour taste in her mouth and looked back at the computer screen. She had been watching her dare devil little sister's crazy antics for as long as she could remember. Stevi tended to push the envelope, especially when she knew it riled Leah up when she did so. Now, though, she didn't appear to be pushing Leah.

"Would you please move out of that window?"

"I'm not gonna fall out," Stevi argued, but thankfully, she moved. It crossed Leah's mind that she moved without argument because all of them considered her fragile right now.

The last damned thing she ever allowed herself to be was fragile. Time to smash all those bad feelings back down her throat and put a lid on them. She had to pull herself together. Leah Hague didn't need pity.

"Who's the lucky guy?"

Stevi flashed her a sweet smile that took Leah back twenty years. Her sister could be a real pain in the ass, but she loved her without condition.

"Just a friend." Stevi shook her head. "Of a friend."

Leah nodded. Took a drink of her coffee. She could push Stevi for more details. But she didn't want to. Stevi was a serial dater, and she owned it. At twenty-eight, Stevi had dated more guys than Leah could claim to know. She had been serious about one a few years ago, but when that romance ended abruptly, Stevi had picked her heart up and dusted it off. After a night or two of crying over wine and ice cream, she was back on the market.

"So, I think Duncan said something about the floors."

Leah nodded. She hadn't talked to him directly, but he texted her this morning—two in the morning, actually—and there were only at least five signs up in the bar downstairs and up the staircase and plastered on the mezzanine floor, and a few more up on this floor where the office was. He had a crew coming in to wax the hardwood floors today. In fact, Leah assumed they would be here any minute, so everything would be done by opening later this afternoon.

Stevi folded her arms over her chest and cocked her head to study Leah. Recognizing that look, Leah searched her mind for something to say to head her off. She couldn't stand another moment of concern or pity.

"Do you listen to much country music?"

Stevi blinked at her, screwed her face up in confusion, and shook her head.

"I'm sorry." She dropped her arms to her sides and stepped closer to the desk. "Did my Frank-Sinatra-loving sister just ask me about country music?"

Already regretting the question, Leah answered with a small smile. She scooted the chair closer to the desk again and reached for the phone. Time to get busy. She would call her distributor and order the Dare Hollow cab now to take advantage of the sale and cross one thing off her list.

"Why do you ask?" Stevi drummed her fingers on top of the computer screen.

Leah ignored her, kept her eyes on the screen. She slid her fingers off the phone and moved them to the mouse to scroll through the rest of her email. She would argue that she wasn't a Frank-Sinatra-loving sister, but nine days out of ten, she listened to the crooners or jazz music.

"No reason," she mumbled. She shouldn't have asked. Because even though she wanted to tell Stevi and Margo, both, about Nashville—the guy, not music city—she knew it wasn't a good idea to make a big deal of it.

"Got an ear worm from the drive?"

Leah chuckled and lifted only her eyes to look at Stevi.

"Really? You think I listened to country music when I was totally alone in my car?"

Okay, so she had. For a little while. She couldn't say why, because she doubted that if Nashville were famous he would be on a little stage in a bar instead of on the road playing for fans. Still, she had searched for local stations as she headed out of Tennessee yesterday.

"Why do you ask?" Stevi whined. Leah groaned. Why had she opened her mouth? Stevi had been the one to wear their parents down when they were kids. Always with the nagging and the questions. The snooping for birthday or Christmas presents. The wheedling to get their mom or dad to let her and Leah have an extra hour of play before bedtime. The way she had always been able to worm Leah's deepest, darkest secrets from her when they lay awake in their dark bedroom and they were supposed to be sleeping.

Not that Leah had ever had much in the way of deep, dark secrets. That seemed to be more Stevi's territory. True, she lived life loud and bold, and she was unapologetic about it. But if either of them ventured into deep and dark, it was more likely to be Stevi than Leah.

"Are there any big-name stars named Trace?"

"Trace Adkins?" Stevi frowned and hitched a shoulder.

Leah managed to keep her mouth from dropping open in shock.

"Why?" Stevi pressed.

It couldn't be the same person. Could it?

"Never mind." Leah shook her head.

"Did you meet him?" Stevi asked. Before Leah could deny it, Stevi rushed around the desk and grabbed for the sleek little keyboard.

"What're you doing?"

"Him?" Stevi pushed Leah's hand away from the mouse, closed Leah's email, and clicked on the Safari icon. Leah sat back as Stevi's pale blue fingernails flew over the keys. She moved her eyes from her little sister to the screen when Stevi looked at her expectantly. "Did you meet him?"

The guy on the screen was most definitely not the man she'd seen in the bar.

"Nope." She was relieved she could be honest with Stevi, because her sister could sniff out a lie better than a veteran detective. Or their mom. Same difference. And yet, she kind of hoped her sister could find the mystery man.

Not that she would do anything about it. But she could listen to his music and see if she liked it.

"No?" Stevi slumped against the desk, obviously disappointed. "But you met someone."

Stevi's laser eyes burned a hole in the top of Leah's head.

"I don't know if I'd say I met someone," she mumbled, and instantly, just like every other time, she regretted that she caved so easily. Stevi turned and rested her butt on the edge of the desk and stood in Leah's personal space and favored her with an enthusiastic grin.

"Tell me."

"Stevi, it's nothing."

"Right, okay." Stevi shrugged. "Tell me anyway."

Leah sighed.

"Did you sleep with him?"

"Are you kidding me?"

Stevi snorted and quickly covered her mouth.

"Who is he?" she asked. "Tell me."

"Nope." Leah picked up her nearly empty mug and stood up. "Not now."

"Because I asked if you—?" Stevi followed her to the door, so close on her heels that when Leah stopped to turn around, Stevi plowed into her.

"Good thing this is almost empty." Leah looked at her mug and then at Stevi.

"Look, I forgot that you have sex like once every seven years. Sue me—"

"Seven years?" Leah frowned. "Really?"

"Seven-year itch?" Stevi asked. "Isn't that a thing?" She waved her hands as if to dismiss the question. "Leah. Did you meet someone?"

"No." Leah shrugged. "I didn't meet someone."

"But?" Stevi grabbed Leah's upper arms and gave her a shake.

"Chill, Stevi." Leah rolled her eyes. "It hasn't been seven years."

"I'm tellin' Margo and Duncan."

"You will anyway."

"So, you did meet someone."

Leah turned away from Stevi and headed out of the office. Stevi followed like a faithful puppy. Or maybe more like a tenacious bulldog, Leah decided as her sister continued the whining to know what Leah had been about to say.

Duncan stood on a chair in the small kitchenette they used as their break room. Hands stretched above his head, eyes on a light fixture, he muttered to Margo, who stood at the counter with her own coffee mug in her hands.

"You got the wrong kind of bulbs," he told her.

"What difference does it make?" Margo asked in a tone that sounded as if she might have already asked once or twice.

"The wattage is wrong. It'll be darker here in the center of the room—"

"Leah met someone last weekend," Stevi announced. Leah cringed when Margo swung her eyes to her, and Duncan's hands stilled on the bulb.

"Was it good?" Margo asked.

Duncan barked a laugh and muttered something about girl talk and cousins and sisters and needing a drink.

"Actually, unlike my immoral little sister here, I didn't leave the bar with him." Leah crossed the room. She snagged the coffee pot from the machine and refilled her cup.

"So, you did meet someone." Stevi nodded and pointed at her. "His name is Trace."

"In fact, even though he was easily the most beautiful man on earth," Leah continued.

"—I'm wounded," Duncan interrupted her.

Leah rolled her eyes and laughed softly. "My first words to him were *I'm not going to sleep with you, Nashville.*"

Stevi arched her eyebrows and tapped a nail on her upper lip.

"Trace. You met a guy named Trace. In Nashville."

"Why's his name Trace?" Margo asked Stevi.

"She asked me if I knew a country music star named Trace."

"Trace Adkins," Margo offered.

"Nope." Stevi shook her head. "Looked him up. Not him."

"Trace Dixon."

"Who's Trace Dixon?" Stevi asked. She took Leah's cup from her hands and took a drink. Leah cocked her head and waited for Stevi to make the usual face at the swallow of strong, black coffee. Her sister was a fan of specialty coffees, heavy on the calories. "Yuck." She shivered and handed the mug back to Leah, her attention still on Margo.

"Tanner Dixon's brother," Margo answered.

"And you know this, how?" Leah asked Margo. "You binge-watching the Grand Ole Opry, Margo?"

"Tanner Dixon and the Lightnin' Congregation," Margo said simply. "You've heard their song 'Tempted.'"

"Nope." Leah shook her head. "Pretty sure I haven't."

"Really?" Stevi's mouth dropped open in surprise. "I love that song."

"Seriously?" Leah glanced at Stevi. She had never heard of the song. Or the band. Or the name Tanner Dixon. But she slid a foot toward the door, anxious to get back to the office so she could search the name Trace Dixon. She wanted to see if it was the same person, and for some ridiculous reason, she wanted to search by herself.

"Tanner Dixon is sex in blue jeans," she heard Stevi mumble as she slipped out of the room.

"Tell me," Margo agreed.

Leah's stomach was a little achy and edgy now, but this time it was anticipation. Had she met Trace Dixon? Seemed possible. If Stevi and Margo believed Tanner Dixon to be sex in blue jeans, seemed possible the Trace she had met in Nashville was his brother. That guy had a beautiful face, bedroom eyes, southern charm, and his body had filled out the denim and left little to her imagination.

She swept her gaze over the elaborate wooden railing and eyed the main floor of the Queen appreciatively. There were times when she would stop here and stand at the rail and admire the dream she and her sister and cousin had achieved. The Queen had made the top five list for bar and grills in town for the second year in a row. They'd landed at five the first year, moved to four this year. If Leah had any say so, they'd claw their way up a notch or two next year.

Her mind on Trace and the denim and the possibility of finding out the guy's last name—not that it mattered—she moved quickly to the office. She set her coffee on the corner of the desk and leaned over the keyboard, much the same way Stevi had just a few minutes ago.

She tapped the keys, fingers fumbling in her excitement, and looked at the screen as she hit enter. Her nails weren't as long as Stevi's, and she needed a manicure, and holy hell, Nashville's dark bedroom eyes stared at her from the computer screen and made her shiver with longing.

Stevi shrieked from just down the hall. Leah chuckled and dropped to the chair behind the desk. Raised her eyes as Stevi crashed into the room, Margo right behind her.

"Are you freaking kidding me?" Stevi gushed. Her cheeks were pink with excitement. "You met that absolutely delicious hunk of man, and you didn't sleep with him? Leah Hague, what the hell is wrong with you?"

Leah huffed out a quick breath and looked away. She wasn't one to jump into bed with anyone too soon. Nor did she get involved in relationships easily. And she'd been away for the weekend to do some...well, not soul-searching, exactly. But to clear her head.

Not get laid.

CHAPTER 4

Trace eyed the mower parts strewn all across his garage floor. He had only planned to change the belts on the damned thing, and now here he was an hour later with grease under his fingernails and on the knees of his holey jeans with the whole mower torn apart around him. He reached for his big tumbler of water and rubbed his other hand over the back of his head and neck. The day had started on the warm slide, and the temperature had climbed by the hour.

He supposed it wasn't a bad thing to go all in with the tune up on the rider. It was getting old—that thought made him laugh and wince at the same time—and it had been a long time since anyone had paid it any tender loving care.

Trace swallowed a mouthful of water and sat back on his booted feet. He had nothing against his aging riding mower, but he could think of other things he'd like to show a little tender loving care. He'd been carrying Leah

Hague's business card around in his billfold for three days now. He had tucked it away the other night when neither Angie nor Kadie was looking, though he figured Pearl had probably noticed.

They hadn't talked again about Leah Hague from Illinois. Maybe Pearl believed he'd moved on.

"Right." He nodded and chuckled to himself. "Moved on."

The hell of it was, Trace could have any woman he wanted any day of the week. Shelly had worked her way into his bed, and from there, she'd batted her eyelashes and oohed and aaahed over Tanner and before long, she'd moved from Trace's arms to Tanner's bed, or more accurately Tanner's tour bus. She hadn't broken Trace—maybe his relationship with his brother, but not his heart. He had never even been tempted to give the gold digger his heart.

But that was the trouble. Other than his first love when he was seventeen, and a girl he met in college, he had never given anyone his heart. Never been tempted by any of the girls that hung around late at night after the shows with Tanner. He wasn't tempted now with the women who hung out at Left Fork.

Except for Leah Hague. Okay, maybe he wasn't ready to box his heart up and ship it to her. He raised his eyebrows, a little bit amused at the thought. It brought to mind stalker movies. The last thing he wanted to do was scare her or make her uncomfortable.

But he did want to...*what, Trace? What do you want to do?*

Music blared from the speakers he hung in the back corners of the garage when he moved in a few years ago. The heavy sounds of Shinedown surrounded him. As much as he loved country music, and he did, he listened to a little bit of everything. He had decided earlier that working outside today called for some rock.

He wasn't going to kid himself. Love at first sight happened in movies; he wasn't pining away for a woman he didn't know. But damned if he didn't want to get to know her. She was beautiful, and she'd handled him in seconds, though the last thing he had intended to do the other night was hit on her for sex.

It had been just a little bit flirty, the way she'd made him wait just a second before turning to him and telling him she wasn't going to sleep with him. She hadn't given him her last name or a phone number, but she had smiled at him.

He'd gone to bed after three that morning, and when he dragged himself out of bed later and made his coffee, he'd pulled her business card from his wallet and read it over and over until he might possibly have memorized her contact information. Coffee mug in tow, he'd sat at the messy, antique desk his grandparents left in the house when they moved into the retirement home and booted up his computer.

Rather than go right to social media, he'd typed Mississippi Queen in the search bar. Hadn't been a surprise when links directing him to the rock band Mountain appeared. Links to lyrics for the song. Pages of links for information on the Mississippi River. Finally, half way through the first mug, he'd added Adam's Bay, Illinois to his search and bingo, he'd struck the jackpot.

Leah Hague was part owner of the bar and grill, Mississippi Queen, located in Adam's Bay on the Mississippi. Her partners were a younger sister and a cousin. Trace had perused the Queen's website, read every last bit of text, but he was disappointed there wasn't much personal info there about the owners. Technically, that was wise; three women owning a bar and grill didn't need to be splashing personal information on the Internet. But, Trace wanted to know more about *her*.

He'd studied the pictures on the site, though most of them were of the building and not the women who owned it. The place looked gorgeous; Sampson would probably trade his sac for a bar like theirs. Sure, Left Fork was a nice place, but Mississippi Queen appeared to be bigger and a bit more upscale. Trace had lost a few minutes to the pictures of the bar and décor; the wooden floors were buffed to a high shine. The bar itself was a thing of beauty. Trace didn't know enough about wood variation to know what the bar was made of, but it certainly commanded attention. He supposed it was the pride of the place.

There were headshots of the three women and a guy named Duncan. Trace hadn't been able to figure out where he fit in. He was listed as a mixologist, and something green and a little slimy-feeling in his gut made Trace roll his eyes at that. Duncan was a bartender; no matter how fancy you wanted it to sound, the guy catered to clientele who wanted a drink. What Trace wasn't sure about was who he was to the women who owned the bar. There was a picture of all four of them together, arms slung around each other's shoulders and faces lit with carefree smiles. If he had to guess, Trace would say the picture wasn't professional; they hadn't posed like that with the intention of using the photo on the website. It looked too warm and comfortable, like the four of them had been laughing together over something, and someone happened to snap a picture of the moment.

Leah stood next to Duncan. Leah, with her longish, dark blond hair wispy and loose around her shoulders, had her arm around this guy. Duncan's bald head shined like the polished floors in their bar. Razor sharp cheekbones drew the eye to his lean, hard face. He looked solid, but not big. Casual in jeans, a gray t-shirt, and flip-flops, the guy had the look of former military. Trace would never admit it to anyone, but he'd spent too much damned time studying the guy's smile, trying to decide if they were all friends, or if Leah and Duncan were more than friends.

Trace gave himself a mental shake now and wiped the side of his face with the tail of his t-shirt. He reached for the new belt he had picked up for the rider, but his head was still on Leah. On the website. They were on Facebook, but he hadn't allowed himself to go look at their page. That felt a bit too much like stalking, so when he'd reached for his mug and found it empty, he'd walked away from his computer and hit the shower.

He most definitely planned to contact her. He just hadn't made up his mind yet how to do it. If he were Tanner, he'd park his tour bus in front of her place and wait for her to come running. He'd asked his brother—when he had crowed about buying the bus— if he was trying to compensate for something with the big, shiny vehicle. Tanner had taken a swing at him, but Trace had simply dodged his fist and walked away.

One thing Trace was certain of. When he sat down beside Leah Hague at the bar and said hello, when she'd looked at him and turned him down instantly, she had no idea who he was. Not that she would have mounted him at the bar if she had known (he'd seen it happen more than once). Trace hadn't met a woman in years who didn't know his face or his name. He was a little bit giddy inside that he'd gotten so lucky that the first woman who didn't recognize him was also so damned beautiful, so sexy, the air around them at Left Fork had vibrated with electric energy.

Oh hell yes, he was going to contact her.

Something to get her attention, though no severed hearts or other body parts. He might be determined to get to know her, but he wasn't crazy.

He scooted closer to the mower deck and wound the belt around the metal pulley.

A phone call might be too much to start with. But he could text her. He had looked on the website and noticed that the first number listed on her card was the bar's number. So he assumed the second was her cell.

Not exactly crazy—

Least I never was before.

Trace hesitated, hunched over the mower deck, and lifted his chin. He stared at the old Pennzoil sign hanging on the back wall of the garage.

But then crazy came to get me

He let go of the belt and winced when it slipped free of the pulley. Muttered as he climbed to his feet and took a giant step over the deck, nearly losing his balance. Eyes wild, he bellied up to the workbench at the wall and dug through his tools to find something to write on. His fingers brushed an old notepad with a now defunct auto parts store logo at the top. He rooted through a bin of junk until he found a short little pencil like the kind at a miniature golf course and scribbled the words down.

When you walked out that door.

The Shinedown song playing now hammered in his head. Trace leaned over to rest his elbows on the bench, but he thought better of it. Pencil still in hand, he reached toward the receiver and turned the volume down.

Head still pounding from the music, heart punching with that adrenaline he loved and needed to feed, he hit the power button and breathed deeply in the sudden silence.

Shoulda told you

Before you walked away

I wish now I woulda said 'em—

All those words I didn't say.

He stood a moment longer and read over the words. Wished he had his guitar. He could mess around with a melody while his brain worked in the background on the lyrics. He laughed at himself and studied his hands. He was a mess from the mower and wouldn't touch Loretta like this, wouldn't touch *any* of his guitars with greasy, oily hands. Nope, he'd just have to finish the tune up before he wrote anymore.

With a quick glance at the paper, he considered going inside to wash his hands. He could grab Loretta, work a bit on what he'd started, and finish this up later. Nope. He knew how that would work out. He'd stew over a song or two, his truck would be in the drive overnight, and the next time he needed to mow the yard—yesterday—his mower would still be strung all over the garage floor.

He huffed out a breath and moseyed back to the mower deck, determined now to get it finished.

It hit him as he squatted down and slowly lowered his knees to the cement.

He'd text her.

And he'd start with something simple and flirty, like *hey darlin'*.

CHAPTER 5

LEAH GRABBED THE CORDLESS PHONE AS SHE HURRIED OUT of the office. As she jogged down the stairs, she looked down at her bare feet and rolled her eyes when she realized she left her shoes upstairs.

"Mississippi Queen." She put the phone to her ear and turned to head back the way she'd come. She still had time before they opened, but she didn't make a habit of running around without shoes downstairs.

"Leah."

She sucked in a quick breath and squeezed her eyes closed as her foot hit the top step.

"Hey, Joe." She whooshed out a quick breath and plastered a smile on her face. This wasn't fair. She needed time to psyche herself up for talks with Joe these days. Didn't he know he wasn't supposed to do this? She had finally pulled herself together last week after the trip to Destin.

This kind of call when she was unprepared for it might send her reeling again.

"You busy?"

His quiet voice was like a nail file shoved too hard under her fingernail, harsh and painful, and she froze in the hallway. She dug her teeth into her lower lip and lifted her arms above her head in a gesture of defeat. *She* needed time to psyche herself up? *What about Joe?* At least she was here, living her life. Joe's whole world—Joe and Kenzi's whole world—had been turned upside down, and now he was more or less shouldering those changes and the fallout they brought on his own.

"No." She swallowed hard. "No. What's—what's going on?"

He hesitated. Leah waited. Counted slowly, though she'd count forever to give him room to say what was on his mind.

"The kids and I just hiked a state park." His voice was small and flat. Leah dropped her arms to her sides but quickly raised her free hand to rub her knuckles over her heart. Her first instinct was to ask who stayed with Kenzi, and she wanted to know who had Edison, but she only rolled her lips inward and kept quiet. He wouldn't leave either of them alone, and she needed to let him talk.

When she trusted herself not to launch the third degree on him about Kenzi and Edison, Leah exhaled softly and nodded to herself.

"That sounds nice."

Joe's answer was slow to come, but he finally grunted and mumbled that it was hot. Leah wondered where he was; she heard steady traffic between his small bullet-like sentences.

"They need more than I can give them."

Leah's throat ached. She looked over her shoulder when she heard someone behind her in the hallway. Duncan arched his eyebrows at her, obviously concerned. When he mouthed Joe's name, she nodded. Sadness moved over his face before he could arrange it in that calm mask that sometimes infuriated her.

Still, when he moved up behind her and slipped his arm around her waist for a quick hug, she melted into him.

"Adelynn had an accident the other day."

Leah's gaze followed Duncan when he let go and stepped around her to duck into the office.

"What? What kind of accident?" She cleared her throat and moved toward the break room. Maybe she should sit down. "Is she okay?"

"Not that kind of accident." Joe sighed. "She was at some girl's house. With friends."

Leah cringed. The way he spat the word out, she figured some kind of mean girl story was coming.

"She started her period when she was there. She had blood on her shorts, and the girls laughed at her."

"Oh man." Leah leaned on the wall just outside the break room. "Is she okay?"

"I don't know. She said she called you, but she got your voicemail."

"When?"

"I don't know. A few days ago."

She closed her eyes and saw Joe's number pop up on the dashboard of her car the day she drove home from Nashville and decided to let the call go to voicemail. Rather than grow a pair and talk.

"I'm sorry," she whispered. Her stomach knotted with guilt. "Is she there now?"

"No." Joe's voice was louder now. It sounded like he was moving, walking somewhere. "They're with Kenzi's mom."

"Mmm." Leah sighed. "How's Kenz?"

Joe's answer was so long in coming that Leah wondered if the call had dropped. She didn't move, paralyzed with the fear that he was still there on the other end of the line, hating her for everything and for nothing.

"No change."

She sniffled and then held her breath.

"I gotta go," he told her.

"Okay." She prepared herself to say more, to remind him that she was here and he could depend on her. Even though she hadn't answered the phone when his daughter had called her. Even though he was in the heart of hell and fighting on his own, and she and the rest of the gang were blissfully unaffected by his heartache.

Not true.

God, no. Not true.

Her phone went dead, and she lowered it to her side.

Sad.

Grateful.

Ashamed.

"Leah?"

She pushed herself away from the wall when she heard Duncan call to her from the office. One foot in front of the other, she made her way to the office, much the same way she'd moved through the past several weeks. Duncan, bent over the desk, glanced at her as he tossed a pen down.

"Hey, Stevi wanted me to ask you if you paid the bill for the produce order that was delivered this morning."

Leah eyed him warily as she put the phone on the desk.

"No. I pay bills monthly, Duncan. She knows that."

"There was a problem with the order," he told her with a shrug.

"Like what?"

"They shorted us half of the arugula and squash."

Leah sighed. She wedged herself into the spot behind the desk and gently pushed him out of the way.

"Did she say anything this morning?"

"Yeah, she talked to the driver, but we both know that's not gonna do any good."

Leah leaned half under the desk and righted her silver heels. Small heels, the curse of being tall, but they were sexy. Not that sexy mattered in her life. She slipped the shoes on and then eyed them on her feet.

"Do you like these shoes?" she asked with a frown.

"Um."

When she looked up at Duncan, he folded his arms over his chest and leaned his butt on the desk.

"I think they'd hurt my feet."

She laughed softly and touched the pointy toe of the right shoe to his leg.

"Yeah. Of course, I do. They're sexy." He shrugged. "And they look like torture."

Leah almost gasped out loud at the wave of despair that rolled over her. She raised her eyebrows at him and attempted a smile.

"I think I might give them to Stevi."

"Why?"

"Why do I need sexy shoes?" she mumbled. She leaned forward to rest her elbow on the desk.

"You gotta let someone in, Leah." He refused to meet her eyes. "I get it. You don't hook up. But you're gonna have to slow down and let someone in one of these days."

She opened her mouth to argue, but she had nothing to say. She shook her head and studied the desktop rather than look at him.

"Hmm." Surprised to see her cell phone half buried under a brochure for a new, local distillery, she reached for it.

"They won't fit her anyway," Duncan told her. "She's tiny."

Leah's sigh turned into a groan of frustration. "Thanks for reminding me."

"You're an Amazon," he said with a grin. "Own it, babe. Men love legs like yours."

"I thought men loved sweet, petite little women like Stevi."

Duncan laughed and stood up to leave the office. Leah glanced at her phone as she climbed to her feet. Still a little off after her short talk with Joe, she wobbled the first few steps as she followed Duncan out the door.

"She might be petite," Duncan called to her. Leah glanced up to see he was already halfway down the stairs. "But she sure as hell ain't sweet."

Leah laughed. Point, Duncan. Stevi Hague was a lot of things, most of them good. But sweet was most definitely not on that list.

At the top of the stairs, she pushed the home button on her phone. A text message popped up from an unknown number.

Hey, darlin'.

CHAPTER 6

LEAH, STILL A BIT RAW FROM THE TALK WITH JOE, SANK TO the steps in slow motion. In spite of the ache in her chest, in her belly, she laughed softly.

Still not gonna sleep with you, Nashville.

Because her legs felt weak, and because she assumed the guy would text again, she simply sat for a moment at the top of the grand wooden staircase, a little like a queen on her throne. Stevi and Margo were behind the bar; Stevi was cleaning, a bottle of furniture oil in one hand and a dust rag in the other. Margo stared at her laptop, elbows planted on either side of it on the bar.

The view was excellent from up here, and she wasn't taking the girls into consideration. The club was trendy, upscale in appearance while still the perfect gathering place for the regular Joe. She felt a stick at the thought; Joe had even suggested they call it Regular Joe's when they'd first started plans to use their inheritance and memorialize their grandfather with the place. Stevi had considered it; Leah knew her well enough to read the look on her face. She didn't like the name; she was just a sucker for Joe.

Well, Stevi liked guys. Nothing bad about that; she truly preferred to hang out with guys and guy friends more than she did girlfriends, Leah and Margo not included. And Kenzi. They all loved Kenzi.

When Leah's phone buzzed in her hand, she drew in a deep breath and sat up straight. Tucking Joe and Kenzi away for the moment, she turned her hand over to read the text.

I'm not that guy.

She knew what he meant, but she answered as if she didn't. It was a distraction, anyway, and what did it hurt to flirt with someone at least four hundred miles away, give or take? God knew, Stevi would flirt with the guy. She might even sleep with him. The thought was like a hot spike of pain in Leah's stomach. She loved her sister pretty much more than anything, but she didn't want her anywhere near Trace Dixon.

You're not the guy who propositioned me at Left Fork?

His answer was instant this time.

You misread my intentions.

Did I?

She stared at her phone expectantly, aware of the tug at her lips.

Did I look like the kind of guy to pick up a woman like that? At a bar?

Leah hesitated. How the heck did she answer that? First of all, she wondered if she looked like the type of woman who would agree to a random hook up. And second, she couldn't very well say what she was thinking, could she? That he looked like sex on a stick, and she wished now she would have taken a lick?

Thumbs hovering over the phone, she felt a frown of concentration draw her face into a pinch. Even that felt different from the weary, sad way she'd been looking at the world lately. It felt better.

"What're you doing?" Margo hollered at her.

"You okay?"

Still puzzling over how to answer him, Leah waved Stevi and Margo off.

I think I'll plead the fifth.

What're you listening to right now?

Surprised by the change in direction, Leah mumbled in response. She looked around the bar, this time tuning into the music Margo and Stevi were playing.

Some 70s song, I think.

If we're gonna be friends, you're gonna have to do better than that.

Leah's mouth dropped open in shock, and a sharp little laugh slipped out.

"Guys, what's this song?" she called to her sister and her cousin.

"What?"

Clearly, Stevi wasn't up to the challenge.

"Margo? Song?"

"Don't know," Margo answered. "Boz Scaggs, maybe?"

"Boz Scaggs?" Leah repeated. "That's the song?"

"Ambrosia," Duncan called from behind her. "The song's called "How Much I Feel." Why do you wanna know?"

"Why do you care?" she hollered back at him. "Thanks, though."

She looked back at her phone, aware that her lips had given in, and now she was smiling.

How Much I Feel. Ambrosia.

Good recovery.

Are we?

Are we what?

Gonna be friends?

Her toes tingled as she waited for his response. It was a good kind of tingle, though. Not the rush of nervous anxiety thing she had been feeling about Kenzi and Joe.

Is that even a question? I'm in.

Leah sucked in a quick breath and covered her mouth with her fingertips.

"What're you doing?" Stevi called to her.

With a long drawn out sigh, Leah looked up and found Margo and Stevi half leaning on the bannister and half creeping up the steps.

"Talking to someone."

"Who?" Margo gave her a tiny shrug.

She jumped when her phone buzzed. Trace Dixon—assuming the guitar-playing cowboy she'd talked to in Nashville was Trace Dixon—wanted to be her friend. And she was keeping him waiting.

Radio silence. Come in, darlin'.

She snorted as she dropped her head back to hang and found herself looking up into Duncan's eyes.

"Stop reading my texts," she said without heat.

"Unknown number, but he called her darlin'."

"How do you know it's a he?" Stevi asked him.

Leah chuckled when Duncan appeared speechless.

"Leave me alone!" Leah tucked her arm to her middle and watched Duncan slip by her on the steps.

"Ohmygod!" Stevi squealed. "Ohmygod. It's him. You're talking to him."

"How dare you talk to him!" Duncan pretended outrage, but Leah heard him when he reached the bottom of the staircase. "Who's him?"

"Trace Dixon?" Stevi smacked Duncan's chest with the heel of her hand. "Like, the sexiest man in Nashville."

"Stevi." Duncan rolled his eyes. Leah laughed when he circled his fingers around her sister's wrist. "You say that, and yet, you fail to recognize you work with the sexiest man in the Western Hemisphere."

Stevi snorted. She faked a cough to hide the word bullshit and then ducked her head and tried to get away from Duncan. Leah watched him pick her up and hoist her over his shoulder.

"Put me down!"

Leah met Margo's eyes as Duncan carried Stevi to the bar, Stevi squealing in protest and Duncan laughing at her attempts to wiggle away from him.

"Is that Trace Dixon?" Margo asked her. Leah gave her a tiny nod, grateful when her cousin nodded her head in the direction of the office.

Leah scrambled to her feet, careful not to lose her balance in her haste. She made her way to the office, the kitten heels be damned, and sank to sit on the couch. Was she too late?

She held her breath and stared at her phone for a moment. Did it matter? She had no intention of sleeping with him. Even if it was truly Trace Dixon. No intention of anything other than...maybe friendship.

I'm here.

And?

She rubbed her hand absently over her stomach as she considered what to say. If this was just a friends thing, why did it feel like she'd swallowed a mouthful of butterflies? She rested her head on the back of the couch and let the feeling slide through her. Attraction. Hell yes, the guy was delicious to look at, and so far, he seemed kind of fun. But that didn't mean anything.

Do you not trust me?

Should I? I met you for five minutes. You hit on me in a bar.

I did not hit on you! I said hi.

Stuck in the memory of that night at Left Fork, Leah snapped out of it and checked the time on her phone.

What're you doing?

What am I doing?

Yes.

All hands on deck. Just talking to you.

Oh my God.

Leah flopped her head back again and let the furious blush color her face and her neck.

You asked.

Well, that's not what I meant. She flexed her thumb over the phone and then added an emoji. The one with red cheeks and wide eyes.

Okay. What did you mean?

Well, now she was just embarrassed to say anything. She started typing, intending to ask what he was doing. As in, if he played in a bar at night, what did he do by day? Uncertain, she backtracked and sat for a moment in thought.

Leah?

Why do you remember my name?

How could she ask him if he was really Trace Dixon? Because, what if he wasn't? She would look pretty stupid, wouldn't she? And then how would she convince him that it didn't matter?

You're kidding. Right?

So not kidding.

Do you believe in love at first sight?

I'm done.

She dropped her phone and shook her head. No. She did not believe in love at first sight. She didn't not believe in it, either, but she wasn't interested. She wasn't interested in anything about love right now, not in her life. Now wasn't a good time, and yes, she was very much aware that she wasn't getting any younger and putting it off wasn't doing her any favors.

Her phone buzzed, but she refused to pick it up.

It buzzed again. And again.

Frustrated, a little bit amused, and sort of curious, she picked it up to look at it again.

A text from Adelynn was sandwiched between two from the unknown number. She blew out a quick breath and opened the one from Adelynn. Her hand shook, though, and the unopened texts from him were like lasers shooting up out of her phone, demanding her attention.

Does anything help? I feel like buzzard shit.

This time, Leah's laugh was a little hollow, a little sad.

Kenzi's daughter might look like Joe, but the kid had every last drop of Kenzi's feistiness.

As she started to answer, her phone buzzed again. She sighed and shoved her fingers up over her forehead, pulled her hair back, and then let it fall again.

Try Midol, babe. Sit with a heating pad for a while.

She licked her lips and switched her phone to look at the texts from Trace.

Wait!

No! No, don't be out.

Leah?

She closed her eyes and shook her head. Should she answer him? Or just let it go and hope he went away? Stevi would tell her to take him for a spin before she cut him loose. Margo would tell her to move on. When she opened her eyes, she found Duncan watching her from the office doorway.

"Do you believe in love at first sight?" She hated that she was asking. Not because it was Duncan there to answer, but because six weeks ago, she'd sworn to whatever the hell highest power there was in the world that she'd never think about love again. No way she would go back on her word now.

Maybe because she'd just talked to Joe, and maybe because she spoke so quietly that her sadness bled through her words again, Duncan didn't tease her this time.

"I believe in a little bit of everything, Leah," he answered. Hands tucked in his hip pockets, he lifted his shoulders in an almost imperceptible hug. "Depends on your way of looking at things."

She blinked, certain there might be a kernel of wisdom in his words, but not a hundred percent sure at the moment what it was.

Her phone buzzed again.

"You're persistent," she mumbled. "I'll give you that."

But it was Adelynn. The ghost of a smile stepped over her lips and walked out before she could hold onto it.

Mom always said running made her feel better.

The text thread from the unknown number tempted her again. She glanced at it, muttering to herself again about love at first sight.

She also knocked back whiskey and a pack a day. Might not work for you.

"Leah."

She swung her legs to the floor and looked up at Duncan. Time to get back to work.

"Love at first sight?'

She nodded.

"Sure. But sometimes only one person feels it." He raised his eyebrows.

"Complicated," she offered.

"Fifteen kinds." He nodded. "Have some fun."

She rolled her eyes when he turned to walk away and looked back at her phone when it buzzed again.

Not much of a whiskey kind of guy.

She groaned out loud.

Multitasking. Sorry. Hang on.

She switched back to the thread of texts with Adelynn.

Try running. Your mom was always on the go. Might help.

Her eyes burned as she tapped the arrow to send her message. Kenzi had been a blur of motion since the day they'd met, which made it that much harder to see her in her current condition.

I miss you.

Me too.

Leah waited for a few moments to see if Adelynn texted again. When she was certain she wasn't going to, she rubbed her eyes and changed back to the thread of texts with Trace.

Sorry. I need to get back to work.

I offended you with my question about love at first sight, but you were willing to talk to me about hooking up.

I turned you down. We didn't discuss it.

Again with the assuming I was propositioning you and with the turning me down stuff.

She laughed softly and rolled her eyes.

I really need to go.

I've played Left Fork damned near every night for two years straight. When I see a woman like you step inside, damn right I'm gonna remember her name.

She'd climbed to her feet, but her knees went a bit weak at his words.

You never told me yours.

You didn't ask.

Nashville works.

Do you know now?

She rested her butt on the edge of the desk and considered how to answer him. Well, what was the point in playing games? She was in Illinois. He was four hundred plus miles away in Tennessee.

Yes.

Okay.

She huffed out a sigh and shrugged. Sort of anticlimactic, she decided as she stood again, ready to tuck her phone in her pocket and get back downstairs to catch up with Margo and Stevi. About the agenda. Not the fact that a country music—sort of star—person was texting her.

She looked down at her phone when it buzzed.

So we're in? Both of us?

Sure. But

Before she could finish the text, another dropped.

And I know, heard you loud and clear. You're not gonna sleep with me.

CHAPTER 7

HOW DID YOU GET MY NUMBER?

"Get her up on stage tonight," Sampson told him.

Head bent over his phone, thoughts on the woman who'd walked out of here last weekend with his heart in her hand, Trace angled his chin and looked at the old man.

"She's not ready." Pearl's tone suggested that she'd said the same words to Sampson more than once in response to his declaration that it was time to put Kadie on stage for a full set. Trace slid his gaze from Sampson—a wiry, old man, both skinnier and shorter than his wife—to Pearl.

"She ain't ever gonna be ready if she don't get used to the stage." Sampson's voice had an edge to it, as if he was tired of the argument. Trace was, too, at the moment. He liked Kadie, but he agreed with *both* Pearl and Sampson. She wasn't ready to sing in front of a big crowd. But Wednesdays—early Wednesdays—didn't deliver big crowds, so this might be the perfect time to give Kadie a shot.

Right now, Trace had about twenty minutes until go time, and he would rather spend that twenty minutes texting Leah Hague than listening to two of his favorite people bicker. Familiar, by now, with the tune even if the words did change from time to time, he ducked his head to his phone and left them to it.

You dropped a business card.

And you scooped it up? Really?

Well, I was talking with the girls. Found a condom wrapper and three business cards.

You found my business card with a condom wrapper? Ewwww.

Trace chuckled softly. He lifted his elbow to rest on the bar and plopped his chin in his hand. People claimed texting was inadequate for communication. He agreed; he would much rather hear her voice right now, much rather be at this bar with her, talking to her and looking at her. But he had to admit this was interesting. Seemed you could learn a lot about a person depending on her emoji usage and her text speak. Or lack of. Thus far, Leah Hague texted in mostly complete sentences. No heavy acronym usage.

He'd like to see her face, watch her lips with the *ewwww* comment, though. He wondered if she'd shivered at the thought of her business card on the floor with a condom wrapper.

"What're you laughing at?" Pearl slid a glass of ice water at him.

"Nothing." He shook his head, his phone still in his left hand, hidden in his lap.

"You think Kadie's ready?" Pearl leaned her hands on the bar. Rather than look her in the eye—after all, she supplied him with the biggest meal of his day most of the time—he lowered his gaze to her hands. Her fingernails were clipped and clean, but her fingers were gnarled with arthritis.

"Good night to try her out," he said as he cast a glance over his shoulder. Just about six o'clock, there were only five people currently in the bar.

"You sided with Sampson last time," she reminded him.

"Did not!"

"Watch your step, Trace Dixon." She leveled him with her steely gaze. The threat in her voice made him swallow hard.

"Yes, ma'am, but I don't even remember what last time was."

His phone buzzed, so when Pearl moved away from him and hefted her heavy front down the bar toward the kitchen doors, he turned his attention to it.

What are you doing?

Getting ready to go on.

So. Why are you like…

Trace stared expectantly at his phone, waiting for more. What was she thinking? Wanting to ask him? Had she been interrupted, or was she hedging?

???

I don't know how to ask.

Just say it.

Why is Trace Dixon the house act at a Nashville bar?

Well. Why, indeed.

He sighed and slid off the stool, heavy and slow like a stealth fighter jet just ripped through his middle. Tossed his phone on the bar and looked around the room again. Sampson had just turned the lights down a smidge, shooting for the evening atmosphere. Trace eyed the taps behind the bar. A cold beer might go down easy now.

"Too much pepper in the soup." Pearl picked up the conversation where they'd left off. He turned to look at her over his shoulder.

"That was six months ago," he muttered. He rubbed his hand over his chest, indigestion licking a trail of fire up his stomach and into his throat.

"Two," she corrected him. He dropped his hand when he saw her watching him. "You okay?"

"Yep."

His phone buzzed, but he didn't rush to pick it up. Pearl

ambled closer to the bar. She leaned in and read the screen without touching it.

"Leah Hague."

He shrugged and rubbed his hands over the seat of his pants. Shook his legs out like a boxer readying himself for the ring.

"Is Kadie even here yet?" He stepped around the barstools and reached for his phone.

"You gonna tell her who you are?"

"Don't know, Pearl," he answered, eyes on the back door.

"How did you find her?"

"What?" He started to tuck his phone in his pocket, but he hesitated. "I got lucky."

Pearl shook her head and rolled her eyes, but Trace saw a knowing smirk on her face.

"God, that's not what I meant," he groaned. "The night she was in here, she must have accidentally dropped a business card. I got lucky and found it."

Pearl folded her arms over her chest and gave him the cool, composed stare he'd grown to dread.

"You're gonna go sniffin' around a woman four hundred miles away? Plenty of women right here in Nashville throwin' themselves at you night after night."

He gave her a curt nod. "That's exactly why I'm talking to a woman four hundred miles away."

To her credit, Pearl didn't comment. Instead, she pursed her lips and scratched absently at an age spot on her wrist. Trace looked at his phone as he made his way to the stage. He picked up Loretta, held her by the neck, but he kept his attention on the phone.

You told me to ask. Did I overstep?

A headache brewed behind his eyes now. Trace scrunched his face up to fight the memories and the bad feelings. Remembered he had started this. He had pursued this woman for a reason. His being the house act at Left Fork was a long story, and not one he wanted to get into at the moment. But he'd rather have this sort of conversation with a woman than have some tipsy little floozy lean into him at the bar and ask him to guess if she was wearing underwear.

No.

He had to say more, but the stage lights were on now. Trace didn't kid himself. People didn't come to Left Fork to seek him out. But he was here to do a job that Pearl and Sampson Allen paid him to do, and now wasn't the time to get into any of this.

???

He laughed softly, set Loretta on the stand again, and stood with his back to the five-person crowd currently mingling in Left Fork and focused on Leah's text.

Can we talk later? Stage lights are on.

To his surprise, she answered him immediately.

Of course.

After midnight.

I'll be at the Queen. Fire away.

Relieved, Trace grabbed a deep breath and nodded to himself. Funny. Talking to Leah made him feel fourteen again. Nervous like the first time he picked up his guitar and played at the school talent show. A little hyper and a little sloppy with the flow of electricity like the first time he'd swallowed liquor.

Leah?

He waited, aware of the seconds ticking by, afraid he'd missed her.

?

What're you listening to?

He wasn't sure why he asked, but he wanted to know. She obviously wasn't a country music person. Being country wouldn't necessarily mean she would be a fan of his or Tanner's, but she would have heard their names, and she would have known who he was a lot sooner than she figured it out. Like before she'd walked out of here the night he'd met her.

Of Monsters and Men.

Music made sense to him at the deepest level; his brain and his heart and soul worked together. He listened to just about anything and liked pretty much everything he heard for one reason or another.

He was curious what song she was listening to right now, but he didn't have time to ask. He did know that the next time he heard the band—he would go looking for their music now—he would think of Leah.

TRACY BROEMMER

He was curious what song she was listening to right now, but he didn't have time to ask. He did know that the next time he heard the band—he would go looking for their music now—he would think of Leah.

CHAPTER 8

LEAH TIPPED HER GLASS UP AND SWALLOWED THE LAST OF the bold, red wine. She leaned on the end of the bar and watched Duncan follow the last patrons to the door to lock up. Feeling Stevi's eyes on her, she stretched and made a big show of yawning to prove how tired she was. Sometimes, after they closed, they hung around the bar into the smallest hours of the morning. Sometimes working, but most of the time just talking and playing silly games. Having a drink and listening to music. Leah loved everything about the Queen, and she sometimes loved those after-hour sessions with her partners and Duncan most of all.

But not tonight. It was well after eleven, and she hadn't heard from Trace yet. Part of her wondered if he was simply going to ignore the fact that he had said they would talk tonight. Maybe she had overstepped earlier when she asked why he was spending his time in a

Nashville bar when he could clearly be doing bigger and better things. Or maybe he'd hit on someone else at the bar, and she had taken him up on the offer.

Leah wouldn't admit as much to Stevi, but she had had a few moments of regret for not taking advantage of the moment. Well, if there had been a moment to take advantage of. *He hadn't hit on her*; but was that because she had shut him down or because he wasn't interested?

The rational side of her brain reminded her that he played live music in a bar. And that bar probably closed at midnight, and even if he quit playing at eleven or midnight, that didn't mean he would be free to drop everything immediately and play some new techno, pen pal game with her.

"I didn't like that wine," Stevi announced.

This time, Leah's yawn was real. She laughed softly and picked her glass up from the bar.

"It was okay," she mumbled.

"Yeah, but don't order it." Stevi turned the lights over the bar off and then turned to Leah, eyebrows arched in question.

"I won't."

Door locked and the closed sign flipped, Duncan whistled to the tune of a Bad Company song that Leah couldn't quite place as he crossed back to the bar.

"Buy you a drink?" He tossed the keys on the bar and grabbed Leah by the shoulder to give her a squeeze.

"No. Thanks." Leah shook her head. She gave Duncan's hand an absent pat and carried her glass to the sink under the bar.

"Stevi? Drink?"

"Yes, sir, may I have another?" Stevi said with a giggle. She stood so close to Leah that she bumped her hip. "Here. Go."

"What?" Leah looked at her when Stevi took the glass from her.

"You've been counting down the minutes since, like, nine o'clock," Stevi told her. Leah started to argue, but her sister tipped her head and gave her that look that their mother used to employ when she wanted the truth. "I can only assume you're expecting a phone call, and due to the bounce in your step, I'm going to—"

"Bounce in my step?" Leah interrupted her. "What?"

Stevi shrugged her lips. "Duncan, did Leah have a bounce in her step tonight?"

"Yes. Bouncing like a six-year-old hyped up on candy and cake frosting and soda, ready to hit the bounce house."

Eyes locked with Stevi's, Leah frowned and finally looked over Stevi's shoulders to Duncan, who was stacking empty boxes to take out to recycle.

"That was oddly specific," she mumbled.

"Go home," Stevi said softly. "Talk to him."

"Stevi, we're not—"

"Look." Stevi set the glass in the sink and took Leah's hands in hers. "I don't know what mental switch got flipped in your head. With Kenzi. I don't know—"

"Don't." Leah closed her eyes and shook her head.

"I don't know. You don't have to tell me. But no one on this earth, especially Kenzi Daniels, is going to fault you for talking to a guy, especially a guy like Trace Dixon."

"Stevi, I'm not interested in—"

"Yeah, okay." Stevi shrugged and squeezed her hands. "I don't get it, but if that's how you feel, okay. Go be *friends* with Trace Dixon."

Leah wanted to argue. Now that Stevi had said it out loud, she wanted to linger here with Stevi and Duncan as if she needed to prove a point. Lips sealed, she drew in a deep breath through her nose and answered Stevi with a smile and a nod.

"Okay."

"Good. See you tomorrow." Stevi leaned in and kissed her cheek.

Duncan followed her out the back door. In the three years that the Queen had been up and running, there had been no reported violence or vandalism in the area. But the business district was uptown, and trouble lived only a few blocks over on the riverfront. Duncan walked them out every night, and the girls had learned not to argue with him.

"Leah, Leah." They stood side by side on the patio out back. Leah's Malibu was parked in spitting distance, and she was thinking again about Trace, but she didn't hurry to leave.

"Hmm?"

"Guys and girls can be friends, right?" He nudged her with his elbow. Leah wasn't sure if he was demanding she answer. Of course, they could. Look at the four of them here at the Queen.

"Yep."

"This guy."

She turned to look at him. Nearly the same height, Duncan's gray eyes stared back at her.

"You know him?"

"No." He shook his head. Duncan was kind of equal opportunity as far as the music he enjoyed, though she knew he favored classic rock. "But. I'm gonna go out on a limb here and tell you he has to think you're gorgeous."

Leah ducked her head to hide her grin. "Aww. Thanks, Dunc."

"Just be careful."

"Thank you." A little bit choked up, her voice was tight and small. "Goodnight."

She leaned in and brushed her lips over his cheek. Duncan rested his hand on the small of her back and held her for a second. He stood watch when she hurried to her car and climbed in. When she pulled out of the lot onto Tolliver Street and looked in the rearview mirror, she saw Duncan wave and tossed him one of her own that he probably wouldn't see. Didn't matter. They'd done this every night since the word go. He did the same with Stevi and Margo, too.

Wednesdays at—check that—Thursdays at 12:22 a.m. provided pretty easy driving. Leah tapped her fingers on the steering wheel as she drove and only remembered her phone was in her back pocket when it buzzed. At the stoplight at 8th and Tolliver, she arched her back off the seat and pulled it out. Her lips did that quick grin when she saw his name on the screen. She'd added it last night after she'd agreed to keep texting him and wondered what people she knew would say if they knew she was texting Trace Dixon. So, she'd found him online; she still didn't have a clue who he was. The name Tanner Dixon didn't ring any bells. Lightnin' Congregation did nothing for her. Maybe she should do some research, but that felt like cheating. That's not how you got to know friends.

Talking. Texting. That left the normal level of mystery in the getting to know each other process.

What're you listening to?

She bit her lip. Was the guy *that* into music? Or did he keep asking in hopes that she would say she was listening to something he sang? Did he have albums out there? Should she look?

Well, she was listening to Frank Sinatra. She wondered what he would say to that.

Fly Me to The Moon.

Sinatra?

Yep. Driving. Give me a few minutes.

She set her phone down when she saw his ok. The light was still red. Leah looked around the intersection in disbelief. Hers was the only car in sight. Should she have stayed at the Queen? Helped Stevi and Duncan make sure everything was locked up? No. She knew better. Duncan could close it all up alone if he had to. Margo had gone home before eight to spend some time with Berkley, and Stevi would probably bug out early on Friday. Nothing said date to Stevi like weekend.

Not quite ten minutes later, she pulled into her driveway and zipped the Malibu back to the unattached one car garage behind the house. Rather than linger outside, though she was tempted to answer him now, she grabbed her phone and her purse. Night sounds followed her to her door. What would he say if she told him she was listening to crickets? And that she *liked* the chirping noise they made as long as they weren't in her house.

She stepped into the kitchen, closed and locked her door, and then pulled her garage door opener out of her purse. She aimed it out the back window and watched the door lumber closed. She hadn't thought to ask Stevi if she would be home tonight, but since she was still at the Queen with Duncan when she left, she assumed she would eventually slip in.

Home.

Busy night?

She carried her purse through the kitchen, navigating the dark by memory and the bit of light from her phone. Sometimes, she had to watch TV to wind down or have a snack because they'd been too busy to eat dinner. Tonight, she slipped through the spare bedroom to the steep, skinny staircase hidden in the closet and climbed the steps to her attic room.

Not bad for midweek. You?

Started slow and picked up as the night went on.

What's your favorite song to sing?

She tossed her phone on her bed, set her purse in the wingback chair, and then stepped out of her shoes. No heels tonight, but her feet still hurt. She sighed with appreciation and then groped under her pillow for her pajamas.

That's like asking me which is my favorite kid.

You have kids?

No, but you know what I mean.

Yeah, but you don't have to be politically correct, because they're songs and you can't hurt a song's feelings.

....

She dropped the phone again and slipped into the tiny bathroom adjacent to her bedroom. It didn't matter what he would say, what song he most liked to sing, because she knew maybe three country songs. No doubt he would catch her if she tried to bluff her way through a conversation as if she was familiar with anyone other than Johnny Cash, Conway Twitty, and Willie Nelson.

She washed her face and brushed her teeth. Finished with all of her business in the bathroom, she returned to her bedroom.

The dots still flashed on her screen. She laughed softly and whispered, "Yikes."

What if he was composing a twenty-page list? She would have to spend all of her free time this weekend researching the songs! She unbuttoned her capris and slid them down over her hips, eyes on her phone all the while.

She tossed the white linen pants to the end of her bed and stepped into a pair of gray pajama shorts.

Impossible. It changes daily.

Hands on the red knit blouse she'd worn at the Queen, she stopped and picked up her phone again.

Okay, so what was your favorite song you sang tonight?

Tomorrow's Mine.

She had never heard of it. To give herself a minute to think, she reached for the hem of her shirt again but hesitated. With a roll of her eyes, she turned her phone screen down and then quickly whipped the shirt off and tossed it to the end of the bed with her capris. She took her bra off and dropped it to the floor, yanked her gray tank over her head, and pulled it down to smooth it over her hips.

??? Tell me you're not googling the song.

Actually, no. I was changing my clothes. But I don't know the song.

...

Leah laughed. She pulled her comforter back and flopped sideways over the bed. Ducked her head and rubbed at her neck.

Changing. Changing clothes.

Trace.

She added the eye roll emoji.

Right. Because friends don't imagine what friends look like in that stage of changing clothes when they have no clothes on.

Right. They don't.

Leah dropped her phone on her bed and squeezed her hands into fists. Funny that she was adamant about not sleeping with him, but the thought of him being affected simply knowing that she'd just changed clothes zapped her body and made her hands shake.

She laughed out loud when she saw his next text.

Gimme a minute.

What are you doing?

Just thinking, I promise.

Ohmygod. Stop!

Heat flooded her cheeks, and even though she was alone in her room, alone in the whole damned house, she ducked her head to bury her face in her outstretched arm. She was too old to feel this way, wasn't she? Giddy and flirty? Good grief, when had she last used an exclamation point? Never in a text, that was certain.

What're you wearing?

STOP IT.

Sorry. Do you know the song?

What song?

See? You're thinking about it, too.

Head still resting on her outstretched arm, Leah held her phone in her other hand and took a moment to wonder when she'd last felt like this about a guy. Maybe college days, but she didn't really remember a specific guy making her insides go soft and gooey. She couldn't even put a finger on how long it had been since she'd had sex, but apparently, it had been far too long.

Was she? Thinking about him thinking about her naked? No. *Well,* okay, so she wondered what he would think of her body. After all, when he'd flirted with her—maybe he hadn't actually hit on her, but he had joined her at the bar to flirt—she'd been dressed, and the lighting had been dim. Wasn't like he got a really good look at her. But no, she wasn't going to dwell on it.

I don't know the song. Should I?

I'm assuming you're not into country music.

Leah laughed out loud and tapped the screen on her phone to send him the emoji with the smile and red cheeks.

Kind of obvious, isn't it?

What were you doing in a Nashville bar if you aren't into country music?

Leah groaned softly and dropped her phone to the bed. Good question, but not one she was ready to answer. Kenzi and Joe were hers, and she didn't want to share their story with anyone. Besides, if she tried, Trace Dixon would probably toss his phone and run away as fast as he could. Still, he was waiting on an answer, so she had to say something. She closed her fingers around her phone and rolled over to lie on her back.

Driving home from Destin. Needed a stop.

Vacation?

Something like that.

Alone?

She held her breath for a second. Finally, she sighed and shrugged and answered him.

Yep.

Leah?

An exorcism, maybe. Needed a break from reality.

She pressed her lips together and waited for him to ask. After all, she'd asked him something that was apparently a personal question, because he'd put her off earlier and still hadn't broached the subject.

Did it work?

She smiled sadly.

No.

Bad breakup?

No.

Marriage on the rocks?

Never been married. I'm okay.

Okay. I'll let it go.

Thank you.

You're not into country, but you do know who I am?

I know you're Trace Dixon, but I guess I have to confess I didn't have a clue at Left Fork.

How did you figure it out?

One hand holding her phone in front of her, she flinched and rubbed her other hand over her belly. Butterfly wings stroked inside her, and the feeling was a little bit enticing and a little bit unsettling. She was attracted to him, and it couldn't happen.

Um. The woman at the bar?

Pearl? She told you?

No, but she called you by name. And I

You what?

I asked my sister when I got home. If she knew a country music person named Trace.

And she didn't say Trace Adkins?

He added the surprised-face emoji.

Leah snorted and chuckled.

Um. Yeah. She did. She and my cousin and Duncan discussed it. Someone suggested your name. And

And what?

I googled you.

Who's Duncan?

What?

???

He tends bar here. At the Queen.

But who is he to you?

He's Margo's stepbrother.

But who is he to you? You look pretty cozy in that picture on your website.

Leah rolled over and scrambled to a sitting position.

You googled me?

Yep.

But.

What? I told you I was desperate.

Wow.

She took a quick breath and squirmed on her bed. The butterflies had kicked it up a notch, and now even her hands felt all gooey and soft.

Double standard much? Are you involved with him?

What? No! I'm just. Not sure a guy's ever googled me before. Haha.

She added the laughing emoji and then after careful consideration, she added the emoji face with only two big eyes, no mouth.

Desperate times. Are you involved with Duncan?

I don't even know what picture you're talking about.

She didn't. Stevi handled the website. It had been weeks— maybe months—since she'd even looked at it.

You with two pretty girls and a guy. The guy has his arm around you.

Um.

Legs crossed now in a pretzel, she ducked her head and scrubbed her fingers back through her hair.

Like we all have our arms around each other?

Yep. But you're by the guy.

Leah felt a weird jolt of—power?—rip through her. He was seriously jealous. Trace Dixon was jealous because Duncan Marks had his arm around her in a picture.

The girl on the end? With the really dark hair. She's my cousin Margo. Duncan is her stepbrother.

Leah.

No! God, no. I'm not involved with him. He's like a brother.

He didn't answer immediately. Leah's breath was shaky and uneven. Didn't he believe her? Did it matter? Why would it matter? She wasn't going to do this. It was one thing to talk to him. But no, she was not going to get involved with him.

As if he was going to hound her. She was a nobody from the Midwest. Trace Dixon was apparently someone, and maybe she needed to do just a little surfing to see just who she was talking to.

Listen to the song.

What?

Goodnight.

No! Wait. Trace? What song?

Tomorrow's Mine.

She waited to see if he said anything else, but after five minutes had passed, she decided he wouldn't text again. She sat for a moment, stunned by the conversation. By the whole idea that Trace Dixon was texting her. Seemed a little bit crazy. One thing to flirt with her in a bar, but to pursue something through text messages? He had to be her age, if not older. To Leah's mind, they were too old for this.

So then, why did it feel so good to flirt with him? Why, several minutes after he had stopped texting, did she still feel tingly and warm inside? She heard the door downstairs. Sometimes, Stevi crept up the steps when she came home to see if Leah was awake. They talked a lot in the small hours like this, but Leah didn't want to talk to her sister now.

Heart beating in her throat, she twisted and stretched sideways to turn the lamp on her nightstand off. Her body hummed with something foreign as she settled against her pillow and looked at her phone again.

She inhaled deeply and tapped the Youtube app on her phone. Typed *Tomorrow's Mine*, and though she knew she was talking to Trace Dixon, it still startled her when a video starring Tanner Dixon and The Lightnin' Congregation popped up. She started to tap the play arrow, but she hesitated. Her eyes roamed over the small screen. The video had over a million views.

Guilt crept up inside her and wormed its way up inside her throat. Mixed with the giddiness Trace had left her with, it created a stomachache. Maybe she should skip this. Walk away.

Stevi's voice came back to her. Kenzi Daniels wouldn't fault her for talking to Trace Dixon. Leah rested her head on the headboard and closed her eyes. Hell, truth be told, if Kenzi were here, she'd tell Joe she was sorry, but if Leah wasn't going to sample the merchandise, she would.

Okay, so she didn't have to sample anything. She wouldn't get involved with him. But she could listen to the song, couldn't she?

CHAPTER 9

Leah blinked at her computer screen; her hands hovered above the keyboard.

"Do what?"

She finally lifted her eyes to look at Margo, perched on the arm of the couch across the room. She tamped down the flash of jealousy. Of course it was okay for Margo to talk to Joe. They were all friends; Leah had no claim on the Daniels family. Besides, she hadn't been great about staying in contact with Joe, anyway, had she? And this was just the beginning of what was the rest of Joe's life.

Margo, feet on the seat of the couch, studied her nails. A spike of regret pulsed through her when her cousin rubbed her thumb over her bare ring finger. Leah dropped her hands to the desk and sat back in the chair.

"How's he doing?"

Margo lifted her head. She wore a small, knowing smile, and her eyes held a challenge. She had known Joe's phone call would ruffle Leah's feathers, just as Leah knew Margo's announcement hadn't been malicious.

Leah sucked in a sharp breath, her chest tight and painful, when Margo turned to look out the window. She wondered for a second if Margo was okay; she looked exhausted, just a little bit sad.

"He's tired, Leah," Margo said softly. "He's tired. Already."

When Margo looked back to meet her eyes, Leah nodded.

"Yeah. I'm sure he is."

"No change." The threadbare words came in response to the question Margo knew she would ask. Already, they were all weary of asking and weary of the answer.

Leah nodded and dragged her eyes away.

"How's Berkley?"

From the corner of her eye, Leah saw Margo's smile. Hard to miss it when it lit up the room.

"The sweetest baby girl in all of baby-girldom."

Leah chuckled as she met Margo's eyes again.

"No bias there at all." She closed her fingers around the mouse and looked at her computer screen again. She had been browsing a new winery's website. Sure, that's what her distributors were for, but Leah enjoyed the entire wine experience. She wasn't willing to put full control of the Queen's choices in someone else's hands, even if her distributors were good. "Hear from Jess lately?"

She hated to ask, but she couldn't ignore the bags under Margo's eyes or the way she sat curled into herself, shoulders hunched protectively.

"Mmm." Margo cleared her throat and shook her head so slightly, Leah wondered if she had imagined the movement. "I need to get moving—"

"Margo—"

Leah's phone dinged, reminding her that she had forgotten to put it on vibrate after she listened to the song last night.

"Get that." Margo winked at her as she climbed to her feet and crossed the room. "It's all good."

Leah sank back in her chair and watched her cousin hurry out the door. It was good, but it wasn't *all good* and hadn't been for a long time. She closed her eyes when her phone dinged again.

She'd liked the song. A lot. Kind of weird that it had rattled around in her head all morning while she showered and dressed. Last night, when she pulled the song up and saw that it was Trace's brother's band singing it, her heart sank just a little bit. She had hoped it was Trace. Sure, she'd heard him sing live, but she hadn't paid much attention to his voice. Now she really wanted to hear it again. Not to mention, she wouldn't mind a good look at him again.

Okay, so the fact that he was in the video mollified her a bit. But he was always in the background. She didn't know cabernets from moscatos when it came to music and musical instruments, so she had no idea what he was playing—bass or rhythm—beyond the fact that it was a guitar. She'd contented herself with watching him, though she had dreamt of watching him—*only him*—on the little stage in the little pub in Nashville.

She yawned as she sat up to grab her phone from the desktop.

What're you listening to?

The familiar question warmed her from the inside out, but a delicious shiver climbed her spine. Laughing at herself, she leaned over the desk.

The Revivalists.

Wish I Knew You?

Haha. No. It Was A Sin.

Mmm. So you listen to a full album? Not just songs that artists release?

I listen to just about anything.

Except country.

Well.

Well?

It's...country.

What does that mean?

It's...whiney. Nasally. Beer drinking music.

You can knock back jack and coke, but you don't drink beer?

I drink beer.

Like what?

Anything. Well...

Well. What?

I don't like light beers.

So you don't like light beer or country music?

Leah tossed her head back and laughed out loud.

I don't listen to country.

Because you don't like it.

I listened to the song.

Yeah? And?

I liked it.

But?

Um.

??? Prove it.

Prove what?

That you drink beer.

"What? How do I prove that?" she mumbled. She tossed
her hands up helplessly and then laughed at herself when

she realized she was answering Trace out loud as if he could hear her.

How do I prove that?

Send me a picture.

Of beer?

Of you drinking a beer.

Leah moved her eyes over the phone screen. 10:24.

"At this time in the morning?" she muttered.

Trace, it's not even noon.

One beer will wreck you?

Are you kidding me?

Dare.

You're daring me to send you a picture of me drinking a beer?

Better yet. Record it.

I'm working!

At a bar.

But I'm working. I don't have time for this!

"Margo acting weird to you?"

Leah jumped and cracked her knee under the desk when she heard Stevi's voice. With a groan and a laugh, she dropped her head to rest it on her arms, folded over the desk calendar.

"Wow."

"What?" Leah asked, face still plastered against the desk.

"You're acting weird, too."

Leah straightened in the chair again and gave Stevi her full attention.

"Good weird," Stevi mumbled. She made her way into the office and stopped to stand behind the desk. Leah watched her glance at her phone. "You're talking to him again, aren't you?"

Leah groaned and rubbed her hands over her face. "I am, yes. I told him I have to get to work."

"Relax, tiger." Stevi offered her a sweet smile. "I love watching this."

"Nothing to watch."

"You look all rosy and happy."

Leah rolled her eyes.

Both of them looked at her phone when it dinged again.

Still waiting.

"What's he waiting for?"

"A picture."

Stevi's mouth dropped open. Her shock delayed the deep-throated mix of a hum and a laugh that finally escaped.

"Stevi Hague." Leah shook her head. "Geez. Get your head outta the gutter."

Stevi cleared her throat and tried to arrange her face in an innocent expression.

"What kind of picture does he want?" She batted her eyes at Leah.

"He wants me to send him a video of me drinking a beer."

"That's…" Stevi narrowed her eyes and shook her head. "That's weird? What? Why?"

"It's not sexual." Leah sighed and pushed her chair back. "He doesn't believe that I like beer."

"Why does he not believe you?"

Leah lunged for her phone when Stevi reached for it.

"Is he sending you pictures, too?" Stevi arched an eyebrow suggestively as Leah curled her hand around her phone and cradled it against her side.

"No. It's just…" She shrugged. "It's…we're just talking. But I don't want you reading the texts."

"Okay." Stevi shrugged her lips. "I get it."

"There's nothing going on—"

"No, I do. I get it." She shrugged. "There're just things you say to someone that you don't want other people hearing or knowing about."

Leah studied Stevi curiously, but she eventually nodded.

"Well. C'mon." Stevi reached for her hand.

"What? Where?"

"You need a beer."

"Oh my God." Leah rolled her eyes.

"Answer him. Tell him to hold his horses."

Stevi says to hold your horses.

Okay. Because after we do that, we're gonna talk about country music.

"Oh my God, seriously?" She sighed as she followed Stevi out of the office.

"See? Now don't do that." Stevi, fingers linked around Leah's, led her down the steps to the bar where Margo and Duncan stood. Duncan was mixing a drink—Leah assumed he was trying a new recipe—and Margo was studying her laptop screen and then eyeing the liquor bottles on the counter.

"Don't do what?"

"Say that stuff. You don't want to share with me what you guys are talking about, so you can't just feed me a line or two."

"He wants to talk about country music." Leah followed Stevi across the main floor to the bar. "Specifically, why I don't like it."

"Barkeep, this woman needs a beer." Stevi smacked her hands on the bar, all but bubbling with excitement.

"Little early for that, isn't it?" Duncan eyed Leah suspiciously as he poured a splash of Iron Horse bourbon into a glass.

"What?" Margo glanced at Leah. "Cat got your tongue?"

"Her friend doesn't believe she drinks beer."

"Oh, I can tell him stories," Duncan muttered.

"No!" Leah shook her head. "No stories from you. From any of you."

"What do you want?" Duncan asked her.

Leah shrugged. She still had a cup of coffee on the desk. The last thing she wanted at the moment was a beer.

"Give her a Trapper," Margo suggested.

Stevi turned and reached for Leah's phone.

"What're you doing?"

"Are you gonna selfie this drink?"

Leah laughed and handed the phone over as Duncan pushed a bottle of Trapper Lager over the bar.

"You could Facetime him—"

"Do not do that." Leah picked up the bottle, but she looked at Stevi quickly. "Please? Don't?"

"Okay, okay." Stevi held her hands up in surrender. "No Facetime. Chug."

Leah rolled her eyes as Stevi lifted her phone to record her.

"I look like shit," she mumbled.

"Thought it didn't matter," Stevi reminded her. "Just friends, right?"

"You look pretty sexy to me." Duncan kept his eyes on his concoction. "Maybe when you finish that beer, you could taste test for me."

"God, no. I still have coffee upstairs."

"Leah. Beer's getting warm."

Leah looked back at Stevi, unnerved with the suspicion that she was already recording.

"Are you—?" She reached for the phone, but Stevi stepped back out of her way.

"Drink."

Leah felt a blush warm her cheeks as she took a healthy drink of the beer. The cold alcohol tasted good going down, but her coffee upstairs had tasted better.

"Trace Dixon, if you want stories about this woman and beer, you just give me a call."

"Margo." Leah rolled her eyes.

"I'm at the Queen."

"Margo." She laughed this time. Took another drink.

"He should just come up here for a weekend," Stevi decided. "We could tell him everything—"

"Okay." Leah stepped closer to Stevi and snatched her phone away from her. She hit the record button to stop it and then watched the forty-seven second video. "Nope. Not sending it."

"What?" Stevi followed her back to the stairs. "What? You better send it, or I will."

"How will you send him anything? You don't have his number!" Leah hesitated at the bottom of the steps.

"I'll sneak into your room tonight—" Stevi launched herself at her. Leah laughed as she reached for the bannister and missed. She swung around to fall gracefully to a sitting position on the third step.

"Send it."

"Why is this so important to you?" Leah asked, still careful to hold her phone out of Stevi's reach.

"You're kidding, right?" Margo called from the bar. Leah glanced at her but held Stevi off with her other hand. "Why wouldn't we want you to be friends with a hot rock star? Gotta be some side benefits for us there."

"He's not all that hot," Duncan mumbled. "Just sayin'."

"He's not a rock star," Leah corrected Margo.

"Leah? Someone puts a smile like that on your face? I don't care if he's hot or ugly as sin." Stevi spoke quietly, but Leah saw Margo nod in agreement. "I just wanna see more of this."

CHAPTER 10

Trace took a drink of his coffee and tapped his pencil on the sheet of paper in front of him. The yellow legal pad was full of his scribbles, though half of them were scratched out. There were doodles down the sides of the paper, but he never claimed to be an artist, so they were unrecognizable. He'd been driven from bed at seven this morning with the need to write. Felt like he'd had the full song in his mind, maybe in a dream, but he'd been working on the damned thing all morning.

His eyes strayed from the paper to his phone. He couldn't concentrate. How the hell could he concentrate when he was waiting for Leah Hague to send him a video of herself? A low laugh rumbled up from his gut. Not even that kind of video, and he was so damned distracted he couldn't think straight.

Thank God he was adult enough that he wasn't writing her name over and over on the paper. He damned sure wanted to, but so far, he'd kept his hand in check.

When he saw the text pop up, he dropped the pencil in exchange for his phone.

Do I really have to send this? I could just send a picture of the beer.

He rubbed his hand over his mouth, aware that the sloppy grin on his face probably made him look like a love struck sixteen-year-old kid.

Please.

Can I just say in my defense that I plan to go home and change before we open?

Send it.

He arched his eyebrows when the video dropped.

Don't put your phone down and walk away now.

God, do you have ESP? How do you know I was going to do that?

He took a deep breath. This could be it. Maybe seeing her in the video would cool his jets. Throw him back to the friend zone. Well, she'd done that already, but maybe seeing her again would bring him back to earth, and he would be okay with the friend zone.

He tapped the screen. Knew already that he would watch it a hundred times to soak everything in. The first time through, though, he would concentrate on Leah. Her hair was piled in some kind of messy twist at the back of her head. A few pieces had escaped the twist, though, and framed her face. No makeup that he could tell. His eyes traced her sharp cheekbones, the hollows under them, her wide, innocent eyes. She held the beer like she'd done it a hundred times before. Tossed back a healthy swallow with ease.

Okay. He was convinced she drank beer. Now to watch it again and listen. Her voice was a little bit sweet, a little husky. He heard her say she looked like shit, which might have amused him, but he listened closer and heard someone else say she thought it didn't matter. *Just friends.* So Leah *had told* someone about running into him. That was something. The guy, though—saying Leah looked pretty sexy. Hell yes, she looked sexy as hell. She was the perfect mix of morning innocence and satisfied woman. Trouble was, he wanted to be the one to tell her that.

He'd like to wake up with her in the morning and whisper those words to her as he slid his leg over hers and smoothed his hand over the warm skin of her belly.

The other girl's comment about stories drew a smile.

Seriously? You're killing me. Killing. Me.

What? I'm watching it.

It's less than a minute long.

I know.

Well??

What?

Convinced?

Yep.

That's it? Yep?

Something came up.

...Like, you have to go? We'll talk later?

Nope. Like I'm looking at a woman who looks incredibly sexy in the morning. Like she might look after a night of satisfying sex.

I don't even remember what mediocre sex is like.

And something came up.

Oh. My. God.

You are adorable when you're embarrassed.

Goodbye.

Don't walk away.

Trace.

We have a lot to talk about.

I am working! Working! You can't say that stuff to me right now.

Because you're working?

That. And because.

Because what else?

We're just friends.

For now. What do you do there in the mornings?

I do some of the purchasing. Inventory. Cleaning or setting up for events. Payables.

As much fun as it was to text her, he wanted to hear her voice again. He didn't answer her last text. Instead, he watched the video again. Listened to her voice. The shaky laughter when the girl—if he had to guess, he would say Margo—said she would share stories.

Are you watching that video again?

This time, he watched her put the bottle to her lips. She licked her lips after she drank; he hadn't noticed that the first time.

Gorgeous.

His dick poked at the fly of his shorts. Trace scooted around on the chair and then reached to adjust himself.

Instead of answering her text, he backed out of the thread and went to her contact information. What if he called her? What would she do? Too much? Too soon?

He shrugged. Looked over the mess on the legal pad, checked out his empty coffee cup, and then glanced at the coffee maker only to find a brown rim in the bottom of the pot, and the orange power light dead. He had been sitting here longer than he realized.

He touched the icon on his screen to call her. Waited with a smile on his face for her to explode. He raised his eyebrows when she declined the call.

Are you kidding me? You're calling me?

Why didn't you answer?

Give me five.

Something come up on your end, too?

Ohmygod. I'm not gonna answer. I will not answer you.

He chuckled and sat back to give her a few minutes. His dick throbbed, but he wouldn't do it. Not now. Totally different to jerk off late at night in his bed with thoughts of her in his head. It felt a little dirty to even consider it here at the kitchen table in broad daylight. Now, if she was here with him? He'd shove everything off the table and take her right here. He'd start with her lips. Lick the same path her tongue had just done. Then he'd flick the tip of his tongue over her throat, dip it in the hollow at the base of her neck. Trace her collarbones.

His thoughts sure as hell weren't helping the wood.

"Idiot." He gave himself a mental shake and squeezed his eyes closed. Pictured Tanner's tour bus with the band on board. The loud music, the beer cans on the table. Five guys on a bus, too close quarters, and not enough fresh air.

Finally, he decided he was in control enough to talk to her.

This time, she answered within seconds.

"Hey."

Her voice was thick like honey, and his dick sure as hell appreciated that thought.

"God, it's good to hear your voice."

"Still not sleeping with you," she answered. Her voice was

light, lyrical, and though he wouldn't push her if she meant no, she sounded like she was teasing him now.

"So if you had to choose…"

"Oh, no. I don't like either or questions."

"Jack and Coke or beer?"

"Beer."

He pushed back from the table and lifted his feet to rest on the chair next to him.

"Why Jack and Coke that night?"

"Why not?"

"I don't know a lot of women who vacation alone several hundred miles from home and stop on the drive back to shoot whiskey."

"I'll bet you know women a hell of a lot more interesting than I am," she answered quietly.

"No." He shook his head. "Nope. I don't."

"Why are you doing this?" she whispered.

"I thought we decided we were going to be friends."

"I won't sleep with you."

He felt the stab of a knife under his heart. Sharp enough that it drew his gaze to his chest. Nothing noticeable on his gray t-shirt, no blood seeping into the shape of a broken heart.

"Okay. But we can be friends, right?"

She hesitated. He heard music, but it was faint enough, he couldn't make it out.

"Sure."

"You listened to the song?"

He held his breath. So what if she said she'd never sleep with him? So what if she meant it? She was the most beautiful woman he'd ever seen, and so far, she was fun and a little bit mysterious. If he couldn't turn her head— but damned if he wouldn't work his ass off to do just that —he would still count himself lucky to call her a friend. Her opinion mattered.

Trace groaned softly and lowered his feet to the floor.

She mattered.

Already.

"I did."

"And?" He hoped he sounded nonchalant. In reality, his heart was hammering out a wicked beat in his throat and his ears.

"I liked it."

He released the breath he hadn't realized he was holding. Not in relief, though, because she spoke with the enthusiasm she might show for lukewarm, backwash light beer on a humid summer day.

"But?"

"What do you mean?"

"You didn't like it much. I can tell."

Trace leaned over to rest his elbow on his knee. The coffee he had savored while he worked burned back up his throat. Unless that bitterness was something else.

"I was just…"

"Just what?"

"Disappointed, I guess."

"Disappointed?" He frowned, hoped she couldn't hear the little tinge of hurt in his voice.

"I was hoping it was you singing it."

"I was singing with my brother's band."

"Yeah, I wanna hear you sing. Not your brother."

Trace jerked upward in his chair, surprised at her words.

"Really?"

"Yep."

"Hmm. Okay."

"Okay? What does that mean?"

"You're working."

"Well, yeah, but—"

"Working tonight?"

"Always."

"Can I talk to you then? Late again?"

He expected her to hesitate. And he wondered what she was thinking.

"Of course."

No hesitation. In fact, she sounded surprised that he would ask.

"Leah?"

He considered telling her he had written the song. Hell, he wrote the majority of Tanner's songs, didn't he?

"Yeah?"

He couldn't, though. Not yet. He wasn't ready to drag any of that up, the stuff with Tanner. And Shelly.

"Can I have Margo's number?"

She laughed.

"The stories they have on you? They're interesting?"

"Goodbye, Trace."

CHAPTER 11

LEAH POURED A GLASS OF SHAMELESS MALBEC AND EYED the growing crowd as she recorked it, set it down, and reached for the Priest Chardonnay next to it. The women across the bar offered smiles and thank yous as she pushed the glasses toward them. She nodded and then carried the bottles back to the cooler at the end of the bar. Thursdays were usually a good bet, and tonight looked to be no different. Trouble was, she was distracted.

The texting this morning. The phone call. She'd had Trace Dixon on her mind all day long. It was one thing to moon over a guy like this. God knows, she'd been attracted to other guys—not quite like this—but still, there was no point in being *seriously attracted* to a man who lived so damned far away. Then again, maybe that was a good thing. He was in Tennessee; she was in Illinois. The odds of them seeing each other in person ever again were pretty low.

Didn't mean she didn't kind of want to, though.

He had sounded…disappointed earlier. When they'd talked about the song. Maybe he didn't want her for himself. Maybe he was scouting out women for his brother. If that were the case, she was definitely out. The younger Dixon brother was easy on the eyes, sure, but Leah had watched a few recordings of live performances online after talking to Trace. Tanner appeared cocky as hell, a little bit brash, and totally the type that would have propositioned her at the bar.

She had hours to go before she could talk to Trace, but she had tucked her phone in her back pocket earlier. Just in case. She doubted he could call now, but it seemed possible he could text a time or two.

Right? Or was she being stupid?

"What?" Stevi leaned into her at the end of the bar. Leah, tall glass of water in hand, looked at her and arched her eyebrows curiously.

"What?"

"Who's being stupid?"

Leah opened her mouth to answer Stevi, but she only shook her head. If she was talking to herself—speaking out loud—maybe she was losing her mind.

"Liam texted me earlier," Stevi told her. "He's got his eyes on a girl at the pool."

Leah grinned. "Yeah, he texted me, too. I told him he's too young for girls."

"Leah." Stevi threw her arm around her back and squeezed her in tight. "Lighten up, babe. He's thirteen, and he's cute."

"Thirteen's too young to look at girls."

"You know what you need?"

Leah drew back from Stevi to eye her warily.

"No, but you're gonna tell me."

"You need to get laid," Stevi told her.

"I agree," Duncan announced as he slid behind them with a customer's credit card in hand. "And I'm here for either one if you need services performed."

Eyes locked, Leah and Stevi laughed softly. Leah rolled her eyes.

"What is getting laid gonna do for me? Complicate the hell out of things—"

"I didn't say go fall in love. Get laid." Stevi shrugged. "Sex is a great way to work out the stress."

"I'm not stressed—"

"Imagine a mind-blowing orgasm right about now."

Leah ducked her head to hide the blush when Duncan sidled up to them and put his arms around them. "Ladies, this is a reputable establishment."

"Find her some love, Dunc." Stevi laughed.

"Wow. Maybe I'll get laid just so *you* feel better, Stevi."

"There ya go. Dante Grant just walked in."

Leah looked toward the door as her phone buzzed in her pocket. Dante Grant usually had an entourage, the majority of them women. Tonight, there was a guy and a woman with him, and Leah caught her breath when her eyes met his across the room. He smiled. Leah smiled back. Good-looking. His caramel-colored skin and golden-brown eyes used to turn her on. The couple he was with—were they a couple, or would the blond chick be ready to toss a drink in Leah's face before the night was over?—grabbed the only open table near the door, near the small stage.

Leah skated her eyes over the front plate glass window. Watched Mick Van Hunt for a moment. She liked him. His music, at least. She wasn't sure in all the time she'd seen him here singing at the Queen she'd ever seen his face. It was always hidden behind a curtain of long black hair.

Dante flashed her a grin from the opposite end of the bar. Leah's hands itched to take her phone from her pocket, but she carried her water glass and slipped away from her sister and Duncan.

"Hey." She smiled as Dante scooted around the bar to hug her. "Long time, no see."

"Out of town," he told her. As she hugged him back, she closed her eyes and breathed deeply, more intoxicated from his scent than the smell of the liquors and alcohol behind the bar. They'd flirted a bit last winter. Shared a kiss. Who knows what might have happened if things had been different for Kenzi?

"You're lookin' good." She backed away and tugged on the sleeve of his white clubbing shirt. He did, too—look good. But not the way he used to. His hair was too dark and thick and curly. His eyes too brown. His skin too warm and dark.

"I missed you." He leaned in and pressed a kiss to her cheek.

"Me, too."

She had missed hanging out at the bar with him. They'd had a few fun conversations about wine and movies, before he had asked her to have dinner with him. She wasn't up for that now, not with a certain Nashville guy in her head. But she could stand here and talk to Dante, ask what he had been up to. No harm there.

"What can I get you?"

The look in his eyes made her uncomfortable, but she held her ground. Dante was a gentleman. He had never forced anything on her, and he wouldn't start now. It just felt a little awkward looking at him with that kiss between them and Trace Dixon on her mind.

"Surprise me." He shrugged. Leah felt her heart kick up a bit. He was reminding her that they'd been around each other enough that she knew his likes, his favorites. She gave him a small nod and turned away to get him a drink. She decided she'd give him a taste of the Braden Valley Reserve. They weren't stocking it yet, but Leah had opened the bottle to taste it and share with favorites and wine connoisseurs whose opinions she valued. Dante certainly fell into both categories.

"I'll cover if you want to leave early," Stevi offered. Leah looked over her shoulder at her sister.

"Stevi."

"You guys haven't seen each other for a while. Go outside and catch up."

"I don't need—"

"Just take a break. I'm not suggesting you grab a quickie in the office."

Leah sighed, ready to argue, but already tired of the argument.

"Do it or I'll text Trace and tell him about karaoke—"

"That's just us having fun." Leah shrugged. One night a week, usually Mondays, after close, the four of them carried on their own little game of karaoke. Although, they sang without music. A line. Ten lines. Whatever the weekly star chose to do.

"No. I mean karaoke at Benson's." Stevi tilted her head at Leah as if she was begging Leah to test her.

"You don't have his number."

"You know me," Stevi reminded her. "I'll find a way."

Leah sighed. Stevi took the Braden Valley bottle from her and nudged her toward Dante. She would rather look at her phone. Read a quick text from Trace. Odds were, he was asking what she was listening to. She wondered what he would say if she told him they had someone here playing. Surely, he wouldn't know the kid; he was local. But Leah figured Trace was familiar with the folk songs the kid played.

She handed Dante the wine, their fingers touching on the stem, and caught her breath when she saw the look on Dante's face. The quick lift of his brow. The tilt of his chin.

Not sure what to say to him, she considered taking his hand and just leading him outside through the back of the building. But considering the kiss they had shared after their one date, it might not be a good idea. She didn't want to give him the wrong impression.

Maybe the fact that she wanted his eyes to be green and his skin to be lighter and his hair to be straighter when she looked at him was reason enough to take a moment and talk to him. If that wasn't enough, the fact that she would much rather hole up upstairs in the office and text with Trace than talk to Dante was reason enough to talk to him. Dante was a good guy, and he was interested, and he was *here*. Trace lived a completely different life, and Leah doubted she would ever see him again.

"Time for a break?" Dante's voice was smooth like expensive whiskey. Leah felt butterfly wings in her stomach, but she was still seeing Trace's eyes in her mind.

"Sure." She nodded. She walked behind the bar knowing Dante would follow her. Her phone had buzzed the second time, and now as she stepped outside and wandered past the small, covered patio area with Dante on her heels, it buzzed again.

She led him out into the parking lot but not into a dark corner, because although it wasn't his style to paw at her or get horny and handsy in public, she didn't want to have any conversation in hearing range of the customers on the patio. She was glad she had worn denim when she hopped up to sit on the neighboring business' loading dock. Dante stood, careful to give her a bit of breathing space.

"I did," he told her in his sincere voice. "Miss you."

She nodded. "Me, too."

"I want you to know—"

"I'm sorry about—"

They both started talking and stopped at the same time. He tipped his head at her with the hint of a smile on his face.

"You first."

"I was just gonna say I'm sorry," she whispered. Right now, she was sorry that she was out here under a starry sky with him and thinking about Trace. That she wanted to rush the conversation and the night just so she could be at home, in bed, talking to Trace.

"It's okay." He stood at her side and leaned his elbows on the dock.

She swallowed hard as she waited for him to finish his thought.

"I know the thing with your friend was hard for you."

Leah winced and looked away. The thing with Kenzi and Joe was more than hard for her, but she didn't want to talk about it. She couldn't put into words what it felt like to lose those relationships, so she wouldn't even try.

"We could start over," he suggested.

"Start over?"

"Dinner." He lifted one shoulder in a careless shrug.

"Dante." If she were ready to date, she would want this to work. But she wanted to want it to work *for them*. Not because she wanted to forget some cowboy who had charmed her a week ago in a Nashville bar and was now— despite all of her protests—claiming her heart.

"Just dinner. I won't rush things."

"I know." She nodded.

"I left town on business. After that night. I've been at the plant since then. I promise I didn't just run out because you said no to a second date."

She ducked her head, a smile playing at her lips.

"I know that."

"Promise?"

She lifted her chin to meet his eyes. The honesty in his warm gaze touched her. Stirred things inside. Mostly guilt, though she was reminded that she had once been attracted to this guy.

Dante moved. Stepped close to her and cupped her chin in his hand.

What had Trace said to her? Was he upset that she hadn't answered him right away?

"Dante." She averted her gaze, gently pulled away from his caress. Fingertips on his collarbone, she gave him a soft push to back him up. "Nothing's changed."

He stared at her for a moment and finally nodded. "Dinner. Just dinner. Next week."

She took a deep breath and considered it. Just dinner. Duncan and the girls wouldn't mind if she slipped out for dinner early in the week. Trace was tied up during the dinner hour—

Guilty for thinking about Trace again, for agreeing to a dinner date because it was at a time when she couldn't talk to Trace anyway, she couldn't meet his eyes when she nodded. "Just dinner."

CHAPTER 12

OF COURSE, TRACE HAD ASKED WHAT SHE WAS LISTENING to. Followed by a text telling her he'd mixed it up and sung a top 40 song. And then he'd warned her not to ask if it was a Taylor Swift song. Leah laughed as she changed her clothes and crawled into bed before she answered him.

At the time you texted, it was a local guy singing a Vance Joy song.

What song?

My Kind of Man.

What is your kind of man?

Ha. The kid's pretty good. He's played the Queen before.

Leah. What's your type?

Leah sighed and propped herself against her pillows.

I don't know. Maybe I don't have a type. Maybe that's why I'm single.

You're not dating anyone?

Ummmmm....well. I had a date before the trip to Florida.

And?

Something. Just something happened.

So no one now?

I'm having dinner with him next week.

She held her breath, afraid he wouldn't text back. The three dots appeared, though, and she worried her bottom lip as she waited to see what he would say.

So tell me about him. Maybe he's your type.

He's...a businessman. His family's into corporate buyouts and takeovers. But Dante runs a chemical plant.

Dante? Really?

Yeah. Why?

You won't go out with me, but you'll have dinner with a guy named Dante?

You never asked me out, and Dante lives here. Not Nashville.

What's he look like?

Nice-looking. Dark hair. Brown eyes.

Has he kissed you?

Trace.

So that's a yes.

Yes.

Is he a good kisser?

Leah dropped her hands to her sides, frustrated with Trace's questions. When her phone buzzed in her hand, she glanced at it.

???

Yeah. I guess so.

Then he's not.

What?

If you guess so.

You're giving me a headache.

Was he at the Queen tonight?

She hesitated. Too long this time. Her phone vibrated in her hand, a long, repeating vibration, which meant a phone call. She took a deep breath as she lifted it to her ear.

"What?"

"Was he?"

"Yes."

"And he kissed you tonight?"

Nerves licked a trail of uneasy heat through her belly and down to her toes.

"No, he didn't."

"Can I ask you something?"

Mouth dry, she tried to swallow.

"I guess." Her words came out like a croak.

"What happened? That drove you to Florida?"

Leah had been expecting a question that involved Dante, so it took her a second to switch gears and think about Kenzi and Joe.

"Um." She breathed through her nose and drew her legs in to fold like a pretzel. Her throat squeezed with emotion.

"Something about him?"

"My friend," she ignored his last question and scrunched her eyes closed. "My friend was pregnant. With her…third baby. She had a stroke during delivery."

"Oh, Leah." He sounded sad for her. She pushed her hair off her face and rubbed her eyes.

"The baby's fine. But, her husband couldn't deal with all of it on his own. So, he moved them all to the east coast. Kenzi's family is there."

"Has she recovered?"

"I guess that depends on how you define recovered."

"I'm so sorry."

"Kenz is actually a few years older than Margo. But we were all good friends."

"Do you still talk to her husband?"

"Yeah." She cleared her throat. "Yeah. Joe calls. He stays in touch with all of us. Her kids do, too."

"I'm sorry. I didn't mean to push you."

Leah considered what Stevi had said to her earlier in the evening.

"It's okay," she mumbled.

"Now I'm not only the guy who hit on you at the bar; I'm the jerk who pushed you to talk about something painful and made you cry."

"I'm not crying."

"I hear it in your voice."

Leah licked her lips and lifted her head to stare at the foot of her bed.

"You said you weren't hitting on me."

His low, sexy laughter went straight to her core.

"Well, I wasn't going to suggest a hook up in the back room."

"We have a nice leather couch in our office at the Queen," she said with a soft laugh.

"And have you hooked up with this guy there?"

"No!"

Stunned by his question, she jumped out of bed to pace her room.

"No. Trace. God, no. He kissed me once. It was a long time ago."

"I would give all the stars in the sky for just a kiss from you."

Leah drew the phone away from her ear to stare at it for a moment.

"Don't say stuff like that."

"But I mean it."

"You're four hundred miles away."

"I have another song for you to listen to."

"Is it your brother's song?"

"Hard Break," he ignored her.

"Trace?"

"Hmm?"

"I'm sorry."

"For what?"

"That I wasn't free to talk to you when you texted."

"Is that your way of saying you were with him when I texted?"

Leah drew the phone away again and blinked at it. How the hell did he know this stuff?

"No," she lied. "I just hate that I wasn't free to talk."

"Goodnight, Leah."

The call ended. Leah stared at her phone in disbelief a third time.

What's your type?

She doubted he would answer her, so she climbed back in bed and turned off her lamp. She held her phone, watched the screen for a few minutes, but when he didn't answer right away, she let her eyes close and pictured him at the bar with her in Left Fork.

She wished now that he would have kissed her.

Several minutes passed, and she was nearly asleep when her phone buzzed again.

Seems obvious.

Wild and willing?

Really? I've never worked so hard for a woman's attention in my life.

She didn't sleep much, thinking about what he'd said, about what she should say to him. Was he upset with her? Hard to tell in a text message, since she couldn't hear his voice. She considered calling him, even went so far as tapping the phone icon and letting her finger hover over his name in her contact list. But she chickened out, set her phone on the nightstand, and curled up on her side with her back to the phone so she wouldn't notice if the screen lit up again.

She tossed and turned most of the night. When she did sleep, she dreamt that she was back in Nashville, and the dream left her feeling empty when she awoke the next morning. There were no new messages, no missed calls, and the lack of something new, the way they'd left things last night made her drag as she gathered clean clothes and headed to the shower.

She stripped down and turned the water on, but before climbing into the shower, she went back to the bedroom and picked up her phone again.

So. You like the thrill of the chase.

She considered the words before she hit send. But she was chilled, and she felt a little bit ridiculous standing in the nude to text him. With a deep breath, she bit the bullet, tapped send, and tossed her phone down on the bed. Not usually one to linger in the shower, unless she was sharing the small space with someone and it had been a long time since that had happened, she flew through this one, anxious to check her phone again.

Wrapped in a towel, she padded back out to her bedroom and leaned over to snatch her phone from the bed. She wondered if Stevi had come home last night. Maybe she'd slept more soundly than she thought, because she hadn't heard her come in.

I like a self-possessed woman who knows what she wants and doesn't throw herself at my feet.

Leah carried her phone back to the bathroom with her. She eyed herself in the mirror. *Self-possessed woman.* Did that apply to her? Maybe. It used to, anyway. Still, the latter part of his answer indicated that he liked the thrill of the chase.

Like I said, the thrill of the chase.

Call it what you want. What're you listening to?

Nothing. I just got out of the shower.

She set the phone down and tugged the towel from her chest.

Would now be a good time to Facetime you?

NO! Ha. Ohmygod. You have to stop. We're friends, Trace.

Are you going to sleep with him?

Leah blinked at the phone, towel still hanging from her hand. She blew out a pained breath and reached with a shaky hand to flip her phone over, screen down. Was she going to sleep with Dante? Was that Trace's business? Well, if Stevi, Margo, or even Duncan asked her, she would answer honestly, wouldn't she? She'd told Trace about Kenzi. She could talk to him about Dante.

Trouble was, she didn't know how to answer him. Did she plan to sleep with Dante when they went for dinner Tuesday night? No. Did that mean she wouldn't sleep with him? Not necessarily. It was too much to text, and she wasn't sure she was up for a phone conversation about something so personal.

Then again, how many nights had she sat at the bar at the Queen and talked face to face with Duncan about sex? About her failed dates? His dates? Conquests?

There's a difference, she reminded herself. And it wasn't something as simple as Leah feeling for Duncan what a sister would feel for a brother. Nope. It was more along the lines of she wasn't attracted to Duncan, and the more she talked to Trace Dixon, the more attracted she was, the more she wanted from him.

Which wasn't likely to happen, even if she hadn't made ridiculous promises to herself and God. When her phone vibrated on the counter, she eyed it, aware that she was getting in deep with someone she simply wasn't going to see often, if ever again. With a sigh, she dressed quickly in athletic shorts and a t-shirt, combed her hair out, and then massaged a handful of mousse into her wet hair.

Finally, she picked up her phone and peeked at it.

??? Off limits? Too personal? Leah?

I'm here. I don't know, Trace.

Don't know?...If I'm being too personal?

If I'm going to sleep with him.

Have you?

Leah laughed softly. She hung her towel over the shower curtain rod and then made her way downstairs, praying not only that Stevi had come home last night, but that by some chance, she was already up, and coffee was brewing.

She glanced at Stevi's closed bedroom door as she slipped out through the living area to the kitchen. No such luck.

You said you've gone out with him. Don't feel like you have to hide things from me.

I'm not ignoring you. I need coffee.

Can't argue with that.

Dante and I have never slept together.

She set her phone down and crossed the kitchen to the pantry. Her insides were jittery enough with the conversation; she probably didn't need coffee. Didn't mean she didn't want it, though. Hard to tell which was pounding harder right now, her head or her heart.

Setting the coffee canister down, she stood for a moment, fists resting on the counter. She swallowed hard and glanced at her phone, surprised that he hadn't answered her yet. Her hands shook as she measured the coffee grounds and filled the machine with water. Again, it hit her that adding caffeine to her already jittery nerves might put her over the edge.

Do you like sex?

Seriously? Did you just ask me that?

Do you?

Yes. It's just. It's complicated, Trace.

You get the full payoff from the experience?

Stunned by his question, she stared silently at her phone. She flexed her fingers and then put the coffee back in the pantry and stood at the open door for a moment. She wasn't hungry; she was scared. Afraid of what he would say next.

Still, the second she heard the telling vibration, she moved back across the room to see what he said.

Can I call you?

No. Please don't.

Are you mad? Offended?

No, but I'd rather not...texting is easier.

Always?

About this.

So. Do you?

Leah carried her phone to the table and carefully pulled a chair out to sit down.

Are you asking because I told you I wouldn't sleep with you? Does that mean something must be wrong with me?

...

She stared at the blinking dots for what felt like an hour, half dreading his response. Finally, she tucked her arm to her side, fingers curled around the phone to wait him out. There was nothing wrong with her. Mentally. Emotionally. Physically. All those things together equaled a healthy woman. But she had always been a bit choosier than Stevi about the men she dated, and she'd been so consumed with fear and grief over Kenzi that sex had been the last thing to worry about.

What would Trace say if she admitted that he was the first man to stir something primal and feminine inside her in what felt like forever?

Your face lit up Left Fork that night. For me. It's not a line.

I was wrecked that night, Trace.

I didn't say your smile. I said your face.

k.

Your first words to me turned me on in ways I can't begin to explain. I hope to hell you don't really think I'm an arrogant jackass who thinks all women should fall at my feet.

Her mouth dry, she tried to swallow.

I don't. This is just so…

What?

I don't know. I never expected to walk into that bar and meet someone like you.

Are you going to answer my question?

The butterflies were back in her belly. Leah smoothed a hand over her stomach as the coffeemaker beeped.

Just a sec. Coffee's ready.

She set her phone on the table and sat for a moment. What was she getting herself into? She liked this guy. Already, she would miss him like crazy if they stopped texting. Flirting with him seemed harmless with a good four hundred miles between them. On the other hand, getting in over her head with a celebrity—on any level— seemed a little crazy. Most definitely not something Leah Hague would normally do.

The pounding in her head hadn't eased, so she finally hauled herself out of the chair. When she heard Stevi open her door, she automatically took two mugs from the cabinet and filled them both.

"Hey."

"Hi." Stevi took the mug she offered. Leah watched her sister lean her back in the doorway, bend her knee, and prop her foot on the doorframe.

"What's up? You look upset."

Stevi shook her head and met Leah's eyes. "I'm fine."

"You sure?"

"Still talking to Nashville?"

Leah laughed softly. "Yeah."

"How did you hook him?" Stevi arched an eyebrow at her. "So unfair that you caught his eye, because you don't even care. He's possibly the hottest guy I've ever seen, he's into you, and you don't care."

Leah grinned. "He's pretty hot," she agreed.

"Okay, so if you're just friends?" Stevi cleared her throat. Leah felt a rush of possessiveness in her throat, but she hoped Stevi couldn't see it. If her sister asked her to introduce them, it would break her heart. "That's cool. But don't forget I'm your best friend, okay?"

"Stevi." Leah's eyes burned. She rubbed her free hand over her face.

"I mean it, Leah." Stevi straightened. She looked small today, a little bit sad, and Leah wondered what was going on with her. "I get that you were close to Kenz. We all love her. We all love Joe. But I'm still here."

"I know that."

"Do you?" Stevi arched her eyebrows. "You don't talk to me much these days."

"We work together—"

Stevi shook her head as she turned to head back to her bedroom. "Not what I mean."

Leah sighed. She watched her sister slip back inside her bedroom and close the door. Nerves jangling again, she went back to the table and sat down.

Sorry. Talking to my sister.

Which one is your sister?

Stevi. The cute little blonde. She thinks you're pretty hot.

Got your coffee?

Yep.

Okay. Answer my question.

Sometimes.

Sometimes? Really?

Yeah. I don't think that's so unusual.

No. No, I don't mean that.

Then what?

Again with the three dots blinking at her.

???

I kind of feel like whatever I say here is going to be wrong.

But you asked me a personal question. I answered it. Tell me what you meant by what you said.

If it were me? If I were the one to touch you that way, I'd do everything I could to make you feel good.

Leah groaned out loud. Frustrated with promises she'd made in a tragic moment. Frustrated by the distance between them. With herself for shutting him down that night in Nashville. Although if she'd have engaged, would they be talking now? Or would she have been just another woman to open her legs to a music star?

Is that okay? If I say that?

Leah rested her elbows on the table and combed her fingers through her hair.

Yeah. It's fine.

It's not fine. I offended you.

No. I just feel like I need a cold shower now.

Why haven't you slept with your guy? Dante? Just tell me.

Leah dropped her head forward and rubbed her neck. Maybe Stevi was right. Maybe she did need sex. A carefree night on the town with someone she enjoyed being around. Dinner. A glass of wine. Sex didn't have to mean she was in a committed relationship. Maybe she needed that kind of intimate touch; it really had been too long.

Okay. Okay. I give.

What? What do you mean?

Stevi suggested last night that I need to get laid. Maybe you guys are right.

CHAPTER 13

How she could take what he had said and misconstrue it as encouragement to sleep with the Dante guy was beyond him. Trace moved through the weekend in an angry, jealous haze. Oddly enough, the only time he was calm was when he was texting with the woman who made him want to punch something. Clearly, she had no interest in him. She'd been a bit flirty here and there, and the comment about needing a cold shower had sent every drop of blood in his body south of the equator. He'd finished that conversation with her with blue balls, taken his own cold shower, and then headed to the gym to work off the restless energy that kicked to life inside him the second he was out of the shower.

If the weekend was bad, the week—Leah hadn't been clear on what night she was seeing her guy for dinner—started out bad and went from there to hell in about five seconds. He woke with her on his mind Monday; well, Trace wasn't sure there was a time she wasn't on his mind anymore. But remembering before he'd even climbed out of bed Monday that she had a date this week had been a pit in his stomach. His coffee had tasted bitter, and it had scalded his tongue and the roof of his mouth when he'd swallowed it, and he'd snapped at his mother when she'd called two minutes later.

"I'm on my way out the door, Mama," he told her as he put the handheld router Sampson had asked to borrow in his truck. He noticed dirt and grease on his hand and almost swiped it on his jeans. But he caught himself and with a mumbled curse, he went back inside the house.

"You're always on the way out the door, Trace Dixon."

He laughed quietly as he propped the phone between his ear and his shoulder and then washed his hands at the kitchen sink.

"How ya feelin' today?" He took a deep breath. Sounded calmer now, though Leah and her date were still in the back of his mind. His mother was a vibrant woman, and she sounded cheerful today. But now and then, Trace heard her age creeping into her voice. The cancer sure didn't help. Remission was a big word, but it always seemed too simple to Trace, and since he'd lost his dad so long ago and because his mother meant so much to him, he didn't trust it. The word. The meaning. The oncologist who used it.

"Good." She sounded almost breathless. Trace dried his hands thoroughly on the dishtowel, a frown drawing his eyebrows down hard. Was she fibbing to him? "I talked to Pearl Allen Saturday morning."

The frown rearranged itself into resignation. Though he loved his mama and Pearl damned near more than anything in life, it was never a good thing when the two women had time to chat. They had nothing in common; nothing, except, of course, Trace.

"Yeah?" He turned to lean his back against the counter and crossed his booted feet. The soft chime in his ear told him he had a text, and because he didn't text often with anyone other than Leah, he had to assume the text was from her. He held his breath, waiting for his mother to spit it out. The funny thing was that Leah might be texting him to tell him she saw a redbird out the back window when she fixed coffee or that the mailman brought her a catalog for a new deli in town, and still, all he wanted at the moment was to tell his mom he'd talk to her later and look at those words.

No matter what she said to him, her texts always sent the sweetest thrill through him. He wondered what she would say about that. What any of his friends would say. Jesus, he was pussy-whipped with this woman, and she had friend-zoned him two seconds into their relationship.

"She says there's a new lady in your life."

Trace flinched. There wasn't. A new lady. As badly as he would like to be more than a friend to Leah, he wasn't. She had made it clear she wasn't interested, and his parents had raised him to be a gentleman. He might pursue her, but he would never push. Apparently, his parents had lived the old saying that the rules were lax for the second kid, because Tanner didn't seem to know how to spell the word, let alone how to *be* a gentleman.

Not that Trace cared.

"She's wrong, Mama. We're just friends."

"Well, then there must be something wrong with her," his mother answered immediately. Trace rolled his eyes. His mother would have him married off to the owner of the first breast he'd signed if she had any say about it.

"Actually, there's not." He sighed as he straightened and then stretched. "I gotta go, Mama. Sampson's got a new side project he wants some help with."

"Yeah, Pearl told me about that beer garden thing he's trying to do out back. Waste a time if you ask me."

"He didn't," Trace reminded her. "Call you—"

"Don't you hang up on me, Trace Dixon. Have you talked to Tanner lately?"

"No, ma'am."

"Why not?"

Trace squeezed his eyes closed and pressed his fist to his forehead. He loved her, but he hated that she still fawned over his little brother like he was a baby.

"Lot going on." His voice was gruff. "And I think Tanner's a little busy, too."

He didn't remind her that not only was Tanner on tour, but he also had Trace's ex on the bus with him so he was working nights and probably burning the midnight oil after the shows. Trace was happy as hell for him to stay busy, because he had nothing to say to him, anyway.

"Trace, he's your brother—"

"Gotta go, Mama. Love you."

A familiar ache wound its way into his neck and his shoulders. He disconnected the call and stood for a moment. His hands itched to check the text that had dropped while he was on the phone, but he needed a moment to push his brother as far from his head as he could before he started talking to Leah.

Happy Monday. The coffee maker decided to quit today.

Oh damn. Not good.

No kidding. Ever make a coffee run at six? A.M? In pajamas?

Um. No. Can't say that I have.

The dregs of the Tanner-induced headache still tucked into his shoulders, Trace picked up his keys and looked around the kitchen. His coffee maker—the bastard that had burned his mouth this morning—was turned off. Water was off. He'd already put the router for Sampson in the truck. Keys in hand. He was ready to go.

Just don't. There were seven cars in front of me at the drive-up window.

Wait. In pajamas? You went for coffee in pajamas?

Don't worry. I didn't get out of the car.

But. What do you wear to bed?

He pulled his back door closed as he stepped into the garage and then jiggled the handle to make sure it was locked. Probably he wouldn't admit it to her, but he had spent many nights since they started talking wondering what she wore to bed. Since it was summer, he doubted she wore anything made of fleece. But did she wear a nightgown? Surely not. Did women drive for coffee in nightgowns?

You're just asking because you wanna know what I wear to bed.

Um. You got me.

Shorts and a tank. It's fine. My point is that I had to wait nearly twenty minutes to get my coffee. Like the SUV in front of me? I swear the woman had nine drinks handed out the window to her.

So was it a tight-fitting tank? Or loose? Either way, the person at the window got an eyeful. Trace climbed into his truck, but he sat for a second. The thought of Leah in a tank top, waiting for coffee, made him hard. Hell, the thought of Leah brushing her teeth or changing a flat tire made him hard.

Was it tonight? Her date? Should he ask? No.

Get a new coffee maker.

I will.

Because if she didn't, he'd go and buy one and ship it to her. Better yet, he would order her one online and have it sent directly to her. Anything he could do to minimize her out running around half-naked.

Why were you up at 6?

When she didn't answer right away, he drew in a deep breath and then started the truck. Naturally, the phone chimed as soon as he backed out of the driveway. He could stop. Pull over and text her back. But then again, he could spend the whole day pulled over on the side of the road texting her. Wouldn't bother him.

Rather than fool with that, he dialed her number and let the call go to Bluetooth.

"Hey." Her thick, husky voice made his dick stir to life the same as it always did.

"Why were you up at six?" he asked without preamble.

"I answered you."

"I'm driving."

"Mm."

The soft sound—a bit too much like a moan—went straight to his heart.

"Couldn't sleep." She sounded tired.

"You okay?"

"Yeah. Just tossed and turned for a while and finally decided to just get up."

"Are you home now?"

"I am."

He could hear the slight echo of her voice in her house, and he wondered what she was doing. Pacing in the kitchen? Sitting in a sunroom to enjoy her coffee?

"I'm heading over to Sampson's house."

"What're you doing over there?"

"He's got it in his head that we need to make the little outdoor area behind the Fork into a bigger beer garden. Pearl says no. I mean, they do well without it, but I have to agree with Sampson, that it would be a draw."

"Left Fork is a gorgeous place," Leah answered. "I would think an outdoor beer garden would go over well."

"Pearl doesn't like change." It was that simple, and that made everything they did there difficult.

Leah laughed. "God, I hear you. My Granddad hated the thought of progress. I'd like to think he'd like what we've done with the place, but he'd probably roll over in his grave if he could see the Queen now."

"You got the Queen from your…grandfather?"

"Yeah." She cleared her throat. "Well, it was a riverfront shack back in the day. I mean, a bar fight might've knocked the whole place over. Could've all ended up in the Mississippi, really. Granddad had money, which surprised all of us, after the way he lived. But we took our money and pooled it and invested in the bar. Duncan and his dad and my dad took some of the old, weathered wood from Granddad's shack and used it when they built the bar in the Queen."

"And your grandmother?"

He heard her sigh. Waited with baited breath for her answer.

"Gram passed away when I was nine. I think that's why the Queen was so important to Granddad. It was steady. His customers were his family, and he needed that when Gram was gone."

"What're you doing?" he asked her as he coasted toward town. There wasn't much he and Sampson could do today, but he supposed they could start drawing up the plans. Sampson had done all the work on Left Fork himself, but then, that had been years ago, and the man had aged since then.

"Sitting on the front porch."

"In your pajamas?"

"Yep."

"Any pileups yet?"

"No. As a matter of fact, no one's even looking at me. Should I flash the next car?"

"Would you?"

"No, that's Stevi."

"I gotta go."

"Talk later?"

"You bet."

He drew in a long, sharp breath as he ended the call.

TUESDAY NIGHT WAS RIDICULOUS, BECAUSE TRACE SORT OF thought Leah had said Tuesdays were slow, which could mean that it would be a good date night. Every song he sang was about cheating or hearts breaking, which was ridiculous, considering they were just friends. He broke two strings on Loretta and ended up having to pull out Lucille, another well-loved guitar, because he didn't have a third spare string to fix Loretta. To make matters worse, he yelled at Angie, was surprised when she sassed right back at him, and ended up in an argument with Sampson over Nascar. *He didn't even watch Nascar.* He'd only wanted to pick a fight to keep his mind off Leah and what she might be doing with her date.

The hell of it was, when he texted her on Wednesday morning—he hadn't bothered her Tuesday night, promised himself he wouldn't be the pathetic pansy texting a woman who was possibly in the throes of orgasm with someone else—she answered as if nothing monumental had happened the night before. Trace didn't mention it, but he wanted to. For one thing, after the intensely personal conversation they'd had last weekend, it seemed like he should ask about her date. But he knew it would come off as him being nosy and jealous, and he refused to be that guy.

Instead, he took it out on the Left Fork crew. Trace often spent mornings at the bar, helping Pearl and Sampson with any little things that needed doing. Sometimes those little things included fixing a kitchen appliance, although Trace was the first to admit the SubZero refrigerator and oven were over his head. Sometimes he helped Pearl with deep cleaning. Taste-testing a new recipe, which he certainly didn't consider a hardship. Pearl was touchy about his help, so he told her he had nothing better to do. She knew he was lying, and he knew she knew, but they both pretended otherwise.

Niall's got some tendon issue in his wrist. Need you back.

Trace blinked at his phone in disbelief. First time his brother had bothered to text him since a week or two after Christmas. Their mom had harped on Trace since then to call Tanner. Trace had no doubt that she'd harped on Tanner with the same directive.

Busy here. No can do.

Left Fork'll always be there. I need you here.

Trace tossed his phone down on the bar as he slid his butt onto a barstool. He rubbed his hands over his face, anger seething inside. He hadn't forgiven Tanner. Never mind Shelly. Women like Shelly Carlyle were easy come, easy go, but Tanner was his brother.

"Why don't you take a road trip?"

Trace dragged his fingers down over his face to look at Pearl.

"What?"

She gestured at his phone.

"Not interested." He shrugged. For all he cared, Tanner and his band could crash from the charts and fall off the face of the earth. No way he was going to pack up his life and go back on tour with the arrogant little bastard.

Pearl snorted softly and folded her arms over her chest.

"That woman's had you tied in knots for over a month now."

Trace frowned and shook his head.

"Go see her."

"It hasn't been a month," he argued, "and that was Tanner."

Pearl, thank God, was on his side. Now and then she paid lip service to the idea of forgiveness and bygones, but she wasn't Tanner's mother and she didn't love him the way his own mother did. She reached for his phone and tapped it, a stern look on her face.

"It has been a month." She stared him down with a no-nonsense look. "You're up and you're down, and you're all over the place. You've made Angie cry three times this past week, and that girl doesn't cry about dead dogs."

Trace narrowed his eyes in thought. It had been awhile since Leah Hague had been here, right here at this bar in Nashville, but he had no idea it had been that long. They talked every day, sometimes by phone, always by text. Now and then she referenced Dante, and Trace knew without thinking about it that those were the times he'd bit Angie's head off and made her cry.

"Who the hell doesn't cry about dead dogs?" he mumbled.

"Take some time. Go see her. Make it right."

Trace shook his head. "Nothing to make right, Pearl. We're friends."

"Never seen a grown man mope around over a woman friend the way you do."

"She's seeing someone."

"Does he know she spends all of her free time talking to you?"

"How do you know that? She's with her sister a lot. Her cousin. She watches classic movies. And she reads—"

"It's an order, Trace Dixon."

"Pearl," he whined. "C'mon. Don't do this. Don't. I'll tell Angie I'm sorry."

"Tell Angie you're sorry for what?" Angie appeared at his shoulder. She set her purse and her keys on the bar and turned a cool green-eyed stare his way. "What's going on?"

"Pearl thinks I need to go see Leah."

"The texty girlfriend?" Angie slid her gaze toward Pearl.

"That's the one."

"She's not my girlfriend."

"You've kind of been a dick since you met her." Angie studied her fingernails. She shrugged, flicked her eyes up to meet his.

"She's seeing someone."

Angie laughed. She stepped closer to Trace and slipped her arm around his shoulder.

"Go find her and swing your—"

"Do. Not. Say. That." He pinned her in place with a threatening look. "You hear me? Do not say that to me. I'm old enough to be your dad—"

"You are not." She rolled her eyes. "You're Trace Dixon. What woman could resist that?"

"She did," he said simply.

"That's making you crazy, isn't it?" Angie grinned. "C'mon. I agree with Pearl. Go see her."

"The last thing a woman would want would be for a guy—"

"Like you to give up so easily," Angie interrupted him. "Man up. I know you've got balls, Dixon. Go fight for her."

Trace blinked at Pearl when Angie walked back toward the kitchen.

"What she said." Pearl nodded her agreement.

Trace pursed his lips.

"Tanner's lead guitarist has an owie. He wants me to take his place."

"You know how I feel about your brother." Pearl harrumphed and turned her back to him. She made a show of wiping down clean glasses.

"I know. But Mama wants things fixed."

He saw her shoulders droop. Pearl and Sampson were his people. Not Tanner's. Not his parents'. And yet, there was some sort of kinship or bond sacred to women, and though Pearl had no love in her heart for Tanner, she cared about their mother.

"That what you're gonna do, Trace?" Pearl asked him. He scooted his phone toward him, but he looked up when Pearl turned to look at him. "You gonna put your dreams on hold again and rescue Tanner? Because that ain't gonna fix Tanner. Or your mama. And letting that woman go now? That's gonna be the last break you can take."

CHAPTER 14

Leah felt Dante's eyes on her as she made her way down the bar. He was with his brother; he never bothered her when she was working. He always said hello, and they talked for a bit, but he didn't demand her attention. She never felt like she was supposed to babysit him, never worried that he wasn't enjoying himself. Still, as she spoke with patrons, refilling drinks and leaning in to hear them better and field any questions they had about the dinner menu, she was a little uncomfortable. She'd gone to dinner with him twice in the past ten days. She'd kissed him goodnight each time, but she felt nothing. There was no fluttery feeling in her belly, no tingling in her toes or fingers. She didn't get breathless with anticipation, and the one time things had sort of progressed beyond that first kiss and Dante had stroked his hand up over her back and touched her bra, she'd backed away. He had brushed her apology away, and apparently, he was the world's most patient man, because he continued to ask her out and he was nothing, if not sweet.

The fluttery feelings and the tingles and all the rest came and went with every conversation she and Trace had. Sometimes they talked for hours about music; she listened dutifully to anything Trace suggested she try. Some of the songs she liked—others, she didn't. What didn't change was her opinion of his brother, but she didn't tell him that. She wondered, still, why Trace was a house musician in a Nashville bar. She'd given in and done a bit more research online. Found two CDs he'd released, one of them nearly ten years ago. She didn't tell him she downloaded them and listened to them and that if she was going to like country music, then his CDs were her favorite.

"Dinner tomorrow?"

Leah cleared her throat as she turned to Dante. She hadn't realized she'd worked her way down to his end of the bar. She wasn't prepared to talk to him. She hadn't spent the day psyching herself up to talk to him, to say yes to the next date. She didn't want to go out with him again. Trying to be attracted to him was getting exhausted.

Joe had called when she was with him last. She'd been tempted to excuse herself and answer the call, but one look at Dante's face had stopped her. What the hell was wrong with her? This nice guy with a good-looking face wanted to be with her, and she simply wasn't interested in more than friendship.

She'd let Joe's call go to voicemail. Texted him later and promised she would call him back. That had been three nights ago, and she had yet to return the call. Adelynn had texted several times and because she hadn't mentioned

Kenzi, she knew there was nothing significant he needed to tell her. No change in Kenzi's condition.

"Dante." She held her breath. "I'm sorry."

She looked around helplessly in search of his brother, but at the moment, Dante was alone at this end of the bar.

"I've been afraid of this since I got back in town," he said quietly.

"I'm sorry," she said again. "Really. I'm just not...I don't know. I'm not ready for this right now."

"Not even dinner?"

She laughed softly. "When we go to dinner, I feel guilty, because I know you want more, and I don't have it to give you."

"I'd never—"

"I know." She nodded. "Believe me, I know. You deserve more."

"Are you kicking me out of the Queen?"

"Never." She moved closer to him and slipped her arm around his shoulders. "You're always welcome here. I just don't think we're right for each other."

"How about New Year's Eve?"

She laughed softly. A Thursday evening, there was no live music, but "Why Am I the One" by Fun played quietly over the speakers. Their crowd was minimal tonight after heavy traffic during the dinner hour. As always, Leah looked forward to closing when she could sneak away to talk to Trace. Margo and Stevi had made her swear she would stick around for a while. Since she'd met Trace, she hadn't been a part of their crazy after-hour antics, and even though she loved talking to Trace, she had to admit, she missed hanging out with them.

"That gives you plenty of time to feel ready."

Leah shook her head. "If you're still waiting on me in six months, I'm going to kick you."

"Kiss me?" He arched an eyebrow at her. When he wiggled it suggestively, she dropped her head back and laughed out loud.

"Go find some gorgeous chick who hangs on your every word." When he stood, she stepped closer to him to hug him. "Well, I didn't mean for you to do it right now."

His body shook against hers when he laughed. She tilted her head up to look at him and lifted her hand to cup the back of his head when he kissed her.

"It's a worthy quest," he said as he backed away from her. "But it seems impossible."

"Are you really leaving?" she asked as he tossed cash down on the counter to cover the drinks he and his brother had had.

"Jax had to go," he shrugged, "and one of the owners of the Queen just dumped me. Might be time to call it a night."

"Dante. No." She touched his hand.

"I'll be back." He nodded. Leah sighed when he brushed his lips over her cheek. "I promise."

"Well, bring a date!" she hollered at him as he headed toward the door. He waved without looking back.

"Cut him loose, huh?" Duncan dropped his hands on her shoulders. She nodded. "'Bout time."

"What?" She whirled around to look at him in disbelief. "You and Stevi are the ones who told me to go out with him again."

"Stevi did," he corrected her.

"Leah Hague!"

She turned to the voice at the other end of the bar and smiled at the girl standing with Stevi. Chantele Bonham. They'd gone to high school together, but she hadn't seen Chantele in years.

"Hey!"

Duncan dropped his hands from her shoulders, and Leah made her way back down the bar to hug her old friend.

"This place is great!" Chantele squeezed her and then released her. "I ran into Margo at the bank the other day. She told me to come in."

"I'm glad you did."

"Chantele's a wine drinker," Stevi told her. Leah rubbed her hands together greedily and raised her eyebrows expectantly. Would she know what she wanted or would she ask for a recommendation? Leah lived for the patrons who loved wine as much as she did.

"What's good here?"

Stevi groaned and shook her head. "Way to push her start button." She patted Chantele's arm. "Good luck."

"Thanks." Leah narrowed her eyes as Stevi leaned in close to whisper to her.

"Someone needs to push it. Did you just break up with Dante?"

"There was nothing to break up, Stevi."

Stevi laid her hand on Leah's back. "I wanna shake you. Live a little, Leah."

"I'm fine, Stevi." She shrugged. "I don't need to date someone to be okay."

"I hope you like red wine," Stevi called to Chantele as she moved away in the opposite direction. "Because Leah does. And she will try to convert you."

"A glass of red a day is good for your heart," Leah hollered after Stevi. Her eyes roamed over the patrons at the bar. She noticed two women who had just come in. One was talking to Duncan, and the other was browsing the drink menu. A guy with a ball cap tugged low. And a middle-aged couple that reminded her she should check in with her parents tomorrow morning.

"I'm good with red," Chantele agreed.

"Do you like cabs?"

"Yes."

Leah selected her current favorite, Dyksta Vineyards 2013 cab, and poured a generous amount in a glass.

"So what have you been up to?" she asked her friend as she handed the glass to her.

"Married Harrison Selby."

"You—? Really?"

"Yeah. We moved to Kansas City about a hundred years ago."

Leah looked around for her own wine and mumbled her thanks when Duncan noticed her searching and retrieved it for her. Again, her eyes skated over the patrons at the bar, catching for a moment on the guy with the ball cap. He glanced up at her as she looked away.

"Thanks," she told Duncan.

"Absolutely." He gave her a curt nod. "By the way, you're up tonight."

He was talking about their after-hours karaoke game. She turned back to Chantele and took a healthy drink of her wine when she heard the word *kids*. Leah loved her cousin's daughter more than anything, but the thought of having her own children made her twitchy. Chantele talked her ear off, and before long, Leah found herself daydreaming about Trace. Trying to figure out how she could wiggle out of after-hours so she could go home and text him. He hadn't asked much about Dante lately, but she wanted to tell him she wasn't going to see him anymore.

Eventually, Margo slid onto the barstool next to Chantele, and Leah was relieved to move away. How anyone could have three kids and so much energy at nine in the evening was a mystery to her. She was always beat after hanging out with Margo and Berkley.

Her phone buzzed in her pocket. She set her glass down and protested when Stevi snatched it up to pour her a refill.

"Know your song yet?" Stevi asked her.

"No." Leah pulled her phone from her pocket and peeked at it. The by now familiar question tugged at her heart.

What're you listening to?

She knew by now that he simply loved music. His question had nothing to do with pushing his music or any country artist on her. He was familiar with the majority of artists and songs she told him she was listening to, and he could talk about any music for hours.

Head cocked to hear the song, she felt eyes on her and figured Stevi was scheming to set her up with someone else.

Lorde.

???

She laughed softly. She should know just to tell him which song, because he always asked.

"Royals."

His answer was instant. Leah took her glass back from Stevi and smiled. Her sister meant well. Maybe Leah should suggest a girls' day. They could hang out Sunday. Do lunch and maybe some shopping. She felt a twinge of sadness. The four of them—Margo, Stevi, Kenzi, and Leah —used to do those fun girls' days. She sipped her wine and looked at her phone again.

Me too.

Something inside Leah slipped, maybe her stomach. Maybe her heart. She lifted her head, eyes darting immediately to the guy at the bar. The one with the ball cap.

"Ohmygod."

His lips twitched, and then that smile knocked her back a step.

"Ohmygod," she whispered.

"You okay?" Stevi stepped closer to her. Leah handed her glass to her sister as she took a wobbly step to get out from behind the bar.

"Ohmygod," she said again, and this time, even though her throat was so tight she could hardly breathe, she was laughing, too. Now she felt all eyes in the room on her as she moved around the end of the bar and came to a stop as he slid off the stool and turned to her.

"Hey, darlin'."

"What're you doing here?"

Breathless, she could only whisper. Her eyes burned with tears as she threw her arms around his neck to hug him.

"I wanted to see you."

Overwhelmed, tears spilled over her cheeks when he slid his arms around her waist and gathered her in to hold her. Thankfully, he held her hard and tight, because she was sure if he let go, she'd be on the floor.

"You okay?" His cheek pressed to hers, his breath was warm on her neck and her ear.

"Yes." She nodded. "Just need a minute."

"Take your time."

She laughed, suddenly aware that they were plastered up against each other with a captive audience watching every move. He smelled like woodsy cologne and fresh laundry detergent, and when she pulled back to look at him, she smelled beer and found herself thirsty.

"How long have you been sitting there?"

"A while." Even with the audience, his eyes were locked with hers, his smile a private gift for her only.

"How many times did I look at you?" She laughed quietly.

"Is it okay that I'm here?"

"Yes." She nodded. "Yes, of course. I'm just…"

"Need to sit down?"

She did, but she didn't want to move from the loose circle of his arms now.

"I'm okay." She took a deep breath.

"Are you sure? Because I don't mind holding on to you."

Embarrassed, she ducked her chin to her chest and shook her head.

"Trace?"

"Hmm?"

She tipped her head and met his eyes.

"Still not gonna sleep with you."

Leah's knees went weak when he threw his head back and cut loose with a hearty laugh. The sound whipped the butterflies in her belly to a frenzy, and her eyes were drawn to the dark beard stubble that covered his cheeks and his chin and part of his neck. Stevi was wrong. Trace Dixon wasn't just hot. He was the most beautiful man she'd ever laid eyes on.

"There's my girl."

Thankfully, he hugged her again, because those words —*my girl*—rendered her a helpless puddle of want. He kissed her, just a quick brush of his lips over her cheekbone, and Leah suddenly remembered that Dante had been here earlier. Had Trace seen her with him?

Did it matter? He knew she was seeing someone. She hadn't lied to him. About Dante or anything else. Except making him believe she was okay with being his friend.

"So."

Leah blinked when she heard her sister's voice. She ducked her head again, rested her forehead on Trace's shoulder.

"You've staked your claim." Stevi's voice was light with amusement. "But can Margo and I just get an introduction?"

Leah lifted her head and aimed a sheepish grin at Stevi.

"No claims." She shrugged. "Stevi, Margo, this is my friend, Trace."

As thrilled as she was to see him and as proud as she was to call him friend, she kind of hated this moment. She had repeatedly told him she wasn't interested in anything other than friendship. Cute, fun-loving Stevi was a completely different story. Leah didn't believe her sister bedded every guy she dated, but even the thought of her sister spending an innocent evening with him made her see green.

"Trace, this is my sister, Stevi." She watched his face, looking for a sign of attraction, she supposed. Trace tucked Leah against his left side and offered his right hand to shake Stevi's. Nothing other than a friendly smile. Not even the private friendly smile he'd given her. "And my cousin, Margo."

"Ladies." He tipped his head. "Nice to meet you."

"It's nice to meet you, too." Stevi took her hand back. "Why don't you go ahead? We can close up."

Margo—sensible, men-are-jerks Margo—turned to Leah with big, dreamy eyes as Trace shook her hand. She nodded in agreement with Stevi.

"No way she's getting out of after hours."

Leah looked up quickly as Duncan approached them. It startled her to realize she had her arm around Trace. When had that happened? Rather than draw away from him and make a scene, she curled her fingers around a handful of his soft t-shirt and held on.

"Duncan, this is Trace." This one was easier. Nothing to be jealous of with Duncan meeting Trace. "Trace, this is Margo's stepbrother, Duncan."

"Nice to meet you, man." Duncan shook Trace's hand, seemingly unimpressed with his celebrity status. "You're on, Leah Hague. Not letting you off the hook."

"Yes. We are." Stevi tugged on Duncan's arm.

"It's okay." Trace shrugged. "I don't mind hanging out here."

Leah laughed. As if she would be able to sing a word with Trace Dixon hanging around.

"Get a drink and go outside," Margo suggested. "Last time I checked, there was no one on the patio."

Leah avoided Trace's eyes. Stevi and Margo thought they needed to be alone to…what? Kiss hello? Make out? Nope and nope. She'd dug herself into a hole with the texts and the phone calls. If she kissed him, she would lose her heart.

"Good idea." Stevi nodded. Leah swallowed hard as she watched her sister hustle around the bar to get Leah's wine for her. Trace leaned to snag his beer from the bar. Had she served him? Without realizing who he was?

No way. He had the bill of his cap pulled tight and low over his eyes, but she would have recognized his voice instantly. She gulped for air when Stevi handed her the wine and Trace took her other hand in his.

"You lead the way."

CHAPTER 15

"You okay?"

Still trying to avoid his eyes, Leah nodded. They stood—alone—on the patio. Without the audience, Leah was afraid she would start shaking.

"Yeah." She nodded again, more forcefully this time. "I'm just..."

"I wanted to see you in your element." He leaned his elbows on the wooden railing, the bottle dangling from his fingers, but he turned his head to look at her. "If you had known I was coming, it would have been...staged. Practiced."

"I'm a little overwhelmed," she admitted.

"And yet, not an ounce of that feeling is about who I am."

She swallowed hard and flicked her gaze over to meet his.

"Who you are to me." She shrugged, dragged her eyes away again. She felt him watching her as she studied the parking lot, the few cars parked out here.

"And that would be…" He nodded his head back and forth. "A friend. Right?"

"Yeah."

He stood and turned to prop his thigh on the railing. Took a drink and studied her when he swallowed.

"Friends hang out sometimes. Right?"

"Of course."

"Good."

Leah sipped her wine, uncomfortable under his heavy stare.

"Are you okay?" she asked quietly.

He hedged. Gave her a half shrug and looked around skittishly.

"How long were you sitting there?"

"Long enough to see the kiss that guy laid on you before he walked away."

Leah took a deep breath and lowered her gaze to his scuffed up, square-toed boots.

"I hope that was your boyfriend and not just someone you served tonight."

One corner of his mouth was tugged up in a lazy smile when she peeked up at him.

"That was Dante," she told him. "But I told him tonight I didn't want to see him anymore."

"That was a goodbye kiss?"

She answered with a slow nod.

"Did you ever sleep with him?"

"Really? We're gonna dive right in?"

"Leah, we've talked about what it takes to get you off," he reminded her. "You can't look at me and tell me if you slept with him?"

She covered her face with her free hand when her cheeks flooded with heat.

"We did not talk about what it takes to get me off." She shook her head.

"I asked," he told her. "And I told you I would push every button until—"

"This isn't..." She shook her head and squeezed her eyes closed.

"I know." He stroked his fingers over her cheek. "I'm sorry."

She licked her lips and stared at him expectantly.

"We didn't discuss exactly *what* it takes to get you off," he grinned, "but we have talked about orgasms and sex. And all I asked this time is if you slept with him."

"Why do you need to know?"

"I would rather not say."

"What does that mean?"

"You've made it clear you aren't interested in sleeping with me, so telling you that I am insanely jealous of any man you've dated isn't going to go well."

Leah laughed and groaned out loud.

"There are a million women out there who would love to have your babies." She took a deep breath. *Time to pull it together.* She and Trace had become fast friends, and she loved him, but she would never tell him that maybe she was *falling in love* with him. He'd just taken their friendship to the next level—up close and personal, face-to-face talking time.

It was up to her to stay cool and stay in control.

"In fact, my sister is one of them."

She met his eyes with courage she didn't feel.

"But not you."

Control. You have to control this situation.

"I don't want kids," she said quietly.

Trace barked out a laugh and rolled his eyes.

"Can I tell you something?"

Leah noticed the slight change in his tone. She nodded when he tilted his head in askance.

"Do you have to get back in there?"

"No, it's fine." She shook her head. "What's up?"

"Tanner."

"Your brother."

He nodded. Leah watched with concern as he paced away from her. He stopped at the end of the patio and hung his head. Leah eyed his long, lean legs and the way his jeans molded his backside.

Something was bothering him. She noticed him tighten his grip on the bottle.

"You never did tell me why you're the house band at Left Fork."

She threw the words out when he remained quiet. She had sensed tension between Trace and his brother before. Trace had given her several songs that Tanner's band sang to listen to, but he never spoke *about Tanner*.

"He thinks I need to come rescue him again."

"What do you mean?"

"His lead guitarist was in a bar fight over the holidays. Had some serious damage done to his hand. Tanner wants me to fill in for a while."

Leah felt a gentle tug inside. Would she and Trace have this friendship if he were on the road with his brother's band? No way to know, of course, but the idea made her miss him, and he was standing right here in front of her.

"And you don't want to?"

"I want to do that about as much as you want to sleep with me," he said quietly. Leah snorted, but she managed to mask her amusement when he turned to look at her. "That was an opening for you to tell me I'm not that bad."

"I didn't sleep with Dante." She offered the words to appease him, but the way his eyes devoured her—head to toe—almost made her regret them.

"Why not?"

She held the eye contact but said nothing.

"Okay, tell me this." He tipped his head to the side. "Did not sleeping with him have *anything* to do with me?"

Leah drew in a deep breath.

"Just give me that much, Leah," he whispered. The intensity of his stare made her fidgety. She cleared her throat and lowered her gaze to the beer bottle in his hand again.

"Can I ask you something?"

"Anything."

Eyes still on his hand, she flinched at his response.

"Why do you push your brother's music at me?"

"Is that what you think I'm doing?" He frowned. "Really?"

"Well, no, not always. But…"

"But what?"

"I wanna hear you." She pressed her lips together. "Not him."

"Leah, every song he's recorded is mine."

"What?"

"I'm a songwriter," he told her. "I have the words. Tanner's the package."

Leah breathed deeply and mulled that over.

"Okay. Then I want to know the songwriter," she said simply. "Not the package."

She half expected a wisecrack about packages, but her words seemed to hit him hard. She watched his Adam's apple bob as he struggled to control himself.

"I feel like every song I've ever written was for you."

Leah staggered under the weight of his words. She lifted her gaze up to meet his again, but her throat and her chest were tight. Her stomach was heavy suddenly, like she was drinking motor oil instead of wine, and her lungs burned when she tried to breathe.

"It's okay." He shook his head. "It's okay. I know you don't feel that way about—"

"Wait. Wait." She stepped toward him. "What is going on? I've never seen you like this."

"We don't see a lot of each other," he reminded her.

"You know what I mean." She waved his words away. "Look, there's a lot going on out here. It's late. You've gotta be tired."

"Sending me away already?"

"No. I don't want you to go anywhere," she admitted. "Including on the road with your brother."

"Good. That's you and Pearl on my side."

Leah smiled at the mention of the woman's name. Trace had told her he was close to Pearl and Sampson; they were like family to him.

"I guess it just feels…fast…to see each other again and to jump into conversations like these."

"It's not, though."

She stared at him silently. He was right, of course. They'd talked about Kenzi and Joe. They'd talked about Leah dating Dante. She'd apparently felt safe enough to admit to him over texts that she hadn't slept with Dante. That she didn't always reach the pay off in sex. He had told her that his dad had passed away when he was barely legal to drink the grief away. He'd talked about his guitars, and he'd shared his favorite songs with her.

He'd teased her and flirted with her, and she'd flirted back when she thought he was several hundred miles away. His proximity made her shy, uncertain.

They weren't strangers. Not anymore.

But sharing secrets while you stared into a person's eyes and he stared into your soul was a whole lot bigger than keystrokes on a smartphone.

"Don't tell me you can't talk to me this way, Leah."

"The trouble is that now that you're here, I'm never gonna want to let go."

"That's what I'm hoping for."

CHAPTER 16

TRACE WAS AWAKE WHEN SHE TIPTOED THROUGH THE SPARE room earlier to get to the kitchen. Rather than admit that, he stayed still on his back, arms stacked under his head, and watched her. Her pink shorts barely covered her bottom, and her breasts had been loose and firm under her tank. She shot a glance his way, and he squeezed his eyes closed so she wouldn't catch him playing possum, and then when she looked away, he looked again. Her hard nipples pressed to the tank had been a shot of lust straight to his dick, and he had to think long and hard about anything and everything else while she showered upstairs.

What he wanted to do was join her in the shower. At the very least, he wished he could see her naked. Not that that would help his aching dick. When he heard the shower shut off, he'd climbed from the bed and yanked his jeans up over his hips. Pulled his t-shirt on and retraced his steps from last night to find the kitchen.

They'd stuck around the Queen until after one. Trace had been more than happy to watch Leah interact with her gang. All of them had included him, and when Leah asked him later what he thought of Stevi, he'd agreed she was cute and left it at that. She *was* cute. Didn't hold a candle to Leah, but he'd gotten sappy enough on the patio and what was the fun in beating a dead horse?

The after-hours game turned out to be a sort of karaoke, but Leach refused to take her turn. Instead, Stevi chose the song, and Trace had stood elbow-to-elbow with Duncan at the bar and listened to her sing "Walk Away." She wasn't Kelly Clarkson by a long shot, but she wasn't bad, and Trace saw in the way she swung her hips and danced while she sang, Stevi Hague was fun.

He'd peeked at Leah a few times. Catalogued the grin on her face and the tap of her foot and decided she was probably just as much fun, if not more, once you broke the lock open on her emotions.

Craving fresh air, he stepped outside. Pulled his phone from his pocket to check in with Pearl. Really, it wasn't like they couldn't do without him. At the first mention of taking some time off, Sampson scheduled four acts to replace him and had three more waiting in the wings. Pearl always handled the bar like a tough as nails bouncer, and Angie had all but planted her foot in his butt to shove him out the door.

Still.

He called Pearl's cell, because he knew she was likely to let the house phone ring until she died.

"Yep."

"Hey Pearl, it's me."

"I seen that on caller ID," she told him. Trace chuckled and shook his head. The woman didn't give him an inch.

"Everything okay?"

"We're all good, Trace Dixon. How about you? You get things patched up?"

He sighed and hung his head. "Nothing to patch up," he told her. "Leah and I are friends."

"Right. Keep working at it."

"Kadie do okay last night?"

It took him a second to realize Pearl had already hung up, and he was listening to dead air. Trace rubbed his eyes. Searched for Kadie in his contact list and sent her a text asking if last night had gone okay. Sampson had scheduled her for a short set. The kid had been a nervous wreck, and Pearl had asked Trace to tell Sampson she wasn't ready. Trace had backed out of the office, hands up in defense, before Pearl finished speaking.

Leah stood with her back against the counter when he went back inside. She had dressed in khaki shorts and a navy t-shirt. Blown her hair dry and let it fall in waves over her shoulders.

"Hey." He grinned. She lifted her mug in greeting.

"You want some coffee?"

"Please."

She turned her back to him giving him time to take in her long, lean legs. The curve of her ass in her shorts. She set her mug down and took another from a cabinet over her head.

"Is this your morning routine?" he asked as he took the coffee she offered him.

"Yeah. Except I'm usually texting you while I'm doing everything else."

He smiled, but when their eyes met, he realized she didn't seem happy.

"What's wrong?"

"Am I one of many?" she asked quietly.

"What?"

She looked at the phone in his other hand.

"Did you step out to call someone else? Since you're with me this morning?"

Surprised at what he would swear was jealousy, he blinked at her and then turned his phone to look at it.

"Um. I called Pearl. To see if everything is okay there."

She winced and looked away.

"Is it?"

"Yeah. But then, the place could be on fire around her, and Pearl would tell me everything was fine."

Leah laughed softly. "That's Duncan."

"They look nothing alike."

"Well. No." She shrugged. "Um. Do you eat breakfast? I have eggs."

"I could fix you an incredible Trace Dixon omelet."

"That seems more like a sexy morning-after breakfast." She shook her head. "Pancakes?"

"You want me to fix you pancakes?"

"I'll make them." She nudged him toward the table.

"How's that different? Than an omelet?"

"Omelets…are made with eggs, and you can toss a lot of other stuff in."

Trace sat, but he turned his chair to watch her as she moved around the kitchen. Pancake mix. Syrup. Butter.

"And?" He shook his head when she turned away from the stove to look at him.

"I don't know. It's…more food. More energy."

"Oh, I get it." He nodded. "When you come up for air, and you're starved. So you need protein so you can go back for round two."

"Or three," she mumbled. "Or four."

"Damn." He groaned and scrubbed his hands over his head.

"What?"

"Well, for one thing, if you're talking round four, someone's given me serious competition and—" He put his hand up to stop her when she started to object to what he'd said. "It's not a challenge, I get it, but now I have the mental image of you in my head."

"Of me…"

He shrugged. "You want me to say it? Topless. Riding someone, preferably me. Head thrown back in ecstasy—"

"What'd you think of Stevi?"

"She's cute," he mumbled. He scooted his chair under the table, hoping she wouldn't notice his erection. "Stop throwing your sister at me."

Leah laughed softly. "Do you date much?"

"Are you kidding me?'

"Do you?" She leaned on the counter, mixing bowl in hand. Trace watched her whisk the pancake mix.

"I don't date, no." He shrugged. "Most women in my world want me to sign body parts. Some want to suck…" He cleared his throat, embarrassed at the smirk on her face.

"Um." She shrugged and looked up at him. "Seems like you reminded me last night that we've talked about what it takes to get me off. So I'm not sure why you're uncomfortable right now."

"Blowjobs." He looked away. "If I had a dollar for every offer, I could buy an island."

"Rough life."

"If they don't want that, they want to sing for me. So I can get them on stage."

"Well, you know I don't want to use you." She shrugged, tossed him a cute smile as she poured pancake batter into the skillet she'd put on the stove. "So, there's that."

"You wouldn't even sing for fun last night."

"Yeah, no." She kept careful watch over the pancakes.

"The rest want a fast track to my brother."

Leah turned to him, a look of surprised horror on her face.

"So." She pursed her lips and hesitated.

"Just ask." He shrugged.

"Okay." She flipped the pancakes and then took the skillet off the burner. Trace watched her plate them.

"Thank you." He met her eyes and took the plate she offered him. "Aren't you eating?"

"Yeah. But these are for you." She went back to the counter and came back with silverware and a stack of napkins. "So. Do you take them up on it?"

He had expected a question about Tanner. About the girls who wanted a fast track to him. Thrown by what she had said, it took him a minute to actually process her words.

"You're seriously asking if I—?"

She nodded.

"I have, but I don't make a habit of it."

"Okay." She arched her eyebrows, but she didn't say more.

"What?"

"Do you have sex with them?"

"With the girls that hang out around the bar?"

"Wow." Leah cringed. "Is that me? Were you seriously hitting on me for sex?"

"I have never hooked up with anyone at Left Fork. From Left Fork. I meant girls…at…other places. Other shows."

"Have you done it since we met?"

"Had sex?" He cocked his head to study her when she set her plate on the table across from him and slid into a chair. Why was she quizzing him? Just evening things up in shares? Or was she probing for the same reasons he continued to ask her about her personal life? Was she jealous? Because if she was jealous, didn't that mean she was interested?

"Well, sure, but I meant the blowjob thing."

"Say that again?" he asked with a grin. The word *blowjob* sounded incredibly dirty and sexy coming from her mouth.

"What? You get a rise out of me saying blowjob?"

"Yes, I do," he admitted.

Leah laughed and shook her head.

"Or are you avoiding my question?"

"I haven't had sex since…I don't know. Last November? And um…"

She stared at him expectantly.

"The other thing right after Christmas."

"You expect me to believe that?"

"It's the truth."

He forked a bite of his pancakes and savored the sweet syrup and buttermilk flavor on his tongue.

"A guy like you not getting any action? Trace, it's almost July."

"I'm not interested in hooking up, and I don't want another nameless girl on her knees in front of me."

"Ouch." Leah flinched. "Thanks for that visual."

"The only action I've had since we met is my hand."

She stared at him for a moment, and when he didn't add anything to what he'd said, she snorted and then ducked her head to her hand. Amused by her reaction to his confession, he stuck another forkful of pancakes in his mouth.

"Okay." She finally looked at him again. She nodded. Grinned and then shook her head.

"I tell you something like that, and that's all the response I get?"

"You want me to spout off about something?"

Trace rolled his eyes and reached for his mug.

"I could ask you why it matters to you."

"You could."

He pushed his empty plate away.

"What's on the agenda today?"

"Would you like to go sightseeing? It's not Nashville, but it's kind of a cool town."

"I would like that," he said sincerely. "What I most want to do is hang out with you."

"Okay. I think we can arrange that."

"Do you need to be at work?"

"Um. There's a country music star in town." Leah stared at him over the rim of her mug. He could swear her eyes twinkled. "I think they'll all be cool with me playing hooky."

"My brother's the country music star," he corrected her.

Leah shook her head.

"Mind if I take a quick shower?"

"Of course not."

She led him out of the kitchen to a bathroom situated between the spare room where he'd slept and Stevi's room.

"She's not home, so sorry, no one is going to join you in the shower." Leah raised her eyebrows, amused to find him eyeing Stevi's closed door.

"Careful or I'll drag you in." He winked at her.

"Wow." She gestured to the closet by the door. "Clean towels. And there is guy soap in the shower, too."

"How come?" He hadn't meant to ask, but the words were out of his mouth before he could stop them. Hell yes, he wanted to know. He wanted to know everything about the woman standing in front of him, her folded arms over her chest now hiding her breasts. Maybe he wasn't interested in playing games, but on the other hand, Leah had been adamant from the word go that she wasn't interested. Trace wasn't used to treading softly, but he was determined to do whatever it took to change her mind.

"Stevi…has an occasional overnight guest."

Trace cocked his head to study her face, to see behind her guarded expression. She wanted him here; he was sure of that. If nothing else, they had become friends, and she had been both stunned and thrilled to see him last night. She wouldn't have thrown herself into his arms with such happiness last night if that weren't the case. She wasn't afraid of him, because they had come to know each other so well through texts and phone calls.

But she was weary.

Of all men? Or was it him? His lifestyle?

Or was she simply not attracted to him? Is that why he had come? Was he pursuing Leah Hague simply because she didn't want to sleep with him?

He remembered the look on her face earlier, before breakfast, when she'd asked if she was one of many women he flirted with via texts and all hour phone calls. Oh, she was interested. More than she wanted to admit, if he read her right. But still reluctant to show him that.

"And you don't?" He edged around her and into the bathroom. Leah cleared her throat and stepped backwards to put more space between them. "Have overnight guests?"

He watched with amusement as she rearranged her face into a look of surprise. He loved that she blushed; when had he last met a woman who blushed when he spoke to her? Not counting the young girls—and even the young ones offered blowjobs and more—he wasn't sure he'd seen a real blush in years.

"I have a queen bed and a bathroom upstairs," she reminded him. "My overnight guests don't normally use this shower."

The way her lips tipped up in a quick smile, the tease of her tongue wetting her lips hit him hard in the ribs. She embarrassed easily, but she was always quick to fire back at him. Just another thing to love about Leah Hague.

He grinned, eyes drawn to her smile again when she dragged her teeth over her lower lip.

"So." He huffed out a quick breath. Time to step back and put the closed door between them. His heart was pounding in his ears, and his dick was probably the shade of midnight by now. "Which one's your favorite?"

Leah had dropped her gaze—shit! Was she looking at his crotch? Because there was no hiding what was happening in his jeans right now—but she lifted her chin and met his eyes when he spoke.

"Favorite?" she shook her head. "Overnight guest?"

He flinched. "The last thing I want is to hear about your overnight guests, Leah." He ground the words out in a small, tight voice.

"Look, Nashville—"

"Song. Which of Tanner's songs is your favorite?"

"I thought they were your songs." Her thick whisper was a caress over his shoulders and down his spine. Trace felt his ass cheeks tingle with lust and wondered when that had last happened. Had it *ever* happened?

"Which is your favorite?"

"Tomorrow's Mine," she answered without hesitation.

This time, he felt a little flutter in his chest, and though his dick and his ass and everything else wanted to invite her to join him in the shower, this flutter felt a little different.

He nodded and stepped backwards, intending to close the door. He needed to bury himself inside her, and short of that, he needed to take care of his hard-on, and at the very least, he needed some time and a cold shower.

"Did I pass?" she asked as he started to close the door.

"What?" He looked up to meet her eyes.

"Was that a test?"

"Unless you want me to drag you in here with me and mess your pretty hair up, you need to let me close this door. Now."

She arched her eyebrows in question.

"Yeah." His voice was gruff. "You passed."

CHAPTER 17

Leah swung her door closed and looked at Trace over the top of the car. Even with shades on, the sun was blinding. She lifted a hand to shield her eyes and watched him take in the view. A tour of her small town had seemed like a good idea, but now that they were at the first stop, Leah wasn't sure she could impress him and she was equally unsure why it mattered to her. Well, okay, they were friends. In the short time they'd been texting, Leah had grown as close to him as she felt to Stevi, Margo, and Duncan. The difference was the electric undercurrent she felt in Trace's presence. They'd talked about sex, and there had been nights she'd gone to sleep with his sexy voice in her head and an ache in her heart and all the other places she'd left long-neglected. But seeing him like this? Whole new level of zing and need. She'd had a hell of a time trying to sleep last night, and sitting with him over coffee and breakfast this morning had been a challenge. Beautiful man, blah blah blah, but when he turned that look on, those eyes lit her on fire.

When they left her house, Trace had offered to drive. Even his damned beat-up Ford pickup had been a turn on, but she'd driven the twelve minutes from her driveway to the Chateau Laurent , and she'd been desperate to get out of the car when she'd pulled into the otherwise empty parking lot. Close quarters with a man like Trace Dixon were hazardous to the woman she'd shoved down inside herself when she'd started making promises a couple months ago. He took up a lot of room in her car, and he'd given her a look of amusement when he turned the volume of her radio up and found she'd last been listening to a country music station. He'd been nothing but a gentleman after his comment about dragging her into the shower with him. He'd ushered her out the back door, and even though she had announced she would drive, he had waited for her to get in the driver's seat and then he'd closed her door for her and gone around to the passenger side of the car.

Likewise, on the drive here, he'd turned just a bit sideways in the seat to look at her while they talked, but he'd kept his hands to himself. Steered clear of suggestive comments and the personal questions that she secretly liked even as she dreaded having to answer them.

Now, though, both of them standing outside the car, Leah missed the closeness the drive had afforded them.

"So, this is the Mississippi River." He shoved his hands in his pockets and ambled around the front of the car.

"Tell me you've never seen the Mississippi before." She rolled her eyes.

"Seen it often." He shrugged and shot her a glance. "But never this part of it."

"We could—" She stopped talking when he turned his back to the bluffs and looked at her.

"What?"

She'd been about to suggest a dinner cruise in the neighboring town of Beaumont, but she decided against it. What if he didn't plan to stay long? What if a dinner cruise insinuated something that she didn't mean?

"Nothing." She shook her head and stepped away from the side of the car. She slipped by him to lead him up to the Chateau Laurent, a castle built as a home on the bluffs back in 1903. Whether it was the summer temperature or nerves, Leah felt sweat on her back. She glanced at him as she walked and wondered if he was one of those guys who lived in jeans. He had to be hot.

"See something you like?" He wiggled his eyebrows. Leah chuckled softly and shook her head.

"So. This castle was built as a home in 1903," she told him. "It's modeled after a French chateau."

She rattled a bit as they went inside. Tours here were self-guided, and as the interior was small and unfurnished, it was a quick tour. But he appeared interested as she led him through each of the small rooms and then back outside.

"Kids do prom pictures here," she added as they stared over the bluff. "Senior pictures. And there are a lot of weddings here, too."

He leaned over to rest his elbows on the stone railing around the chateau.

"Tell me about the Queen."

Leah blinked and shook her head.

"It was just a house."

"Your queen."

"Oh." She shrugged and took a deep breath. "Um. My grandfather…well, my grandparents…owned a little shack down on the waterfront. It was a hole-in-the-wall tavern, but the town loved Granddad. Stevi, Margo, and I spent a lot of time there when we were kids. We knew almost everyone who'd come in and out there. Granddad let us help out, but never with the beer or liquor. Kind of gave us the boot when we got older. Demanded that we go to school. Do something better with our lives than he did."

"What did you study?" he asked. Even with the vivid green bluff and the Mississippi thriving below them, Trace had eyes only for her. "In school?"

"Business. Stevi did, too, but she was interested in marketing. Margo took some business classes and some engineering classes…but…"

"But what?" He turned sideways at the rail, giving up all pretenses of admiring the view.

"She didn't graduate. She's probably smarter than Stevi and me together, but she just…didn't focus on school," Leah answered quietly. "I guess she didn't need the degree. The Queen's okay. We struggled a bit at first, but we're running in the black now. I think she regrets dropping out, but she has Berkley."

"Is she married?"

Leah winced and shook her head the tiniest bit. "She was crazy about Jess. And he was kind of a jerk. Promised he loved her, but he didn't want to give up the drinking and the girls. They lived together for a while, but she kicked him out right after Berkley was born."

"Nice." Trace rolled his eyes.

"Jess isn't a bad guy," Leah mumbled. "He just needs to grow up."

Trace nodded. "I know the type."

She eyed him curiously for a moment, but she looked away when he turned to her again.

"So you went to school for business."

"Yeah." Leah cleared her throat. "When Granddad died… we were all shocked to learn that he had money. You would never have guessed it from the way they lived. But there was money, and they left it for us. It was kind of an unspoken agreement that we didn't want to take it. Unless we did something for Granddad. Something in his memory."

"Hence the Queen."

Leah nodded. "Yeah. He called his place the River Queen. We decided to keep the Queen, but to make it ours, too."

Trace considered that and offered her a small smile.

"How long have you been in business?"

"Is that your sly way of asking how old I am?"

He shot her a panicked grin and held up his hands in surrender.

"A gentleman never asks a woman her age."

Leah laughed softly. "We've been open four years, and I turned thirty last winter."

"Still a baby." He eyed her silently for a moment. Leah felt paralyzed by his gaze.

"Yeah. Right."

"Where does Duncan fit in?"

"Um. Duncan's father married Margo's mom about ten years ago. So…they're steps. But they've always been friends. Easier, I think, since they were older. Margo was seventeen when her parents divorced. And it was amicable. I think that made a difference."

Leah turned her attention to the view and considered the ways her world had changed in the past four years. She and two people she loved more than life had gone into business together, and then Duncan had jumped in headfirst to round out a great team. They had struggled the first couple of years, no secret there. There were still slow nights and slow nights that turned into slow stretches that were hard on the bottom line, but little by little they were making a name for themselves. Leah couldn't be happier with their success or more excited for their future.

It was Kenzi's future, Kenzi's family's future that took her breath away and scared the hell out of her.

"...gorgeous."

A zap of excitement bolted through Leah, effectively nailing her to the ground. She swallowed hard and turned her head to look at Trace, a little bit relieved to find him looking the other way. What was gorgeous? Good grief, she liked this guy, and she loved his voice, and hearing him say the word gorgeous set her heart fluttering in her chest. Flirting was fun, but what would she say if he was talking about her?

"I mean, Left Fork isn't your average tavern," he continued as he looked back at her. "Sampson made that bar in there himself. He built it from the ground up. Sanded it and stained it."

Leah watched him as he talked. He was talking about the bar, about the Queen. Comparing it and Left Fork. She wasn't disappointed, though, because his thick eyebrows were drawn just so over his mysterious eyes, and she wondered now if he'd shaved, because already she could see the hint of beard stubble on his face. He cared about Sampson and Pearl, and as if she needed anything sexier than the body and the smile and the eyes, Trace Dixon had a heart for love.

"God, he'd love the Queen." Trace finished talking. "Where do you guys put your musicians?"

"Up front by the window."

He nodded, obviously picturing it in his head.

"How many nights do you have someone in?"

"Um." She shrugged. "Eventually, we'd like to do every Thursday, Friday, and Saturday, but we're not consistent yet."

"Business better with live music?"

"Not necessarily," she answered truthfully. "Some people bring in more of a crowd, but there are some weekends when we're jammed without it."

Standing about a foot apart, Leah nudged his boot with the toe of her sandaled foot.

"Is that what this is?" She arched an eyebrow at him. "A little corporate espionage?"

Trace's wide grin flashed perfect teeth and a dimple over the corner of his lips. How had she not seen that before? She loved his eyes, but her gaze was drawn to the dimple. She jumped when he cleared his throat and lifted her eyes to his, mind still on dipping her tongue there and then maybe flicking it over his lips, rubbing it over his.

"I don't know." He raised his eyebrows. "Would a little corporate espionage turn you on?"

The sharp note of laughter that escaped her lips apparently surprised him. He covered his heart with his hand and shook his head.

"No sleeping with spies, huh?"

Leah pressed her lips together, but she couldn't help but smile at him. Dangerously close to leaning in to him, to kissing him, to sticking the tip of her tongue in his dimple, she cleared her throat and stepped back.

"So. Let's...the bridge. It's prettier at night," she announced as she stepped around him to lead him back to the car. "The city lights it up. Special colors for special occasions."

"That bridge?"

He caught her hand in his and tugged her back to stand with him. Leah glanced over her shoulder at the Adam's Bay Bridge in the distance.

"Yeah."

"Can we wait?" His voice was gruff again. "See it at night?"

"Of course."

"Where did Stevi stay last night?"

Leah blinked and then tipped her head, confused by his question.

"What?"

"Where did she stay?"

"At Margo's."

"Because she thought we were going to sleep together?"

"No." Leah shook her head. "Just to give us space to hang out."

"Does she stay at Margo's a lot?"

"She's interested if you are," Leah told him, but she held her breath waiting for his answer. It would kill her to see him with her sister, but she couldn't be greedy. He was a friend; she wouldn't play games with him. At least if he got involved with Stevi, he would stay in her life.

"I'm not." He shrugged.

Leah closed her eyes when he squeezed her fingers.

"Would you really be okay with that?" He spoke slowly, as if it pained him to ask.

"What?"

"Me. Being interested in your sister."

Leah blinked her eyes open to find his dark, intense eyes watching her closely.

"Are you?"

"You think…what?" He stepped closer to her. Mouth dry, Leah couldn't swallow. Her throat was tight with emotions, with her heart, all the pieces of it that she was still trying to put together. "I looked you up on the Internet and saw a picture of Stevi and thought maybe I'd drive up here and wrangle an introduction? Is that it?"

Leah felt her eyes burn.

"Wrangle?" she repeated, but the attempt to lighten the mood only made the air between them sizzle.

"I drove up here for one reason, and it's not corporate espionage and it's not your sister, no matter how many times you try to push me her way."

She rolled her lips inward and ducked her head when he stepped closer to her. He still held her hand in his, and when he squeezed her fingers again, she squeezed his back.

"No." Eyes closed, she gave him a tiny shake of her head.

"No what?"

"Why are you pushing this? I told you I'm not gonna sleep with you, Nashville."

"No what? One thing at a time."

"No. I wouldn't be okay with you and Stevi."

She closed her eyes again when he lifted his free hand to cup her chin and force her to look at him.

"Okay." He nodded. Leah's heart skipped, and her belly flopped as he leaned toward her. Anticipating his kiss, she closed her mouth and drew a deep breath through her nose, flooding her senses with his fresh, woodsy scent. "That's a start." He pressed his lips to her forehead and then turned his head a bit to rest his cheek on her head.

CHAPTER 18

T HE KISS—THE FOREHEAD KISS—WAS A SORT OF TORTURE, but one Leah craved more of. Trace had stood for a moment, but then he'd moved and fingers still linked with hers, he'd led the way back to her car. Still caught up in the sweet gesture and his soft words, in the flirty fun when he'd asked her if corporate espionage turned her on, she'd been off-balance as they climbed back into the car, and she drove to the next stop she wanted to share with him. They toured the George Adam Mansion and then lingered on the grounds for a bit, simply walking hand in hand. Leah tried once to tug her hand from his, but he wouldn't let her go. Though she thought his kiss earlier had been sweet and honest, she suspected that he was enjoying her discomfort.

They followed the tour of the mansion up with lunch at the park. She would have preferred to make sandwiches herself, but she didn't have cold cuts or fresh bread at home, and she had no desire to waste a beautiful summer day—with Trace Dixon—inside a grocery store. Instead, they grabbed sandwiches and sat together on a picnic table in the park.

"How long can you stay?" She kept her eyes on the sandwich in her hands. Her stomach was a mix of hungry and fluttery nerves, and she knew she would never get two bites down, let alone the whole thing.

"How long do you want me to stay?" He leaned into her and flashed a grin when she peeked at him. "I don't know. Sampson and Pearl weren't concerned about me leaving, if that's what you're asking."

"Already found a new musical cowboy, huh?"

"I'm not a cowboy, Leah." He twisted the cap off a bottle of water and took a long drink.

She answered with a slow nod. "No, you're not. Maybe a little southern, but definitely not a cowboy."

"Too southern?" He arched an eyebrow. Nudged her foot with his boot. "You like the boots, though, right?"

She did. Like the boots. But when she dragged her gaze up over his outstretched leg and then over his hard abs—a slice of skin showed where his red t-shirt had ridden up—to meet his eyes, she couldn't find her voice. Instead, she could only nod.

"Pearl told me to get up here and figure this out."

Leah frowned, eyes drawn to his throat when he swallowed another drink.

"Figure what out?"

"You and me."

Leah winced and looked away. "You didn't tell her there was a you and me, did you?"

"Nope." He sounded frustrated. "In fact, I told her there definitely wasn't a you and me, but she insisted."

"So you're here to make Pearl happy."

"I'm here because Pearl….well. All the ladies at Left Fork were tired of me being an ass."

Leah licked her lips. She set her sandwich down and reached for her water.

"And why were you being an ass?"

"Something about you and your friend Dante."

Leah hunched over to rest her elbows on her knees.

"There've been a few late nights when you haven't answered my texts."

From the corner of her eye, she saw him shrug, but she knew by now that the nonchalance was a show.

"Easy to assume you were busy with him."

Leah shook her head. "You were being an ass to the ladies because you thought I was having sex with Dante."

"Call me crazy," he mumbled. "Not really something I want to think about."

Leah groaned and pushed her hair back from her face.

"Can I tell you something, Nashville?"

"Can I tell you what it does to me when you call me that?"

She turned quickly to look at him, wondering if he disliked the nickname she'd given him. He stared back at her with an intensity that made her tremble.

"What does it do?" she whispered. "Because you're the best thing I remember about Nashville, Tennessee."

"Jesus, Leah." He grunted and sat up, not trying to hide it when he adjusted his crotch. She glanced at his hand and then looked at him wide-eyed, unable for a second, to breathe.

"You ever bargain with God?" She turned away from him.

"What do you mean?"

"You want something so badly, you tell God you'll do anything to have it?"

When he didn't answer immediately, she glanced back at him. He'd moved again, and now he copied her position, hunched over his knees.

"Yep."

She shrugged, looked away when he tilted his head to look at her.

"When Kenz was in labor," she licked her lips, "and she had…"

Trace nodded. "Were you there?"

"Mmm. Yeah." She sighed. "Joe was with her, but it was a really long labor, and the doctor let me and Stevi and Margo come in for a few minutes. Not together; that would have been too much. But...before her labor had progressed too far...one at a time, we went in to wish her good luck. I was there...when it happened."

She flinched when she felt Trace's hand on her back. "She was talking, laughing. Giving Joe shit about getting her pregnant, telling him she was too damned old for babies. And she was telling him he had to get it fixed...no more sex until he had a vasectomy. She couldn't....she couldn't get the word out. Just kind of started shaking and her speech was all slurred, and then she was just...out. Unconscious."

"Oh, Leah."

"The baby was in distress. Joe was a wreck. They had to cut her open...to do an emergency c-section, and one of the nurses was pushing me out of the room. Joe was trying to be strong. They were trying to hold him back, too, and I..."

"You made a bargain with God."

She nodded as she wiped at her eyes.

"I did."

"What did you promise to live without? To keep your friend alive."

Leah glanced at him. "Love. The kind of love that Kenzi and Joe have. The kind of love that makes beautiful babies like they have."

"And how long are you gonna stick to that bargain?"

"I don't—"

"You know that's ridiculous, right?"

"Yep." She nodded. "Because it doesn't mean anything. I don't want kids. I don't want anything to do with that life. There's no way in hell I could do that now after watching what happened to her." She rubbed her eyes again, though they were dry and tired—not blurred with tears—and took another quick peek at Trace. "Easy for me to promise to give that up when I don't want it in the first place."

Her words had the opposite effect of what she'd intended. Trace leaned into her, his palm still splayed over her back.

"You don't want someone to love you?"

"I don't wanna love anyone." She couldn't look away from his magnetic gaze, so she closed her eyes to hide from him.

It might have been her imagination, but she thought he sighed. When she opened her eyes again, he'd sat back, giving her space.

"So." He cleared his throat. "Are you telling me you definitely weren't entertaining Dante in your bed when I texted? Is that the point of the story?"

"I've never slept with him, as I told you last night, and before that in texts," she reminded him. "And I'm telling you this so you know why I won't sleep with you."

He was quiet for a long moment. Leah wondered if he would pack up and drive back to Tennessee now. If the game was over, since she'd clearly defined her reasons for saying no.

"Tell me about Kenzi."

"What?" Hands over her face, Leah squeezed her eyes closed.

"Where did you meet her?"

"She was a couple years ahead of Margo in school. They played ball together. Margo's three years older than me. I met Kenzi through Margo. They hung out a lot. Eventually, the four of us were together all the time. And then she got married, and we all loved Joe. Her kids are like a niece and nephew to me."

"Did the baby make it?"

"Yes." She nodded. She hadn't bonded with Edison, though, because she'd been so damned angry with him for Kenzi's stroke.

"Kenzi's not gonna die if you find love."

Leah swallowed hard.

"You know that's not how it works. Whether you believe in God or fate or some other obscure, all-knowing being."

"I know that, but…" She shrugged helplessly. "But what if I'm wrong? Kenzi can't die. She's got kids who love her. Who need her."

"Did Margo and Stevi make the same bargain?"

"Margo and Stevi weren't there when it happened, but if they had been, you bet your ass they would have made that same bargain. Kenzi was…she's bigger…than life. Anyone would want to save her."

"Leah."

She licked her lips when she turned toward him again.

"I'm not giving up." His eyes searched hers for a long moment. Leah held her breath, painfully aware of the seconds ticking by. The park was quiet; only one car parked in the lot near hers. She hadn't seen anyone else, though, and she figured it was possible someone was hiking the trails.

The sun was hot through her top, and she considered scooping her hair up off her neck. But she didn't want Trace to think she was flirting, suggesting anything. As much as she wanted his hands on her, she couldn't give in. Not even for a second.

"And when I still don't sleep with you?" she finally whispered.

"Darlin', I'm not talking about sleeping with you." He shook his head. She swallowed hard, her mouth like cotton, as he leaned in. This time his lips brushed hers, just the corner of her smile. Leah turned her head slightly, but Trace dropped a trail of soft kisses over her cheek and then pressed his lips to the skin under her ear.

Leah's heart pounded, and her stomach quivered. She dragged her teeth over her lip when she felt the tip of his tongue flick the pulse point in her neck.

"Do you want me to head back to Nashville?"

She shook her head quickly. "No. I don't. But I don't want to lead you on, either."

"You let me worry about that."

She laughed softly. "Yeah, and when you do get back to Left Fork and you still haven't sewn any wild oats, Pearl's gonna hate me."

"Pearl knows this isn't about wild oats, Leah Hague." He drew back, leaned in once again to press a kiss to her cheek, and then sat back to look at her.

"Why me?" she whispered.

"How could it not be you?"

CHAPTER 19

"So how do you do it?"

Leah stretched out on the couch and tossed her arms up over her head. Across the dark room, Trace's fingers froze on the guitar strings and the soft sounds of the acoustic guitar—the one he called Loretta—stopped abruptly with a muted twang. When he didn't answer, when several moments of silence ticked past, Leah rolled to her side and propped her head up on her elbow.

She could barely make his face out in the gray of the room. They had come home after midnight; Trace promised he didn't mind sticking around the Queen after closing, but Stevi had shooed them out almost the second Duncan flipped the lock. Leah hadn't particularly wanted to hang out for kicks—not when she had Trace here all to herself—but Margo had gone home early to be with Berkley, and she felt guilty for leaving Stevi and Duncan again. But Stevi had been persistent, and Duncan had shrugged indifferently, raised his water bottle in a toast, and winked at her as she led Trace out the back door to his truck.

When they had come in earlier, she'd turned the light on over the stove, and together they whipped up grilled cheese sandwiches and then stood hip to hip at the stove to eat them. Now, that light was the only one on in the house, and Leah struggled to make out Trace's expression.

"Do what, exactly?" he finally asked. She saw him lower his hand—the one that had strummed the guitar—to his lap.

"Um." Safe in the shadows, she allowed herself a grin and wondered just exactly what he thought she meant. "Write music."

"Oh." He took a deep breath and then ducked his head over his guitar again.

"What did you think I meant?"

"I don't know." He sounded distracted, but when he lifted his head to wink at her, she felt it like a thousand jolts of electricity in her heart. "I was just hoping you weren't asking me how I sign body parts."

"Well, I would assume you'd do that with a permanent marker," she said with a small smile. "Have you done that often?"

"More times than I care to remember," he told her.

"So you've had your hands on a lot of women, then." She arched her eyebrows. "Between the ones you sign and the ones you do."

His laugh was sort of resigned, like maybe she was right. It made her belly hurt to think about it.

"One girl asked me to sign her lips." He looked up at her suddenly, and even though their eyes met, she could tell he was a million miles away.

"And did you?"

"No, I talked her out of it." He zeroed in on her and turned his nose up. "That was just too weird."

"But you're happy to sign anything else?"

"I wouldn't say I'm happy about it, no," he mumbled. "But. Yeah, I've done it."

The idea of Trace's fingers wrapped around a marker and women's tits just so he could sign and leave his mark on their skin made her head throb. Made her heart throb, too, but not in a good way. The windows were open, and her curtains moved with a cool, gentle breeze, but her skin was hot and sticky. Her stomach, other things clenched at the thought of taking her clothes off and asking Trace to sign her body.

No denying how badly she wanted him. Not even to herself now that she'd spent a few days with him. He hadn't touched her, not in any way that could be misconstrued as a sexual advance. He had no qualms about touching her, taking her hand while they walked or sliding his arm around her waist at the Queen when he leaned in to talk to her. But he hadn't kissed her again. Not on her lips. Or her forehead. Part of her was pleased that he'd listened to her, that he respected her answer, her reason for saying no. Part of her wanted him to argue that her promise to God had no bearing on real life. God wouldn't punish Kenzi and her family if Leah fell in love with someone.

"So." She cleared her throat, desperate to change the subject. Her body was ready to implode from the mix of jealousy and desire for the man across the room. She reminded herself it was better this way, because missing him when he left was going to be a new full-time job. And if she gave in and made love with him, Trace Dixon would walk away with her heart, and then it wouldn't matter what God did or threatened with Kenzi, because she would be ruined for any other man.

"I don't know." Seemingly completely unaware of her struggle, Trace's fingers moved on the strings. Mesmerized by the beauty of the movement, she stared at his hands and wished just for a moment that he would play her that way. "I wrote my first song when I was about sixteen, maybe. It wasn't good, but it was good enough then that I knew."

"That you knew…" She flicked her eyes up to his when she realized he was watching her watch him.

"That I wanted to do it. That I had to do it."

"Play it." She arched her eyebrows hopefully, but he most likely couldn't see her face that clearly.

"Nope." He shook his head. "Told you it wasn't good."

"What's the first song you wrote that was good?"

"'Fireflies and Moonlight.'"

"I haven't heard that one." She shook her head.

"You said you don't know my music," he reminded her.

Should she tell him that she found two of his CDs? That she downloaded them?

"Sing it for me."

"No."

"Why not?"

"Because I don't like it."

"Do you write for other people?"

"I'm a songwriter," he hedged. "And it's a business."

"And?" She shrugged.

"Yeah. A lot of artists have recorded my songs."

"You never answered me."

"About what?" He dropped his hands to his lap and leaned on the ottoman at his back. Leah laughed softly when she saw him wiggle his eyebrows suggestively. "You asked if I took the girls up on blowjob offers, and I admitted that now and then I do. What else could you ask me?"

"Yeah, well, let's not forget that you said the words *what it takes to get you off* to me." She was glad for the darkness because her cheeks were on fire. "I think you scarred me."

"You never did tell me what you like."

"And I'm not going to," she told him simply. "Because we're not having those kinds of conversations."

"Do you talk to Duncan like that?"

"Yes, I'm close to Duncan, but no, Duncan has never asked me and I've never told him what I like."

"Can I ask you something?"

Leah groaned and buried her face in the couch for a second. "I was reminding you that you haven't answered my question. How is this fair?"

"How long are you gonna hold yourself to the fire?"

His voice, the darkness, his forearms resting on his denim-clad legs lit that fire inside her all over again.

"I get that a bargain with God is serious business." He spoke quietly. "But you can't deny yourself forever."

If it was about sex, she would crook her finger at him now and lift her hips to slide her jeans off. But already, it was more with him, and she couldn't give in.

"You can't wait me out, Nashville." She licked her lips and averted her gaze again. Why couldn't she have met him last year at this time? Before Kenzi was pregnant with Edison?

"Don't tell me what I can and can't do, darlin'."

Leah wasn't sure if his words were a threat or a promise, but her toes and her fingertips tingled and pounded with her heartbeat.

"Why are you the house band at Left Fork?"

"I told you I'm just a songwriter."

"You're not *just* a songwriter," she fired back at him. "You just told me that you write for a lot of artists. You've written several big hits for Tanner. And you had four top twenty singles of your own, two of which climbed to number two before falling."

"Don't." The low, guttural growl shocked her. She watched him set the guitar aside and climb to his feet. It wasn't fear that rocketed through her now, but it wasn't just lust, either. She'd pushed a button, and she had no idea what she said to set him off. Trusting him to talk when he was ready, she scooted to sit up on the couch and drew her legs up in front of her.

He'd tugged his boots off after they snacked in the kitchen, and Leah found herself looking at his bare feet as he paced the gray room. Presented with the jeans that rode low on his hips, the way the denim hugged his ass and made her mouth water, the soft gray t-shirt that stretched over his shoulders and back, she was looking at his feet. What would it feel like to lie with him in bed? Naked. Her bare feet fitted over his bare calves. His naked thigh thrown over her legs, his toes pressed against the inside of her ankle?

She realized he'd stopped pacing, and when she lifted her gaze to look at him, she felt that same zap of electricity hit her. He was watching her study him.

"Don't what?" She meant to ask boldly, because they were past the awkward new phase of friendship. But her heart was in her throat, and her hands shook so badly with desire, with the need for him to see it and the fear that he would. She circled her arms around her legs and rested her chin on her knees.

"Tanner." He huffed out a big, angry growl.

"Was it a woman?" she asked quietly.

"What?" Trace turned away from her and paced to the door. She'd opened it when they'd come to sit in the living room. Now she watched him fold his arms over his chest and prop his shoulder in the doorway.

"Is that why you don't get along?"

He dipped his head and rolled his shoulders.

"You were in love, and she left you for him."

"I wasn't in love with her," he corrected her. "But yes, she is now on the road with the Congregation."

"It's okay," she offered. Her voice came out a little thick and maybe sulky, and Leah closed her eyes for a moment to consider that.

"What's okay?" He lifted his chin and turned his head a bit, but not enough to look at her.

"If you were in love with her."

"I wasn't," he repeated. "I liked her. But things hadn't gone that far."

"You weren't sleeping with her?"

"I was. But we hadn't said the L word." He turned in the doorway to watch her.

"And what? You came home one day, and she said she was hooking up with a traveling band?"

"No. I walked in on her and Tanner all over each other. My house. My girlfriend. My brother."

Leah watched him for a moment, but his face—carved in stone—gave nothing away.

"I'm sorry."

"Women like Shelly are easy to find," he said quietly. He shrugged his right shoulder and tilted his head.

"But it was Tanner—"

He growled again and shook his head.

"Trace?"

"Just don't, Leah." He took a step out of the doorway and reached up to thrust the fingers of both hands through his hair. "I don't wanna hear your voice say his name."

Eyes glued to his as he moved toward her, she pressed her lips together and finally offered him a slow nod.

"Okay. But…"

"But what?" He sounded resigned. Tired of an argument—if he could call it that, and Leah wasn't sure he could—that had just started. He stood directly over her now; his eyes bright with emotion. Suspicion? Anger? Jealousy. She wanted to comfort him. Promise him that she had no interest in his brother. And yet, a promise like that might mean more to him than she intended.

"Nothing." She shook her head and lowered her gaze to his knees and finally to the floor.

"Tell me what's on your mind, darlin'."

"Jesus, Trace." She sucked in a sharp breath when he squatted down by the couch. "Look, I can't do this. I can't do this. I can't do this with you."

She was stunned to see her own hand caress his face, startled to feel his skin, his beard stubble against the palm of her hand. He narrowed his eyes at her, but he didn't move. Didn't speak.

This won't happen again, she told herself. You will never be this close to this beautiful man again. So look your fill. Touch him. Make sure he knows what you can't say.

Scared to breathe, to break the moment, Leah tried to swallow, but her mouth was dry. She slid her hand just a bit and felt it low and heavy in her stomach. A flash of desire. A longing to love him. To tell him she loved him.

"I won't say his name if you don't want me to say his name," she whispered. "Ever. Because he doesn't matter to me."

"I don't want—"

"Not like you do."

Trace dipped his chin to his chest. Leah watched his shoulders expand on a deep breath. Heard him release it in another low growl.

"I just don't want my worlds colliding." Head still lowered, he covered her hand with his and then turned to press his open lips to the palm of her hand. "I don't want you anywhere around him. Not even in my thoughts."

Her heart pounded in her throat, and his lips on her hand made her whole body throb to the beat. He licked her hand, and rather than feel suggestive, it made her feel warm, safe, and when he finally looked at her expectantly, she could only nod.

"If you don't want me, I get it." He leaned forward to rest his knees on the floor. "I won't push you. But I wanna be part of this. Part of your life. And I wanna keep coming back, Leah."

She wanted him to keep coming back. She wanted to know that when he left this time—whenever that would be—that it wasn't over. That he wouldn't chalk her up as crazy or frigid and forget her. She wanted to matter, and she wanted to know that he was part of her life.

What she didn't want was the way it hurt to push him away.

"Goodnight." He turned her hand over and kissed her knuckles, and then he stood and slipped out of the room, and she was alone on the couch with their longing and her heartache.

Trace slept much better than he thought he would after the emotional scene with Leah in the dark. He walked out of the living room the night before with his heart in his throat, his arms aching to hold her. She wasn't ready, and she might never be ready for what he wanted. There was a difference in teasing her and flirting with her and taking advantage of her in a heated moment, and Trace was man enough to understand that. He had crawled into bed with her voice in his head, thick and buttery with emotion when she had repeated to him it couldn't happen between them.

Now, he lay on his back, hands stacked under his head, and stared at the ceiling. Should he dig a hole and bury his head in it for being such a pansy last night? There was a small part of him that regretted it, the honesty he'd given her, but mostly, he felt good about it. If they weren't going to be lovers, he did want her in his life in some capacity, and he already thought of her as his friend. No point in pretending to be someone he was not, especially since he had pursued Leah for that reason to begin with.

On the other hand, he had no intention of dragging today down with that same intense emotion and hang dog crap that had boiled to the surface last night. He had every intention of having fun here with Leah; there was nothing better than making her laugh.

She wasn't making much noise upstairs, so Trace hoped that meant she was still sleeping. Did she sleep on her stomach? With one arm up under her pillow? Or was she curled up on her side? Trace closed his eyes and pictured Leah's bedroom. He'd never gone up the steps just on the other side of the closet door not even three feet from where he slept, but he sure would like to. He imagined her curled on her side, the strap of her tank a bit loose, and the front of it gapped just enough to give him a glimpse of her breast.

His dick—unhappy with the just friends thing his brain and his heart had agreed to—throbbed to life. He groaned out loud, even lowered his hand and slid his fingers inside his briefs to cup himself. But he couldn't do it. Had nothing to do with the fact that she might come down those stairs any minute and catch him. It just felt a little disrespectful to promise her he was good with being friends and then lie here in her spare bed and jerk off while he thought about her asleep, upstairs.

Instead, he huffed out a long sigh of frustration and sat up.

"Sorry, man." He gave his buddy a squeeze and threw his legs over the side of the bed. He would make coffee for her this morning. She'd been up first and made coffee all four mornings that he had been her guest. Why not get up and do something nice for her? He yanked his jeans on but neglected the shirt at the foot of the bed. Coffee makers were pretty universal creatures. He could start the coffee and grab a shower. If Leah was still sleeping after he showered, he would call home and check in with his mom and with Pearl.

Plan in mind, he shuffled out to the kitchen. Usually bright and airy with morning sun, the room was shadowed and gray. Trace sauntered over to the windows and watched the raindrops roll down the glass. Judging from the thunderhead clouds hanging low over the house, he and Leah would not be doing any picnicking or any other outdoor adventures today. They had spent most of their daylight hours together outside. Leah had shown him the sights of Adam's Bay, and though it wasn't Nashville, he liked it here. It was a pretty town, and spending his evenings at the Queen with Leah and her family was as much fun as being at Left Fork. More, because he'd rather hang out with Leah than text her.

So, they would have to find something to do indoors to keep them busy today. He snorted when his dick stirred to life again.

"Not happening, man." He adjusted his crotch again and then went back to the business of making coffee. When he took the coffee and filters from the pantry, he took a moment to peek at her snack items. At the way she organized the shelves. The neat stacks of empty Rubbermaid containers on the top shelf.

He considered making her an omelet for breakfast, but after their discussion from his first morning here, he decided against it. Instead, he filled the glass carafe with water, poured it in the back of the machine, and then scooped enough coffee into the basket to wake them both up.

Another glance at the window as he crossed back to the pantry to put the coffee away told him it was coming down harder now. He stood for a moment, transfixed by the sideways rain, and finally rousted himself and moved. He would grab a quick shower now and check in at home before Leah was up.

When he closed the pantry door and turned to head back out of the kitchen, he ran into Leah. All soft, warm skin and slender but strong body, she moaned softly in confusion as they collided and then took half a step back.

"What's—?" She blinked at him and looked around the room as if she were lost.

"I made coffee." He tried to hide his amusement, but Leah apparently saw through him. Either that, or his eyebrow had arched or his lips twitched or something. She swung her gaze from the window back to him and blasted him with a frown. "What?" He lifted his hands up in surrender. "I made coffee, and you're killing me with the laser eyes."

"You're laughing at me."

Trace lost his struggle to keep his eyes on her face and groaned out loud when he lowered his gaze to her shoulders. The skimpy little gray straps. All that skin that he imagined was still warm from being covered up in her bed.

"I am...so...not laughing." He shook his head. "In fact, I'm kind of in pain right now."

"Trace."

When he flicked his gaze back up to hers, he caught the disgusted eye roll. But she crossed her arms over her chest and drew his attention back to her shoulders. The hollow at the base of her throat and her slender collarbones.

He took a deep breath, intending to look up, but she added a little shrug and her tank top twisted and gapped a bit, and he had an eyeful of the creamy skin of her curvy breasts.

"Not helping," he mumbled.

He held his breath, hoping his comment didn't offend her. Afraid to look her in the eye and unable to look away from the eyeful she'd accidentally given him, he whooshed out another frustrated sigh.

Her throaty laugh filled the room and finally broke the spell. This time, he threw his hands wide and drew his shoulders up in a deep, exaggerated shrug.

"Now you're laughing at me!"

She let her arms fall to her sides, and she pressed her lips together, but her eyes shined with amusement, and when he cocked his head at her, another small laugh escaped. She lifted her hand—fingers curled around her phone—to cover her mouth.

"Um." She cleared her throat and eyed his bare chest and arms. "What about you, Mr. Dixon? You're topless in my kitchen."

"Giving you any ideas?" He poured on the charm, hoped his voice sounded smooth and seductive. He called on every ounce of heat in his body to hit her from his gaze.

She arched her eyebrows and actually studied him, studied his naked chest and arms and abdomen, like she was considering it. Touching him? Kissing him? Sleeping with him? He'd take any or all of the above.

"I didn't know it was supposed to rain today." She broke the magnetic hold he'd had on her and looked toward the window. When she turned her back to him and moved to stand at the window, Trace took the opportunity to adjust his dick again. She folded her arms over her chest again, but now his eyes were on her sweet, little ass and her long, lean legs.

"Rainy days are good days for sleeping in."

She yawned and nodded. "I know. I didn't even hear my alarm go off this morning."

"Why do you set an alarm?" He took a step toward her. "You don't need to be at work until later."

"I don't always," she said softly, "but I don't want to stay in bed when you're here."

Her voice traced a shiver up his back. She turned her head just a bit, but Trace wasn't sure if she was looking at him or just getting a different angle on the rain outside.

"We'll have to find something to do indoors today." He tucked his hands in his hip pockets and raised up on his toes for a second when she turned toward him.

Leah tilted her chin, but she didn't say anything.

"I know what we can do. It'll be a fun way for me to learn more about you."

Her lips parted with a small gasp of surprise. Trace watched her skin flush. She did want him. She'd made a bargain with God, and she was desperate to keep her friend safe, and he respected that. But just now, that rush of heat in her cheeks and the doe-eyed look of innocent desire on her face told him everything he needed to know.

"Trace." Her jagged whisper scraped his heart.

"That's not what I meant."

He took a step closer to her and pulled his hands from his pockets. She watched and waited silently when he lifted his hand and brushed her hair off her shoulder. When she didn't shy away from him, he brushed his fingertips over her neck. Her warm, soft skin made him hungry for more, but he drew his hand away. She watched with big eyes when he reached to rub the back of his neck.

"No?"

Trace squeezed his eyes closed, half wishing he was anywhere but here. Back home in Nashville. Upstairs in Leah's bed with his arms wrapped around her. She had asked once if he liked the thrill of the chase, and he did. What hot-blooded man didn't love the thrill of chasing the woman he wanted more than any damned thing else there was? But her desire and her guilt for what she wanted and wouldn't allow herself ate at him.

When he opened his eyes again, he found her watching him, her own hunger evident in her eyes. She wet her lips, and his eyes were drawn to her tongue.

"Leah."

He stood still, one arm at his side and his other hand cupped around the back of his neck. The kitchen was hot, a little bit sultry, and the smell of strong coffee lingered in the air around them. Desperate to gather her in his arms, he forced himself to wait. She took a step toward him. And another. Until there wasn't an inch of daylight between them. She lifted her free hand and touched him. Just a gentle press of her fingertips on his neck. Trace imagined she felt his pulse hammering under her fingers.

He flinched when she dragged them down slowly and then smoothed them over his shoulder and finally his chest.

"Leah."

Her name was a prayer and a warning on his lips.

Eyes on her fingers splayed over his skin, she flattened her palm on his chest and parted her lips on a soft sigh.

Trace clenched his jaw, afraid to move. When she pressed into him, he groaned and raised his eyebrows.

"I can't help what you do to me." His voice was low and tight. She didn't back away, though. Instead, she flicked her thumb over his nipple. He hissed a string of four-letter words. His fingers twitched at his side.

"I can't sleep with you, Nashville," she whispered.

He nodded. "I know."

She still didn't move. When he lifted his free hand and brushed his fingers up over her hip, she only stared at him. He let go of his neck and then before he could stop himself, he cupped her face and leaned in close enough to kiss her. He didn't, though. Not at first. And then, after several torturous seconds, just a sweet chaste kiss on the corner of her mouth. She stretched and angled her head just enough to give him access when he pressed his closed lips to her neck.

"I want to."

He felt her tremble against him. Her skin was warm and soft, and her fresh, flowery scent made his dick so hard, it hurt. His hands moved on their own, sliding over her bottom and her bare arms like feathers, soft caresses that drew goosebumps to her flesh.

"Leah."

She turned to him, and this time, when their lips met, he needed more. He lingered there, waited for her to say no. To say yes. She didn't speak, but her breath was soft and warm on his lips, and she smoothed the palm of her hand low on his chest and then around to his back.

He rubbed his lips over hers, once and then twice. Slow and soft, the need to claim her at war with the need to cherish her and protect her from his desire. She kissed him back; her lips moved with the same mix of curiosity and pleasure under his.

As if reading from a script, they both drew away just enough to breathe. Trace moved his gaze over her face, from her lips and up to meet her eyes.

"I can't do this," she whispered.

"Okay." He lifted his hands from her arms to her neck and leaned in to rest his forehead against hers. "It's okay."

He meant it. It was okay. It would kill him to walk away, to watch her slip out of the room and hurry upstairs. He would get in the shower and give his dick one stroke and maybe bite his arm to keep from calling out her name when he shot his wad. But it was okay. He would get dressed and spend the day playing board games or watching movies or anything she wanted to do. But he would wait.

He might wait forever for Leah Hague.

Because no one else would make his heart race like this ever again.

"Just…" Her voice was thick, swollen with longing and tears. He'd heard her cry once, when she'd first told him about her friend. "Just one."

"One what?"

One kiss? Hell yes. One time together? One chance to make love to her?

He wanted to say he would give Leah Hague anything, but he wasn't sure he could make love to her one time and then step back into the just friends role.

"One kiss." Her whisper was soft on his lips.

He nodded. Rubbed the pad of his thumb over her lip and then followed with his lips. His tongue. She whimpered, and then suddenly the whimper was a cry of frustration, and the hand that had been pressed tightly against his back was on his chest and pushing him to step away.

"Leah?" He held his hands up in surrender again and backed up a step. She shook her head and held her phone up. Trace saw that it was lit up and vibrating in her hand. She looked at it for a moment and then looked up at him with big, wet eyes.

"It's Joe."

CHAPTER 21

She wanted to wait to answer it. She needed to put some space between Trace and Joe, to catch her breath and push that kiss out of her mind before settling in to talk to Joe. To catch up about the kids. And Kenzi.

But she couldn't. She couldn't get up the steps to her room that quickly, and she felt like she'd put Joe off the last few times he'd called. Besides, Leah suspected that kiss, *almost-kiss*, the moment in the kitchen, would haunt her no matter how much distance she could put between herself and Trace.

Even when he packed his bag and went back to Nashville.

When she thought she could speak without a tremor in her voice, she hit the talk button on her phone.

"Hey."

Okay, so she sounded funny, and her heart was still

pounding in her throat and her ears, and she was out of breath, but hopefully Joe wouldn't notice.

"Hey. Are you okay?" He sounded concerned, and Leah hesitated as she stepped into the spare room, the room where Trace was staying. A little wobbly on her feet, she lifted her free hand and propped it in the doorway. Still a bit lightheaded, she took a deep, cleansing breath, only to fill herself with his scent. The smell of his cologne that lingered now in the sheets on the bed and in the air itself set her heart racing all over again.

"Yeah," she spoke so softly, Joe might not even hear her. "Yeah. I'm fine."

Her gaze fell on the bed, the comforter and sheet tossed aside when Trace got up. To make coffee. The thought of Trace Dixon at home in her kitchen, making coffee while she was upstairs asleep, rolled over her like a tidal wave. Dragged her under and caught her in an undertow.

"You sound out of breath," Joe announced. "Are you sick?"

"Nope." She cleared her throat. She had to get through this room and upstairs. "I'm okay. Just had to find my phone."

She hated lying, and that was stupid, because she told those kinds of fibs all the time. Who didn't? The guilt that festered in her belly wasn't just about a lie. It was that she'd just had an intimate moment with a man she was attracted to, a man she wanted to get to know better, and she'd made that damned bargain with God, and so she felt like Joe had caught her doing something wrong. It wasn't like Joe even knew about those fervently whispered prayers in the seconds before Leah was led out of Kenzi's birthing room.

"Okay." He sounded mollified, which only made her feel worse. She stepped on into the room, relieved that her legs were working okay, because she felt a little bit lovesick. But when she rounded the end of the bed, she made the mistake of trailing her fingers over the comforter, and then while Joe was telling her that Adelynn had joined the swim team, she moved up the side of the bed and smoothed her hand over the pillow Trace slept on.

"That's great," she heard herself say, and she meant it, but her throat was tight with her heart squeezed inside it. She lifted her gaze and peered through the gray bedroom to the door she'd just come through. What was Trace doing? Was he angry with her? Did he think she was a tease?

She cleared her throat and then turned her back to the bed, to the room at large, and hurried up the steps to her own bedroom. Still no sunlight, but there was a bit of rainy daylight coming through the window where her curtains were parted. Best of all, she didn't have to look at the bed and think of him lying there and wonder if he slept on his back. With his arm tossed up over his head. Or if he was more comfortable sprawled out on his stomach when he slept.

"What's going on with you?"

Leah paused in the act of gathering clean clothes to put on after a shower. She wished she would have had a chance to grab a cup of coffee when she was downstairs, but

really, she wished she would have had a chance to taste
Trace on her lips and her tongue, and that kind of
thinking was dangerous.

"What do you mean?" she hedged. Was Joe suggesting that
she was hiding something? She closed her fingers around
a gray t-shirt, pulled it from her drawer, and then leaned
into the drawer to push it closed.

"I haven't talked to you for a while. Are you guys staying
busy at the Queen?"

Leah pursed her lips and released a quiet sigh. "Yeah, we
are. I love it there."

"I know you do," Joe said with a quiet laugh. "Margo said
Berkley's starting to chatter a lot these days."

"Sure, but I'm not sure what language she speaks." Leah
felt a sad smile cross her face.

"She also said Jess has been calling her."

"What?"

"Yeah, I was afraid she hadn't told you that."

Leah perched on the end of her bed and rubbed her
fingers over the bridge of her nose. "No. She hasn't."

"I get the feeling she hasn't told any of you that."

"Is she seeing him?"

"She says she's not."

Leah heard what Joe didn't say. He didn't believe it.
Margo had kicked Jess out when he failed to clean up his

act after Berkley was born. She was adamant that he wouldn't waltz in and out of their daughter's life and damage her in the process. But Leah thought Jess had walked in and out of Margo's life often enough to hurt her, maybe damage her. Margo hated him, but she loved him, and though she would protect Berkley from him, she had a weakness for something about him.

"Do you think I should talk to her?"

"No. She's an adult, Leah. I just…I worry about her."

"You don't need to worry about any of us," she reminded him. "How's Edison?"

What she really wanted to know, of course, was how Kenzi was doing. But she couldn't ask. She couldn't make her mouth form the words.

"He's growing," Joe told her. "And Liam has a girlfriend."

"Liam is thirteen." She rolled her eyes. "He should be playing baseball and riding a dirt bike."

"He is."

Leah heard the laugh in his tone. He sounded okay, and so she allowed herself to relax. She couldn't quite let herself remember the moment in the kitchen, the one that Joe's call had interrupted, but she was glad to hear Joe's voice minus the sadness that had been so profound lately.

"His girlfriend races dirt bikes."

"Oh." She laughed softly. Pushed her fingers back through her hair and wondered again what Trace was doing.

Maybe he'd called home to check on things. Maybe he was in the kitchen, sipping his coffee and talking to Pearl.

Or maybe he was scrolling through his contacts on his phone, hoping to find someone to hook up with when he made it back to Nashville. She'd been firm early on that she wouldn't sleep with him, but she'd started something downstairs and then she'd walked away from him. Who could blame him for wanting to move on?

"Kenzi's talking, Leah."

Stuck in her thoughts, her regrets about Trace and what she wanted and wouldn't take, it took a second for Joe's words to hit her.

"What?" She sat up straight, ice in her veins. Her heart hurt a little, and she couldn't breathe, but this time, it had nothing to do with the man in the kitchen and the way he'd almost kissed her. The feel of his velvety, warm tongue flicking over her lip before she pushed him away.

"It's slow. And it's painful, and it's awkward, but she said my name yesterday."

"Oh my God." The whisper fell from her lips, and tears streaked her face. Since she'd been awake after the stroke, Kenzi Daniels had suffered from aphasia and partial paralysis. The prognosis was less than hopeful. Her doctor hadn't said she would never recover, but he hadn't been overly optimistic for a full recovery, either. "Oh, Joe."

"I miss her, Leah."

The throb in his voice ripped a hole in her heart.

"I've been moving so fast every damned day just to keep the kids going, that I had no idea how badly I missed my wife. Until I heard her say my name after her therapy session yesterday."

"She knows you."

"She knows us," Joe assured her. "She knows all of us. She reacts when the kids and I talk about you guys. But she's locked inside herself. No voice. No way to communicate."

"This is huge, then."

"Yeah."

"Joe?"

"What?"

"I love you guys so much. If there's anything—"

"Leah. Just keep living. That's all you can do for me and Kenzi right now."

Leah climbed to her feet and paced to the window. Rain still pelted the glass. She considered what might have happened if Joe hadn't called. Trace had kissed her, but she'd stopped him. Would she have kissed him back? Of course, she would have. But, what then? If Kenzi was making progress, did that mean Leah was keeping her end of the bargain? Would she relapse if Leah fell in love?

As if in answer to her question, thunder rolled in the distance.

Of course not. She wasn't naïve, and she wasn't terribly

religious, and she knew that what she did had no bearing on Kenzi's recovery.

Except...she'd made a promise, and she didn't do that lightly.

"Do the others know?" Her voice was gruff, and she knew that had been her opening to tell Joe she'd met someone. In fact, odds were, he knew she was spending time with Trace Dixon, because Stevi or Margo would have told him. Maybe even Duncan. Still. She wasn't ready to discuss Trace with Joe.

"I talked to Margo. She said Stevi was there this morning."

Leah flinched. Stevi had been staying at Margo's since Trace had shown up here. Leah had argued that it wasn't necessary, but she had to admit that having the house to themselves had been nice, even if they were simply getting to know each other as friends.

"Okay." She nodded. Was he waiting for her to tell him about Trace? Did the fact that she didn't want to mean something?

"I need to go."

"Okay."

Joe ended the call, and Leah stood lost in her thoughts for a moment. Kenzi would love Trace Dixon. She would insist that Leah sleep with him and then share all of the details over margaritas. After all, Kenzi loved to kiss and tell. There were days when Leah found it hard to look Joe in the eyes after the things Kenzi shared with them.

She watched raindrops slide over the windowpane and thought about fate. Or maybe God. Testing her? Or giving her someone to love? If it hadn't been for Kenzi's stroke, if Joe hadn't packed his family up and moved them all to the East Coast to be closer to Kenzi's family, Leah wouldn't have needed a trip to Destin to clear her head. She wouldn't have set foot inside Left Fork.

And she wouldn't have met Nashville.

What did that mean?

Fall for him and lose a dear friend? Or fall for him and be...happy.

No closer to answers, Leah stirred to life. Nashville was waiting for her downstairs.

CHAPTER 22

THEY SPENT THE DAY AT HER HOUSE. WHEN TRACE suggested something to get to know her better, he meant that he wanted to look at photo albums with her so he could get to know her through all those awkward childhood and teenage years. Leah balked at the idea, but Trace dared her, as if she could possibly back down from a dare. And so they sat together in the living room, huddled together on the floor, and pored over her photo albums.

It wasn't as simple as looking at pictures, though, because Trace quizzed her on so many of them. He asked about her parents; she had introduced them the day before on a drop in at their house. They had visited for a while; Leah could tell her mom was floored that a country music star was sitting at her kitchen table. Her dad seemed less in awe of that and more interested in the work Trace told him he and Sampson were preparing to do at Left Fork.

Leah had been afraid that Trace would be angry about the phone call, about the way she'd led him on. But he hadn't seemed affected at all. Well, other than the way he looked at her and the way he had fought to catch his breath when they stood toe-to-toe in the kitchen. And his obvious arousal pressed into her at that same time. He wasn't angry. He didn't refer to what happened all day while they talked over the photo albums and lunch—they had pizza delivered and ate in the watery gray kitchen light—while thunderstorms raged on outside.

They watched a movie later in the afternoon, and Leah fell asleep on the couch. She loved *The Breakfast Club*, but there was something so soothing about rainy days and pleasant company that she couldn't fight the temptation. Trace, on the floor, head propped in his hand, teased her when she blinked her eyes open to the credits rolling on the TV. She noticed his phone on the floor and wondered if he was texting someone, but she didn't ask.

At five, they changed clothes and headed to the Queen for the night. He hadn't worn the ball cap since the first night when he'd shown up out of the blue. Leah got a kick out of the girls and women who did a double take when they saw him. Some looked at him as if they knew who he was but couldn't believe someone like Trace Dixon would be in Adam's Bay. Others just looked at him like he was the best-looking man they would see for the next ten years.

She was proud that he was with her, but when those gazes lingered, she felt a twinge of jealousy. Though Trace seemed oblivious to the attention—never rude, but he seemed to have eyes only for her—it chafed a bit, wondering how it would feel to watch him drive away. Knowing that there were women, girls—he'd told her he'd been propositioned by girls he doubted had legal drivers' licenses—all over the place, especially in his hometown who would gladly give him what she had held back.

Because it hurt to consider it, to imagine Trace with any other woman, she tried not to think about it. Better to have fun with him while he was here and deal with the jealousy when he left and eventually texted and told her he'd hooked up or had some fun after a set.

Even Margo liked him, and Margo had been a champion of batteries and vibrators for years, even before the bad scene with Jess. Leah watched him now, dancing a little bump step with her cousin, to a seventies song. Boz Skaggs. "Lowdown." Trace had certainly taught her to pay more attention to music—all music—and there was no hardship in watching him enjoy pretty much everything they played at the Queen.

Margo's mom had Berkley tonight, so Leah expected Stevi to cut out early for a date. When the dinner hour came and went, and Stevi was still sticking around, Leah watched her for a moment. It wasn't that she didn't trust her sister. Even though Leah had told Stevi several times that she and Trace were just friends, Stevi would never make a move. Still, Trace had that charm, something in his smile just made you want to inch closer and closer until you could feel the warmth radiating from him. She wouldn't blame Stevi for getting caught up in that rush.

She was surprised to find Stevi at the other end of the bar with Duncan. Leah stood at a tall table near the back door, talking to two couples who had quickly become regulars, but she watched Duncan lean in to say something directly in Stevi's ear. Stevi threw her head back and laughed at whatever he had said.

Intrigued, Leah let her eyes roam the length of the bar to find Margo. When their eyes met, Margo tipped her head in Stevi's direction, and Leah answered with an exaggerated shrug. She looked back at Stevi, amused when her sister slipped down the bar to say something to Trace, and he dropped an arm around her shoulders.

He fit. Trace Dixon, country music star—funny that he claimed he wasn't famous, when his voice was her favorite—and award-winning songwriter, fit in her world. He liked her family; he liked her world. And her family liked him.

She wondered not for the first time what Joe and Kenzi would think of him.

"Leah, can we get a bottle of the Dykstra Chardonnay?"

"Absolutely." She turned back to the customers at the table with a smile and a nod. "Four glasses?" When they agreed that they all wanted a glass, she asked if they needed anything else. Their answer being no, she moved to get their wine and glasses.

"Tell me you've at least kissed him." Stevi stretched to her tiptoes to lean close and whisper to Leah as she selected a bottle of Dykstra Chardonnay from the cooler behind the bar.

Leah laughed softly. "Okay. I have kissed him." She nodded and then looked around helplessly when Stevi's squeal of excitement cut through the bar noise. "For God's sake, would you chill?" Fingers wrapped around the neck of the Chardonnay, Leah threw her other arm around Stevi's shoulders and clapped her hand over her mouth.

"But, really?" Stevi peeled Leah's fingers away. "You really kissed him?"

"Really. I did kiss him."

"Like…" Stevi dogged her steps as she moved to set the bottle down and reached for a foil cutter. "More than that cute little pecky stuff that you did that first night he was here? Right? More than that?"

"I know why Mom and Dad never let us get a dog." Leah kept her eyes on the bottle as she cut the foil.

"What?" Stevi sank back on her heels and eyed her with a frown. Leah snuck a quick peek at her and laughed out loud.

"We didn't need a dog, because we had you." Leah tapped Stevi on the tip of her nose and set the foil cutter down.

"Leah, he's just—"

Leah looked at her when Stevi stopped talking. Wide eyes looking at something over Leah's shoulder, she wasn't surprised when Trace moved up behind her and settled his hands on her hips.

"Did you make this playlist?" she asked him over her shoulder.

"Why would you ask me that?"

She twisted around to look at him, prepared, but that smile—the one he saved for her—still took her breath away.

"Not sure I've ever heard Dwight Yoakam in here before." She shrugged.

"I put a lot of thought into this playlist." He crossed his fingers in an x over his heart. Leah reached out and touched his hand, gave it a squeeze without a second thought. Of course, he would put a lot of thought into the playlist. He loved music, and he wanted everyone to love music with the same intensity that he did.

"I downloaded your CDs." She had considered telling him several times and ended up keeping it to herself. For some reason, the words just rushed out now. Stevi still watched him, but she stood a few feet away now, and Leah doubted she had heard what Leah said.

The Queen faded away, and it was just the two of them and the moment, and Trace stared at her with big eyes. Leah felt a quiver in her belly as she waited for him to say something. Was he angry? Surely, he wouldn't be angry that she had listened to his music. But he didn't seem excited about it, either.

"And?" He cleared his throat.

Leah watched him toe the floor with his boot. He looked around helplessly and finally met her eyes again and shrugged impatiently.

He was scared.

Trace Dixon was afraid of her opinion.

Aware that they weren't alone, Leah simply stepped closer to him and rested her hand on his arm. His skin was warm and soft, and for a moment, they were back in her kitchen, and she wanted to kiss him.

Not the pecky stuff like the first night he'd come here, and she had been so thrilled to see him. Not the almost-kiss from this morning. She wanted to kiss him. She wanted to stroke her tongue over his lips and slide it against his. Leah wanted to be free to love him. Except, no matter what that meant for Kenzi, it would leave her heartbroken when he headed back home to Nashville.

"I would rather listen to them than anything I've heard on this playlist."

He stared at her for a moment, as if he was waiting for a punch line.

"There's a reason Tanner's out there on tour." His voice was gruff.

She nodded. "You wouldn't have been at Left Fork if you were the one on tour." She barely breathed as she whispered the words. "I already told you you're my favorite part of Nashville."

Leah felt his eyes on her as she gathered four glasses, snagged the bottle of Chardonnay, and carried everything to the table by the back door. She talked with the ladies at the table as she poured. One of them was mesmerized by Trace; Leah sidestepped the question of his identity and simply said he was a friend of the family. The other one asked her several times how Margo and Berkley were doing and when Margo might bring Berkley in again. Leah promised them Berkley would make an appearance soon, though she knew Margo wouldn't bring her daughter in any time after dinner hours.

When the music changed to "Cleopatra" by The Lumineers, Leah looked up to find Margo and Stevi standing at a table out front, huddled together and singing. Trace and Duncan were engrossed in conversation behind the bar. She wandered back to the bar slowly, curious what they were discussing. As she watched, they both shifted to look out the front window. It crossed Leah's mind to wonder if Trace was asking Duncan something about Stevi.

The thought was there and gone so fast, she ducked her head and combed her fingers back through her hair. He wasn't interested in Stevi. She hadn't exactly thrown her sister at him, but she'd suggested more than once that Stevi would love to entertain him while he was here. Trace hadn't shown the tiniest bit of interest in her, beyond the fact that she was Leah's sister.

She snagged a couple of dirty pint glasses from the bar and carried them to the sink, but she still watched Duncan and Trace as they talked. Duncan was now gesturing wildly, arms swinging wide to indicate something. Leah watched them for a moment, but she looked away when she saw Margo slip away from Stevi and head up the stairs. When Margo tugged her phone from her back pocket, Leah glanced at Stevi and raised her eyebrows.

Stevi shrugged and shook her head.

"Was it Aunt Liz?" she asked when Stevi joined her at the bar.

"I don't think so." Stevi sighed. "Jess has been texting her."

Leah yawned and shook her head. "Have people asked you who he is?"

"Trace?" Stevi glanced at Leah with an arched eyebrow. She shook her head. "Well. Yeah. But I haven't told anyone. A few people knew without asking."

Leah leaned on the end of the bar and pulled her phone out to see what time it was.

"So. The kissing?" Stevi nudged her with her elbow.

"Did you talk to Joe today?" Leah asked her.

"Leah, I have been living out of a duffel bag for a week." Stevi whined. "Just gimme something."

"Am I one of many?"

He had stepped up behind her without her seeing him. She leaned into him when he dropped his hands on her shoulders and squeezed.

"What?" She still held her phone in her hand, but she turned her head slightly to look at him over her shoulder.

"You're here at the Queen, checking your phone." His lips brushed her ear when he spoke. "You got some other guy texting you, Leah Hague?"

"You're it, Nashville." She winked at him.

"Do you know how happy that makes me?" His whisper was gruff in her ear.

She dragged her eyes from him when Stevi tugged on her arm.

"What?" She considered smacking her. One little swat on her cheek to back her off. She'd done it once or twice when they were kids and landed herself in some hot water.

Stevi handed her a beer and then tapped her own to the bottle. Leah grinned and took a drink.

"I gotta ask." Stevi rested her hand on Trace's forearm. Leah blinked at her sister in disbelief. What the hell was she going to ask him? Something about kissing Leah?

"Hit me." Trace shrugged. "I'm an open book."

"Careful," Leah mumbled.

"Hit you?" Stevi wiggled her eyebrows. "Like, can I misunderstand—"

"Behave." Leah threw a sharp elbow at her.

Margo appeared behind the bar singing along now to the Bruno Mars song, "Treasure." She linked her arm through Leah's and tugged her away from Stevi and Trace. Leah glanced at him, but his smile reminded her that he was hers for the taking.

She danced away from them arm-in-arm with Margo.

Later, near time for Duncan to lock the doors, they still had several patrons at the bar and four tables on the main floor were full. Nine people crowded around one of them. Duncan had watched the group carefully, making sure there was at least one in the crowd not drinking alcohol. Leah was a strange mix of tired and restless. She wanted to go home, to curl into the quiet darkness with Trace. But part of her had enjoyed tonight so much, seeing him mix with the people she loved most, talking and dancing a bit, waiting on their customers like he was just a new bartender Duncan had hired, that she didn't want it to end.

When a few of their patrons started dancing at the front window, Leah and Stevi exchanged a look and shared a small smile. Margo sat at the west end of the bar, eyes on her phone. Duncan moved up behind Stevi and wrapped an arm around her neck. Before Leah could wonder about it, Trace stepped up beside her and slipped an arm around her waist.

"You know what I really wanna do with you before I have to leave?"

The word hit her in the heart. She flinched and tried to smile when she looked up at him.

"Told you I won't do that, Nashville," she reminded him.

He moved to stand in front of her as the music changed again. She'd listened to enough country music now that she could name a few of the artists. This one was Garth Brooks, but she wasn't sure what the song was.

Trace grinned at her and settled his hands on her hips.

"Dance with me, darlin'."

CHAPTER 23

HE GAVE HER PLENTY OF SPACE, ROOM TO SAY NO, AND NOT feel like the rest of the room would notice. She didn't, though. She laughed softly and stepped closer to him. He curled his fingers into her hips as she closed hers around the back of his neck.

Duncan had asked him to throw a playlist together when they'd first walked in. Trace wasn't sure if it was a test. Would he try to cram too much country in? Was he supposed to go heavy on instrumental? But he loved music of all kinds, so he had thrown together what he thought was a good variety, all with this moment in the back of his mind. He wanted to dance with Leah.

They stood right where they were, near the back of the bar, and swayed to the music. Leah was almost pliant in his arms. Trace hoped that was as much to do with her finally feeling comfortable with him as with the beer he'd seen her drink. They talked as they danced, mostly conversation about the people still here enjoying themselves at the

Queen. Trace loved it here; Duncan had shared some of their ideas for the future with him regarding live music and the possibility of a mystery dinner theater the following year. Trace wanted in; he wanted to be part of everything they were doing, but mostly he wanted a place in Leah's life.

When the song changed again and the Black-Eyed Peas started singing "I Gotta Feeling," he wanted to kick himself. He loved the smile on Leah's face, and sure, it was a treat to watch her cut loose and have fun with Stevi and Margo, but he wanted her in his arms, dancing with him. He wanted her to himself.

Still, she linked her fingers with his as she turned to face the girls. He supposed he could do worse than dancing with three pretty girls. But, he would still rather have Leah to himself.

Duncan had made him an intriguing offer. He needed to mull it over, but the words had been a lifeline. It was true that Pearl and Sampson were doing well, and Pearl's main concern anytime he called to check in was whether or not he'd fixed things up here with *that girl*. But Trace felt a little bit guilty to be up here enjoying himself every night, instead of back at work, on that little rinky dink stage with his hands on Loretta's gorgeous neck.

He missed her. Loretta, not the stage. He had played around a bit for Leah, but it wasn't the same thing.

Duncan's invitation had been just what the doctor ordered, just what Trace needed without having to ask.

But what would Leah think about it?

The last thing he wanted to do was make her uncomfortable.

She had floored him earlier when she told him that she downloaded his CDs. Wasn't just that she had done it, but the way she told him. As if it was the most natural thing in the world for her to do. He had squirmed under her bold gaze, afraid for the first time ever, that he wasn't good enough to do what he did. Afraid that if Leah would have had a choice between him and his brother, she would have walked away on Tanner's arm.

Her reasoning that she wouldn't have met him if he had been the one on tour had been a fist around his heart.

He considered stepping back now, sliding to the bar to watch her mingle with Stevi and Margo, all three of them dancing now with the big group gathered around one of the tables. Leah held his hand, still, so when he shifted to move away from her, she turned quickly and shook her head.

"Tell me a music man like yourself has some moves tucked up his sleeve." She moved closer to him and offered him a flirty smile.

"I might have a few moves tucked up my sleeves," he said with a grin, "but you've told me repeatedly that you aren't interested."

She laughed softly and swung her hips gently to the music.

"I don't want you to go."

She spoke so softly, Trace wasn't sure if she said the words or if he imagined them.

"Do you mean that?"

Eyes locked with his, she answered with a small, quick nod.

"Leah."

"When?" She frowned. "When do you have to go back?"

"We can—"

"Because I know Pearl sent you up here, but they have to want you back. Who's playing while you're gone?"

"There's no shortage of musical talent in Nashville, darlin'."

"But there's only one you."

"Leah."

"What?"

"It's only four hundred miles."

"Only." Her laugh was soft and sad. "I like waking up in the same house as you, Nashville."

Stunned, he only stared at her.

"I mean…" She cleared her throat and lowered her gaze to her hands on his chest. "Don't get me wrong. I live for the texts, but being with you…"

"Me, too." He gathered her in his arms and held his breath as she relaxed against him.

"Leo Sayer?" she asked a few minutes later. She lifted her head to look at him, and the joy in her smile lit him on fire. "My Gram loved this song."

"Told you I wanted to dance with you."

The crowd thinned out as they danced, until there were only three people at the front of the place talking to Duncan and Stevi. Still, Leah stayed in his arms, warm and soft against his chest, her arms over his shoulders and her hands on his neck.

"I think some of those girls dancing were plotting to murder me." She turned her face to his neck. Trace smoothed his hands over her back and pressed a kiss to her head.

"Why would they do that?"

He felt her snort, and when he looked down at her, he saw a smirk on her face.

"Maybe because the most beautiful man in the room is dancing with me."

His face against her head, his grin pulled her hair just enough that she lifted her head to look at him.

"How much did you have to drink?"

"Two beers."

He gave her a slow nod.

"I know exactly what I'm saying," she told him.

"I'm pretty sure I've never been called a beautiful man."

Leah stroked her fingers up into his hair and lifted her eyebrows.

"Maybe you need some new friends, Nashville."

He laughed and shook his head.

"I don't know why you're here, but I'm so glad you are."

"What does that mean?" he asked as he twirled her around and danced her just under the staircase. The shadows and the stairs themselves gave them a bit of privacy, and though he expected nothing, Trace wanted just to flirt with her in private.

Her eyes wide with innocent desire again, she stared at him silently.

"I told you why I'm here." He moved his hand from her back to her neck and traced circles under her hair.

"Because Pearl sent you."

He held her gaze for a long moment, and then slowly, he leaned into her and rested his forehead to hers.

"I'm not here because Pearl sent me," he told her. "And you know that."

She pressed her lips closed, and Trace saw her nostrils flare when she took a deep breath.

"I know."

Desperate to be closer to her, he moved his hand down her back again and pulled her in tight against his chest. With her face turned to his neck, her warm breath on his skin was delicious torture. Around them the lights turned low, and the conversation grew quiet. Music still played, and Trace still swayed her gently in his arms.

He heard Stevi and Duncan talking at the bar, and Margo hollered something from upstairs. Leah didn't react. She simply held onto him, as if she would never let go.

"Leah."

She moved her hands, just enough to rub her fingers over the crewneck collar of his shirt. One handed molded his shoulder and then fisted around his shirt, and the other slipped around the front of his neck, and she nuzzled the skin under his ear with her lips.

He gritted his teeth, but no amount of control was going to hold the erection down. Leah Hague kissed him. He had thought about this moment a million different times, but nothing he had ever imagined felt this good. Her lips were soft and warm on his neck, and then suddenly, she parted them and nipped at his skin.

"Leah."

Fire in his veins, he groaned out loud when she kissed a trail over his cheek to his lips. When their lips met this time, he wasted no time in claiming her. Still afraid that she would change her mind, he was cautious, but he stroked his tongue over hers before she had time to think.

"Nashville," she whispered, but she didn't stop him. Instead, she kissed him back, her tongue dancing with his, her hands sliding and smoothing and claiming his shoulders and his arms and his neck.

"Still don't wanna sleep with me?"

CHAPTER 24

BREATHLESS, SHE COULD ONLY STARE AT HIM FOR A moment. Lost in his kiss, she blinked him back into focus, saw that the lights had been turned down in the bar. Margo and Stevi were head-to-head over the bar. For a second, Leah worried that they were discussing her and Trace, maybe placing bets on what was going on. But they appeared to be in a serious conversation, and at the moment, Leah didn't give a damn about anything but the man in her arms.

"Kiss me like that again, and I might change my mind."

She was only half-joking, and she held her breath waiting, hoping that he would kiss her again. He had been a perfect gentleman, and she loved that he'd shown respect for her reasons for saying no. But one more kiss, and she was all in with him.

"Don't say things like that if you don't mean them," he warned her.

Leah, middle pressed to his middle, felt his arousal against her. Breathless with excitement, she felt her heartbeat in her nipples and wondered if he felt it against his chest. She stroked her fingers over his chin and his lips, eyes locked with his, and waited.

He kissed her again, his lips warm and soft on hers. She moved her hand only slightly and thrilled at the feel of his stubble on her skin. They played for a moment with those soft, chaste kisses, and his breath on her lips, on her face, was warm and soft. Fingers of her other hand on the back of his neck, she feathered them in his hair and moaned softly when he finally licked the seam of her lips with the tip of his tongue.

Hungry for the taste of him, she met his tongue thrust for thrust, and she held on tight with her arm over his shoulder, because her knees were weak with desire. When he pulled back for a moment, she followed him, kissed him again and then kissed her way back to the spot under his ear where she felt his pulse against her tongue.

"Take me home, Nashville," she whispered.

"Are you sure?" He slid his hands down over her back and molded her bottom.

"Yes."

He kissed her again, but he cut it short and turned away from her. He curled his fingers around hers as he moved toward the bar. Leah followed a step behind, eyes searching for Stevi's.

"You guys need help—"

"Nope." Margo cut Trace off before he could finish his question.

"Did you—?" Duncan leaned over and rested his elbows on the bar, as if he was settling in for a long conversation. Leah tuned him out. Her body vibrated with need; her hands shook so badly, she tugged loose of Trace and tucked them in her pockets.

Margo coughed and stepped closer to Duncan. Stevi stepped around the bar and sidled up to stand beside Leah.

"Go." She slipped her arm around Leah's waist and gave her a squeeze. "Whatever Duncan thinks he needs to say can wait until tomorrow."

Leah nodded.

"Night, guys." Stevi patted Trace's shoulder and then stepped between them and the bar, chattering to Duncan about a woman who had mentioned wanting to host a fiftieth birthday party for someone next month. Trace glanced at Leah and reached for her hand when she only arched an eyebrow in response.

Behind them, Duncan talked with Stevi about the prospective party, but Leah knew he wasn't that clueless. Even if he hadn't seen Trace kiss her just minutes before when they were dancing, he had to get it now the way Stevi and Margo were ushering her and Trace out the door.

Hand in hand, he led her to his truck parked out back. It was warm, but the breeze felt cool on her feverish skin.

She reveled in the feel of it, the gentle wind fingering through her hair and around her neck. But she wanted Trace's hands there. His mouth on her neck. On her belly.

At the truck, she lifted her head to look at the stars. Wondered if it was too late to pray. Were there words she could say to take back what she'd promised? Was God watching her, ready to snuff out Kenzi's life the second Leah gave in to Trace? No. She didn't believe that. She didn't make the decision lightly, but she didn't believe that God or fate was vindictive and watched and waited for her to go back on her word just to exact revenge.

"What're the odds of seeing a cop on the way to your house?" Trace grinned as he pulled her door open for her.

She laughed softly.

"In a hurry, Nashville?"

To answer her question, he leaned over and dropped a kiss on her forehead. She hesitated as she stepped to climb up into the truck. Looked at him over her shoulder. He met her eyes, but neither of them spoke. When she settled in the passenger seat, Trace swung the door closed and then moved around to the driver's side.

"What's your favorite?" he asked after several moments of silence. He had reached for her when he pulled the truck into the street, and now he drove with his hand on her leg, like he couldn't bear to be separated from her.

She knew he was asking which of his songs on the CDs was her favorite. She loved them all, but then was she ready to tell him that she loved to listen to them when she was lying in bed at night? That she closed her eyes and thought of him singing to her?

"'Just You.'" She covered her hand with his. From the corner of her eye, she saw him look at her. Rather than look at him, because somehow that would make the drive seem longer, she squeezed her hand around his fingers on her leg.

He goosed the gas just a bit, and Leah laughed softly.

"They know."

She turned to him, amused by the look on his face.

"What?"

"Stevi and Margo know what's going on. Don't they?"

"Going on?" She cleared her throat. "Trace, you drove—"

"They know that we were dying to get out of there tonight because I'm dying to get you out of those clothes—"

"No."

"No?"

Impatient when he hit the brakes again, she glanced out the windshield to see that they were at a four-way stop on Montgomery Street near her house.

"They know me." Her whisper was thick with lust.

"What?"

"You kissed me, Trace. Dancing with me, you kissed me. They saw me kiss you back."

"And that's a big thing?"

"I've told them both a hundred times that we're just friends."

He slowed again, but this time, it was to turn into her driveway. When he parked, they sat for a moment. Leah turned toward him, hungry eyes roaming over him in the dark.

"Change your mind?"

He unbuckled his seatbelt and leaned across the seat. Leah moved willingly toward him. She gasped out loud when he threaded his fingers in her hair and kissed her again, his velvet tongue hot and wet against hers. Fingers trembling, she fumbled with her own seatbelt, and then Trace's hand covered hers, and he pushed the button and the belt slipped free.

They climbed out of the truck at the same time, the sounds of the doors closing jarring in the quiet neighborhood. Leah fished for her keys in her purse as he followed her to the back door.

"God, I'm shaking so much, I can't do anything." She laughed. Leaned into him as he reached around her and held her purse steady for her.

"Why are you shaking?" He pressed his lips to her ear, and the warmth of his breath and vibration of his voice there sent a sharp, powerful shiver to her toes.

"Because I want you," she said simply.

"Dammit, Leah." He sank his fingers into her hip and pulled her back to rub her bottom against his erection.

"Stop it!" She laughed again. "I'd rather not do this right here."

She wanted to sing in triumph when she finally closed her fingers around her keychain. Trace steadied her hand as she unlocked the door, and then they stepped inside and Leah fell on the door to close it. He moved in to kiss her, but when she gathered his shirt in her hands, he pulled back and shook his head.

"No?" Her mouth dry, she managed to whisper.

His reaction made her heart hurt, and before he could step out of her reach, she slipped her hand under the tail of his shirt and spread her fingers over his smooth, hard abs.

"We're not doing two minutes on the kitchen table." His voice was gruff. He caught her hand in his and pulled it from his stomach.

"Gimme at least three minutes, Nashville." She licked her lips and reached for him with her other hand. He groaned as if he was in pain when she hooked her fingers in the waistband of his jeans.

"I hope to give you all night, but I want you in your bed."

"All night?" Back pressed against the door, she watched him as he peeled her fingers from his jeans and linked them with his.

"You said something about round three and four," he reminded her. "I've got some work to do to impress you."

"You really don't," she whispered. "This all feels new to me. Right now."

"Leah." He dipped his head to kiss her again. She pushed off the door and slipped her arms around his shoulders. He kissed her with hunger, but Leah needed more. Her knees trembled, and her inner thighs burned with a fire that only he could quench.

"Please?" she whispered. "Please make love to me, Trace."

She turned him in a small circle, unwilling to let go of him to lead him out of the kitchen and to the steps to her room. Finally, he let go of her and nodded for her to take control. She reached for him, though, and took him by the hand to lead him through the dark, all those nights that she hurried through the house to get upstairs and talk to him on her mind.

In the room where he was staying, she slowed. Breathed deeply and considered that his bed was closer, and they could touch each other faster, now, but Trace stepped up behind her and nuzzled her neck with his lips.

"Your bed. I want you in *your* bed, darlin'." He nipped at her earlobe. "I've been thinking about you alone in that bed since the first night I saw you, and I want your sheets on my skin."

Her heart raced in her chest. Weak with desire, she lifted her arm and wrapped it around his head. Turned her face toward his and kissed him. Because she didn't want to, because it would be much too easy to kiss him again, to turn to him and undress, because he *would* take her here, she moved again and led him to the stairway to her room. On the bottom step, his body wrapped around her from behind her and his hands on her hips, she lifted her head and wondered how her bedroom could be so far away.

She moved quickly, and at the top step, she turned to him and backed toward her bed, ready for him. Ready to love him. She'd dropped her purse somewhere, but it didn't matter. She didn't need her keys or her phone, only him.

Leah watched him take it in, his eyes roaming quickly over her room, only a shade lighter than darkness from the moonlight outside her window. And then his hands were on her, and she watched, breathless, as he made quick work of the buttons on her blouse. When he opened the last one, he studied the horizontal slice of skin, the lace of her bra between her breasts, and then lifted his eyes to meet hers.

"Are you sure?"

"Trace—"

"I don't wanna wait, Leah." His voice was tight and hard. "I want to spend the rest of my life making love to you."

She bit her lip and then started to answer him, but he shook his head.

"Just you. And I wanna start the rest of my life right now. But if you need to wait, I understand. I want—"

Leah reached for him. Touched her fingertip to his lips.

"Please."

He nodded. Parted her blouse and looked his fill at her flat stomach and the pale pink lace that covered her breasts. With slow, precise movements, he pushed her blouse over her shoulders and then pulled her close enough to press his open mouth to her neck.

She moaned his name as her knees buckled. He kissed a trail up over her neck to lick the shell of her ear, and Leah struggled to free herself of the blouse. Trace refused to let her move, though, and she whimpered when he dropped kisses over her cheek. She kissed him when he slid his mouth over hers and sighed, frustrated, when he continued and kissed her other cheek and then treated her other ear to the same flick of his tongue.

"You're beautiful." His tone reverent, he loosened his hold on her blouse, on her wrists. She wiggled out of the sleeves and let the material fall to the floor. "I knew you would be beautiful, Leah."

"Kiss me," she whispered. She pressed her lips against his as he smoothed his hands over her upper arms and her shoulders. "Trace, I'm burning up. I need you—"

"Leah, southern boys don't get in too much of a hurry." Hands splayed over her back, he pulled back to offer her a grin. "I'm gonna take my time and enjoy the hell out of your body."

"Could you hurry just this one time?" She laughed, but they both heard the throb of need in her voice.

"No, ma'am." His voice was low and sexy, and Leah shivered and ducked her forehead to rest on his shoulder.

"Please touch me." She wound her arms around his waist and slipped her hands under his shirt. "I know you want to touch me."

"You're first, darlin'." He reached one hand behind his waist and circled her wrists with his fingers, and then suddenly with a quick movement, her bra gave and he flattened his other hand over her back.

"Me? First?" She parted her lips and bit gently on his collarbone. "I want you inside me. I want you—"

"I've been thinking about this since the night you walked into Left Fork," he reminded her. "Night after night and day and night. You're playing with fire."

She laughed softly.

"I've thought about you, too," she admitted.

"Yeah?" He gave her a lazy stroke on her back and then slid his fingers down inside the back of her jeans. "Jerkin' off in the shower?"

She turned her head to rest her flaming cheek on his chest and felt the rumble of his laughter roll through her.

"No." She flinched in protest when he moved his hand again. "More like thinking about how you're the best thing about Nashville, and I walked away. Wondering how many women had their hands on you while I was here missing you."

"Two, including Pearl always pushing me around at the Fork and Mama—with the hugs and the love pats."

"But not on your ass, right?"

"No, darlin'," he assured her. "No one's had her hands there—"

Leah moved quickly and slid her hands over his back and down over his butt, cussing the denim all the way.

"Leah."

She lifted her head to look at him and gasped at the raw, dark need on his face. Her mouth watered when he moved again, this time to slide her bra straps from her shoulders. She watched when he plucked the lace from between her breasts, his fingertips tickling her skin. He took a moment to admire the lace, Leah's nipples hard with desire as she waited.

Her mouth went dry when he lifted his eyes to hers.

"Guess you've seen a lot of those in your line of work, huh?"

He shrugged her question away. "Prettiest I've ever seen right here." He dropped her bra and let his eyes fall to her breasts. "You're beautiful, Leah Hague."

"Yeah?" She laughed softly, suddenly worried about the many other women Trace Dixon had touched. "You wanna sign them?"

"No way." He sounded reverent again. "But I want to kiss them. Lick them."

Her eyes fluttered closed as he stroked a calloused fingertip over her nipple.

"Please do," she whispered.

"Lick them?"

"Yes."

"Suck them?"

"Do what you want with me, Nashville." She tried to take a deep breath, but she was so lightheaded, she swayed in his arms. "I'm yours."

"Tell me what you like."

He watched her, his gaze intense on hers, as he curled his fingers around the curves of her breasts.

"Just you," she answered. "You and me. Your hands. Your mouth. Please."

She expected more of the slow, languid touches, and though they were torture, every second with him was perfect. But when he moved this time, he claimed her. His hands roamed over her stomach and around her waist, and he bent his head and sucked her taut dark nipple into his mouth. She gasped out loud and wrapped her arms around him, desire ripping through her when he rolled her nipple with his tongue and then flattened it against the roof of his mouth.

"Do you like that?" he asked as he drew his lips away. Leah whimpered in protest when the air in her room made her wet flesh pucker, and then he engulfed her other breast in the heat of his mouth and plunged his hands into her jeans again.

"Yes." Her voice was small, because she couldn't catch her breath.

"Leah?"

He walked her backwards a few steps until her legs hit the edge of her bed. Grateful for a soft place to land, she pulled him with her when she went down and captured his mouth with hers.

"I am so in love with you." It was still a whisper, but a thick, heady whisper, and she meant it. Trace slowed the kiss, pulled back to look at her, and wiggled his hands free of her jeans. She held her breath as she waited what felt like an eternity before his lips quirked up in a small smile.

"You might wanna wait to make sure I can deliver before you say things like that."

She laughed and opened her legs, making room for him to lie between her thighs.

"I'm sorry." She swallowed hard. "I didn't mean for that to come out."

He cupped her breast in his hand and played with her nipple. Rocked against her to remind her that he was aroused and ready to make love to her.

"Taking it back that quickly?"

"No." She walked her fingers up his back and rubbed his neck. "I have no doubt you're gonna deliver, Nashville. I seem to remember you telling me you would do everything you could to make me come."

"Pressure." He wagged his eyebrows. "And me with a hard-on for you for at least a month. Six weeks."

"Do that, like two more times, and I'm there," she said when he rocked against her again.

"Leah."

"You don't have to say it, Trace. You don't have to feel—"

"Earlier? When you first brought me up here. Before these girls distracted me?"

She laughed out loud and rolled her head on the bed.

"Do you remember what I said?"

"Of course I do."

"Tell me."

She blinked at him and licked her lips.

"Nope. You're not gonna distract me again."

"The rest of your life," she whispered.

"What about it?"

"Making love to me."

"I meant it. Just you. Forever."

She combed her fingers up the back of his head.

"I really want you inside me."

"We'll get there." He nodded.

"Not if we both keep our pants on."

CHAPTER 25

Trace's whole body—even his teeth—vibrated with arousal. And something else. Hell, he'd known he was in love with her, but hearing her say it—those words, the throaty, sultry moan, *I am so in love with you*—had filled him with fire. He'd slowed things down for a second, against his better judgment, against his dick's wishes, just to make sure he'd heard her right. Made light of it, tried to tease her, see if she would admit to just rambling, sweet talking, dirty talking, whatever it was she was doing.

She said she meant it. She meant it. Leah Hague was in love with him. Jesus, he'd almost jumped off of her to dance across her room like an NFL star who had just scored a touchdown. But her eyes were hot with need, and he could feel her heartbeat under his hand when he touched her breast.

And he wanted to be inside her. He wanted to climb in balls deep and feel her body close around him, tight and hot. He wanted that delicious friction, the drag of her tight glove over the head of his cock. Her legs around his waist. Her lips on his face, at his ear.

She kissed him now with an intimacy that felt raw. She needed him the same way he needed her, and damned if he didn't want to deliver an orgasm that would make her sing. He wanted her fingernails in his back and his name, like a prayer, on her lips.

Without breaking their skin-to-skin contact, he slid lower over her body. She moved under him, arching her back and rocking her hips just enough to tease him. He tasted the skin of her belly, dipped his tongue in her belly button, and then eased the button of her jeans open with his hands. Leah rubbed her hands over his shoulders.

"Dammit, Nashville." She gathered his t-shirt in her hands and pulled at it, at him, until he propped himself up so she could ease it over his stomach and chest. "Take it off," she ordered him with a desperate laugh when it bunched under his arms. Eyes on hers, he unzipped her jeans and pulled them open.

"I might die of a heart attack tonight," he told her when he saw that she was wearing pink lace that matched the bra he'd taken off her earlier. "Just so you know."

"Then you better get busy, because I need you to make love to me before that happens." Her eyes twinkled in the moonlit room.

He wanted his shirt off now as badly as she wanted him to take it off. He wanted her soft hands on his shoulders. But he wanted to push her, to make her crazy with desire. Instead of sitting up to take his shirt off, he leaned forward and licked a line from the edge of the pink lace up to her belly button.

"You're cruel," she whispered. "I'm begging you to take your clothes off and get inside me."

He slipped his hands under her bottom and tugged half-heartedly at her jeans. When she lifted her hips, he pulled them down around her thighs, but to throw her off, he sat up on his knees and whipped his shirt over his head.

"Beautiful." The word was soft and sweet.

Trace let his gaze fall slowly from her face and over her bare breasts and stomach. He slipped his fingers just under the waistband of the lace and pulled them down a fraction of an inch.

"Killing me." She sighed. "You are killing me."

"I'm gonna love you back to life," he promised her.

Her smile was weak, and her eyes fluttered closed when he dragged his thumb up the seam in the lace, careful to put pressure on her center.

"Look at me."

"Please make me come."

"Open your eyes." When he slipped his fingers inside the lace and touched her, she blinked her eyes open and stared at him with lust. "Take 'em off."

She wasted no time. Sat up and reached for her panties. Trace kissed her and eased her back down on the bed. Before she could protest, he pulled her jeans off and then hooked his fingers in her panties and slid the wet lace over her thighs.

"Leah."

"Yes."

He pressed his mouth to her core and slid his fingers inside her. The soft hum of pleasure she made filled him with the need for more. Leah shifted beneath him and then cupped the back of his head. She combed her fingers through his hair, her fingernails gently scraping his scalp and drawing a hard shiver of desire up from his gut.

She murmured his name on a soft, dreamy sigh, and he lifted his head for a moment to look at her. The fingers of her other hand were splayed over her breast, but as he watched, she smoothed her hand low over her belly and lifted her head to look at him.

"I'm so close," she whispered. To remind him that she needed him, she rubbed the back of his head again and shifted her hips under him. He wanted to draw it out, to make her wait, but she had already begged him, and he wasn't sure how much longer he would last. Damned if he wanted to shortchange her when he finally buried himself inside her.

He stroked her again, and he was rewarded with another soft moan and her hot, velvet fist clenching around his fingers. Leah drew her knees up, and he lowered his head to kiss her again. When she exploded with pleasure, Trace lifted his head to watch her. Her body clenched tightly around his fingers, her face fluid with pleasure, and her breasts rose high and proud as she panted and called out for him.

He wanted to move. To jump up and shuck his jeans and boots. He was desperate to get his cock inside her and feel the waves of her orgasm around his body. But there was time. He could absolutely give her more, and he wanted this moment for Leah. Rather than move, he continued to move his fingers inside her in small, slow circles over the bundle of nerves. Hanging out in bars and in the country venues, he'd heard all kinds of talk through the years. He'd heard women and girls of all ages say all sorts of things about what they could do with his cock. He'd had all sorts of females offer him all of their body parts; he'd heard girls and women share what they liked and how it felt when someone bit their nipples or their clits and that they'd screamed until their throats were raw when someone hit their G spots.

None of that mattered to him. It never had. Wasn't to say he hadn't taken a few of them up on their offers through the years. Wasn't to say he didn't look when a girl offered a peek. But he'd never seen or heard anything as beautiful as Leah Hague in the throes of orgasm, and he hoped to hell she'd never felt anything like what he was doing to her at the moment.

A deep red flush climbed from her chest up over her neck and her face. Her lips were parted on a constant repeated prayer—at the moment she was talking to God, but Trace had heard her mention Nashville a time or two—and her nipples were still taut with arousal. She thrashed on the bed; one hand still curled around the back of his head and the other now up over her head, grasping for purchase. He watched her fist the sheet in her hand and then lowered his mouth to flick the tip of his tongue over her center one more time when she slid her feet over his back and locked her ankles.

"Leah?" he murmured her name, lips pressed to her lower belly now.

"Mmm."

"I've never seen anything so sensual in my life," he said quietly.

Her hand limp, she moved, let it fall to the bed. He watched her squeeze her fingers in and out for a moment and listened to her breathing slow to normal.

"Right." She stretched her legs now, slid her feet down his denim-clad legs. "Because you have porn chicks in leather and lace offering you their bodies night after night."

"I've never been in love with a porn chick." He lifted his head to meet her eyes and offered her a smile.

"The last time that happened—"

He moved. Scooted off the bed and stared at her.

"Nashville, it was my vibrator." She lifted her arms over her head again and watched him unbuckle his belt. "In my hand."

"Yeah?" He dropped his belt and then sat on the edge of the bed to tug his boots off. "When was the last time a guy made you come like that?"

"Maybe never," she said softly. "You don't make love with your boots on?"

He stood again and looked at her with a grin. "Well, I could. But I wanna be naked with you. Can't get the jeans off with the boots on."

"Will you?"

"Will I what?"

"Make love to me? With your boots on?"

"Now?"

"Tomorrow?"

He pushed the denim over his hips and kicked the jeans aside.

"This is gonna happen tomorrow?"

"God, I hope so," she whispered. Trace stood still as she moved her gaze boldly over his body.

"I will make love to you however you want me to make love to you, Leah." He cocked his head and watched her. When she finally dragged her eyes back to his, he lifted his hand and licked the fingers he'd used to drive her wild. "I have no shame when it comes to you."

"I'm sorry."

"There's no room for those words here." He shook his head.

"For making you wait."

He shrugged. "I would have waited forever, Leah. You're it. This is it. I'm crazy about you."

Her eyes on him, he reached for his jeans, and pulled his wallet from the back pocket. She sat up when he found the one condom he always carried—a precaution he hadn't needed for a long time—and reached for it. Trace dropped his jeans again, tossed the wallet to the floor, and then as she opened the foil package, he hooked his fingers in his gray briefs and pulled them down over his hips.

"Was my business card really on the floor with—?" She took the condom from the packet, but when she lifted her gaze to his nudity, to his long, thick cock practically waving at her, she stopped talking.

"Your business card was on the floor with a silver foil condom wrapper," he said with a nod. "Kadie noticed all of it. She and Angie were making a joke about it. I was angry that we had a condom wrapper there. And then I saw your name."

Still speechless, she lifted her eyes to his. Her struggle to swallow made him vibrate with need. He gave his cock a long, slow pull and drew her eyes back down.

"Let me." Her lips barely moved, but Trace heard her throaty voice say the words. She scooted closer to the edge of the bed, to him, the condom still in her hand. He sucked in a sharp breath, one that hurt like knives in his ribs, when she touched him. He fisted his hands at his sides as she stroked her fingers over his balls and then up the length of his cock. She moved before he could stop her and flicked the tip of her tongue over his head, but he grabbed her chin gently and lifted her face.

"I want to be inside you when I come." He gave her a soft push and followed her down to the bed. The feel of her soft, smooth skin over his legs and his waist and his ass cheeks was almost more than he could bear.

Desperate now, he raised up on his knees to straddle her. Her hands shook as she rolled the condom over his cock.

"What do you like?" His voice was small and tight. She cupped his balls and then dragged her fingers down his inner thigh.

"I'm yours," she reminded him as she lay back again and reached for him. He gripped her hips and eased into her, feeling every inch of her sweet, hot desire as she took him in.

Her contented sigh drew his eyes from where their bodies were joined. Smoky eyes on him, she licked her lips and arched her eyebrows.

"Is it okay if I still call you Nashville?" She grinned.

"You can call me anything," he said through gritted teeth. "But gimme a second."

"You make me so happy," she whispered. "I don't know how you found my card. I don't know what made you walk off that stage—"

"Darlin'." He leaned forward and pressed deeper inside her. She gasped, and her eyes fluttered closed. "I would walk off any stage in the world for you."

She whispered something; Trace thought he heard the word never, but he couldn't wait any longer. Leah opened her eyes when he moved again, when he rocked her hips in a slow, easy motion.

He read her lips, saw *I love you* there as they moved together. She held on like it was love, but she moved with him, as hungry, as aroused as he was, and when she rolled her head on the bed and moaned his name again in pleasure, Trace ducked his head to her shoulder and chanted her name over and over, until the last of his release shuddered out of his body, and he was spent. Breathless and skin slick with sweat, he eased his weight down to lie on her and then inched to her side. Leah twisted on the bed and curled up against him, her head resting in the crook of his arm.

CHAPTER 26

Leah squeezed her eyes closed and laughed softly. She stretched her arm up under her pillow and took a moment to feel Trace's chest pressed to her bare back, his skin warm and soft, and his heavy thigh thrown over her bottom, pressing her into the mattress.

"I think we made some music." She spoke with her eyes still closed, but she knew it was morning.

"Oh, we did, darlin'," he agreed.

She shivered when he traced his fingers from her shoulder to her elbow and then back.

"I'm kind of glad Stevi didn't come home." She blinked her eyes open and lifted her head to look at him over her shoulder.

"You said they knew what we were up to when we left."

"They would have to be blind not to see what we were up to." Leah grinned. "But I'm glad she wasn't here to hear me. Wouldn't wanna make my little sister jealous."

"Your little sister's cute, but she doesn't hold a candle to you." He pressed a kiss to her cheek.

"She was hot for you, but she would never have acted on that." Leah turned over to lie on her back. Trace propped his head on his hand and touched her lips. "Not after the first time you texted me."

"Even though you weren't interested?"

"Nashville, I was always interested." She lifted her hand and pushed his hair back from his face. "I don't know a woman alive who wouldn't be interested in this."

"What changed your mind?"

She swallowed hard and then puffed her cheeks up with a deep breath.

"That bargain with God?"

He winced. "We could have waited. I told you I was willing—"

"Shh." She touched his lips with her fingertip. "It wasn't about sex. I promised not to *fall in love*, and I did. I fell so damned hard for you, no matter how many times I said I wouldn't."

"Me, too." He kissed her fingers.

"When Joe called?"

"Yesterday?"

"God, was that yesterday?" She stretched again and then lay still when he did the same. When he dragged his toes over the inside of her ankle, she squeezed her eyes closed and grinned.

"What? What'd I do?" He pulled away from her to look down their bodies and then looked up at her with a curious frown. Leah pouted and reached for him, cold where he'd moved away from her. "I wanna know so I can put that look on your face again. I didn't touch any girl stuff."

She laughed out loud and feathered her fingers back through his hair. Lifted her head to kiss him and then fell back to the pillow and simply stared at him.

"Your toes on my feet," she said softly.

His face so close to hers she could feel his breath on her lips, he frowned. Gave her a small headshake.

"That's sexy? You have a feet thing?"

"I have a you thing," she answered simply. "And yes, I thought about what it would feel like to lie with you like this—"

"When you say like this, do you mean—?" He angled his eyebrow for a rakish look. Leah giggled.

"Yes. I mean naked. Post-coital."

"Let's say naked and satisfied."

She shrugged. "I wanted all of you. Touching all of me."

He groaned. "And when did you decide that?"

"The night you played Loretta for me."

"The night you said you couldn't do this."

She nodded.

Trace drew his fingers over her lips and then down over her neck.

"Joe said Kenzi's..." She hesitated. She couldn't say that Kenzi was making progress, because she wasn't naïve or stupid, and just because Kenzi had said Joe's name didn't mean she would be fully recovered in x number of days. "The stroke left her partially paralyzed. And it affected her speech."

"I can't imagine how he would feel." Trace's voice was thick was emotion. "If something like that happened to you."

Leah flinched. Her heart squeezed painfully hard in her chest.

"Her family is out there. He had such a hard time with the decision. Taking her from here, when we love her. But, in the end, he needed family. So she's in a nursing home. It's supposed to be a really good facility. And she does therapy. I don't know...physical therapy. Speech therapy." Leah shrugged impatiently. Trace nodded to encourage her to keep talking. "She said his name the other day."

"Wow." Trace rested his head on Leah's forehead. "That must have been incredible for him."

Leah breathed deeply as she smoothed her hand up over his back.

"Like a first kiss."

She waited for him to go on.

"Ya know? Something you need so badly. Something where you might die if you don't get it." He moved to his back, pulling her with him. Leah rested her head on his chest. "You need that first kiss when you're so in love with someone. Because…"

"Because what?" she whispered.

"Because you know you'll feel it. You'll taste it. If she loves you, too."

Leah closed her eyes and slipped her arm over his middle.

"I would think she needs to hear his voice right now, to keep her tied here, to help her fight for recovery. And he needed to hear her voice that same way. Hearing her love has to renew his energy."

"Jesus, Nashville." Her throat was tight with emotion. Lips pressed tightly together, she drew in a long, deep breath through her nose. He fought her when she moved, but finally, she wiggled away from him and climbed off the bed.

"What're you doing?"

She glanced at him as she ducked into the bathroom. Wrecked by the night with him, by the tenderness of his touch, and by his words just now, she lowered herself to sit on the side of the tub. She covered her face with her hands and let the tears come.

How in the hell was this going to work? She loved him so much the thought of him going back to Tennessee broke her heart.

"Leah? You okay?"

She cleared her throat and rubbed her eyes.

"Coming," she called. Love and fear and sorrow and the purest happiness she'd ever known at war inside her, she stood and moved to use the bathroom since she was there. Her legs were weak when she stood to wash her hands.

He sat on the side of the bed when she opened the door. She fought down a wave of panic when she saw that he had pulled his jeans on. But his briefs and socks were at the end of the bed. She saw the top of one boot on the other side of the bed.

"You okay?"

"Yeah." She nodded.

"No regrets?" He stood, but he stayed where he was, giving her plenty of space.

"Oh, I have one huge regret, Nashville," she admitted.

"Leah." Pain flashed over his face and ripped her heart out. She shook her head instantly and moved toward him.

"Not us. Just those four hundred miles." She shrugged. "I fell in love with you when you were four hundred miles away, and I can love you that way for the rest of my life."

He took her hands in his, rubbed his thumbs over the backs of her fingers.

"But?"

"I don't want to."

"What does that mean?"

"I want you to stay." She gulped the words out on a thick whisper. "I want you to stay, and I have no right to ask you for that."

"Darlin', you've got every right to ask anything of me," he reminded her. "Let's talk about this."

"When do you have to go back?"

"Whenever I decide to go back," he answered. He turned and looked at the bed long enough that Leah wondered if he was going to throw her down and take her again. "Here." He moved around the end of the bed and then leaned over to snag his t-shirt from the floor. She took it when he put it in her hands, but she only stared at him.

"Put it on." He lifted his hand to press his thumb over her cheek and the corner of her lips. "I'm fixing you breakfast."

She laughed softly.

"We're just getting started, Leah." He watched her pull his shirt over her head. Leah closed her eyes and reveled in the feel of the soft gray material over her bare skin, Trace's scent that now surrounded her.

"I don't know if I have that much food downstairs." She grinned and reached for her underwear when he handed them to her.

"Together." He stepped closer to her. "This life. I'm not talking about sex. I'm talking about forever."

She stepped into the underwear and met his eyes as she settled the lace over her hips.

"Although, I'm up for a post-breakfast treat."

"Me, too."

Leah followed him downstairs, still uncertain about the future, but relieved that he seemed committed to being with her. She laughed softly as they made their way out of the staircase and wound their way around the bed he had been sleeping in. They stepped over the sandals she'd kicked off at the foot of his bed, and Leah noticed her purse on the floor when they reached the kitchen.

She went straight to the pantry to get the coffee, and Trace moved directly to the refrigerator to gather omelet items.

"You look better in that shirt than I ever will," he decided as he set the carton of eggs on the counter.

"I don't know about that," she eyed him with a small smile. "You make a t-shirt look pretty sexy."

"So do you." He slipped behind her and cupped her breasts in his hands as if to show her what was sexy in the shirt.

"Are you a shirt and tie guy?" she asked. He took over scooping the coffee as she squatted down to get a skillet from the cabinet. His grunt caught her attention. She looked up at him and laughed.

"I own shirts and ties," he answered. "And I can and will wear them. If I have to."

She stood and set the skillet on the counter. "And I bet you look smokin' hot in a suit and tie." She grinned and nodded. "But, I like the relaxed look."

"Oh, I do, too." He eyed her from head to toe and nodded.

"Tell me about your mom."

He sighed and shifted back to the business of making omelets. Leah put the coffee filters and the canister away and then took plates from the cabinet and set them on the counter.

"Mama's great." He shrugged. "Except when she decides her baby can do no wrong."

Leah winced. "Did you love her, Trace?" When he slowed his hands and looked at her, she arched her eyebrows. "It's okay. I know I'm not your first woman. You don't have to lie if you were in love with someone else."

"I wasn't, though." He turned his attention to the bell pepper in his hands. She reached around him to grab a small cutting board for him. "I liked her. We'd gone out a few times. We were sleeping together, yes. And yes, there had already been girls who used me to get to Tanner. That was going on even when Tanner was in high school."

"I'm sorry." She leaned on the counter next to him and watched him slice the orange pepper. "Stevi and I have always been so close. I can't imagine what that would be like."

"Well, yeah, you'd think family would mean something there. But not to Tanner. He's fun. He's good-looking, I guess. But he's kind of a dick, too."

"Does he love her?"

"I think Tanner loves Tanner," Trace told her, eyes on the cutting board and the knife. "We were close when we were younger. Ya know? I did a lot for him. Taught him to turn on an inside pitch and take a ball down third baseline. Taught him to play 'Love Me Tender' on his guitar. I took lessons when I was a kid. He didn't. I showed him a few things, but he just took off one day. Guy plays a guitar like a woman's body. Makes love—"

"You play baseball?" she interrupted him. Because she didn't particularly care about Tanner. She'd meet him. She'd be nice to him. She'd accept him as someone in Nashville's life. But right now, she was greedy for details —big and small—about Trace Dixon. Not Tanner.

"When I was younger." He glanced at her. She wiggled her eyebrows. "You like baseball players?"

"I like baseball," she answered simply. "What else do you do, Nashville? You cook. You play a pretty mean guitar, and you played my body like no one else."

Trace slowed his hands again and set the knife down. Leah noticed a neat pile of diced peppers on the cutting board.

"Tell me no one will play you like that again. Just me."

"No one will ever touch me like that again, Nashville." Her voice was thick with need. "No one, but you."

"Promise me."

"I'll promise you that every day." She nodded.

Apparently satisfied, Trace turned his attention back to breakfast. Leah watched him dice two sausage links, whisk the eggs and milk in a bowl, and then pour the concoction into the skillet.

"Do you play other instruments?"

"Play the piano some. I can play a banjo, but not well."

"Wow." She folded her arms over her chest. "That's so cool. I can't play anything, and I have no rhythm."

He looked at her with smoldering eyes. "You have rhythm."

"You were telling me about your mom."

Trace nodded. "She's tough. She's smart. She took it hard when Daddy died, but she was strong for me and Tanner."

"Does she openly favor him?"

"She's very forgiving." Trace shrugged. "She gets upset with him. She worries about him. I know she loves us both, but I think she just knows...I'm not reckless. Tanner is."

"It must be hard for her with him on the road so much."

Trace considered her words as he tossed the peppers and sausage into the egg mixture.

"Do you want anything else in these? Tomatoes? Cheese?"

"Cheese." She tilted her head to study his face. "I wanna take my coffee and my omelet and sit down with you and learn everything there is to know about you."

He cringed. "Well, we don't need to learn everything."

"Oh, but we do," she said softly. "And if you don't wanna tell me funny, embarrassing things, I bet Pearl would."

"That's cruel." He pointed the spatula at her, but he laughed.

"Do you see her a lot?" Leah asked. She turned to grab mugs from the cabinet. "Your mom?"

"I do." He nodded. "I bought my grandparents' house when they decided to move to a smaller place. They're in a retirement village now. I'm about thirty minutes from Mama. But she's not...she's not a busy body. She's got friends. She's always doing something, so she doesn't stick her nose in my business a lot."

"Just sometimes." Leah looked at him from the corner of her eye as she poured the coffee.

"I think that's a mom thing."

"Amen." She nodded.

"Hey." The back door opened. Leah looked over her shoulder, heat rushing her neck and her cheeks to be caught in her underwear, obviously enjoying morning-after coffee with her lover. Stevi grinned at her. "Can I have a cup of that?"

Leah looked at Trace, but she only blushed again when he grinned and winked at her.

"Why?" Leah cleared her throat as she reached for another cup. "Why are you here?"

"I texted you." Stevi looked from Leah to Trace and back to Leah. "Seriously. I called twice. Texted when I got voicemail."

Leah avoided her sister's eyes as she crossed the room to take her coffee.

"What's going on?"

"You haven't taken time to check messages?" Stevi's eyes grew wide. "Oh God. I'm sorry. I just...I thought I'd slip in and out and..." She eyed Leah's bare legs and then let her gaze jump to Trace, who was now plating the omelets.

"Is everything okay?" Leah asked quietly.

"Yes. I just..." Stevi rubbed her face and laughed. "Damn. I'm sorry. I just wanted to grab some other clothes and stuff. I didn't mean—"

"You can sit down." Leah looked at Trace in askance. He shrugged and nodded, seemingly at ease with Stevi there.

"No, it's okay. I'll just grab—"

"Stevi, you live here," Leah reminded her. "It's fine."

"I can't just sit down here with you when you're in his shirt and your underwear, and your face is flaming red."

"You've seen me in my underwear a million times," Leah said as Trace carried the plates to the table.

"Yeah, but not like...after...not with a guy. Ever."

Leah noticed Trace's sharp look, but she refused to look at him. She sat down by him and looked up at Stevi.

"Joe called earlier," Stevi announced. Leah blinked and looked at the microwave, shocked to see that it was after nine. "Where's your phone?"

"No idea," Leah mumbled. "In my purse, maybe? On the floor over there."

"Damn." Stevi cut loose a dreamy sigh and sank down into a chair across the table. Leah watched in disbelief as she reached over the table to knuckle Trace. "This is awesome."

"Oh my God." Leah shook her head. "Stop it."

"Margo wanted to watch porn last night."

Leah snorted and covered her face with her hands.

"Leah's been on a long, dry stretch," Stevi told Trace. "This is something to celebrate."

"Oh my God." Leah groaned. "First? This is not your business. Second, how do you know?"

"Leah, if this guy didn't have the control he does, I think you'd have been banging him upstairs in the office at the Queen."

"That's more your style." Leah rubbed her eyes.

"It is," Stevi said with a chuckle. "You guys were burning the place down last night. That's all."

"We did kinda do that," Trace reminded Leah. She laughed again and dropped her hands to the table.

"Okay. Yes. Uncle. We did. Be glad you weren't here, Stevi."

"Just tell me it wasn't here on the table."

Leah snorted and covered her mouth when she barked a harsh laugh. Stevi picked up her mug and started to back away, but Leah shook her head. "No. We didn't. I promise."

"So. Joe called."

Leah took a drink of her coffee. "Did Margo watch porn?"

"I dunno. Duncan and I hung out at the Queen until almost four. She was sound asleep when I got in."

"What the heck were you and Duncan doing until four?"

"Playing cards," Stevi answered simply. "Joe called Margo's, so we were on speaker phone."

"Is he okay?"

"Yeah. Um." Stevi yawned and dragged her fingers back through her hair. Leah noticed the dark circles under her eyes. "He was with Kenzi."

Leah's eyes filled when Trace reached to cover her hand with his.

"She said hi." Stevi sniffled and ducked her head. She sat for a moment, and Leah knew she was trying to pull herself together. "I mean, I think that one word exhausted her. But she said hi to me and Margo. And Joe sounds… so…happy."

Leah glanced at Trace. The memory of his words earlier made her shiver and ache with love for him.

"Look, Joe asked where you were. He called, and you didn't answer."

Leah nodded. "So you told him."

"Well, I didn't tell him that you were busy setting the house on fire, but I told him you're in love with some guy from Nashville."

Leah laughed softly and met his eyes again.

"I told you they know me too well."

"He said he would call you later."

Leah nodded.

"And Duncan said..." Stevi stood up slowly. She pushed her chair in and looked at Trace uncertainly. "To call him before zero tonight. He was going to draw up some ideas."

Trace answered with an enthusiastic nod. Leah watched him closely, but he didn't look at her.

"Okay. I'm gonna grab a few other things, and I'll get out of here."

"Stevi—"

"Omelets, Leah," she said with a grin. "I get it."

CHAPTER 27

LEAH WAITED UNTIL SHE HEARD STEVI'S BEDROOM DOOR close before she turned to Trace.

"Sorry."

"For what?" He shrugged. "That she knows for sure we had sex? Or that she took some of that coffee we need?"

"I don't need the coffee when I have you." She wiggled her eyebrows. "And no, I'm not sorry she knows, but, if that was a little weird for you—"

"It wasn't." The corner of his lips turned up in a smile. "I hope this is a regular thing, Leah."

"Breakfast in our underwear with my sister?"

"I'm dressed," he reminded her. "And you having breakfast dressed just like that for the rest of my life is perfect. And yeah, hanging out with your sister. Your family."

"I feel kind of bad that she's basically moved out," Leah whispered. "But I love having the house to ourselves."

"Your bedroom is upstairs. Did we make that much noise?" When he finished his omelet, Leah stared at his clean plate in disbelief. He shrugged and winked at her. "Fuel."

"Why does Duncan want you to call him?"

"You've never done this before?" Trace reached for her mug to see if she needed a refill. When he saw that she didn't, he stood and carried his own mug to the counter.

"Done what...before?" Leah asked with a frown. Her stomach growled, and she decided she needed fuel whether they made it back upstairs for another round or just to shower and get dressed. She picked up her fork and dug into the omelet.

"Had male guests for breakfast?"

"Very few who stayed the night. And never breakfast with...Stevi...around..."

"Why?" He scratched his belly and then rubbed his chest as he returned to the table to sit by her.

"I'm not sure what you're getting at," she said as she put her fork down in exchange for her mug. "But I promise you, I wasn't a virgin last night, and there've been guys who stayed overnight. But none that wanted to stick around, and none that I wanted to stick around for a big family breakfast."

"Except me."

"Except you." She watched him over the rim of her mug. "I loved a guy when I was in high school. First love. Gave him everything. We dated for a long time—"

"How long?"

"Couple of years," she said quietly. "We went to football games together. Prom. He was my first. We broke up when he went to college."

"Anyone else?"

Leah took a deep breath.

"It's okay," he reminded her. "I know I'm not the first guy you've been with."

She laughed softly when he fed her words back to her.

"No. Not really. Yes, I was involved with a few guys." She shrugged. "But nothing that ever amounted to anything."

"What about Stevi?"

Leah stared at him silently.

"Leah, darlin'." He reached for her hand. "I'm just getting the lay of the land. I like your family. I want to be a part of it."

"You don't need to know the lay of Stevi's land, do you?"

"You said Margo was involved with someone and had his baby. What about Stevi and Duncan?"

"Stevi and Duncan." Leah frowned. "What?"

Trace leaned over the table and kissed the corner of her mouth.

"Either of them have a significant other?"

"No." She brushed her fingers over his eyebrow. "They don't. Actually, they both date a lot. I don't think Stevi cares to find more. And Duncan can't find enough."

Leah pushed her plate away. She'd done some damage to the omelet, though she hadn't been able to finish it.

"Why does Duncan want you to call him?"

Trace pursed his lips. Leah watched him look over his shoulder and then turn back to her with a mischievous grin on his face.

"How long do you think she's going to be here?"

Leah laughed softly as she leaned into him to kiss him.

"As long as she's here, tell me what Duncan wants."

"He mentioned wanting to build a stage."

"Really?" She tipped her head to study him when he sat back in his chair. He drank from his mug and then looked at her with his slow, sexy smile.

"Really."

"Hmm." She ducked her chin to her chest and rubbed her forehead with her fingertips.

"You don't think you should?"

"No, it's a good idea." She looked up and shrugged. "We talked about it before. But we haven't ever had consistent..."

Trace raised his eyebrows when she let her words trail off.

"You can't do that, Nashville." She shook her head.

"Why can't I?"

Leah licked her lips and tried to swallow. "Because you have a life in Nashville. Because you're *someone* there. You can't give that up for us." She pushed her chair back to stand up, but when Trace shook his head, she stayed in her seat.

"I'm a songwriter, Leah," he reminded her. "I can write music anywhere."

"But." She held her hand up to stop him. "You have a…a thing. You work with Pearl and Sampson. People love you there—"

"And someone I love is here."

"Trace," she whispered. "God, yes, I want you here. I want you here every day. But. I can't ask you to walk away from the music—"

"I would only be walking away from Tennessee. I still have music." He reached for her hand and when she placed her fingers over his palm, he pulled her gently from her chair to sit in his lap. "I still have my guitars. And I have you."

On her knees, straddling his lap, Leah leaned forward to rest her forehead on his shoulder.

"What about recording studios? I mean, I know the writing is more important—"

"Let me figure that part out." He closed his hands around

her back. "Okay? We could just try it this way for a while and see what happens."

The fear that she'd battled down earlier came back now, but Trace simply held her and she breathed in the comfort he gave her.

"So, what you're saying is when I wasn't looking, you went and got yourself tied in tight with my family?" She turned her face toward him and kissed his neck.

"That okay?" His lips in her hair, his voice was a low rumble in her ear. She shivered and lifted her head to give him the eye.

"I saw you in cahoots with Duncan last night." She framed his face in her hands to study him. His emerald eyes were dark and sincere, but his face was relaxed as if he didn't have a care in the world.

"In cahoots?" he repeated. Leah raised her eyebrows when he grinned.

"And there it is."

"What?" he asked innocently.

"That smile." She rubbed her fingertips over his lips. "I love your smile."

"You said *cahoots*, city girl." He nipped at her fingers. "I'm rubbing off on you."

"I'm okay with that," she decided. "I think I might be okay with just about anything you do, Nashville."

"Duncan mentioned that your act for the weekend cancelled." He shrugged. "And I offered to step in and help out. From there, the conversation snowballed to talk about building a small stage. Duncan was adamant about it being small. He said you guys had all talked about it, and you had agreed it needed to be small but on par with the bar itself."

Leah considered it, the fact that Duncan had discussed Queen business with Trace Dixon. She didn't mind; no doubt if she had known that the music act had cancelled on them and she and Trace had ended up in a conversation about it, she might have mentioned that they'd talked about building a stage, too. They had weighed the cost of building a stage—minimal, if Duncan did it—against the benefits of having something a bit more permanent, a bit fancier for the musicians. Perhaps something less makeshift would be more appealing to the musicians and end up pulling in more acts.

The fact that Duncan felt comfortable having the discussion with Trace spoke volumes, though. He wasn't an equal partner in the business, though she, Stevi, and Margo considered him as such, and he had mentioned buying in. The four of them had a strong relationship, business and personal, and they debated and flat out argued things often. But none of them were ever eager to discuss bar business with outsiders. In fact, they didn't, other than occasional talks with their parents.

But Duncan had apparently been open about their current discussions, and he had included Trace. Which meant that Duncan liked him. Not that Leah had expected anything less, and not that Leah needed anyone's approval to fall in love. Hell, her heart hadn't listened to her head, so she knew it wasn't going to listen to anyone else.

That Duncan felt comfortable talking business with Trace warmed her heart. It made her happy. It made things feel right, even though she worried that Trace might decide he wasn't happy here in Illinois.

"Leah?"

"Hmm?"

"Are you okay with this?"

"The stage?" she whispered.

"With us. With me being around for a while?"

"Yes."

She wondered what would happen when he got bored here. What would happen if Pearl and Sampson needed him. Or if Tanner demanded Trace join him on tour. Did she love him enough to let him go? And if she did, and he took her heart with him—because there was no question that he would—how would she go on without him?

"Leah, have you seen my—oh for Pete's sake," Stevi groaned. Leah looked up as her sister strode back into the kitchen, a navy blouse in her hands. Trace—back to Stevi —lifted his hands in the air as if to prove his innocence, as Leah climbed off his lap. "Do I need to look for a new place?"

"No!" Leah shook her head. "God, no. We were just talking."

"I'm teasing." Stevi rolled her eyes. "Sort of. I just don't wanna get an eyeful."

"It's all good," Trace promised her as he stood. Leah noticed that he took a moment before he turned half way to look at her then. She lifted her eyes to his, and they shared a smile.

"Have you seen my white shorts?"

"Did you look in the laundry room?"

"Yep."

Leah shrugged. She leaned over the table to grab her plate and stacked it on top of his.

"Did you leave them somewhere?"

"Not funny!" Stevi laughed, but she was embarrassed by Leah's teasing.

"I haven't seen them. Maybe they're at Margo's house."

Stevi stared at the blouse in her hands as if it might lead her to the shorts.

"Did Duncan tell you he talked to Trace about building the stage?"

"Yeah." A sharp frown creased her brow when she looked up at Leah. "Why? You didn't know?"

Leah rinsed the plates and reached without looking to open the dishwasher door.

"Um, we were a little distracted last night," she cleared her throat, "didn't do much talking."

When Stevi didn't say anything, Leah shot her a quick glance and noticed the sparkle in her eyes.

"I think I like you, Mr. Dixon." Stevi nodded.

Leah snorted and then dropped her head back and laughed out loud.

"Feeling's mutual," Trace told her as he stepped up behind Leah.

"So does this mean you didn't know Trace is bringing Nashville to the Queen?"

Leah tamped down a little flare of temper and shrugged her eyebrows at Stevi.

"Right." Stevi nodded. "Okay. I'm outta here. See you guys later."

Leah watched her cross the kitchen and disappear through the back door without another word. When she was gone, she turned to Trace and folded her arms over her chest.

"Did you discuss this with all of them first?"

"No. Just Duncan. He must have told Stevi."

She tipped her head and narrowed her eyes at him. "Funny. Duncan told Stevi, but you didn't tell me."

Trace stepped closer and pinned her between his body and the cabinets at her back. She let her eyes slide closed when he rested his hands on her shoulders and dug his fingers into her muscles.

"Darlin', we didn't do much talkin'. Remember?"

She fought but lost the battle with the grin.

"Dammit, Nashville," she said with a laugh. She opened her eyes and lifted her hands to rest on his chest. "What am I gonna do with you?"

Trace moved one hand behind her neck, and Leah moaned appreciatively when his fingers started working on the muscles there. He lifted his other hand to play with her hair.

"Funny you should ask." His eyes were hot above his hundred-watt smile.

CHAPTER 28

TRACE WAS EXCITED ABOUT BUILDING A STAGE FOR THE Queen, happy to work with Duncan on the ideas he'd drawn up. He didn't need a stage to play, but he had to agree with Duncan and the girls. They had room for something small, and if it was as visually appealing as the rest of the Queen was, it would add to the ambiance. Might draw in more musicians, though Trace knew plenty who could and would pick up a guitar in a crowded corner booth in a diner and sing their hearts out.

He was ready to get back to the music, though he wouldn't miss Nashville. For one thing, it was an easy drive, and one he could foresee doing whenever he might need anything for business or if he wanted to visit family and friends. He had told Leah the truth; he considered himself more of a songwriter than a performer, always had. The CDs he released weren't an embarrassment, but they hadn't hit the Top 25 on any chart. Except maybe

Leah's, and hers was the only opinion that mattered to him these days.

She didn't argue with him over his decision to stay. In fact, she had asked him if he planned to stay with her at the house, and when he'd teased her and acted as if he was considering anything other than staying there, she'd launched herself at him and tried to hold him down to tickle him. She'd crowed the other day when she had figured out he was ticklish, especially in the ribs. But she wasn't strong enough to hold him down long. Didn't bother him at all, and she didn't seem to mind when the tickling and rough-housing turned to messing around and making love.

Still, there had been a few times when he'd caught her staring at him anxiously, her teeth nibbling on her lip or her brows drawn down and a deep groove in her forehead. They talked about logistics, and he thought she was okay with the plans. He would play here at the Queen for the weekend before he left, though there would be no big advertising push. Trace didn't believe his face or his guitar or his ass—as Margo had suggested—would bring in any extra business, but he also understood that the Queen pushed any live music night, so of course, they would want to do *something* to let the district, the public, know he was there. He didn't want them to go to any extra expense, though, to hit the marketing hard, since their original act had cancelled. They'd agreed on a poster with his picture in the front window for this time and to revisit the subject the next time he was needed in a pinch.

He admitted to Leah that he wanted to be needed. In a pinch. Or just whenever. He wanted to play; he missed his guitar time. And he wanted to do anything he could to be part of the Queen and the family.

After this weekend, he would head back to Nashville and start the process of moving here. Except Leah had pointed out that he didn't need to move furniture or any big items. Just instruments he wanted handy. Any other sort of equipment—she'd waved her hands here, as if grasping for words or the equipment itself—like amps. Clothes. Cowboy hats. He reminded her then that he wasn't a cowboy and didn't do hats, and she reminded him that he wore boots. His response had been to throw her on her bed and undress her, shove his jeans down over his hips, and make love to her with the boots on.

After, Leah wondered if it was better with his boots on because they gave him more traction or better with nothing on, because she still had that thing with his bare toes on her feet and her ankles. Trace simply offered that it was something they should research further.

He hated the thought of leaving, even for the sole purpose of going back to pack up and move to be with Leah every day. The fact that she hated his leaving as much as he did made him feel a little better, but he was anxious to get everything taken care of and to be back with her. He'd known when he started performing at Left Fork—and he'd eased into that more for comfort, to feed his need to play rather than perform—that it wasn't his life's work. Pearl and Sampson knew that, too. Neither of them wanted to kick him out and send him packing after Tanner the way his mama did, but they had always known he would eventually move on.

He told Leah that, too.

She asked about what his mother would say. As much as Trace loved his mother, he didn't need her permission to move north, to fall in love, to live with the woman he loved. Leah laughed at his reaction and said she didn't think that. But what would his mother think about him being so far away? Wouldn't she miss him?

Trace worried about her, sure. But her battle with breast cancer had been victorious so far. And he reminded Leah again that Nashville wasn't that far away; it was certainly drivable and besides why was it okay for Tanner to be living his dream all over the country and not okay for Trace to live his dream with the woman he loved eight hours away via Routes I-24 and I-64?

He asked Leah if she wanted to go with him, and she did, but he noticed her hesitation. She still felt guilty for leaving the Queen when she took off and headed to Destin for a quick vacation. And with the 4th of July coming up, Leah wanted to be at the Queen. All of them had been talking excitedly about the holiday celebration in Adam's Bay, a lot of which would happen in Douglas Park, a beautiful square block just out the front door and across the street from the Queen. Business, Trace figured, would be booming, and they would need Leah there to help.

Trace strummed Loretta now, half his mind on Leah and strumming her body just so, the touch he'd learned would make her sing damned near every time. If she hadn't enjoyed the full payoff from sex every time, Trace had to assume she had been with some selfish or lazy lovers. Either that or her body simply responded to his on every level. Come to think of it, that was probably it. No woman had ever done to his body, his heart, the things Leah Hague could do with one look.

Crashed on the couch, she lifted her arm above her head and let her other hand rest on her stomach, her finger marking her place in the book she was reading. She stretched now, and Trace's eyes were drawn to her long, lithe legs. She turned her face toward him to watch him, the hint of a smile on her lips.

He felt a rush of love so full, so overwhelming, it hurt his chest to breathe. Though they had agreed on him moving here and hanging out for a while, they hadn't planned too far ahead in the future. He wouldn't rush her; hell, he would be happy with the status quo if this was as far as things progressed. Spending the rest of his life with Leah was his only plan. He believed in the forever kind of love in songs and in the movies, and he believed in marriage, because he'd seen some damned strong couples in his life. But if Leah didn't want to be married, he would let it ride.

She hadn't said a lot about her bargain with God. Trace knew she still thought about it and that now and then the pinched expression on her face had to do with the guilt she felt. But she also promised him, when he asked, that she had no regrets about being with him. The more Trace was around her family, the more times he heard the names Kenzi and Joe, and the more he wished he could meet the people—the woman—who had such a hold on Leah's heart. She had talked to Joe the other day. Trace had picked up his coffee to leave the room and give her some privacy, but she had touched his hand and when he looked at her, she shook her head and raised her eyebrows.

So he stayed. She didn't put the call on speakerphone; she wasn't ready for that yet. But she talked freely to Joe while Trace sat with her in the kitchen, her feet propped in his lap. She talked to both of the older kids, and Trace's heart melted at the way her voice went a bit soft and sweet with love for them. She had told him she didn't want children, but he believed her words were driven by fear. Trace was as crazy about Berkley as the rest of them were—who could resist the sweet little imp with the chubby cheeks and coal black hair? But if Leah didn't want children, he would agree to that, too.

He was in love with her, and the rest of his life stretched out in front of him with Leah at his side was the most incredible vision he'd ever had.

"Nashville."

He lifted his chin again—he'd turned his attention back to Loretta, the notes of something new in his head as he picked at the strings—and watched Leah turn to lie on her side. She looked drowsy and sexy, and knowing that her soft skin would be warm right now made his groin tighten.

"Hmm?"

He considered putting Loretta down and going to her. Kneeling on the floor beside the couch to talk to Leah. But talking to her would lead to kissing her and touching her. The other night they got carried away on the couch, and Stevi and Margo had come crashing into the kitchen all giggles and loud whispers. Thankfully, things had not progressed too far, and Leah was able to scramble off his lap and situate her clothing. Maybe they had managed to look more like guilty teenagers caught in the act, rather than being two nude adults so drunk on each other they didn't realize they were being watched.

Leah wanted Stevi to move back in, and Trace agreed that they couldn't expect her to just stay with Margo indefinitely. Stevi continued to put them off. She would agree to it, say yes, of course she was coming back, but she hadn't gotten around to it yet. He had overheard them—Leah and Stevi—loudly whisper-arguing about it yesterday morning in the kitchen. Stevi insisted that she didn't want to be a third wheel, and Leah had been adamant that she and Trace were completely capable of controlling themselves and keeping their private life private. When Stevi continued to argue, to tell Leah that she was so happy for her that she didn't mind making herself scarce for a while, Leah had snapped back that Stevi made her sound like there was something wrong with her, as if she had never been with a man before.

Trace had stood just out of sight in the living room wondering if he should just walk in and interrupt the argument or if he should clear his throat and give them some warning that he was coming, that he could hear their discussion.

And then Stevi had said of course it wasn't that Leah had never been with a man before, hadn't she walked in on Leah with Evan Wieman that one time? Trace had felt vicious stabs of jealousy from head to toe when he heard Leah laugh. Not particularly a visual he wanted. But then Leah had mumbled something about this being different, that Trace was different, and Stevi had simply said, "bingo."

He almost busted into the kitchen then, because he had a ridiculous notion that there was a guy named Evan Wieman in the room with them, and he needed to put his arm around Leah and claim her as his—stupid, yes, but he had learned jealousy does that to a man in love. Plus, he kind of needed to see their faces, and he wanted to know what *bingo* meant in this instance.

But before he could move, he heard Stevi's voice again.

"You think we don't all see how different he is? I've never seen you in love, Leah. You're glowing so bright, I gotta stay at a distance to look at you guys right now."

He'd blown out a deep breath he hadn't realized he was holding, and then, because his body hummed with adrenaline and happiness, he had backtracked through the living room to the bathroom and slipped inside and closed the door. He didn't need to use the john; he just needed a minute to breathe and get his rapidly beating heart under control. He had taken a peek in the mirror, too, just to see what a man in love looked like. To see what *he* looked like in love. Turned out, he looked pretty normal. Well, normal with a goofy, lopsided grin. He could deal with that.

"Promise me something?" Leah's soft voice drifted to him from across the room.

"I've promised you everything, darlin', remember?" He tapped Loretta's well-oiled curvy body and tipped his head to Leah. "You ask, and it's yours."

"Yeah, about that." She wiggled an eyebrow at him. The suggestive grin on her face sent a thrum of excitement through his veins.

"My answer's yes," he said with a grin. Leah's delicious laugh rolled over him. His stomach did a little flip-flop—he would lose his man card if anyone knew Leah had that power over him, but he didn't care—when she rubbed her hand over her eyes. The book she was reading fell to the floor, and she lost her place, but she didn't seem to care.

"Nashville." She tried to sound serious, but he could still hear the laughter in her voice.

"What?"

"When you go home?" She took a deep breath and propped herself up on her elbow to look at him.

"I'm coming home," he said quietly. "As long as you'll have me, Leah, I want this to be home."

She stared at him for a moment, a sweet smile on her face. "When you go to Nashville…no…Just…whenever…"

"Whenever what?"

"If he calls you, I want you to work things out with him."

She was talking about Tanner. Stomach a little soured now with the mention of his brother, Trace put the guitar down. Tanner had called the day before yesterday, and Trace had talked to him. There hadn't been any working anything out; like usual, Tanner demanded Trace drop everything and hit the road to lend a hand. Trace hadn't even mentioned Leah; Tanner had made light of any responsibilities Trace had at Left Fork and foisted all of their mother's pleas on him. They sounded a lot more doable in Mama's voice, though, and when she asked Trace to help Tanner out, he could almost envision himself saying yes. As it was, he had told Tanner no, he was too busy. And he had suggested that Tanner hire a new lead guitarist.

"Why?"

He wasn't suspicious. Or jealous. Leah loved him; she wasn't a wannabe star using him to get on stage, and she wasn't a groupie. She had never heard of him or his brother before she walked into Left Fork that night.

"Because he's your family," she answered simply. Her answer surprised him. He had expected that Leah worried about his mother. That she would join forces with her to put the brothers back together for the family, for Mama's sake. She had yet to meet his mother, but he knew they would get along just fine. Mama would love Leah, no question, and Leah already seemed to have utter respect for his mother.

"Leah."

She grimaced and shook her head.

"What?"

"You're annoyed with me," she answered, and before he could deny it, she continued, "you only call me by my name when you're annoyed."

"That's not true."

"I'm not asking you to leave me and tour the country with him. I'm not asking you to fix it all for your mama."

"Then what?" He gave her a pointed look. Okay, maybe he was a bit annoyed with her.

"When you told me that day about how you taught Tanner to turn on an inside pitch and go down third baseline?"

"What about it?" he hedged, unwilling to bend at all as far as Tanner was concerned.

"You were all puffed up with…pride…" She scooched around to sit up on the couch. Her hair tumbled around her shoulders. Made him want to scoop her up and drop a hundred kisses on her face. "And love. And I hate to see you—"

"I told you I wasn't in love with Shelly—"

"I'm not talking about her," Leah argued. "I get it. You didn't love her, but still. He's your brother, and what he did hurt you. It still hurts you, Nashville, or you wouldn't avoid him like you do."

"So because I would rather be here with you and your family means I'm avoiding—"

"I'm not the enemy," she interrupted him. "I'm not asking you to do anything but talk to him."

CHAPTER 29

Leah swept the room with her gaze and noticed most of the women in the Queen were watching Trace. There was no stage yet, though Trace and Duncan had been working on the design. While they were all excited by the idea now that Duncan had asked for Trace's opinion, none of them wanted to hurry the process. They had been excited like little kids opening presents before they opened The Mississippi Queen, but they hadn't allowed that excitement to rush them then, either. For now, their musicians—currently Trace Dixon—had a small area up front near the plate glass window, with atmospheric—though still inadequate—lighting, and the option to sit on a barstool. According to Trace, it was more than enough, and after seeing him at Left Fork, Leah believed him.

Still, it had been a while since she had seen him play like this. He claimed he wasn't a performer, but there was something in the way he moved, the way his voice throbbed with gritty emotion—need and love and sometimes pain—the way he played Loretta, that made women want him and men enjoy his music. Leah wasn't necessarily jealous as she watched the room full of women want him—at least just for the night. In fact, she understood. She found herself almost leaning toward the front of the bar to be nearer to his voice, the way a smaller tree might lean around a bigger tree to find sunlight for nourishment. His upbeat songs filled her with joy, but the love songs—about good love and love gone wrong—made her yearn for his touch.

Over and over throughout the night, people stopped her to ask how in the world they had landed Trace Dixon for the Queen. Once, someone called him Tanner, and Leah snapped her pencil in her hand. She laughed it off, and then simply explained that she and Trace were together. She didn't say he was her boyfriend, because that felt too high school. And she didn't say they were lovers, because that was no one's business. For her, the word *together* said it all, and judging from the looks most of the women gave her when she answered them, it was all she needed to say.

He sang her favorites. He talked to the crowd, and there was a crowd tonight. Margo had elbowed Trace earlier, between sets, and said she told him so about his ass drawing a crowd. Cheeks red with a sweet blush, Trace had reminded Margo that it was a beautiful summer weekend and that might have something do with the crowd. Margo had given him a slow, patient nod, and then she'd eyed Stevi and Leah as if to say *whatever*.

He played songs she'd never heard and songs she suspected she wouldn't love if anyone else sang them. He talked to Leah, too, and about Leah, and she blushed wildly a few times, although he never said anything inappropriate. Stevi slumped over the west end of the bar late in the evening and watched him and listened.

"Does he have any other brothers?" Her sigh was wistful, and she looked as love struck as the rest of the women here when she turned her big eyes to Leah. Trace had shared some stories about Tanner and the band. Some of them were fun, things that made them all laugh. Some painted Tanner truthfully, as a fame jockey more interested in a show than being a true musician. Trace didn't tell any of them about his ex and how she was now Tanner's girlfriend. Leah kept her mouth shut about him, because she didn't know him, and because he was Trace's brother. No matter what had happened, they were brothers, and she hoped that one day they would be friends again.

Still, no matter what had been said and what Trace and Leah had kept to themselves, Leah's family seemed to know instinctively that Trace was genuine and maybe Tanner wasn't.

Leah grinned at Stevi and rolled her eyes.

"Or maybe a cousin?" Margo joined them at the bar. "He's dreamy, Leah. I'm in love."

"You can't be in love with him," Leah argued. "He's mine."

"Did you feed him a love potion?" Stevi pushed her hair back from her face and sighed again.

"Stop it." Leah laughed. She slipped her arm around Stevi's shoulders and gave her a squeeze. "And no. It just happened."

"That's the best kind," Stevi whispered.

"Best kind of love," Margo agreed.

Leah leaned around Stevi to narrow her eyes at Margo.

"You don't even like men."

Margo snorted. "Don't say that so loud."

"She'll have women hitting on her," Duncan agreed as he slid onto the stool beside Margo.

"Oh no, not tonight." Stevi shook her head. "Every woman in this place is drooling over that delicious hunk of man with the guitar. God, just look at him."

"Stevi Hague!" Leah squeezed her sister again.

"You sleep with him every night." Stevi rolled her eyes. "At least let the rest of us just look."

"He's a nice guy." Head turned toward the front of the bar, Duncan shrugged. "Nice-looking, sure. But there are other men around, Stevi Hague."

"Really?" Stevi made a show of looking around the room. "None that catch my eye, Duncan."

"Ouch!" He laughed and clutched at his heart. Stevi shook her head and rolled her eyes again. "You've worked side by side with me how long? Hello?"

She chuckled and held her hand up to her eyes as if to block a light.

"Oh, there you are. The lights are shining on your head." She reached over the corner of the bar and grabbed his hand. Leah watched her give him a gentle shake, as if to say she was just messing with him. "You're not bad, Duncan." She winked at him.

Duncan ran his free hand over his head and then arched his eyebrows suggestively.

"The ladies like to touch my—"

"Nope." Stevi shook her head as she ducked away from Leah. "Not going there. Table four needs refills, and it looks like seven is looking for a check."

"Overkill, much?" Margo glanced at Duncan. Leah stared at them with a frown, but when she heard Trace say her name, she snapped out of her thoughts and moseyed down the length of the bar.

"Leah, this couple over here would like to know how we met." His voice was deep, and it carried through the room. Leah felt it rumble inside her, felt her heartbeat pick up in response.

"We met in Tennessee," she said simply as she turned to the older couple that Trace had gestured to. "At a place called Left Fork. Nashville hit on me at the bar."

He chuckled and took a drink of his water. "I didn't hit on her. I approached her and said hey."

Leah grinned when he met her eyes.

"I was in love. One look," he continued with a deep shrug. To Leah's embarrassment, a few of the guys in the Queen hooted and hollered as if to agree with him. "She told me to drop dead."

Leah threw her head back and laughed loud and hard.

"And so, when she left and I thought I would never see her again, I wrote this song for her."

Her heart pounded in her throat and her ears now, as Trace picked the guitar strings slowly. He leaned close to the mic, and his deep, southern drawl filled the room. He sang about being crazy, about watching her walk out the door, and how he loved her then and loved her now, even more. She hadn't heard the song before, and while at first she was embarrassed to be called out in front of her crowd, she was enthralled by the end of the first verse.

Hot, sticky tears tracked her face, and then someone was behind her, and because her knees were weak, she leaned. Stevi was shorter, but strong, and she held Leah up as Trace sang. He closed his eyes once or twice during the song, but mostly he held her gaze, and goosebumps broke out on her skin.

She loved the Queen, but if he asked her to, she would pack her life up and stick it in a U-Haul truck and move to Nashville just to be with him. She would marry him in a heartbeat, if he asked her to.

When he finished the song, the crowd erupted in applause and whistles, and Stevi gave her a gentle shove to propel her across the floor to Trace's open arms. She wouldn't ask him again if he was sure about moving, about leaving Tennessee. There was no doubt he was meant for her, and within a week, they would start their lives together.

CHAPTER 30

HE SPENT MONDAY DRIVING, THOUGH THE ORIGINAL PLAN had been for him to leave Sunday. Leah had stretched against him Sunday morning in bed, dragged her toes up the inside of his calf and found him ready and willing with her warm, soft hand, and slid over to straddle him. Who the hell could leave that kind of loving, even if it was necessary to get on with the rest of their lives? He finally understood it, too—her fixation with his bare toes on her skin, because she had lit him on fire with that slow drag of her skin over his. They spent the better part of Sunday in her bed, only venturing out for French toast early in the day and a long walk later in the afternoon, and when she tried the same move on him again Monday morning, he only kissed her and promised her he would be back as soon as he could get away.

He crossed the Tennessee state line around seven, on into Nashville, and drove on to his house first. As much as he loved the place, and as much as he thought Leah might like the house, it felt empty to him now. He took his bags inside, but when walking through the house didn't settle the restlessness inside him, he went on to Left Fork for a beer. He needed to catch up with everyone, and he thought it might be a good test for him. Why not pass an hour or two in the place that had given him more comfort even than his home and see if the thought of leaving there, leaving his friends, for Leah would bother him?

Kadie was on when he walked in, and he thought she sounded pretty damned good. Pearl apparently did, too, because Angie said Kadie had earned a weekly spot since he had been gone. So, it was only two weeks. That was a big deal in Pearl Allen's world.

He wanted to talk to Pearl and Sampson, but the Fork was pretty busy with summer tourists, so conversation was light. That was okay, too. Trace was happy to sit at the bar and soak up the atmosphere. The music was good, though if he was pressed, he would admit that he had enjoyed a bit of variety at the Queen. That variety in styles would be even better at the Queen once they were able to draw performers in for live music consistently. When Pearl ended up a bit swamped at the bar—Trace noticed, because she would certainly never ask for help—he drained his second beer and joined her. He didn't want another, anyway, and he'd spent enough time behind the bar at the Queen to enjoy himself. Tonight was no different. He had fun pulling beers and mixing drinks. Maybe he didn't have the flare for it that Duncan did, but he was sure capable of serving alcohol. He enjoyed talking to the patrons at the Fork, always had; but, being behind the bar instead of on the stage gave him more opportunity to do that. He thought Pearl enjoyed it, too, but getting her to admit that would be more work than scrubbing the floor with a toothbrush.

He missed Leah, though. Okay, he missed all of them. Even Duncan. The guy was okay. After meeting him face to face, it was obvious to Trace that there was nothing between Duncan and Leah. Not even in Duncan's head. He missed Stevi's carefree laughter, the way she teased Leah. He missed Margo, too, though she still wasn't as openly affectionate with him as Stevi was. And Berkley. How could he help falling in love with her? Those big blue eyes and the black ringlet curls had captured his heart in about 0.3 seconds. She'd puckered up and given him a sweet, soft kiss when he dropped in at the Queen earlier to say goodbye. A little bit slobbery, but Trace had melted when she'd wrapped her little arms around his neck and said goodbye. Or something that sort of resembled goodbye.

Of course, Berkley made him want for things Leah said she didn't want. Of course, he wanted a baby with Leah Hague. What a beautiful baby they would make. What a beautiful mother Leah would be. But he wouldn't push it. Maybe once he had moved up there and things were settled, they could talk about it. Until then, Trace would be more than happy to be an honorary uncle to Berkley.

As long as he had Leah. Nothing mattered if he had Leah in his life.

After closing, he watched Gunnar Flynn pack his guitar up and head out. Kadie had finished strong with one of Trace's songs earlier. Sampson was long gone, Chino didn't care one way or another what Trace did with his life, and Pearl was tired. When he started to tell her that he was moving, that he was giving them notice, she had simply waved his words away and gone about the business of closing down. She was right. They could talk in the morning.

Trace slept a solid eight hours, called Leah when he awoke, and spent a good twenty minutes just talking to her and another ten having phone sex with her. Leah purring over the phone as she touched herself drove him wild, and he wasn't sure he would last two days here, let alone the week or two it might take to get things ready to leave again.

Restless after talking to her, after hearing those throaty moans and his name on a heated whisper from miles away, he went for a long run and then hit the shower. While both worked for killing the hard-on for Leah, neither soothed the way he missed her. In just two weeks, he had grown so used to spending his days with her—whether he was downstairs behind the bar bullshitting with Duncan or playing around on Loretta in the office while Leah did the books—he felt like he had left half of himself there at the Queen. Leah's house. Wherever she was, Leah carried his heart with her.

Showered and dressed for physical work—Sampson had started the patio project, and by all reports from Pearl and Chino and the girls, it was going well—Trace headed to the Fork to see what he could do to help. According to Pearl, Sampson had been putting in early morning hours out back, trying to beat the heat. Wouldn't matter if he beat Sampson or everyone to the Fork, because he still had a key. In fact, the thought of handing that key back to either of the Allens gave him a little bit of indigestion.

He parked behind the old tavern and saw Sampson's truck in the first spot behind the building. He need not have worried, he realized, after a glance at his phone. It wasn't that early anyway.

"Finally dragged your sorry self out of bed, Trace Dixon?"

Trace turned his head when he heard Pearl. Found her squatting in the corner of the patio, eyeballing a few pieces of lumber. Sampson worked on a ladder across the patio. Trace glanced at him and decided his first move would be to get the old man off the ladder. His tan forearms were above his head, the ropy muscles in his arms taut as he drilled through a 1"x6" piece of lumber to connect it to a truss for the roof of the patio.

Before he could move, though, he heard a distinct harrumph from the corner, and he turned to see Pearl stand slowly, a wooden beam in her hands.

"What are you doing?" Trace moved to her side quickly and reached for the beam. True, the stout woman might make two or three of him, and Trace would grudgingly admit that she could possibly bench press him. That didn't mean he was going to stand there and watch her haul heavy, awkward woodwork around.

"Been working like this more years than you've been around, Trace Dixon." She challenged him with a direct stare.

"Well, I'm around now, so you don't need to do that. Sit down."

Pearl arched an eyebrow at him, but Trace wasn't sure if she took issue with him ordering her around or if she was mocking his declaration because he'd started to tell her last night that he was leaving Left Fork for good.

"I'm not gonna sit down or that fool man'll work himself to death."

Sampson tutted at her, but it was lost in the noise of the drill. Trace glanced back at him as he leaned forward, further off the ladder, to secure another section of the beam and the truss.

"Sampson—" Trace shuffled half a step that way, but he swung his gaze back to Pearl when he felt the lumber in his hand. Pearl pushed it at him somewhat gently and then dropped her hands to her sides. He wondered if Leah and the girls had been involved with building the bar at the Queen. If they would want to be involved with the stage he and Duncan were going to build, or if Duncan would simply move forward on his own, while Trace was here.

He assumed Leah, Stevi, and Margo were very hands on, and that they would want to be part of the stage-building process. He hated the thought of Leah's soft hands on power tools and raw lumber. He didn't particularly want to see Pearl Allen handling either, but on the other hand, there wasn't a damned thing about the woman he could describe as delicate. Nothing other than her age, maybe. Leah appeared delicate, right down to her dewy skin and her pretty, well-manicured nails. But he had seen her unload freight and carry cases of wine down to the wine cellar. He had seen her drag heavy bar tables around either to resituate them or just to polish the floors beneath them. He also knew her well enough to know that she wouldn't appreciate him thinking of her as delicate.

"I suppose you want coffee." Pearl propped her fists on her thick hips. He didn't, really. He'd brewed a few cups at home before coming here, but if it gave Pearl something else to do, he wouldn't say no.

"That would be great, Pearl." He flashed her a grin, and though she was old enough to be his grandmother, he saw the pink in her cheeks. Amused by her response—as always—he watched her steamroll her way back through the kitchen to fetch him a cup.

"She'll have a heart attack one day," Sampson told him. Trace turned his attention back to the man as he set the drill down on top of the ladder and then grabbed the ladder to drag it further over the patio. Trace, still holding the beams in one hand, stretched to grab the drill before the vibrations in the ladder sent it skidding off and it either whacked Sampson in the head or fell to the ground and broke. "The likes of you flirting with her."

"Flirting with her," Trace muttered. "I'm just trying to stay out of the doghouse, old man."

"She's ready to move you in there permanently," Sampson eyed Trace for a second and then dropped his head back to eyeball the truss he was working on.

"The Fork was supposed to be a temporary thing," Trace reminded him half-heartedly. He felt a pang of homesickness. So, he *would* miss it here. The atmosphere —both the fact that they were in Music City and Left Fork itself. The people. But he couldn't imagine never going back to Leah. To the Queen. "It's been a coupla years now."

Sampson coughed as he climbed back up the ladder. Sounded like he had a lung lodged in his throat. Trace looked away as the old man picked up a Styrofoam cup and spit a wad of something unidentifiable in it.

"I ain't talking about you leavin'."

When he reached for the drill, eyes still on the wooden beam and the truss above him, Trace carefully placed it in his open hand.

"You're not?"

Tired of holding the beams Pearl had foisted at him, he stepped to the edge of the patio and leaned them on the wall.

"Nope."

Trace waited, but Sampson didn't say more.

"Then what? Why am I in the doghouse now?"

"You never called about that girl."

Trace drew back in surprise. "Sampson, I called here every day I was gone."

"You didn't tell Pearl nothing about that girl. How things was going."

"She never let me say a word. I asked how it was going here. She said fine. And hung up. Times ten."

The door swung open, and Pearl appeared, two mugs in hand. The late morning sun burned a hole in the back of Trace's neck, and sweat licked at the ends of his hair. He had mentioned needing a trim, but Leah had threatened him not to come back to Illinois all neat and groomed. He had laughed, but she had pinned him down on the living room floor to exact a promise from him. Truth be told, he could have flipped her over easily, but when a woman like Leah straddled his waist and leaned over to hold his hands down on the floor and her breasts—clothed or not—hung in his face, why would he fight?

"So, I sent you off to find that Leah woman so you would quit moping, and now you're moving to some Godforsaken place called Adam's Bay, Illinois."

The sun was hell, and Pearl's scrutiny wasn't helping. Thankful he had stopped after two beers last night—though, to be honest, he couldn't remember when he last had too much to drink—Trace took a mug from the woman. He sipped the coffee and remembered that these two drank it weaker than he cared for. It was hot, and most of the time that was something positive to say about it, but today, not so much. He swiped his fingers over his brow and then wiped them on his khaki cargo shorts.

"So you did hear me last night." He studied her over the rim of the mug and took another drink. Leah liked her coffee strong and serious. No frills. She saved those for the bedroom—from the soft, feminine décor to the sweet and sexy silk and lace she wore to bed when she slept with him.

"Heard you," Pearl answered as she cast her gaze on Sampson. Back in the day, Trace might have assumed the other coffee was for Sampson, but he knew the two of them much too well to think that now. "Just not sure I approve."

"This was temporary, Pearl," he said the words again, but this time they stuck inside. He cleared his throat. Dammit all, this might be as hard as telling his mama that he was moving. "Two years ago."

Pearl turned back to him with a puzzled look and then waved her hand at him as if he was a fly to be shooed away.

"I ain't even talkin' about you leavin' the Fork." She shook her head and drank from her mug. Trace thought of the way Leah drank deeply from her mug in the morning and then paused to savor the taste and the experience. Come to think of it, Leah did that with anything she tasted. Including him. His dick twitching in his pants was most definitely not a good thing right now, not while he baked on the blacktop in the bright summer sun, with two people who had probably had sex a few times in their day but probably hadn't used those parts in decades.

At least that's what he preferred to think.

"What're you talkin' about then?" He moved. Decided maybe those thoughts, unpleasant though they were, were just what he needed to kill the hard-on for Leah. He took another drink of his coffee and wandered over to stand at the ladder by Sampson. "Why don't you take a break? Let me do that for a while?"

"You think I can't handle the heat?" Sampson didn't spare him a glance or even bother to put any feeling in his accusation.

"No, sir," Trace answered immediately. "Thought you might want a coffee break."

"She want your money?" Pearl sank into a lawn chair that had seen better days. Trace glanced at her, noticed her ample hips barely fit in the frame of the seat, and looked back at Sampson.

"What money?" He shrugged.

"She wanna get closer to Tanner?"

"She doesn't know who Tanner is," he answered, bristling a bit at Pearl's questions.

"Trace Dixon, there ain't a woman alive don't know who your brother is," Pearl told him. "Anymore than there's a woman who walks into Left Fork and don't want to bed you."

Trace snorted and hung his head for a moment. Heat flared in his cheeks, because as much as he loved Pearl Allen, he didn't care to discuss his bed and whom he kept in that bed or even the word *bed* as a verb with her.

"She didn't know me, either, Pearl," he said quietly. "She's not a country music person."

"And you trust her?"

"I do."

"You trusted that other girl," Sampson reminded him. Trace pursed his lips and then blew out an angry sigh. They cared about him. These people cared about him, and unlike his mama, they knew how deep the incident with Shelly and Tanner had bruised him. Not because he lost Shelly, but because his brother—his flesh and blood—had been willing to take her when she'd so obviously used him.

"Leah's different."

He could try to put into words why she was different, but Trace knew he would just sound like any other lovesick guy, crazy about his woman. With another swallow of the hot coffee, he looked back at Pearl to find her watching him with a shrewd frown.

"She makes me happy, Pearl."

"She damned well better make you happy," Sampson announced. "You packin' up and moving up there for her."

Surprised that Sampson had shared his thoughts in such a blunt way, Trace looked up at the man to find Sampson watching him.

"You sellin' your granddaddy's house?" Pearl asked him.

"No." Trace took another drink. Tired of the hot coffee, tired of standing around and not getting anything done, he leaned over and set the mug on the ground near the wall. "Let me take a go at that for a bit, Sampson."

"Keeping it because you're not sure."

From the corner of his eye, Trace saw Pearl nod. She was looking away, at the parking lot, and she appeared to be lost in thought. But she was nodding to herself, as if she knew she was right.

"No." Trace stepped out of the way as Sampson backed down the ladder and then grabbed the ladder to hold it steady as he climbed up. He reached up with both hands to test the beam and truss Sampson had been working on. It was solid, no surprise there. He backed down the ladder again, scooted it closer to the other side of the small patio area, and climbed back up. "I'm keeping it because it's a place for Leah and me to stay when we're in Nashville."

"You bringing her back here?" Sampson asked incredulously.

"I have family here, Sampson. I own the house outright, so when we're in town for a visit, we have our own place."

He thought he saw Pearl's lips twitch, but she did nod her head slightly, as if in silent approval.

"I want her to see it," Trace mumbled, though he didn't believe he needed to explain himself to anyone. "I want her to see my home, my life, too."

"She's a looker," Sampson said. Trace thought he might have said more, but he coughed again and reached for his Styrofoam cup. Trace glanced at Pearl as Sampson disappeared inside.

"When did he see her?" He eyeballed the beam above his head rather than look at Pearl.

"Found her on that website for her bar."

Trace froze, arms over his head. He leaned his face around his elbow to look at Pearl in disbelief.

"You? And Sampson? Stalked Leah online?"

Pearl turned her head slowly and gave him a baleful look. "No. Angie and Kadie did. 'Course Sampson and I had to look."

Trace chuckled softly and shook his head. Okay, so maybe he'd count Angie and Kadie when he counted family here in Music City.

"And? What'd you think?"

"She's got family." Pearl nodded. "I like that."

Trace arched his eyebrows, eyes back on the beam and the truss, though his heart was in Adam's Bay.

"Sampson liked that bar," Pearl announced. "Thought it was even better lookin' than your Leah."

This time, Trace burst into laughter and rolled his eyes. "Of course, he did."

His phone buzzed in his pocket. Before he met Leah, he would have let it go until he was free to talk. Now the thought that Leah might be calling or texting made him drop his arms and stick his hand in his pocket. He pulled his phone out, a smile already on his face, ready for Leah to ask him what he was listening to. Wouldn't she get a kick out of this conversation?

I need you on the road. Just finish this tour for me.

Trace sighed and dropped his phone back in his pocket. His mama wasn't around, and Leah wasn't, either, so he had no intention of answering his brother's text.

CHAPTER 31

Leah dropped into the chair behind the desk and stared at Stevi's phone where it lay face up on the desk. Her name was thick and a bit clunky, but hearing Kenzi's voice after all this time traced shivers up her arms.

"Kenzi." Her own voice was soft with wonder, but a bit too tight and small to control her emotion. As much as she needed to gush and sob and cry, right now was not the time for it. "Oh, Kenz. It's so good to hear your voice."

She lifted her eyes to find her sister on the couch across the office. Stevi's hundred-watt smile lit up the room a thousand times brighter than the afternoon sun flooding through the window and falling over the hardwood floor. Tears streaked her face, and Leah knew without a word between them that they were tears of joy and relief and even some residual sadness, because Kenzi had lost so much time with her baby, with her kids, and Joe. And there was still so far for her to go for recovery with no guarantee that she would ever find her way back to the woman she used to be.

"Leah."

"It's me." Leah laughed softly and dashed at the tears on her face. "Oh. Man. Joe? Are you there?"

"I'm here."

"Wow." She leaned back in the chair and took a deep breath.

"Liam is at Kenzi's mom's house. And Adelynn is at the pool."

"Swim practice?"

"Yeah." Joe sounded happy. Leah wished she could hug them both. She looked at Stevi again, and this time they shared a smile.

"How's Edison?" Stevi called from the couch.

Leah rolled the chair forward and reached for a pencil. She was restless, but she didn't want to make noise and be rude, so she twirled it in her fingers.

"Growing," Joe answered. "He's good. He's got a pretty wicked grin."

"Like his daddy," Stevi said with a nod.

"Joe."

Kenzi's slow, dull voice drew another chill from Leah. She

sucked in a deep, silent breath and ducked her face to her hands.

"Yep, Joe's got a nice smile, huh, Kenz?" Stevi called.

"Yesh."

Leah's heart pounded in her ears and her throat. She wished she could just run out to her car and drive across town to the house where Kenzi and Joe used to live. She wished she could throw her arms around her friends. She couldn't wait to tell Trace that she had talked to Kenzi.

"Leah, what's this I hear about you burning up the sheets with some country music star?"

Leah snorted and lifted her head to look at Stevi.

"Did Stevi tell you that?" She tipped her head as she watched her sister. "Are you spying on us?"

"Hey, I just told him my sistah's in love!" Stevi shrugged and laughed with Leah.

"I'm hearing it from everyone at the Queen," Joe answered. "Even had a few regulars tell me about you."

"Our regular customers are telling you Nashville and I are burning up the sheets?"

This time Joe laughed out loud. Leah thought she heard something in the background, a small bark of laughter. She wondered if it was Kenzi. She wondered if Joe had an updated prognosis, if there was something new to learn about Kenzi, but she wasn't sure she should ask when he was on speakerphone with Kenzi listening. She wasn't sure she should wait, though, and ask later, because that felt sneaky and underhanded. They had never been about secrets; the whole bunch of them had always been very open with each other.

Things had changed, though. Leah was stumbling around in the dark; well, they all were. No one wanted to leave Kenzi out, but talking openly ran the risk of upsetting her.

"Okay, I filled in the blanks," Joe told her, "but from what I hear, you're pretty cozy with him."

"Yeah." Leah was breathless, suddenly overwhelmed by how much she missed Trace. He'd been gone only two days, but to Leah, those two days felt like months, and even though they had talked several times, and he still texted her to ask what she was listening to, she was so ready for him to come back that she felt like a kid the day after Christmas, waiting on Santa to come back the following year.

"Cozy." Stevi rolled her eyes. "Guys, he's moving up here."

"You got some hot-to-trot cowboy giving up the limelight to live with you, Leah Hague?" Joe whistled, and Leah heard that harsh bark of laughter. She could imagine the look on Kenzi's face and wished with all her heart that Kenzi could tease her, too.

"He's not a cowboy," Leah answered. Her thoughts turned to the times Trace had told her that. He was southern born and bred, but he was not a cowboy. He didn't wear a hat, and he didn't ride horses.

"He wears boots," Stevi reminded her. Leah ducked her head as her cheeks flooded with an embarrassed heat. He did wear boots, and he had worn his boots with his jeans shoved out of the way while he made love to her. The boots were sexy, and they gave him traction, but she liked being skin-to-skin with him, too, head-to-toe.

"He does," Leah said with a nod. She rubbed her face and cleared her throat as she lifted her head to look at Stevi again. "But he's not a cowboy."

"Kenzi thinks he's hot," Joe told her. Now Leah was glad they were on a phone call, because she was blushing again, and her friend would call her on it. Then again, it would feel damned good for Kenzi to tease her again.

"He is." Leah met Stevi's eyes. Stevi grinned and nodded. "But he's not a cowboy. And he isn't into limelight."

"But he's a performer?" Joe prompted her. "Right? You met him in a bar? And he was performing—"

"He played at a bar called Left Fork. On a small stage. He's a songwriter. His brother is the star."

"Kenzi says your guy's hotter."

"Damn right he is," Leah said quickly. She ignored Stevi's amused snort. "He's moving up here to help out at the Queen—"

"He's moving up here, because you guys have that sick lovey dovey thing going on all over the place, Leah. That guy's so into you, it's not funny."

Leah stared at Stevi silently. She was so into Trace, it was terrifying. They'd fallen hard and fast, but the future stretched out in front of them, and the fact that they hadn't talked about it scared her. When Trace was here, when he held her, when they laughed together as they shared ice cream sundaes or slaved together behind the bar, he made her believe none of that mattered. They could do anything together. But now that he was gone, there was a big hole in her life where all of her doubts had come to pile up and taunt her. Yes, she believed he loved her. She loved him. But there was so much that could go wrong—

"Stop it."

Leah blinked to find Stevi standing in front of the desk. She spoke so softly, Leah doubted Joe and Kenzi had heard her. She pursed her lips, but she said nothing and tuned in when she realized Joe was talking again.

"…wedding. You know that, right?"

Leah swallowed hard and stared at Stevi silently.

"What?" Her voice shook, so she cleared her throat again.

"You gotta hold off for a while for a wedding. Give Kenzi some more recovery time."

"No one's talking about weddings, Joe," Leah argued.

"Live big, Leah." Joe laughed, but she thought it sounded strained. She wished again that she could be there, that she, Stevi, and Margo could be closer to Kenzi so they would know the truth about how she was doing.

"Margo's still talking to Jess," Stevi announced. Leah was relieved to be out of the conversation spotlight, but she wasn't sure throwing Margo under Joe's bus was a good idea. All of them used to like Jess. Maybe all of them still did like Jess. He was a good guy. Sometimes. Big hearted and generous, Jess would give anyone the shirt off his back. The trouble was, Jess often took the shirt off his back, along with his pants, and he was a bit too generous with his sexy smile and his body, when he had already promised all of it to Margo.

He drank too much, too, and the more he drank, the friendlier he got with every woman in a room. Often while Margo watched. Margo had finally called it quits and sent him packing, because she didn't want Berkley to grow up with a father who was either falling down drunk or hung over twenty-four seven. She'd argued for a while after Jess was gone that his flirting—that she called it flirting and not cheating seemed a big problem to Leah— didn't bother her. That they weren't exclusive and never promised to be. But when Jess had been gone three weeks, Margo packed Berkley off to her mother's house for the night, and the four of them—Margo, Stevi, Kenzi, and Leah—went out for a girls' night. It started fun, but Margo eventually caved and admitted how badly it hurt her that she wasn't enough for Jess, that she was head over heels in love with him, and that she missed him so much she didn't sleep at night.

The next day, she'd had a ferocious hangover, and she'd demanded promises from all of them that they weren't going to discuss Jess. Ever again. She had told him when he left that if he cleaned up his act and quit drinking, he could see Berkley. Jess had vanished. Only now, he had apparently resurfaced. Leah worried for Berkley and

Margo, and she knew Stevi and Duncan well enough to know that they did, too.

And now, so did Joe.

Leah didn't want to sit here and talk about Margo and Jess—they had promised not to do that, although Margo had apparently forgotten how he broke her heart. She also didn't think Joe needed more on his plate right now with his struggles with Kenzi and the kids.

"Yeah, she told me he's been calling her." Joe sighed. Leah thought he sounded pensive, but she shot Stevi a look of disbelief. Margo was talking to Joe about Jess?

"What else did she say?" Stevi asked cautiously. She stared at Leah with big eyes and shrugged dramatically.

"She doesn't say a lot," Joe answered. "But she sounds sad."

Leah winced. What would she feel if something happened, and she couldn't be with Trace? It would rip her heart out already, and she and Trace didn't have the time involved that Margo and Jess did, let alone a child together.

"She did say she likes Leah's guy."

Joe's chuckle and his words made her think of Trace, and thinking about Trace made Leah flush with warmth and love. She shivered and rubbed her hands up and down her arms.

"You're gonna love him," Stevi told him. "He's perfect for Leah."

"Leah."

Leah met Stevi's eyes when Kenzi spoke again. They shared a private smile.

"Kenzi says put a ring on it, Leah," Joe told her. "We're gonna go, guys. Kenz is tired."

"Thanks for calling." Leah stood, but she leaned over and flattened her hands on the desktop. "Love you guys."

"Yep," Stevi chimed in. "Love you."

Leah and Stevi stared at each other silently when the call ended.

"Do you still pray?" Stevi asked her. "For them?"

"Every day." Leah's voice came out gruff with emotion.

"Me, too," Stevi whispered.

"You tell Joe that me and Nashville are burning up the sheets?" Leah arched an eyebrow playfully.

"Um." Stevi sniffled and cleared her throat. "I might have."

"Just guessing?" Leah asked softly.

"I might have heard you a time or two," Stevi mumbled. She shrugged. "You did tell me I could come back home."

"Just as long as you didn't hear me Tuesday."

"Trace left on Monday," Stevi reminded her.

"Yep." Leah nodded and winked at her.

"Damn," Stevi whined. "You guys are having phone sex? He's four hundred miles away, and you're still having more sex than me."

"You were the one who suggested I needed to get laid."

"And I was right, wasn't I?"

Leah laughed softly as she straightened. "Maybe now it's time to find you the right man."

"Please." Stevi rolled her eyes. "I've been looking for the right man forever. And it's never going to happen. You don't even go looking for a man, and you get the perfect guy."

"I don't think you're really looking, Stevi," Leah said simply. She tucked her hair behind her ear and picked up her mug from the desk.

"Leah."

"Hmm?"

"Stop looking for trouble with Trace, okay?"

"What?" Leah took a sip of the coffee, but it was lukewarm. This time the shiver that slid down her neck and over her back was more like the willies. Warm coffee was gross, and whatever Stevi was about to say made her stomach hurt.

"He's moving here to live with you. To be with you. Because he loves you. The rest of us? The Queen? We're icing on the cake, and sure, I'm even a scoop of ice cream on the side."

Leah rolled her eyes, but she laughed as she moved out from behind the desk.

"But Trace is in love with you, and he wants a future with you."

"We haven't even discussed a future," Leah argued.

"Yes, you have. You discussed him living here with you."

"Stevi, we haven't talked about marriage. And kids. I don't want…What if he—"

"Leah." Stevi stood beside her and slipped her arm around her. "You guys love each other. The rest of it is a bunch of details. Fun and happy and exciting as hell details. Don't get scared of the possibilities. Just let it happen."

Leah blew out a deep breath and nodded. "Maybe you're right."

"Always am," Stevi agreed.

"I hate it when you're right," Leah said quietly. She glanced at Stevi as they made their way to the door. Stevi raised her eyebrows. "But this time I want you to be right."

"Then you're in luck." Stevi gave her a squeeze. "By the way, Duncan said you guys were going to inventory the wine cellar today."

"You call that luck?" Leah whined as she led the way into the break room.

"Spending the day meal planning with Margo or hanging out in a wine cellar…" Stevi nodded her head back and forth. "With Duncan. I'd take door number two if I had a choice."

"Tellin' Margo," Leah sang.

"Tellin' me what?" Margo called from behind them. Leah and Stevi turned as Margo's foot hit the top step. Laptop tucked under arm, she carried a coffee mug in one hand and a stack of unopened mail in the other.

"Joe called," Stevi answered quickly.

"Stevi likes Duncan better than you." Leah crossed the room, tossed the warm coffee in the sink, and then filled her mug again.

"Who doesn't like Duncan better than me?" Margo shrugged. She hovered in the doorway now as Stevi grabbed a bottle of water from the refrigerator. "He's funny and charming. Things I'm not."

"You're both," Stevi answered. "He's in the wine cellar today. Who doesn't want to spend the day in the wine cellar?"

"Me." Leah waved her hand and smiled. "Send rescue if we aren't back upstairs by noon."

CHAPTER 32

Being gone from Leah for two weeks nearly did him in. But once he was back in Nashville and he saw Sampson working on the patio, he couldn't leave the old man hanging. Chino helped quite a bit, and the three of them had the place looking pretty nice before Trace headed north. They had added the partial roof, so there was protection from the weather, for sun and rain. Sampson had hired out a little concrete job so that most of the patio was now concrete, rather than the blacktop of the parking lot. Pearl had argued that they should leave it blacktop and make people sweat and maybe order more drinks. But Trace had reminded her that they weren't open until later in the afternoon, so the baking asphalt wouldn't be a factor the way it would be in a place like an amusement park. Sampson argued that everything just looked better with the concrete patio area, and Trace agreed with that, too. It cost him a half dozen cookies while he was there, but Kadie had snuck him a couple on a few different occasions.

He took some time to pack the belongings he didn't think he could do without, which amounted to enough clothes to get by without having to do laundry every other day, three guitars, two amps, and his granddad's banjo. He wasn't good on the banjo, but he did like to pick it now and then. Mostly, he needed to be with Leah, so by the time he had helped Sampson, visited with his mama, and done two more nights at Left Fork—they actually billed it as his goodbye show, as if it mattered to Music City if Trace Dixon moved away—he was champing at the bit to get on the road and get back to her.

It took some talking to smooth his mama's ruffled feathers over his relationship with Leah. Not so much that it existed, but that he hadn't introduced the two of them and that Mama didn't know anything about her. Over iced tea and grilled chicken out on his mother's deck, he filled her in. Told her how he and Leah met, how she'd shut him down so instantly. He had expected her to be indignant on his behalf, but instead, she'd laughed with delight and announced then and there that she liked Leah Hague. He told her how he got lucky finding Leah's business card—although he left out the part about the condom wrapper near it on the floor. And though he didn't recite every conversation he and Leah had shared, he did say that he was in love with her before he ever saw her in person again.

His mother had decided it was all very romantic, and she had gushed about meeting Leah. Trace promised her that they would come to Nashville soon so that he could show Leah off. After all, he and Leah had already agreed to a visit soon, just not the part about showing her off. She didn't know he was calling it that; she thought she was going to meet the people he considered family. He might have left his mother's house happy if she hadn't had to drag Tanner into their visit.

She had served him a piece of cherry cobbler—homemade, of course—and then she'd casually mentioned Tanner and how she had just talked to him the night before. Did Trace know that Tanner's guitarist was having trouble with his hand? Did Trace think he could fill in a show or two for Tanner? Trace knew how that would go. Tanner had been asking the same, but Trace knew he would probably end up on the remainder of the tour with the band, and he had no desire to do that, with or without Leah waiting at home for him.

She asked, too, if Tanner knew about Leah, and Trace had struggled to be patient. To stay calm. Hell no, Tanner didn't know anything about Leah, because for one thing, Trace did his best not to talk to Tanner any more than he absolutely had to. Even a lot of their business conversation either went through Tanner's manager or else he and Tanner texted. Second, why was Leah any of Tanner's business? He didn't doubt Leah's love for him. He didn't worry that she would magically fall under Tanner's spell if they met. But neither he nor Leah were as into Tanner Dixon and the Lightnin' Congregation as Tanner was. Leah had started listening to some country music, but that didn't mean she was ready to buy a pair of boots and a plaid shirt and learn to line dance. Leah was more of a Sinatra lover, and Trace was a Leah lover, and being at the Queen, being involved in Leah's world, had brought him more joy than he remembered since he was a kid, before his dad died.

Mostly, it just rankled that he and his mama couldn't have a conversation that didn't circle back around to Tanner. Some days, he thought Tanner could rob a bank or two before he took the stage and their mother would shrug and pat Tanner on the head and tell him next time just to ask her for a loan.

He'd finished the cobbler and iced tea, changed two light bulbs for his mama, and given her a big, long hug before he left. He loved her, and he worried about her, even if he did tire of hearing her rave about how wonderful Tanner was. Honestly, he missed his little brother, but the guy he missed was long gone and seeing Tanner now wasn't the same, anyway. So he hadn't shared that little kernel of knowledge with anyone but Leah. Then again, sharing that much with Leah had probably prompted her to exact his promise that he would work things out with Tanner.

His final shows at the Fork were fun, even if Trace thought the whole *Farewell Trace Dixon* thing Pearl and the girls did was over the top. The bar was packed, but then again, Left Fork usually was on summer weekends, so no, he didn't believe he was the draw. Angie had swiped his phone earlier in the week and stolen Leah's phone number. So Angie and Kadie texted his girlfriend a few times. He supposed that was fine, but it did make him nervous when the two of them, heads bent over their phones, giggled about something. He had nothing to hide from Leah, nothing bad, though he was certain the two of them had come up with embarrassing stories to share with her. Rather than get mad, he texted Leah and reminded her he would be living in the same house with her and her sister and working with Stevi, Margo, and Duncan on a regular daily basis. Leah's response was simply the smiling, pink-cheeked emoji.

Angie recorded a lot of his Friday show, and so he dedicated a song or two to Leah. In his heart, every love song he sang was for her, but he said it out loud a few times Friday. During the Saturday show, Kadie Facetimed Leah, and so, apparently, a few of the Queen's regular patrons saw him sing to Leah from Nashville.

He didn't mind. His only regret was that Leah hadn't been able to come with him on this trip. He did promise the crew at the Fork that he would bring her back down. Pearl had harrumphed and tutted at him both as if meeting Leah wasn't that important to her and as if to say he damned well better bring her down to officially meet them. Chino and Sampson had both been happy to hear that Leah would be back. Chino had whistled at the picture Kadie showed him; Stevi had snapped it one night when he and Leah had been standing together behind the bar at the Queen. Sampson had nodded and reckoned how she was *good-lookin'*. When Angie scoffed at that and told him that Leah was hot, Trace only looked at her and arched a suspicious eyebrow. They'd laughed together that night. All of them. And it hurt a little bit to walk out of the Fork when he headed home.

Nothing that seeing Leah wouldn't cure, though. In fact, he drove with a heavy foot and told himself that a speeding ticket would be justified if it happened. Told himself that even God or fate or something approved of his relationship with Leah when he made it to Illinois without a ticket. Desperate to see her, Trace made himself go to the house first, before calling her. Odds were, she was at the Queen, but he had to unload his stuff from the truck first. He hadn't seen any evidence of crime around the Queen, but still. His equipment was expensive, and why not take the extra time to unload his bags and sound equipment and then head down to the Queen?

He was surprised to find Leah's car in the drive when he pulled in. It was only four, but the gang spent most of their time at the bar. Then again, even as much as they loved the place, they probably all needed time on their own and time away from the bar, too. He had been intent on using his key—the one Leah had given him—to unlock the door to the house, and he was amused to find that he was almost disappointed not to use it. But that feeling was gone quickly, when he stepped inside and heard water running somewhere in the house.

"Leah?" he called as he leaned over to set a duffle bag on the floor in the kitchen. "Is that you?"

When no one answered him, Trace moved through the kitchen to the living room to look around. The bathroom door opened as he did, and there she was. It took her a moment to realize he was standing there, and in that second, he worried that he would scare her. But she stepped out of the bathroom and yawned and then her eyes lit on him, and there was that smile. It was the one he'd seen the night he had surprised her at the Queen the first time, when she'd hurried out from behind the bar and thrown her arms around him and clung to him.

"Nashville." She took a step toward him, and when it looked like her knees might buckle, he was there, and he swept her into his arms. "You're back? You're here?"

"I'm here." He pulled her close and buried his face in her neck to breathe her in.

"You're home." Her voice was soft with wonder. "Right? You're home?"

He pulled away from her, just enough to see her face, to look into her eyes. Dropped a kiss on her forehead.

"I'm home," he agreed.

"How long, Trace? How long are we gonna do this?" Arms over his shoulders, her eyes roamed over his face and hung up on his lips.

"Leah, I packed my bags—"

"I know." She nodded. "But there's so much we haven't talked about. So much about the future that we don't know. That we might not even agree on—"

"Darlin'." Trace circled one arm all the way around her back and lifted his other hand to stroke her cheek. "We agreed we love each other, right?" When she only stared at him in response, he arched an eyebrow.

"Yes." She held the eye contact. "Yes. We do. I know."

"Then nothing else matters," he reminded her.

"Nashville."

"What's going on?" He tipped his head, curious why underneath the happy, he sensed her worry.

"I'm just…" She licked her lips and shrugged.

"Just what?"

"I think you deserve more than me."

"There is no more than you." He shook his head. "You're all I want. All I need."

"I wanna be the woman you need, Nashville, but I can't. I'm not…I don't want a family. I don't want kids. I want to be able to give you that."

"Yeah?" He grinned and swayed her back and forth a bit. "And I wanna give you twelve inches and two hours, but I can't do that."

Her laugh was delicious and sexy, and when she dropped her head back and exposed her throat to him, he leaned in to nip at the cords of her neck.

"But you can." She combed her fingers up the back of his head. "You have."

"I don't have twelve inches anyway you look at it, darlin'."

"Pretty damn close," she whispered in his ear. "Maybe you should give it to me now, just so we can check."

"Yeah?" He stroked his hands down over her back and cupped her bottom. "You want it now?"

"I do." She outlined the shell of his ear with the tip of her tongue and then tugged at his earlobe with her teeth.

"Maybe we should go upstairs?"

"Mmm." She kissed a trail from his ear to his lips and slid her hands down over his back. Trace assumed she was backing away to lead him up to her room—no, their bedroom—so when she put her hands on his belt buckle, he blinked at her in surprise. "I think that's too long to wait."

He laughed and looked around the living room.

"Are we alone?"

"Yes, we are." She gave him a slow, lazy nod. "Stevi's at the Queen."

"The drapes are open," he reminded her when she worked his buckle and then unbuttoned his jeans.

She glanced to her left, where the drapes on the window behind the TV were indeed open. But when she looked back at him, she only grinned.

"But if we move a few steps this way," she slipped her fingers inside the waistband of his shorts and tugged him gently toward her, "no one will be able to see us."

"I missed you," he told her as he followed her closer to the wall, out of view of the window.

"I missed you, too."

"Why all the worry, darlin'? We're together now. We face everything together."

She leaned back on the wall, eyes locked with his.

"We all talked to Joe and Kenzi the other day."

"But you said everything seemed to be going well."

Leah had told him about the phone call. That Kenzi had said Leah's and Stevi's names. That they had talked to Margo and Duncan, too, later that same day.

Leah nodded now. "I know."

"But?"

Trace's mouth went dry when she moved. Her hands went to her shorts and before he knew what she was doing, she slipped them down over her hips and stepped out of them. He glanced at the denim material on the floor and did a double take when he noticed the scrap of red lace inside them. Heart racing in his chest, he dragged his eyes back up over her bare legs and let them linger at her thighs.

"Leah."

Breathless, he watched her slide her fingers between her legs and then rub herself suggestively.

"I've been doing this for two weeks, Nashville."

He licked his lips and tore his eyes away from her, though he could watch her touch herself for hours. Or forever.

"It's okay." She shrugged her eyebrows. She moved her other hand under her t-shirt now. "But I like it a whole lot better when it's you doing this to me."

"You have any idea how sexy you sound when you touch yourself and moan my name over the phone?"

"You liked that?"

"I did."

His dick hard like steel, he stepped closer to her and bent his head to kiss her.

"I have something for you," he told her.

Her throaty laugh shot a spike of electricity through him.

"Not that."

"Whaddaya got then, Nashville?"

He patted his pockets to find his phone. Time to toss it aside. He didn't want any interruptions right now.

"You got something for me in your pockets?" She stared up at him with dreamy eyes. "We quit using condoms."

"I know we did." He grinned.

"You're not gonna pull any diamond rings out, are you?"

"What kind of man do you take me for?" he asked with a laugh. "When I propose to you, it's not gonna be while you're half naked on a wall, and I have my pants down around my ankles."

She grinned. Moved her hands and tugged his jeans down over his hips.

"I just got scared while you were gone," she whispered, suddenly serious again. "I thought maybe you could find someone better than me."

"I love you," he said quietly. "I love you, Leah Hague, and I'm not playing house here. I'm in this for keeps."

CHAPTER 33

THEY MADE IT TO THEIR BEDROOM EVENTUALLY, AND though they wanted to linger there for the rest of the evening, they got up and showered—together, which took some time—and dressed to head to the Queen. Except that when they stepped past Trace's bag in the kitchen, they went outside and saw his truck behind her car and remembered he still had stuff to unpack. Leah laughed softly when he glanced at her and wagged his eyebrows. She helped carry in what she could, but he handled most of the equipment. He did let her carry the instruments inside, and Leah mumbled that it was sort of terrifying to carry Trace Dixon's guitars, especially Loretta.

"Based on how well you handle the rest of my equipment, I trust you, darlin'."

The comment, delivered as they crossed back over the drive to the house, made Leah laugh. And wish that they could simply go back inside, go back to bed, and love each other.

Stevi texted her on the ride to the Queen.

"Stevi wants to know where I am," she said with a small grin.

"Well, you can tell her now." He shrugged.

Trace is home. He had to unload his stuff.

She tucked her phone between her knees after she answered Stevi.

"So, was your mom upset?" she asked him.

"Just upset that you and I've been seeing each other, and I hadn't mentioned you to her at all."

"Is she gonna hate me?"

"Actually, no. She thinks you're awesome, because you told me you wouldn't sleep with me."

Leah laughed and rolled her eyes. Her phone buzzed, so she snatched it up to look at it.

"I'm glad I did sleep with you," she announced.

"Yeah?"

When she looked at him, he shot her a quick grin and a wink.

"You have a pretty high-tech vibrator," he reminded her. "You don't really need me."

"Mm. It's nice," she agreed. "But it doesn't kiss me. And it doesn't have big, hard shoulders to hold onto. It doesn't throw a leg over mine when we sleep. And it never says *goodnight, darlin'*. Or *I love you, darlin'.*"

"You like me better? Is that what you're saying?"

"I do."

"Well, that's a relief."

"What about Pearl and Sampson?"

Trace shrugged. "I got the standard we're gonna miss you from all of them, Leah." He glanced at her again. "And I'll miss them, too. But I have no regrets. No doubts that I'm supposed to be right here with you."

"I don't have doubts, Nashville," she whispered. "I just don't want to disappoint you."

"If you wanna shack up until we're old and gray, I'm happy. If you want marriage, I would be so happy to give you my name. We can elope. We can have a big wedding. We can do whatever you want."

"I'm not against marriage," she said simply. "It's just the whole family thing."

"Okay." He shrugged. "Can we get a puppy?"

"You want a puppy?"

"You got something against dogs?"

"No!" She laughed. "No. Not at all. I just picture you with a lab or something. A big dog."

"I picture me with you," he answered. "And a wiggly little puppy climbing all over you. Trying to lick your face."

"I like puppies," she whispered.

"Can I ask you something?"

"Of course."

"Is it that you don't *want* kids? Or are you…"

Leah avoided his eyes when he glanced at her this time.

"It's okay," he promised her. "I'm just…if you can't or if you just don't want a pregnancy, or if you just don't want children, it's okay, Leah. I just want to know what you're thinking."

She nodded. Throat tight with emotion, she tried to take a deep breath. Glanced at her phone and snorted with laughter.

"What's funny?"

"Stevi." She rubbed the bridge of her nose. "I told her you were here, and that you had to unload your stuff."

Trace barked a laugh and shook his head. "You walked right into that one."

"'Wow. I did," she agreed with another soft laugh. "Duncan added a bit to the sketch of the stage. Did I tell you that?"

When Trace didn't answer her right away, she glanced at him. Eyes forward, his hands loose and relaxed on the steering wheel, he didn't appear upset. She didn't want to talk about this now. About babies. And that was part of the reason she worried, because if he wanted babies, she should be willing to talk about it at least. So much easier just to avoid the whole subject.

"You said he made a few changes." Trace glanced at her. "I talked to him a couple of times while I was gone."

"You did?"

"Yeah." Trace shrugged. "That okay with you?"

"It is perfectly okay with me that you talk to anyone in my family."

And it was. It still kind of took her breath away that she met someone—not that she met *Trace Dixon, country music songwriter*—who loved her and wanted to spend the rest of his life with her. Someone she loved and needed in her life just to love him. Just because loving him made her happy. It was okay that he was close to her family; it was better than okay, it was perfect.

But that didn't mean it didn't overwhelm her now and then. This whole forever kind of love thing.

"Speaking of which, I saw Angie and Kadie doing a lot of giggling over their phones during my last two nights at the Fork."

Leah only grinned.

"Well?"

"Is that okay?" She turned his question back around on him.

"Yes. Both of them are dying to meet you, although Angie said she thinks you're hot, so I'm not sure about that."

"It's okay. Women can say that about each other and not mean anything by it."

"Yeah, but you are hot," Trace pointed out. "I don't know which way Angie swings, but I mean, women share shoes and clothes and stuff, so when you meet her, if there's any ounce of attraction on your part, I'm gonna worry. She could probably give you a lot more than I can."

Leah considered his words and gave him a playful smile. "I gotta tell ya. I've seen some beautiful women, and I've seen some sexy women. And I do love shoes. But I'm all yours, Nashville."

"Good to know."

"You are one hundred thousand percent stuck with me."

"You can borrow my shoes, ya know."

"Your boots?"

"Sure." He nodded. When he slowed at the stoplight just down the block from the Queen, the smolder he shot her burned. "You're welcome to wear them anytime you want. Only one condition."

"Oh?" She arched her eyebrows in question. Trace looked back at the light and eased his foot off the brake.

"When you wear them," he crossed the intersection and then made a left turn into the parking lot behind the Queen. Full of love and pure joy that he was back, that Trace was home and they were officially starting their lives together, Leah was restless as he pulled into a spot next to Duncan's black car. The niggling worry over marriage and family tamped back down by Trace's presence, Leah wanted to get out of the truck and shout for the world to hear that Trace Dixon belonged to her. "You can't wear anything else."

She unbuckled her seatbelt and then turned to him. She held her phone in her lap with one hand and rested the other on the dash.

"Honestly, Trace, that's not a sexy picture."

"The hell it isn't."

"But me? In your boots? Babe, they look just right on you. Not for me."

"You think I'd be looking at my boots, darlin'?"

She smiled. "I am the luckiest damned girl in the world."

"And you know what I am?"

She eyed him for a moment. "Sexy. Probably horny. Hot."

"I'm sensing a theme."

She tossed her hands up as if to say *what're you gonna do?*

"I'm hungry."

"We should have grabbed something before we came down here."

"I'll find something." He sounded unconcerned as he popped his seatbelt release and opened his door. Leah twisted around to open her own door and climbed out. She started toward the back door, but when she realized Trace wasn't behind her, she turned to see what was keeping him. She tucked her hands in the hip pockets of her khaki capris and watched Trace as he leaned back into the backseat of the truck cab.

"What're you doing?" she finally called to him. From the patio behind her, she heard music, and she tuned in for a second to hear what was playing. It hit her as she did that noticing music and identifying songs and artists was important to her now, because music was Trace Dixon's passion. She decided the song was "Magic Carpet Ride," but she wasn't sure who the artist was. "Who is this?"

There was muted conversation on the patio behind her, and Leah thrilled to the sound. She loved the clinking of glasses, the music, the sounds of traffic on the streets surrounding the bar. Summer nights here at the Queen couldn't be beat. Summer nights here, winter nights, any night now with Trace would be perfect.

"Steppenwolf," he answered as he stepped away from the truck and closed the door. He had something in his hand, but Leah didn't look closely to see what it was.

"Hey. Did Tanner—"

Trace shook his head as he approached her. "Not tonight. Okay? No Tanner tonight. We have the rest of our lives to deal with…him. Let's celebrate tonight."

"Okay." She nodded as he stopped to stand in front of her.

"This is for you." He held up a white cowboy hat. Or, Leah decided, a cowgirl hat.

"For me?"

"Yep." He set it on her head and gave her a once over.

"You got me a cowgirl hat?"

"I did." He dropped his hands to her shoulders. "I thought you might like it."

"I do." She laughed. "How's it look?"

"Looks good." He nodded and then dragged his gaze down over her shoulders and her belly to her feet. "I think it'll look good later when you take everything else off."

She laughed as she threw her arms around him. "Nashville, I can't make love with a hat on."

"You can if you ride me." He rubbed his hands over her back and dropped a kiss on the tip of her nose.

She hissed and pressed her face to his chest. "You say that and expect me to walk inside like everything's normal?"

"Darlin', your panties might be wet, but no one can see that. I got a bigger problem."

"Twelve inches." She patted his chest as she looked up. She kissed the corner of his mouth and then took his hand. "Let's go, Nashville. Let's start our life together."

CHAPTER 34

DURING THE SECOND WEEK HE WAS BACK—THE SECOND week he was home, he liked the sound of that better—Trace helped Duncan tackle the stage they had talked about. Trace studied the sketches Duncan made, decided he liked the minimal changes and additions, and the two of them climbed into Trace's truck and headed out to Becker Lumber, a place owned by someone Duncan knew. Although the girls liked the idea of the stage and all five of them pored over the sketches and discussed it all at great length, they still stood in the back door snickering at him and Duncan when they left.

Trace even checked his fly before he climbed into the truck. Duncan waved the girls away, though he passed it off as a wave goodbye, and told Trace he would have to develop thicker skin if he was going to live in the presence of these three women on a daily basis. Trace laughed and hunkered in for the drive out Broadway, happy to listen to Duncan telling tales on the girls.

There were stories about disastrous dates. Sounded like Stevi had the most disasters, but then it also sounded like Stevi dated more than anyone he knew. There were stories about disastrous kitchen experiments. Trace's mind jumped to several very successful kitchen experiments he and Leah had performed, though he doubted those were the sorts of kitchen experiments to share. The best of those stories sounded like Margo's attempt at apple pie. According to Duncan, she mistook cumin for cinnamon, which made the pie taste interesting. Then again, the story about Leah forgetting a soda can in the freezer until it exploded through the middle of the night and scared her and Stevi so badly they called Duncan was pretty good, too.

Things that were obvious to Trace as Duncan shared stories on the girls were that the four of them were very close and had been since Margo's mother and Duncan's father had started seeing each other several years ago. Trace had recognized that closeness in the pictures he had searched for on the Internet before he and Leah started talking on a regular basis. He would be envious of it now, but without hesitation, they had all welcomed him into the group. Not simply as a friend, but as the man Leah was in love with, and therefore, family. He also decided Duncan Marks would take a bullet for any and all three of them and that the guy was over the moon for Berkley.

Trace loved all of the women they were discussing, including the shortest and sweetest of them. He had brought her a pair of cowgirl boots, guessing on a size that she would grow into soon, and assuming that since she was a little girl, she would like something colored.

He'd foregone the pink, though, and when Margo's eyes welled with tears when he showed Berkley the lavender boots, he knew he'd made the right decision.

The girls teased Leah about the hat he brought back for her. But she'd worn it all that first night he moved back. Tipped it a time or two to a few of their patrons, always with a nod to Trace. Word had traveled some around Adam's Bay, and it seemed someone came in every few nights looking for him. Leah didn't hover or paint the word mine on his forehead. Nor did she pretend that they were just friends.

She wore the hat when they got home that night, too. When they made love and she straddled him and rode him to mutual orgasm. Then she'd sort of purred, tossed the hat aside, and lowered her body to his side.

The stage took only a few days to build, and since they started working on a Sunday, they finished it midweek and didn't have to close the Queen down. Trace worked side by side with Duncan, swinging a hammer and lining up wooden beams and felt more at home with the guy than he'd felt with his own brother in years. He worked behind the bar, pulling beers, learning cocktail recipes, and taking dinner orders with all of them. He took inventory, and he handled phone calls when the rest of the crew was busy. He spent time with Leah's parents, and he noticed that whenever he happened to pick up Loretta to do anything around the Queen—not often with the construction job, but a time or two—her parents were there, tapping their toes, and nodding their heads.

There had been a time in the beginning when he wondered if there was more to Kenzi and Joe and Leah's bargain with God. If her reaction to Joe's calls—early in their relationship—had something to do with guilt and if that guilt had something more to do with her and Joe than with her living a strong, healthy life after watching Kenzi stroke out during labor. But being completely immersed in Leah's life, in the world of the Queen, he understood it wasn't that sort of guilt at all. Kenzi was simply a part of the girls' group, had been since she and Margo had gone to school together. They loved her the same as they loved each other. They loved Joe the same as they loved Trace. And Leah happened to be the one in the birthing room at the moment when Joe and Kenzi's life had imploded and changed, and the trauma of the stroke, of seeing her friend's life shrink from all the world to her own mind— to being trapped in her body—had simply been too much for Leah to handle.

Duncan and Stevi filled Trace in some of those details. Leah and Margo were upstairs in the office handling the books. As good as business was, there appeared to be some question on the cost benefit of serving dinner every night of the week, so those two were knee deep in numbers and that left Duncan and Trace at the bar, playing with mixology. Trace remembered that he'd rolled his eyes at the word when he first found the website for the Mississippi Queen. Now that he considered the guy a friend, he was fascinated by his artistry with liquors and cocktails.

Stevi hopped up on a barstool to watch them. She set her

phone down and rubbed her eyes. When she looked at them, she tried unsuccessfully to tamp down a yawn.

"Your date keep you out too late last night, Stevi?" Duncan liked to rib her about the serial dating, though Trace noticed he was never vicious with the teasing.

"Hmm?" She folded her arms on the bar and rested her head on them. "No. My date had me home by nine, thank you."

"Yeah? Bingo with Dennis Cardero?"

"Eew." Her dramatic full-bodied shiver made Duncan laugh. "No. I've been texting with Joe."

"Yeah? How's our girl?"

"Adelynn won that swim meet last weekend. Or she won first in her events, I guess." She met Trace's eyes and shrugged. "I don't know anything about competitive swimming."

Trace raised his eyebrows and shook his head. "Beats me."

"Kenz is kind of at a standstill."

Stevi sounded sad, and watching her talk about their friends reminded Trace of the way Leah looked when she talked about them.

"What do you mean?" Duncan asked Stevi. He leaned over and eyed his pour carefully. Satisfied that he poured the perfect amount of vodka into the shaker glass, he capped the bottle and set it aside.

"She's not making any progress." Stevi took a deep breath. "Hasn't since we talked to her a couple of weeks ago."

"But she's not…backsliding?" Duncan asked hopefully.

"No. I don't think so." Stevi sat up again and looked around. Trace watched her study their new stage. All done except for the stain they would apply over the weekend. "But Joe said you can tell she's down. *Joe* sounded down."

"You remember that time Kenzi danced on the bar at Twilight?"

Stevi laughed and rubbed her forehead.

"She danced on a bar?" Trace couldn't hide his surprise. "Joe was okay with that?"

"Oh, she didn't take any clothes off," Stevi shook her head, "but she'd had a few too many, and someone turned the jukebox on. I guess it *was* kind of sexy, her body moving to Marvin Gaye."

"Are you for real?"

"I am so for real." Stevi nodded. "In fact, that might be the night they went home and made baby Edison."

Duncan laughed out loud. "I think you might be right."

"I think Joe was more upset that she was dancing on the bar, instead of down on the floor with him."

"Do they know what happened? What caused the stroke?"

Stevi shrugged. "She was thirty-five. Smoker. She was smoking a pack a day back when she went to school with Margo. God, we begged her to quit. Joe asked her to quit.

She did when she was pregnant with Adelynn. Went back to it after she was born. She tried to quit when she was pregnant with Liam, but I know I caught her smoking several times then. When she got pregnant with Edison, Joe asked her again to quit. And she wouldn't. She said she'd smoked some with Liam, and he turned out fine, so Joe should quit worrying."

"She had high blood pressure," Duncan picked up the story when Stevi got quiet. "It was a high-risk pregnancy. And unfortunately, Leah saw it happen."

Trace looked from Duncan to Stevi.

"She told me she made a bargain with God." He spoke quietly, sort of worried that he was breaking Leah's trust in him. But he worried about Leah, even now that Kenzi had started to make a small recovery. "That she would forgo love…" Trace cleared his throat and waved his hand around to make his point. He saw Duncan nod as he grabbed for a bottle of piña colada mix. "If he would save Kenzi. Bring her back."

"She never told me that," Stevi whispered. "But I figured it was something like that."

"I just…when I first came up here, she was adamant that we were just friends. I wanna say I would have been okay with that." Trace glanced at Duncan. "Anything to be part of her world. You know what I mean?"

"Yep." Duncan nodded without further explanation.

"And then…things changed really fast. I would never ask Leah to forget what she…what happened. But I…"

"Want Leah to forget what happened," Duncan finished for him.

"Kinda." He shrugged. "Does that make sense?"

"Yep."

Trace looked at Stevi for support.

"Leah's still got some demons to chase as far as Kenzi goes, and I can imagine what they are, Trace. But I know my sister, and I know she is absolutely in love with you."

"Leah's heart is as big as Texas," Duncan mumbled.

"He's from Tennessee," Stevi reminded Duncan.

Duncan cut her a threatening look, and Stevi grinned.

"She's the girl who finds a nest in the backyard and has to save the birds. She's the girl who sees a little kid lose a balloon and feels that kid's loss in her chest like someone yanked her lungs out." Duncan looked at Trace. "You get what I'm saying?"

"I do."

"She's always gonna hurt for Kenzi and Joe. But that doesn't mean she can't love the hell out of you, Trace."

Trace nodded at Stevi.

"You helping her Sunday?" Duncan asked Stevi.

"Helping her what?"

"She said you guys were staining the stage on Sunday."

"News to me." Stevi shrugged. "But yeah, I'm free. I'll be here."

"No date? No Sunday movie matinee?"

"Shut up, Duncan." She said it without heat, so Trace knew they were kidding around.

"Stevi's a little bit like Leah. She feels bad for dateless guys, so she goes out with a lot of nerds. Lot of old dudes who've lost their wives."

"Twice." Stevi mouthed the word to Trace and rolled her eyes. "I went out with Grant Deavers last night, Duncan. He's not so nerdy, is he?"

"No, he's a walking steroid, Stevi," Duncan answered without hesitation. "The dude could probably bench press my car," he told Trace. "Looks like one of those body builder types. Kind of looks like he forgets most of his leg days, though."

"I like his legs just fine," Stevi said simply.

"Yeah? Was he all oiled up for you? How does that work? Do you slip and slide on him?"

Stevi snorted and then laughed out loud.

"You are terrible!"

Duncan looked up at her with a grin. "Hey. The guy's a tool. Only one reason you're going out with someone like that."

"So, can I ask you guys something?" Trace cleared his throat to pause their banter. Both of them turned to him,

Duncan still with a satisfied smirk on his face, probably for tagging Stevi, and Stevi looked as if she was trying not to be amused by a seven-year-old's bad jokes. When she looked at him, though, her face lit up with curiosity.

"Oh my god." Her mouth hung open in shock.

"Stevi?" Margo called from the top of the steps.

Stevi scooched around on the barstool so that she was on her knees and leaning over the bar. "Just a sec, Margo."

"Can you come—"

"Just a second! Be right there."

"You wanna swim in my new cocktail recipe, Stevi?" Duncan was clearly amused, but Trace also noticed that from Duncan's angle, Stevi's cleavage was probably on display. Trace laughed softly and shook his head.

"So?" Stevi asked Trace. "Really? Already?"

"Too soon?"

Flustered now, though he wasn't exactly thinking about engagement rings as Stevi thought he was, Trace stuck his hands in his pockets and rocked forward in his shoes. Since they'd been working on the stage, and since Trace had been down here at the Queen working in daylight hours in general, he'd started wearing cargo shorts and tennis shoes. Leah had informed him she liked his legs— she loved his legs—but she missed the jeans and the way they molded his butt.

"Does it feel like it's too soon to you?" Stevi asked him

quietly. Duncan, still adding dashes of this and that to his concoction, hung on every word.

"Every second that goes by is too long to wait." He shrugged.

"Oh, God," Stevi moaned. "I'm glad Leah found you, but I want a man like this, Duncan. God, can you find me a man like Trace Dixon?"

Duncan raised his eyebrows. "Kiddo, I don't know a man alive who could handle you." He shook his head and then added, "And I don't mean handle you the way Grant Deavers handled you last night."

Stevi groaned and turned her attention back to Trace.

"It's not too soon for me," he told her. "I feel like my whole life has been leading me to this. To Leah. I'm just afraid I'm rushing her."

He expected Stevi to argue with him, to push him to buy a ring, and pop the question if for no other reason than she loved the romance playing out in real life. Then again, they had just talked about the way Leah was happy with him and still broken for their friends.

"She always wanted a summer wedding." Stevi bit her lower lip. "Something small. Lots of flowers, but not anything too...perfect. Natural. Simple. She wanted a summer wedding, a house of her own with the guy she married, and three kids. Because she said there were times when we were kids when she was mad at me and she wished she had another sister or brother to play with."

Stevi met his eyes and laughed. Trace's whole body vibrated with Stevi's words. She wanted three kids. *Leah wanted kids.* So why had that changed?

"Then again, we had Margo, so maybe she'd be okay with two kids if they had cousins." Stevi glanced at Duncan and shrugged.

"Don't look at me," he argued. "Not dad material here, and Margo's already got a kid."

"Mm-hmm." Stevi nodded. "A kid who has *not dad material* Uncle Duncan wrapped around her little finger and is well on her way to having Uncle Trace wrapped around the other one."

Trace liked the sound of that.

"I was thinking more of a..." He sighed and shook his head. "I think for Leah, it's too soon for a ring. But something."

"Something less scary than an engagement ring and something a little less obnoxious than a cowgirl hat that she can wear when she's at the Queen that lets all the guys out there ogling her know that she's taken."

"That." Trace nodded at Duncan.

"Wow." Stevi looked at Duncan with big eyes. "You *do* get it."

"I do," he agreed as he picked up his shaker to mix all the liquors he'd just poured. "Try this."

"You kidding?" Stevi eyed the glass he poured the new

drink into and pushed toward her dubiously. "I gotta get up those stairs to see what your stepsister needs me for."

"I'll carry you," he told her. "Fireman's carry. Throw you right over my shoulder."

"Wow," she said again. But Trace watched her pick up the glass and sip from it. "Oooh. That's good."

"I'm good." Duncan winked at her. "Drink more and tell me your thoughts."

Stevi's laugh this time bordered on wild and flirtatious. "Duncan, you might run the other way if I drink all of this and start telling you my thoughts."

"You're right. I might." He nodded, but he propped his hands on his hips and watched her take another drink, a pleased look on his face.

"Trace, Leah likes white gold," Stevi said as she slid cautiously from the barstool. "And of course, we all love diamonds."

"Anything else?"

"Pearls," she answered. "But nothing…stodgy."

Trace raised his eyebrows and nodded. "Great. Nothing stodgy. What the hell does that mean?"

"If you're looking at necklaces, go with a pendant, not a string."

He considered that and shook his head.

"He's thinking rings," Duncan told her.

"How do you know that?" Stevi and Trace asked at the same time.

"Because she's behind the bar a lot. And she's waiting tables a lot. And people see her hands. He wants everyone in the Queen to see that his woman has a ring on her hand."

Trace blinked at him silently. Duncan was exactly right. No diamonds yet, but he most definitely wanted to put some sort of ring on her finger.

"How do you know that?" Stevi asked him again.

"Because if I had a woman here, I'd feel the same damned way."

"Duncan, guys don't ogle us—"

"Stevi, if there's a guy in this bar that doesn't ogle you," Duncan leaned over the bar to make his point, "or Leah or Margo, he's blind."

CHAPTER 35

Leah hesitated at the door of Stevi's car. It felt like the humidity was in triple digits already, and the temperature was climbing quickly. The thermometer on the dash of Stevi's car said 88, and the forecast was calling for a high of 95. While the sun had a way of making the world bright and cheery, Leah could do without it today.

"What's wrong?" Stevi asked over the top of the Acura.

Leah rested her hands on top of the door, but she yelped and pulled them away when the hot metal burned her.

"Do you smell that?" She sniffed and then shuddered at the smell of decay in the air.

Stevi took a deep breath through her nose and flinched.

"Yuck." She stepped away from her car and looked back at Leah over her shoulder. "Something's dead."

Leah swallowed down a wave of nausea and followed Stevi across the parking lot. She glanced at the loading dock of the neighboring business as they passed it. Whatever was dead had curled up just under the dock for its last breath. Leah saw fur and blood. She grabbed for Stevi's hand as her stomach heaved in protest.

"What?" Stevi whirled around immediately, fingers curling around Leah's protectively.

"Something's dead right there." Leah shuddered again and hurried past Stevi on wobbly legs. Stevi stood a few seconds longer to stare at the dead animal. Leah rushed to the back door to wait in the shade.

"Should I call animal control?" Stevi wondered as she joined Leah at the door. Leah's stomach still rolled; the coffee and eggs she and Stevi had shared with Trace before leaving the house threatening to make a reappearance. She watched Stevi's face as her sister unlocked the door, and then she hurried into the cool, dark space the second Stevi pulled it open.

"You okay?" Stevi asked quietly.

"Yeah." Leah shivered. "I'm fine. That just really got me."

"Should I call animal control or just call Duncan?"

Leah moved on through the back room to the main bar. Because they were planning to stain the stage today, she had pulled on old athletic shorts and an old Def Leppard concert t-shirt, and she'd pulled her hair up in a messy twist. She tossed her purse on the barstool nearest the door and slipped behind the bar to grab a glass. Her hands shook a bit as she filled it with water and sipped it.

Without ice, the water was tepid, but maybe that was better. She wasn't tempted to gulp it down, which would surely be a bad idea right now.

"I don't know," she mumbled when she realized she hadn't answered Stevi. But when she turned to look at her, Stevi already had her phone to her ear and her other arm crossed over her middle.

Leah took a deep breath and sipped the water. The eggs this morning had tasted a little rubbery, but Stevi and Trace hadn't seemed to notice. In fact, Trace devoured a plate full of scrambled eggs. It helped to be out of the sun; that was certain. In an effort to control her breathing and settle her stomach, she paced the length of the bar twice and then carried the glass to the front window to study the stage.

It wouldn't take them that long to stain it. It was a small stage in a small area. The design was a little bit intricate; Duncan and Trace had used a router to put some fancy notchings in the wood, but that wouldn't make a difference in applying the stain and varnish. Leah had been excited about working on it before today. She was anxious to do some sweating over it, to say that she had contributed to the project, as they all had with every step they took at the Queen. Also, she had looked forward to hanging out with Stevi. Margo had offered to come in and help, but Stevi had told her to stay home with Berkley. Leah agreed that Margo should be with Berkley, but at the moment, the dead animal most likely still stinking up the area behind the bar, Leah wanted nothing more than to be back at home. Maybe in bed. Drapes pulled. And a cool cloth on her forehead.

"So." Stevi's voice was far away again. Leah blinked and looked back over her shoulder, but she didn't see her sister. "When does he write?"

Leah swallowed another wave of nausea. She carried her glass back to the bar and flinched when Stevi turned the lights up.

"That work?" Stevi called. Leah saw her near the back door.

"Yeah. That's good." She looked up at the golden lights over the bar and the sconces on the wall behind the stage. The lighting would have been best outside, but the guys had built the stage inside with part of it adjacent to a wall, so they were stuck with working indoors. She sipped the water and then took another deep breath when Stevi approached her, a gallon of stain in her hand. She carried the brushes in her other hand.

"I called Duncan." She harrumphed as she set the can down in front of the stage. "He said he'd take care of it."

"Good."

Leah watched Stevi head to the supply room in the back, most likely to get something to jimmy the gallon can open. She should've done that, but the thought of going back near the door and the dead thing was enough to make her feel faint again.

"So does he have a set time, or does he just write when he gets the urge?"

Stevi tossed a handful of rags and a tarp down on the floor and then squatted beside the can. Leah watched her tap a hammer on the end of a screwdriver and then lift and set the top of the can on a rag.

"He kind of does both," Leah answered her. She took the tarp and spread it out over the hardwood and then picked up a brush. "Like, whenever he has something in his head, he grabs anything he can find to write it down. He wrote something on a brown paper bag the other day. But there are times when he gets down to business, too. Ya know? Like sits down with his guitar and with the lyrics he's working on. I think there are times when things are really smooth for him, but there are times when…" Leah shrugged. "He said it's like sometimes he goes fishing, but the river's run dry. And it's more like work, then. But he'll stay at it for a specified amount of time."

"It's kind of cool, don't you think?" Stevi eyed Leah and then dipped her brush in the can.

"Trace?"

"Well, yeah. I mean…everything about watching you fall in love with him has been fun," Stevi said with a grin. "But just…the process. Knowing what goes into the songs we hear, the ones that we like. The songs that yank our hearts out or the anthems that we live by."

Leah nodded. "It is."

She admired Trace for his songwriting. Not just as a starstruck fan, because she would definitely say she would be a fan of his music, his songs, even if they weren't involved. Sure, it was easy to get caught up in his stardom, to hang on his words when he talked about meeting Sam Cassidy and Tommy Archer. Margo had come undone when he told them about rubbing elbows with Roni Matthews and Christina Folgers. But that stuff was only skin deep, and while Leah was human enough to think it was cool and somewhat exciting, she admired the man who wrote the music. The man who lived a life that inspired him to write. The man who loved all genres of music and who experienced life to its fullest and had that innate ability to express emotions everyone feels, but everyone thinks they feel alone. Trace Dixon's songs reminded people—at least they reminded her—that everyone loves and everyone loses, and kindness and heart make life more enjoyable.

"He loves you so much." Stevi sounded dreamy and distant. Leah watched her for a moment and wished that her sister would find someone to love her the same way. If that was what Stevi wanted. Hard to tell, really. Her little sister used to daydream about falling in love with the perfect boy and getting married. Stevi wanted a family; at least, she had always said she wanted a family. Leah wondered now if that had changed, and if so, why. Same reasons Leah's dreams had changed or had Stevi just become a new person? Granted, her sister had changed a lot since they were younger. Leah didn't believe anyone could say the same of her.

"He does."

"I mean. It's just...Leah, it's...I just want you to know I'm happy for you guys."

Brush dipped in the stain can, Leah eased forward to her knees and crawled to the corner of the stage. She dabbed at the base but froze suddenly as a new concern hit her. Her stomach rolled again, but she ignored it. She looked at Stevi over her shoulder, watched her sister working on the other end of the stage.

"What?" Stevi finally asked her. "We should have turned some music on. Do you think?"

Leah wasn't sure she wanted music on right now. Between the heat, the stench just out the back door that had made her sick to her stomach, and the smell of the stain, her head was pounding now.

"Stevi?"

"Hmm?" Stevi flicked her eyes toward her, but she looked quickly back at the brush in her hand. The two of them were perfectionists, and Leah knew that in a minute or two, Stevi would give her heck for interrupting her when she needed to pay attention to what she was doing. A little something they owed to their dad.

"Trace didn't…" Leah barely shrugged her shoulders. "He didn't say…something to you, did he? About us?"

Stevi peeked at her again and then went back to the brush and the stage and the stain. Leah waited, and a few seconds later, Stevi stopped what she was doing and focused her attention on her.

"What?"

"I mean…" Leah licked her lips. "About future plans?"

Stevi eyed her silently, almost suspiciously, Leah thought.

"Um. No." Stevi tipped her head. The frown on her face was so severe, it was almost comical. "But, he did just pack up and move here from Nashville, Tennessee. And he's living in our house. Sleeping with you."

Leah nodded. It was enough. Before—well, if she couldn't be honest with herself, she had a problem—before what had happened with Kenzi and Joe and Edison, she wanted a husband. And a family. Three kids, she had always told Stevi, so that when one got mad at one brother or sister, he or she would always have a spare sibling. Now, the idea of being pregnant scared the hell out of her, and so the thought of Trace wanting marriage and a family scared her. She didn't want to disappoint him. She didn't want him getting any ideas about rings or engagements, because she couldn't marry him.

She shouldn't have let him give up his life in Nashville to come up here. Well, if she was going to think in shouldn't haves, might as well start at the beginning. She shouldn't have fallen in love with him, and when she realized she was very much in love with Trace Dixon, she shouldn't have told him so. And she should never have invited him into her bedroom.

The throbbing in her forehead suddenly so intense she couldn't bear it, Leah groaned softly. Another wave of nausea rolled over her; like the ocean waves when she'd stood on the beach just a couple of months ago, each one was stronger and bigger.

"What?"

Leah closed her eyes and breathed deeply, but it didn't help. She swallowed hard and cracked her eyes open a smidge to look at Stevi.

"What's wrong?" Stevi asked quietly.

"I'm gonna..." Leah grimaced as it hit her again. She shook her head and set her brush down on the tarp near the can of stain.

"Leah?"

She stood quickly, but then she wobbled in place for a second, and finally she dashed back through the Queen to the ladies' room. Glad she was dressed in ratty clothes and tennis shoes—as lightheaded as she felt right now, she couldn't imagine that short run in anything other than tennis shoes—she crashed into the bathroom, hand flat on the wall, groping for the light switch.

"Leah?" She heard Stevi call, her voice much louder than it would be if she was still at the front of the bar. She didn't particularly want to be sick in front of her sister. Who did like an audience when they were bent over a toilet, covered in sick sweat, throwing up and feeling like death?

She reached down to lift the seat of the toilet and opened her mouth to answer Stevi. But her stomach heaved, and this time, she gagged and coughed and vomited. She supposed it was the breakfast she had eaten not so long ago, but she squeezed her eyes closed to steady herself.

"Holy cow." Stevi rubbed her hand on her lower back, the same way their mom had always done when they were little girls and they were hit with the flu. If Leah's hair was down around her face, she knew Stevi would pull it back for her. As humiliating as it was to be in this position with someone watching, it was also comforting to know her sister had her back. She would certainly do the same if their roles were reversed.

"I'm sorry." Her voice was a cross between a thick whisper and a low, guttural moan. She started to straighten, but another round of nausea racked her body, and she leaned over again. There wasn't as much to throw up this time, but she waited to make sure she was done. Spit a couple of times, though nothing she could do would get rid of the taste in her mouth.

"Here." Stevi reached forward and pressed a tissue into her hand that now cradled her stomach. "Wipe your mouth."

Leah did as Stevi told her. Shivered in disgust as she crumpled the tissue and tossed it in the toilet. Her hand shook as she reached to flush, and then she straightened. Not sure if that was it—yesterday, she'd thrown up three different times before she came downstairs—and also, embarrassed and afraid to look at Stevi, she stood for a moment and took a slow, deep breath.

"You okay?" Stevi's voice was gentle.

Leah took another deep breath and then swallowed to test her stomach. Her knees were weak, and she was covered in a sheen of sweat, but she thought her stomach was okay for the moment.

"I'm gonna go get you some water." Stevi stroked her hand

up over Leah's back and rested it between her shoulder blades. "Okay?"

"Thank you." Leah nodded. But Stevi only leaned around her and put the seat and the lid down.

"Sit. I'll be right back."

"I'm fine."

"You're green," Stevi said simply. "Sit down for a second. I don't want you to pass out while I'm gone. I'd rather not have to scrape you up off the floor."

Leah laughed softly. "I can still pass out if I'm sitting down. And then, I might fall backwards into that corner. Imagine scraping—"

"Sit. Down." With gentle hands, Stevi turned her away from the toilet and then pushed her shoulders to make her sit. Leah's legs trembled as she eased herself to a sitting position. Still skittish about meeting Stevi's eyes, she covered her face and rubbed her eyes as her sister backed slowly out of the room.

It was almost funny, definitely ironic, but she felt like two-day old road kill and didn't have it in her to laugh again. Not even a quiet chuckle. Since being in the birthing room with Kenzi, she'd been scared to death of this. Probably every woman to ever carry a baby the first time feared the unknown. Not just the day-to-day surprises during a pregnancy. Not just the exhaustion. The weird craving for foods at particular times—though Leah hadn't experienced that yet. The need to pee a bucket or two every hour. The worry that the baby was healthy. But surely every woman—even those who were excited to be pregnant, those who welcomed a foreign little body inside theirs—got twitchy nervous about the actual delivering of that baby. The unknown. No amount of diagrams in an ob-gyn's brochure or on their office walls could tell anyone exactly what the experience would be like. Didn't matter if a woman watched ten different birthing scenes either in popular movies or sex ed classes in high school. You feared labor and delivery at least until you experienced it, and Leah figured some women feared it every time. Sure, it was a beautiful experience, pushing a baby out of a body. A fully-developed little human being. Giving life to that precious little human being.

It was also terrifying, because so much could go wrong.

Like, the mother could have a stroke.

"Here."

Eyes closed, Leah didn't realize Stevi had returned. She jumped slightly, still feeling a bit weak, and the whole moment—everything in the Queen right now—felt surreal. She blinked her eyes open and stared at the glass of water Stevi held out in offering.

If the cat wasn't out of the bag yet, it was definitely clawing at the opening to get out. Stevi wasn't stupid. Leah wasn't stupid, either, and though she'd played hard at denial for the past couple of weeks, she'd known exactly what was going on. She was on the pill, so when Trace made love to her the day after the first time—when she'd known without a doubt that they were together forever—she'd suggested they didn't need condoms. She had known he would enjoy sex more without them, and she liked it better without the barrier, and she was on the pill, so she'd assumed they were safe.

Leah sat up straight and breathed deeply through her nose. She fought the urge to lick her lips, afraid of what she would taste there. She smoothed her hands over her shorts and then shuddered when she hit the cool, clammy skin of her legs. Still avoiding Stevi's eyes, Leah took the glass from her and sipped.

"Why are you here?" Stevi propped herself in the doorway and crossed her arms over her chest. She spoke quietly, which sort of made Leah feel better, but sort of worried her more.

"What?" Leah took another small drink.

"Is it really a good idea?" Still calm, Stevi stretched her leg out and nudged Leah's shoe with her toe. "Inhaling the fumes of the stain?"

Leah started to argue. She opened her mouth to inhale and then to speak, to argue. To deny. But the words wouldn't come, and then to her horror, her eyes filled with hot tears, and her chest ached so badly, she couldn't breathe. It was almost worse than that dizzy, sweaty anticipation she'd just felt standing in front of the toilet, ready to vomit.

"Stevi." It was all she could manage. And even that was enough to break her. She sobbed softly, but when Stevi moved to squat in front of her, Leah shook her head and pushed Stevi away.

"Why didn't you tell me?"

"Lemme out of here," Leah whispered. "Please?"

Stevi reached for her hand, and Leah stood, linked her fingers with Stevi's, and let her sister lead her out of the bathroom. The cool air in the main part of the bar kissed her skin and made her shiver. Still weak, and now outed and afraid and uneasy about all of it, Leah stared at Stevi, willing her to make it all better.

"You shouldn't be in the building right now." Stevi groaned and looked back toward the stage. She threw her hands up helplessly. "Why don't you just call Trace? He'll come and get you, and maybe Duncan can help me. Then again—"

"No." Leah's firm answer seemed to startle Stevi.

"I can probably just do it my…" Stevi's words trailed off. She stared at Leah with wide, disbelieving eyes. "Leah."

"No." She shook her head. "I'll call Margo."

Stevi pursed her lips and finally let out a long, loud frustrated groan. "He doesn't know?"

"No."

This time, Leah's voice was just barely a whisper.

"Why not?"

Leah swiped at her eyes. God, she hated to cry. The only thing she hated more than crying was crying in front of someone. Which is what had driven her to run to Destin, to isolate herself from her friends and family, and cry over Kenzi and Joe's tragedy. To cry over her own broken dreams and ideas. And that desperate attempt to deal with something her sister and her cousin had handled just fine —like fully emotionally mature adults—had led her through Tennessee, to Nashville. To Music City.

To *Nashville*. Her heart.

Why hadn't she told Trace what she suspected?

"Stevi, I can't have this baby." She spoke through clenched teeth. She wobbled again on her feet and reached out for something to hold onto.

CHAPTER 36

STEVI STARED AT HER FOR A MOMENT WITH BIG DOE EYES. Leah gulped down a burst of nerves. In all the years that she and Stevi, and sometimes Margo, had played house and pretended to be married either to cute boys from their classes or their celebrity crushes, in all the times they'd stuffed their dolls under their shirts and pretended to be pregnant, none of them had ever uttered anything close to what Leah had just said.

The moment frozen around them, Leah was suddenly aware of the silence. Now she wished for music. Or a room full of bar patrons. Or a do-over of the past few weeks. She didn't want to wish Trace out of her life. Just the baby. Maybe if they could go back to the first night they'd spent together. When they awoke the following morning, instead of stopping Trace when he reached for a condom, shaking her head when he had looked at her in askance, she would let him go. Help him roll the protective barrier over his erection before taking him inside her body. Or if she could rewind to the time she had apparently forgotten her pills. She'd been wrecked emotionally after what had happened to Kenzi. She'd taken off to Florida and left half of her belongings here. Her swimsuit. Her toothbrush. The birth control pills. She had come home with the same nightmares, the same sadness, and the same guilt—what right did she have to feel this way, when it was Joe and Kenzi dealing with the stroke and the damage it had caused—and she'd been in such a funk, it had taken her ages to remember her pills every morning. Obviously, she'd taken longer than she thought to get back into that routine.

At the time, it hadn't mattered.

Right up until Trace Dixon showed up at the Queen and swept her off her feet, it hadn't mattered if she was scatterbrained and careless with her birth control. She hadn't had a man's body inside hers in at least six months, if not longer, and she hadn't believed she would let herself be involved with Trace Dixon.

She was no smarter, no more mature than a sixteen-year-old girl who thought having sex one time, the first time, without protection, wouldn't hurt.

Stevi stared at her like she'd just announced that she was thinking about selling the house and moving to Mars. Leah felt a swell of regret. Of course, she *wanted* this baby. This baby was a miracle she and Trace had created together. But that didn't mean she could *do* it. Just because she and Trace Dixon had been blessed to find each other and then to make a child together, that didn't mean she could carry it to term and then deliver it.

It.

She flinched and looked away from Stevi's accusing stare.

"Why—?" Stevi stopped herself. She cleared her throat, gave herself a mental shake, and looked around the Queen. "Let's go upstairs."

"What?"

"Let's go up and sit down."

Leah waved her hands out at her sides. "Chairs right here, Stevi."

Stevi seemed to consider what Leah said, but then maybe not, because after a few seconds of silence, she shook herself again. Only this time, she shook herself hard as if to loose some wicked thought from her head. Maybe to swallow her feelings, her words. Eyes averted, a look of tired resignation on her face, Stevi stepped forward and took Leah by the hand again.

Maybe Stevi should be the older sister. She was certainly acting more maturely than Leah. In fact, Leah wanted to stop. Just stand here, as if her feet were planted in the hardwood floor, and stretch Stevi's arm as far as it would go, and then pout and refuse to follow her when Stevi looked back at her.

Because going upstairs meant sitting in the office. On the couch. And sure, it sounded comfortable, and Leah was tired—again. But it would mean Stevi could sweep in with the platitudes. The promises that Leah would be fine. That just because something bad had happened to Kenzi didn't mean anything bad would happen to Leah.

She would insist, too, that Leah tell Trace.

Leah didn't want to hear any of it.

But she followed Stevi upstairs, because the smell down here was getting to her again. She still had that headache, though her stomach had settled finally. As Leah had known she would, Stevi led her into the office. But once there, she took the water glass from her and put it on the desk.

"C'mere." She turned to Leah and before Leah could say a word, Stevi gathered her in her arms and held her. It was an awkward pose, and not because Leah was the older sister, but because she was so much taller. Still, it was comforting for a moment to lean on Stevi. When they pulled away from each other, they both moved toward the couch and dropped to sit on opposite ends.

"You wanted an outdoor wedding. And you were going to go to Greece for your honeymoon, which I always figured had something to do with that movie. The one about the girls who shared the pair of jeans." Stevi drew her knees up and rested her chin on them. "When we were little, that's all there was to it, of course. To the honeymoon. When you were eighteen, we didn't play house anymore, but you told me you were going to have hot sex in Greece, with your husband."

Leah stared at Stevi silently.

"And then after the honeymoon, you and your husband would come back home. He would be a doctor. You were going to be a lawyer, if I remember correctly. And you were going to have three kids."

"Yeah, well, you were going to run for mayor, remember?"

"True." Stevi shrugged.

"Is that what all of your dating is about? Looking for votes?" Leah felt bad the second the words were out of her mouth. She winced and started to apologize, but Stevi simply shook her head.

"This isn't how I imagined learning about my first niece or nephew."

Already sick with guilt over what she'd said downstairs—that she couldn't have the baby—and sick about carrying the secret suspicions around for two weeks, Leah ducked her head to her hands to hide. Tears wet her face and her fingers, and she hiccupped a tiny sob.

"How can you love him like you say you do and not tell him you're pregnant?"

The word was so heavy it dragged Stevi's voice down to a low throb of a whisper.

"I do love him," Leah argued. She rubbed her eyes and looked up at Stevi.

"I know you do." Stevi nodded. "Margo and Duncan know it. Mom and Dad know it. He knows it. So how can you keep this from him?"

"First of all, I don't even know for sure—"

"Leah." Stevi tilted her head and stared at her as if she were her mother instead of her little sister. "Maybe you haven't seen a doctor yet. Maybe you haven't even peed on a stick yet—"

She hadn't. Peed on a stick. Because she and Trace were living in close quarters now. Sure, her bedroom was spacious and her bed was big—not that it mattered, because she loved sleeping up against him with his arm around her—but the bathroom was tiny. Not much bigger than a small closet. There was no way she could buy a home pregnancy test and use it without him noticing it. In fact, she sort of thought it was amazing that he hadn't noticed she hadn't had a period this month. Unless it was just new to him, living so closely with a woman that all of those private things hadn't yet become quiet, simple shared knowledge. She knew he awoke every morning with an impressive erection that had nothing to do with her. She knew that erection was a pain in the butt for him in the bathroom. But if he had noticed a lack of feminine products used or even that she hadn't begged off sex or said she had cramps, he hadn't said anything.

"His brother wants him to go out on tour with him."

"I think Trace has made it pretty clear how he feels about his brother."

"Stevi, listen to yourself. They're brothers. They're like you and me. And they had a falling out. I don't want that to be the end of Trace's relationship with Tanner."

"So...what? You have him move in, and then you're gonna kick him out to live on the road? You think he wants to be living on a tour bus, when he's got you and the house and the Queen?"

Leah shook her head and breathed deeply. She swiped at her wet eyes and then looked back at Stevi.

"No. He doesn't want that."

"But you do?" Stevi's frown was one of genuine confusion. "You're gonna chase him away? Now?"

"No." Leah rubbed her fingers over her neck, her throat aching with the knife of emotion. "I don't want him to go anywhere. But I don't want him to walk away from his brother. They used to be close. His mom wants them to work things out—"

"I know!" Stevi nodded eagerly. "Leah, I know. He's talked about this. But what does it have to do with anything? Even if he did a show or two with Tanner, this is home now. You are home for him."

"I can't do it." Leah sniffled. She touched the tip of her tongue to her upper lip and dragged her eyes away from Stevi. "I can't have this baby."

"And what? You're...gonna push him to leave with Tanner? So you can get rid of it?"

"Of course not!" Leah yelped. "God, no, Stevi. No."

She moaned softly, the horrible thought a pit in her stomach. A huge, yawning pit that threatened to swallow her and the baby, and then there would be nothing left for Trace at all.

"Then what, Leah?" Stevi shook her head. "What's your plan?"

Leah squeezed her eyes closed and smoothed her hands back over her messy hair. She didn't have a plan. What Stevi suggested was horrifying. She wouldn't abort a baby.

No matter who it belonged to. She couldn't just terminate her pregnancy. And yet, she didn't plan to carry it to term and deliver it, either.

"I don't know!" she wailed. "Stevi, I don't know what to do!"

"What happened? Why are you so—?"

Leah opened her eyes when Stevi stopped talking.

"Oh," Stevi said with a slow nod.

"What?"

They both jumped when the phone on the desk rang. Leah blinked the office into focus and wondered who would be calling the Queen. Stevi patted her hips and looked at Leah curiously as she climbed up from the couch. Leah slumped over on the couch and watched Stevi take a few nimble steps over to the desk and snatch the cordless handset off the charging base.

"Mississippi Queen."

Leah mentally braced herself, though for what, she couldn't say. It didn't matter in the least who was on the other end of the line. No one but Stevi knew what she suspected. Well, she supposed it was beyond suspected now.

"Sure. Yes. Thanks." Stevi carried the phone back to the couch and sat down. "Oh. Our phones are downstairs... Leah's—"

At this, at whatever was about to come out of Stevi's mouth, Leah felt the blood drain from her face—her whole upper body, really—and pool in her gut. Her lungs went the other way, pushed up into her throat, and she struggled to breathe. Who was Stevi talking to?

"She got a little overheated. And that smell got to her...I think he's working?" Stevi looked at Leah and phrased that last part as a question. "I think he said over breakfast this morning..."

Leah's stomach rolled at the mention of breakfast.

"Awesome. Thanks, Duncan."

She clicked the end button on the phone and dropped it in her lap. It took her a second to look at Leah. Made Leah feel even worse that her little sister was disgusted with her.

"Duncan scooped it up," she said in a flat, quiet voice. "It was a cat."

Leah moaned and clutched her stomach to ride out the nausea again.

"You're scared." Stevi still spoke quietly, but there was a hint of concern in her voice this time. "Of—"

"I'm just not ready," Leah argued. She wasn't ready to admit to her ridiculous fear of something women had been doing since the beginning of time.

"Yeah? You're thirty. Remember that?"

"Margo was thirty-two."

"You have it now!" Stevi roared. She pushed off the couch and paced the office. "You have everything you wanted.

You have your education. You have a career in a great place. And you have the greatest guy so in love with you. And you're not ready?"

Leah swallowed hard. "I'm sorry."

"Don't *I'm sorry* me!" Stevi reached the far end of the room and turned back toward Leah. She threw her hands in the air in defeat. "I'm not jealous. I'm not angry that you have it all. I'm angry that you're being a coward."

"Stevi."

"I get it. You're scared."

"You weren't in that room when it happened."

"No, I wasn't. And I'm sorry that you were. I'm sorry for Kenzi and Joe, and I'm sorry for you. But just because it happened to her doesn't mean—"

"You're afraid of spiders."

Stevi shrugged. "I am. So I avoid them. You're stuck. You have a life growing inside of you, and you either have to call the women's clinic and take care of that. Or you have his baby."

"She was talking to Joe. She was ripping on him. Giving him hell. No more sex until he was fixed. And then she started shaking. She couldn't talk, couldn't say—"

"And she was thirty-five. She smoked more cigarettes than I could afford to buy on a week's paycheck. And she had high blood pressure. She was high risk. Her doctor told her when she found out she was pregnant that it was a high-risk pregnancy."

"Mom told us not to play in the street, because we could get hurt. So we don't. If I can avoid—"

"Okay, sure if you never got pregnant, you could stay safe. Avoid any possibility of this. Adopt a kid. A dog." Stevi shrugged. "But you got pregnant, Leah. You know you're pregnant."

Leah climbed to her feet and lumbered away from Stevi, every step as heavy as if she wore chains on her shoes.

"How'd you let this happen?" Stevi whispered.

"It's my fault?"

"I'm not the one who wants to blame someone," Stevi answered. "Because I'm happy for you guys."

Leah stared Stevi down, but her sister only raised her eyebrows and offered her a weak smile.

"I forgot my pills when I went to Destin," Leah mumbled.

Stevi tipped her head. "Are you sure this is—"

"And..." Leah sighed. "I guess I was just....messed up. Emotionally. Took me a while to get myself together once I came back home. Forgot to take them."

"Really?"

"I found the last half of May and part of June's supply in the medicine cabinet the other day."

Stevi's mouth dropped open in surprise.

"Yeah, I'm an idiot. So freaking upset over Kenzi's thing that I ran away and so traumatized that I forgot to take the pill for several weeks. Putting me right in the spot I most wanted to avoid."

Stevi took a step backward and perched on the edge of the desk.

"Trace is the only guy I've been with since way before last Christmas."

"You have to tell him."

"What if he thinks I did it on purpose?"

"He won't," Stevi promised her. "Because he knows... you've made it no secret to him that you don't want kids. And second, I don't think it would matter anyway, because he wants you and the house and babies and puppies and a cabinet full of Gerber baby food and soccer vans and—"

"Stop." Leah shook her head. "Please, stop."

"What're you gonna do?" Stevi pressed.

"I don't know, but you have to promise me that you let me handle this."

"Leah."

"I'm serious, Stevi. Please keep this between us."

Stevi sighed and toed at the floor with her shoe.

"You can't just wish this away." She looked at Leah with narrowed eyes. "You get that, right? You're gonna start showing. And you're with me and Margo and Duncan every day. You're sleeping with Trace every night."

"I know that." Leah nodded. "I just need some time."

"Okay." Stevi stood. She reached half-heartedly for Leah, but her hands dropped to her sides and left Leah cold and lonely. "But the longer you wait, the harder it's gonna be to justify keeping it from him at all."

CHAPTER 37

July in the Midwest was brutal, and business flourished with the stage and—though he argued about it —Trace's presence at the Queen. First of all, word got around fast that Trace Dixon had moved to town. Leah got a kick out of the first few times she'd overheard snippets of conversations about him. Some people claimed it was all a hoax, the way so many of the Facebook and other social media stories about celebrities are a hoax. Others believed that he'd moved to Adam's Bay, though they didn't know exactly why. And still others—definitely regular patrons at the Queen who had become friends—knew Trace Dixon was here because of Leah Hague.

They had more music acts interested in performing there now, too, and they all knew—even when Trace denied it— that the sudden influx of interest was about the fact that Trace Dixon was at the Queen every night. Maybe some were connected to Trace to begin with—Leah loved watching him reconnect with people he'd met on the road or in Nashville—though Leah figured a lot of them were coming out of the woodwork to sing at the Queen just in case Trace Dixon had connections to push them further along in their careers. That had bugged her at first, but Trace had shrugged it off and reminded her it was simply the nature of the business. Leah supposed he was right. Someone had heard Trace's first song and liked it and pushed for someone else to listen to it and to like it and share it, until it snowballed and Trace Dixon, the songwriter, was born. He seemed genuinely interested in helping others the same way. Leah had been tempted to bring up his ex, but she realized before she opened her mouth that it was a different situation. Trace's ex had manipulated him to get to Tanner. She'd slept him with him, probably promised him the same things Leah promised him—the difference being that Leah meant everything she said to him with her heart and soul.

Leah spent the few weeks with Trace worrying and wondering if people would say he had made a mistake in coming here from Nashville, in giving up stardom for a girl like her. Surely, there were people out there who said so, but she didn't hear them. She also held her breath almost constantly, worried either that someone else—Trace—would figure out her secret or that Stevi would spill the beans. Each night she went to bed with him, curled up in Trace's arms, Leah resolved that tomorrow was the day she would tell him.

Each morning, she found a new reason to chicken out.

Funny thing, though. Stevi pointed out that as long as Trace was living with her, he was going to figure it out sooner rather than later. Leah had never been a heavy drinker, so no one had noticed—so far—that she'd stopped drinking altogether. She might let Margo pour her a glass of wine or Trace pull a beer, but she always opted for water and left the alcohol set, mysteriously forgotten.

The longer she waited to tell him, the bigger the issue it would be when he did figure it out. Not the pregnancy itself, but the fact that she hadn't told him.

Still. She held out, as if by some miracle she would wake up one day and realize it had all been a bad dream. Or maybe not a *bad* dream, because if it was a *dream*, she could be happy, excited about the baby.

Stevi alternated between hovering over her—and with that tenderness came an excitement about being an aunt that made Leah feel guilty—and shooting daggers at her for keeping the baby a secret. From everyone, most especially from Trace.

Trace holed up in the office sometimes when they were at the Queen. He scratched out lyrics like a strung-out druggie at two in the morning. He played riffs and chords and sang lines all day every day, and Leah learned the joys —and frustrations—of songwriting. And loving a songwriter. On days—or nights—when she heard him struggling, she went to him to offer support or comfort. Or sex. He spent the small hours of the morning in the basement, and though there was a portion of it that was finished, Leah and Stevi didn't spend much time there, so hanging out with him there was a new experience for her.

He fielded phone calls and text messages. He made his own calls. He checked email daily. He changed his address and got checks in the mailbox, and finding his mail in her mailbox filled her with a contentment that she figured was ridiculous and even childish. He talked to Pearl daily, though the woman kept those phone calls short and to the point. He talked to Angie and Kadie often, but then, Leah did, too. They'd moved from stories about Trace—Leah liked the one about the night he broke a guitar string, kicked over a bottle of water, and then bumped his microphone over, all because of a sexy girl watching him from the bar. Leah had eyed him with humor as Angie shared the story, and Trace promised Angie had mixed stories together, because there had been one night when he'd done those things—he was young and there was a record producer there, not a sexy woman—and the sexy woman story was actually much more recent, when he'd gone to the bar to talk to her and she'd simply said she wouldn't sleep with him.

She told him one night, curled up in his arms on the couch in the basement, that she was afraid. It was after three in the morning, and the basement—finished only with a remnant of oatmeal-colored carpet, the couch Stevi had brought with her when she had moved in, and an end table and lamp—was damp and chilly. When they had come in earlier, home from the Queen, Trace had climbed the stairs to her room with her and kissed her goodnight. She had wanted to make love, but she was so exhausted she couldn't keep her eyes open, and Trace had noticed. Instead, he tucked her in, kissed her forehead, and took Loretta down to the basement. But she had only slept for an hour at the most, and when she awoke, still tired, she wanted to be near him. He had been sacked out on the basement couch, Loretta in the stand he had brought here with him from Nashville. Leah had watched him for a few moments, overcome with the need to smooth his hair off his forehead and kiss his cheek and hold onto him. Boots toppled over on the floor at the end of the couch, Trace slept on his back, one arm thrown up over his face. Leah had tiptoed around to peek at him, to look at the angles of his face, thrilled that she could just see his right eye under his arm. His long, thick eyelashes and the dark stubble over his cheeks and his neck made her want to reach out and stroke her fingers over his face. She let her eyes roam over his broad shoulders in the pale green t-shirt he wore, over his hips and down over his long legs in the well-worn denim.

When he spoke, his voice was gravelly, and his lips twitched as if he'd seen the way she had jumped even with his eyes closed. He had asked her if she liked what she saw, and she had laughed and eased herself down to lie half on the couch and half on him. She reminded him that their bed was bigger; Trace had grunted something about how he liked the sound of that, and she told him then.

"It's not that I don't want to have your babies, Nashville," she had whispered into the night, lit by the golden glow of the lamp. "I'm just scared."

"I know, darlin'." He had lowered his arm to slide it around her and pin her there against him, and she opened her mouth to say more, to tell him, only to feel his chest rise and fall in a deep sleep. Instead of saying it, instead of confessing to him that she was pregnant, she had slipped her hand under his t-shirt to touch his warm skin and gone back to sleep in his arms.

Maybe she should have tried again the next morning, but the lamplight wasn't cozy in the daytime. And Stevi was in the kitchen when they had come upstairs for coffee. Trace had gladly accepted the mug from Stevi, dropped a quick kiss on Leah's upturned face, and gone upstairs to shower.

Joe had taken to calling the Queen just to catch them all at the same time. He called late mornings, and they gathered around in the office to catch up on Kenzi's progress and to hear the latest about the kids. Leah introduced Joe and Trace via speakerphone and when Kenzi said Trace's name—except she called him Nashville—the lot of them laughed and cried together.

Leah thought of the calls as therapy sessions, right down to the fact that she was hiding something huge and pretending everything was fine. Seemed like any character in a movie or book who went to therapy to get better only sabotaged herself by keeping the very secret that had driven her there in the first place. Margo said she felt like *Charlie's Angels* when they all gathered in the office to talk to Joe and Kenzi.

Trace adjusted to life around the Queen easily, but Leah doubted it was much of a stretch since he had helped

Pearl and Sampson with nearly every aspect of running Left Fork. Leah asked him a couple of times if he missed performing, but he would only remind her that he wasn't a performer. Never had been. She decided he was happy, and he did step up behind the mic every now and then, sometimes to sing a line or two with their musical talent for the evening or to fill in for someone who couldn't make it. He'd even played a few nights for the hell of it, even when they hadn't advertised live music at the Queen.

After the phone calls from Joe—he usually called on Wednesdays, as Kenzi had a break in her therapy schedule on Wednesday mornings—the five of them went about their business. Leah had pushed Stevi into helping with the wine tasting and schmoozing the distributors. She was more than happy to inventory what was in the cellar and order when something was low, but she passed all the new stuff to Stevi to taste and decide if they wanted to stock.

"Wait." Trace took her hand as she straightened in front of the desk. Stevi shot Leah a look over her shoulder as she followed Duncan out of the office. Margo and Berkley were in the break room; Berkley was shrieking and giggling that delicious baby laugh. Leah realized when her eyes met Stevi's that she had crossed her arm over her stomach, and she dropped her hand to her side as she looked back at Trace.

"What?"

Afraid that he had somehow guessed that she was keeping something from him, Leah bit her lip. He stepped closer to her and put his arms over her shoulders.

"I have something for you," he told her.

Leah eyed him curiously and then looked around the office. Stevi would spend the day working on the fall and winter special events schedule. Hard to believe it was that time already, but Stevi had reminded her they had two big parties scheduled already in September, an art festival that would happen in October to align with the city's Octoberfest celebration, and with the sudden jump in popularity, it really wasn't too soon to start thinking about holiday events. The thought had given Leah a headache.

Duncan had probably already left. He had planned to spend the day in St. Louis at a trade show for liquors and cordials. Leah thought he should have left earlier, but he got caught up in Joe's phone call and stuck around. The trade show and tasting event was a two-day thing, so Duncan would stay there tonight. Leah supposed if that were the case, he didn't necessarily need to be there first thing, so she hadn't questioned him when he slipped into the office in time to say hi to Kenzi and Joe.

"You wanna give it to me here?" She wiggled her eyebrows suggestively and laughed when Trace arched his in response.

"I've got fantasies of laying you out on that beautiful bar downstairs." The grin tugged at the woman inside her. Heat flooded her cheeks, and she dropped her head back to laugh again.

"Okay, you got me there," she admitted. He moved closer and nibbled on the exposed skin of her neck.

"You wanna know what I would do to you on the bar?"

"Mmm." She cleared her throat. "I do, but no, because we have all damned day and night here, before we can be alone."

He drew away from her and watched her with an intensity that lit her on fire.

"So do you want it?" he asked her. Eyes glazed a bit with lust, and his voice low with desire, Leah wobbled backwards to lean on the desk again.

"Oh yeah." She took a deep breath, but she was laughing again. "I do. Dammit, I just told you I do."

"Not that." He rolled his eyes.

"Sure." She nodded, but when he reached into his hip pocket, she held her breath. Looked up to meet his eyes when she saw the black velvet ring box.

"Nashville."

"It's okay." He shook his head. "Darlin', do you really think when I propose to you, I'm gonna do it like this?"

Heart still hammering uncontrollably in her chest, Leah offered him a lame shrug and a small laugh.

"No?"

"Make no mistake," he cupped her chin in his hand, "that's happening. But not now."

"Okay."

"Just something I wanted to give you," he continued. "To remind you I love you. And to remind all those guys that belly up to the bar night after night that you're with me."

Leah tried to swallow, but her mouth was dry. She lifted a hand to cover his and turned her face to kiss his palm.

"I thought that's what the cowgirl hat was for."

His laughter was genuine, and Leah reveled in the way they could tease and love each other all at the same time.

"You mentioned that the hat messed your hair up," he reminded her.

"Gave me hat head." She nodded her agreement.

"Well." He rubbed his thumb over her lip and then let go of her. She watched him pop the box open and then marveled at the stunning pearl ring nestled inside the velvet pillow. "I promise you this is gonna be gorgeous on your hand."

Leah blinked, but there were too many tears to hold them all back.

"It's beautiful," she whispered, too awestruck to speak louder.

"Will you wear it?" he asked. Leah watched Trace's usually nimble fingers—the same fingers that plucked wire strings and made beautiful music and played her skin and her body and made her *feel* beautiful—fumble with the delicate band of silver.

Leah lifted her eyes from the ring and realized he was

watching her. Tears streaked her face as she held out her left hand to him.

"Yes." She pressed her lips closed as he took her hand and slid the ring up over the knuckle of her ring finger. She felt a pang of excitement for their future, for the day Trace put a wedding ring there, though looking at the pearl now she couldn't imagine anything prettier, anything she would like better.

"How did you know?" she whispered. Eyes back on the ring, she fluttered her fingers and felt the movement—definitely just nerves—in her belly. She *had* to tell him about the baby.

"Stevi," he answered. "She said you love pearls, but she warned me it couldn't be something stodgy."

Leah laughed and swiped at her eyes.

"It's perfect."

"Not stodgy?"

"Not at all."

He moved in to hold her, and Leah threw her arms around him to hold on.

"Nashville," she whispered against his shoulder.

"Hmm?"

"I need to tell you something."

"Okay."

Pressed face to face, his five o'clock shadow rough against her cheek already this early in the day, Leah breathed deeply. His simple, clean cologne was familiar and comforting. She could do this. She could tell him. And as long as they were together, she could have this baby.

"I should have—"

"Leah?" Margo's frightened shout sent them jumping apart from each other. "Leah? Can you come here?"

She met Trace's eyes, and without a word, they both turned to rush out of the office and down the short hall to the break room.

"What happened?" Leah gasped as she ran inside the room. Margo stood with her back to the door, head bent over her hands, over the sink. Berkley smiled up at them from her high chair, cereal and maybe apricots smeared from ear to ear.

"I didn't know…" Margo whispered.

"Margo?" Leah stepped closer to the sink, but Margo turned a bit, and Leah saw that she had a handful of blood. "Oh, Margs. What did you do?" She tried again to go to her, but her stomach twisted and pitched and rolled into her throat. She ducked her head and pressed her mouth to her shoulder.

"I didn't realize there was a knife in the sink." Margo's voice was weak. "I sliced—"

"Lemme see." Trace gently edged Leah out of the way. He moved in close to Margo to examine her hand. Leah heard him grunt, and Margo sucked in a quick breath.

Berkley banged on the tray of her chair and let out a string of babble that sounded a little bit animated and a little bit serious, too.

"Where's Stevi?" Leah mumbled. She needed to tend to Berkley. To get her out of the chair and wash her face. But maybe first she would just run to the bathroom and throw up. Again.

"She decided to go with Duncan."

Leah had turned her back to them at the sink, because if she saw the blood again, all bets were off, and she would lose it all over the floor. But she glanced at Margo now as if she hadn't heard her correctly.

"Okay. Leah?" Trace looked back at Leah. He did a double take and looked at her with a frown. "Are you okay?"

"Yeah." She nodded. "I'm good."

"You're green."

"It's the blood," she whispered. Her stomach convulsed again, and she winced as she clutched at it. She silently begged Margo not to say anything, not to ask her what she was talking about. She had never been one to faint or to get sick at the sight of blood.

"Okay. You stay with Berkley. Okay?" Trace arched his eyebrows. "You stay with her, and I'm gonna take Margo to the ER. I think she needs some stitches."

Leah nodded. "Okay."

She looked away as Trace wrapped Margo's hand in a

clean dishtowel, the crimson stain spreading through the white cloth immediately.

"Sorry…" Margo mumbled as Trace turned her toward the door. "Leah—"

"We'll be fine," Leah promised her. "Just get the blood out of here."

CHAPTER 38

WHEN TRACE HUSTLED MARGO OUT OF THE BREAK ROOM—funny how he moved so swiftly without rushing Margo and making her panic—Leah battled down her nausea and then plopped down in a chair next to Berkley's highchair. Hoping to calm herself—she knew Margo would be okay, even if she did need stitches, but Leah's body was still on fight-or-flight mode—Leah drew in several deep breaths and released each slowly. Berkley's big blue eyes watched her every move, her thin, barely-there eyebrows sliding up and down in rhythm. Leah laughed softly when it hit her that Berkley was trying to mimic her deep breathing.

When Berkley saw that Leah found her funny, she squealed with delight and patted her cheeks with her fat, little hands.

"Oh goodness, kiddo." Leah winced as those little hands pushed up into the black ringlet curls that covered her head. "You're making a mess."

"Mum mum mum mum." Berkley scrunched her shoulders up and cackled when Leah chucked her chin with her finger.

"Mum?" Leah leaned close to drop a kiss on Berkley's head. "You want Mum?"

"Mum." Berkley grinned.

"Mum will be back," Leah told her. "What do you say we wash that pretty face?"

Leah wasn't sure if Berkley's sweet little babble was agreement, but since she was smiling, she decided to go with it. She stood, rocked back and forth a bit to test her knees, and decided she was okay.

"Were those good apricots?" she asked as she squeezed the levers on the highchair tray. Berkley lifted her arms as Leah reached down to unbuckle the little safety belt. It hit her, as she hauled Berkley up from the highchair and settled her on her hip, that it wouldn't be long before she would be holding her own baby. A baby she and Trace made.

A baby she had been about to tell him about when Margo yelled for help. Remembering then that Trace had just put a ring on her finger, Leah rested her cheek on Berkley's head and held out her left hand to admire the ring. Might not be an engagement ring to the rest of the world—not even to Trace, since he would probably go to the ends of the earth to make it a special, romantic affair when he did give her one—but it was to Leah. This ring marked her as committed to Trace Dixon, not that she needed any material things to be committed to him. But it told the rest of the world that she was in love with someone, and that she was living her own happily ever after.

Berkley reached her hand out to touch the pearl. Leah grinned and turned her face just enough to brush a kiss over those black curls.

"Pretty?"

"Mum."

"Well," Leah laughed softly, "yes, Mum's pretty, too."

She stifled a wave of disappointment. She'd been ready earlier to just tell him. To come clean and to bear the weight of Trace's disappointment, maybe even his hurt feelings because she hadn't told him sooner. And now she would have to pull herself together again to share news that shouldn't make anyone afraid or anxious.

Still holding Berkley on her hip, Leah moved efficiently to grab a small washcloth from the cabinet and wet it with warm water. Berkley twisted and fought her as she smoothed it over her little heart-shaped mouth.

"Let's read a story," Leah suggested as she folded the washcloth and set it on the back of the sink. "I bet you have a book in your bag, huh?"

Berkley's grin was back now that Leah was done washing her face. She patted her hand over Leah's lips as Leah made her way back to the table, where Margo had left the diaper bag. Leah breathed deeply, inhaling through her nose, and slowed her hands for a moment. Beneath the smell of the fruit and cereal Margo had just fed her,

Berkley smelled like baby shampoo and lotion, maybe with a touch of lavender.

She dug into the bag and immediately closed her fingers around a little board book.

"Oh, animals," Leah said as she pulled a little board book out to examine it. "Sounds good to me."

"Me." Berkley nodded.

"You?"

"Me."

Leah carried Berkley on her hip and the book in her hand back to the office where she sat down on the couch to snuggle Margo's little girl. She opened the book to read, and Berkley plopped her hand on Leah's arm. Leah started reading, but overcome with emotion, she stopped for a second. What was she carrying? Would she give Trace a sweet baby girl to capture his heart or would she give him a son?

"So. Wait." Stevi shook her head. "You did what?"

Margo, head back on the couch with her eyes closed, groaned softly.

"Cut my hand."

Stevi shot a look at Leah as if to say *is she for real?* Leah shrugged. Trace had stayed with Margo at the emergency room while the doctor there sewed her up. Leah had read to Berkley and put her down for a nap in her playpen right there in the office with her. Margo was pale and clammy when they came back, her hand—wrapped in white gauze—as big as a boxing glove. Leah had insisted she go home, that she and Trace and two guys they had recently hired could handle a Wednesday crowd with no problem. Margo had agreed; she'd asked her mom for a ride home and an overnight babysitter. Leah supposed the rest overnight had helped, but it might take a few days for Margo to feel up to working at all. She had asked her mom to bring Berkley home, but Leah suspected she regretted it now. Mothering a baby was definitely a two-handed job.

Leah had waited for Duncan and Stevi to get back in town before leaving the Queen to come by and check on Margo. Fortunately, they opened late enough in the afternoon that it didn't matter when Stevi left Trace and Duncan there to follow Leah over to Margo's house.

"I was washing some dishes." Eyes still closed, Margo's voice was small and flat. "I forgot the knife was in the sink."

"Why was that big knife in the sink?" Stevi glanced at Leah again.

"Because I cut that pineapple up," Margo reminded Stevi. "I picked the knife up and had my hand around it before I realized what I'd done."

Stevi shuddered much the same way Leah had the other day when she'd seen the blood pooled in Margo's hand.

"What made you decide to go with Duncan to the trade show?"

"Wasn't much of a trade show," Stevi argued, but she added a shrug. "I dunno. He sort of threw it out there, and since it's usually quieter on Wednesdays and now that we have more help—"

"It's fine, Stevi," Leah interrupted her. "I'm just curious."

"What I learned is that I'm not much of a bourbon drinker, but I'd choose it over scotch."

"Your top choice is always gonna be cold beer." Margo opened her eyes. Leah watched her wiggle her fingers, her wrist propped on a bed pillow at the end of her couch.

"You got it," Stevi agreed.

The three of them turned to look at Berkley—parked in her bouncy seat—when she sailed her pink dragon rattle across the floor.

"I'm gonna have to ask Mom to take her again tonight," Margo mumbled. "You should see the diaper job I did on her. Ever change a diaper one handed?"

"Can't say that I have." Stevi arched her eyebrows.

"Which reminds me." Margo's voice was suddenly louder, and she scooted around to sit up straighter on the couch. Leah drew her eyes away from Berkley to look directly at Margo.

"What?" Leah covered a yawn with her hand and then stretched in the recliner across from the couch. "You need diapers? Anything else? I'll go to the store for you."

"No." Margo shook her head. "Actually, I'm wondering why you got so pale yesterday. You looked like you were gonna barf all over the table in the break room."

Leah licked her lips. Heat rushed her cheeks, and her heartbeat pounded in her ears. The longer she scrambled for an explanation, the less likely Margo was to believe anything she said.

"Um. If you remember right?" She tipped her head and eyed Margo with a calm she didn't feel. "You had a handful of blood. Like, it looked like something out of a slasher movie."

"Except it was just in my hand and not all over the walls and my face."

"True." Leah nodded.

"And I had clothes on."

The three of them laughed, but Margo wasn't ready to let it go.

"Yeah, well, I remember a time when Stevi was about five, and she fell and cut her head on the steps. You were seven, and you were like the medical director. You totally handled it, while your mom flipped out."

"Margo—"

"And the time my mom got the sewing needle stuck through her hand? Remember that? She was making Halloween costumes for us, and you and I were in her sewing room and we were playing, and she kind of gasped in pain. We looked up and saw that needle in her hand. I got all clammy, and I threw up on the carpet. You were all calm, and you hollered at my dad. And then you mothered me all night—"

"Is there a point?" Leah asked her with a deadpan expression.

"Because she might deliver the kid before you get to it." Stevi stretched her feet out on the couch and leaned back.

"Stevi!"

Stevi shrugged. "Leah, she knows. It's not that hard to figure out. She's right. Nothing makes you queasy. You could do brain surgery while you eat lunch. And you got lightheaded the other day when Duncan had a splinter in his finger."

Leah sighed and groaned softly.

"Does he know?" she whispered.

"What?" Margo snapped, her voice so shrill and loud, Berkley jumped. Stevi scrambled off the couch to rescue her as her eyes filled and her lip quivered.

"Duncan doesn't know, but pretty soon, everyone's gonna know."

"You're pregnant?" Margo watched Stevi haul Berkley up to her shoulder and pat her back, and then she looked back at Leah.

"Yeah." Leah nodded. "I am."

"Like. You're late? Or you're pregnant?" Margo pushed. "Like you peed on a stick pregnant?"

"I'm late, and I peed on a stick, and my ob-gyn says I'm pregnant."

"Wow." Margo mouthed the word. "Why didn't you tell me?"

"She hasn't told anyone." Stevi turned to look at Leah, accusation in her eyes.

"She told you," Margo reminded her.

"She got sick at the Queen. I was there."

"Why keep it a secret? I think you and Trace will be awesome par—"

Leah looked away. Guilt was a knife in her throat at the moment, so there was no point in trying to speak anyway.

"You haven't—?" Margo sounded exasperated. "He doesn't know?"

Leah kept her eyes on the floor. With a weary sigh, she smoothed her sweaty hands over her thighs and then covered her ring with her fingers. Not to hide it, because Margo and Stevi had both seen it, of course. But to remind herself that yesterday had happened. That Trace loved her, and even though she had been wrong to keep this from him, she would tell him tomorrow, and things would be fine.

"No."

"Why wouldn't you tell him?"

Leah swallowed hard and lifted her eyes to meet Margo's.

"Does he not want kids? Because he's awesome with Berkley."

"He wants kids." With the guilt still stuck sideways in her throat, Leah's voice was only a whisper.

"Then what the hell is the problem?" Margo threw her hands up in frustration. Her sudden wince shot a blade of sympathy through Leah.

"Take it easy," Stevi reminded her.

"I'm gonna tell him tomorrow."

"Tomorrow." Stevi repeated with a nod. "Right. How far along are you now, Leah? Because—"

"I was gonna tell him yesterday," she started. When Stevi rolled her eyes, Leah climbed from the recliner to plead her case. "Listen? Please?"

"I'm so mad at you." Stevi shook her head. "I get that you're scared, Leah. But who better to be with you through this than Trace?"

"Scared of what?" Margo asked. Leah and Stevi turned to watch her slide to the edge of the couch and climb unsteadily to her feet. "That he'll be mad? Why?"

"Scared of the baby." Stevi looked at Leah.

"Are you afraid of my baby?" Margo asked Leah. "I mean, you just...you'll know. It's the scariest damned thing in the world knowing you have a tiny life completely dependent on you, but you'll know the minute—"

"Kenzi." Stevi dropped the name quietly, but it shut Margo up.

"Oh." Margo winced. "Oh. Honey. It's not…that's not gonna happen to you."

"You think Kenzi went in to deliver Edison thinking it would happen to her?"

"Kenz was a basket case, Leah. She had high blood pressure. It was off the charts before she got pregnant. You're healthy."

"I just wish…" Stevi rubbed the bridge of her nose. Berkley, thumb in her mouth, rested her head on Stevi's shoulder, face turned to her neck. "I just wish you would tell him."

"Look." Leah drew in a deep breath. "I see Dr. Hendricks tomorrow—"

"You just said you were gonna tell him yesterday."

"Can I finish? Please?" Leah tipped her head at Stevi and continued when Stevi nodded, "I see my doctor tomorrow. Hopefully, I'll have a due date. She did do a blood test to confirm the home test, but I haven't actually had an appointment with her yet. I planned to talk to him after that. But when…" She pushed her hair back from her face and then lowered her hand to look at her ring. "When he gave me the ring…I knew I had to tell him then. Because…it's wrong to keep him in the dark, regardless of how long I could get by with it. He should know."

"Amen." Stevi shrugged. "So why didn't you tell him?"

"Because I sliced my hand open," Margo answered with a look at Leah. "Right?"

Leah answered with a half-hearted nod.

"You could've told him when they got back to the Queen."

"We were rushing to get things done then. Getting ready to open."

"How about last night? When you crawled into bed with him?"

Leah licked her lips and shook her head. "I was so tired…"

"I don't get it," Stevi muttered. "I don't get why you're keeping it from him. You're living with him. You're in love with him. You can't hide it forever. He's asked you to marry him—"

"It's not an engagement ring," Leah argued, but Stevi's no-nonsense look was overbearing, so she closed her mouth without saying more.

"I'm just really disappointed in you, Leah," Stevi whispered. "You've never been a coward."

CHAPTER 39

TRACE SWIPED THE SWEAT FROM HIS BROW AND PULLED AT
the flaps on the case of wine. He wondered what time it
was. Leah should be getting here soon. He pulled two
bottles of the cabernet from the sleeves in the box and
eyed the rack in the cellar. This one was Leah's favorite.
The thought of watching her sip a wine she loved, the
look of pleasure on her face, made him smile. The thought
of putting that look of pleasure on her face made him
hard. Again. She'd been a little bit frisky this morning, not
that he was complaining.

He heard someone on the steps. Figured it was Duncan,
so he wiped the goofy grin from his face and continued to
stock the wine. After they made love this morning, he had
made coffee and then run through the latest melody he
had written while Leah showered. Dressed in bright red
capris and a loose white eyelet blouse, she had come
downstairs to kiss him goodbye. She told him she had a
few errands to run, but she also told him she wanted to

talk to him about something when she met him at the Queen later. Normally, that whole scene might make a man balk, but Leah's smile and the sparkle in her eyes promised that whatever she wanted to talk about would be okay with him.

"Your brother got a big-ass tour bus?"

Hunkered down between the case and the wine rack, Trace lifted his head to look up at Duncan when he peeked around the rack. He thought it was funny now that he had wondered what sort of relationship Duncan and Leah had before he met them. The guy was like a big brother to all of the women here, and Trace liked him for that and just because he was an okay guy.

"What?"

"Tanner. Big, fancy tour bus? Sleek and silver?"

Dread tap danced over Trace's chest, hit him square in the heart. Slowly, he stood. Eyed Duncan warily.

"Yeah."

At least the last he had seen of Tanner and the bus, it was sleek and silver and had a lightning decal down the side. Trace didn't want to know how much the bus had set his brother back, though he guessed it was an obscene number. He also wouldn't be surprised if Tanner had already traded up. The guy was full of himself, and his ego knew no bounds. Trace just hoped he had some good liquor and a few loyal friends around if and when things went bottom up. No one stayed at the top forever. Sooner or later, there would be an up and coming wannabe that would at least threaten Tanner's star status.

Trace sure didn't plan to be around to nurse him back to life.

"He's parked out front."

"Come again?" Trace shook his head. He rubbed his hands on his khaki shorts and then propped one on the wine rack at his side.

"Big tour bus just pulled up at the curb."

Trace sighed. Yep. That's what he thought Duncan said.

"You gotta be kidding me."

"Stevi's already drooling." Duncan rolled his eyes.

"Just a pretty face," Trace mumbled. "Maybe some decent moves—"

He broke off with a laugh at Duncan's scowl. It crossed his mind again that he might have had things partially right back when he had first found the picture of the Queen's crew online. Maybe Duncan had a thing for one of the girls, but maybe it was Stevi and not Leah. The guy turned and gave him his back before he could ask. Just as well. None of his business, anyway.

Besides, if Tanner was here, he had bigger things to wonder about. For starters, what was Tanner doing here and a close second, how to get rid of him. Fast.

With a groan, he followed Duncan up the steps to the main level of the Queen. He regretted telling Tanner where he was now, what he was doing. Sure, Tanner was passing through the Midwest heading on to the last leg of his tour, so Adam's Bay, Illinois wasn't completely out of his way. By Trace's calculations, he had played Kansas City or St. Louis this week.

Still. Trace had no interest in playing catch up over a cold one. He didn't particularly want Tanner around Leah. Or Stevi or Margo, for that matter. Leah was his. Period. He'd fight Tanner for her, not that he believed Leah would be interested in Tanner or anyone else. But he had no intention of letting his cocky little brother worm his way into Stevi's or Margo's heart or head, either. No way he would let him hurt anyone he cared about. It was bad enough that Tanner's second career in life seemed to be setting their mother up only to hurt her. The guy phoned it in like nobody's business. Lip service, rah rah rah. *Love you, Mom. You're the best.*

Never had time to show up, though. Never had time to slip in a visit to her, even when the band wasn't on tour. Tanner hadn't seen their mother for a holiday in ages—except maybe St. Patrick's Day three years ago. Trace seemed to remember Tanner had accidentally dropped in on their mom in the middle of the afternoon just in time to take her to a corned beef and cabbage dinner to celebrate the holiday at Holy Family's parish center. Mama had been thrilled, but Trace had clocked the stiff smile on his brother's face as irritation later that evening when Tanner brought Mama home and Trace was there fixing a drag in her screen door.

Mama still touted him as the greatest thing since sweet tea, though, and that burned Trace. No way would he let Tanner ingratiate himself with the women here at the Queen.

"What're you doing here?" Trace asked, surprised to find Margo at the bar. God, please don't tell him that Stevi had called her when the tour bus showed up. Tanner was easy on a woman's eyes; even Trace got that. But there were guys here for Stevi and Margo. Trace had seen several ogle both women many nights here at the Queen—not that he loved watching strangers or even familiar bar patrons eyeball Leah's sister and cousin.

Margo shrugged her eyebrows. "I'm behind after being out two days."

"You're also injured," he reminded her. He held up his hands and wiggled his fingers. "Kind of hard to type like that, isn't it?"

She grinned and tipped her head in acknowledgment. "I can make notes. I need to get the menu for the next few weeks squared away."

"Your boss is a slave driver," he teased her. "You know that?"

"I do." She nodded. "Leah back yet?"

"I don't think so." He tapped his knuckles on the bar and finally drew in a long, steady breath. Maybe a shot of something bold from behind the bar would better prepare him to deal with the devil in the street, but Trace had never been one to drink to chase away demons. He had seen too many good men taken over by the bottle when maybe the demons they were trying to outrun would have been easier on them.

"Jess called me last night," Margo mumbled. Trace glanced at the window, but at Margo's muttered admission, he turned back to her quickly. He had never met Jess, and he and Margo had never talked about him directly. But Leah and Stevi and Duncan, all three, had a lot to say about the guy. Rather than comment, Trace studied Margo's face. She was pretty, like Leah, and yet, she didn't look a lot like her. Darker hair, green eyes, and thin lips added up to a pretty face. She wasn't quite as tall as Leah, and her hips were just a touch fuller.

Right now, the dark skin puckered around her eyes made Trace wonder if the pain in her hand had kept her awake last night or if the phone call from Jess had done it.

"You okay?" he finally asked her.

She met and held his gaze. Parted her lips, as if to answer him, and then closed them and answered with a dramatic shrug. "I don't know."

"Leah hasn't said much about him," he admitted to her. Was that a good thing? That Leah hadn't shared Margo's secrets? Okay, yes, Trace cared about Margo and wanted to be in the know. But maybe Leah had been sworn to secrecy, and it should make Margo happy that Leah had been trustworthy.

"He loved me." Margo propped her elbows on the bar. "And just about every other woman he met."

He winced.

"I kicked him out after I had Berkley."

"So he knows about her?"

Margo nodded. "Yeah. Missed her birth, because he was drunk. Hitting on some woman at a hole-in-the-wall bar on the south end of town."

"I'm sorry."

Margo's eyes filled. She offered him a tired smile and then shook her head. "I'm fine. Just tired."

Trace eyed her for a moment, knowing it was obvious that he was doing a visual assessment.

"What's he want with you now?" Trace leaned into the bar. True, he would avoid the scene in front of the bar as long as possible, but he wondered if Margo wanted to talk. It wasn't often that she offered up anything personal, and it seemed like a bad idea not to listen when she did.

"Um. He just said—"

"Okay, so, for the record," Stevi announced as she jogged down the stairs. Trace and Margo both swung their attention to her and saw her pointing at the window, and unless she was blind, the bus idling at the curb. "I reserve the right to look. Maybe even to drool a little bit. But I'm Team Trace, all the way."

Trace laughed and opened his arms to Stevi as she hit the bottom step and crossed the wooden floor to the bar.

"Thanks for that, I think." He gave her a quick hug.

"Well, Leah thinks you're the most beautiful man on earth." Stevi turned toward the window again. "I'm inclined to agree with her, but I am a woman. I have to look."

"Sunsets are beautiful." Trace rolled his eyes.

"And puppies are cute." Stevi shrugged, but she kept her eyes on the window at the front. "As I said, I think she's right on this one."

"Right about what?" Duncan asked as he appeared from the back room.

"Nothing."

Trace kept his mouth shut, but he shot Duncan a quick glance. The guy set a case of wine on the floor behind the bar and then straightened and watched Stevi watching for a sign of stardom out front. So far, Trace hadn't seen anyone moving out there. Just the obnoxious bus. He pulled his phone from his pocket to see if Tanner might have called or texted, but there was nothing there but the picture of Leah he'd taken one morning and then set as his wallpaper. Leah in a gray tank, no makeup—which she hated and he loved—and her hair in a messy twist at her neck. She held a mug of coffee in her hands, her natural full lips tilted upward in Trace's favorite smile. It was the one she wore after they made love.

"Leah thinks Trace is better looking than Tanner," Margo told Duncan. Trace snorted and looked at Margo, relieved to see the sadness, the uncertainty gone from her face. He wondered if he should mention it to Leah or not, that Jess had called her.

"Leah thinks Trace is better looking than the rest of the male species," Stevi corrected Margo. "These days, I agree."

"These days?" Trace yelped. "What's that mean? I have an expiration date?"

Stevi laughed softly and looked at him over her shoulder. "It means, maybe one day I'll find my own most beautiful man on earth."

"You stop looking for beautiful and start looking for perfect, babe, and here I am."

Trace and Duncan exchanged a grin.

"You're a doll, Duncan Marks," Stevi told him. "You're also my cousin."

"Good thing for you," Duncan mumbled with a nod. He turned his attention back to the wine bottles he'd carried upstairs.

"Why good thing for me?" Stevi finally moved from her sentinel spot and sidled up to the bar to lean over it and talk to Duncan. Trace found it easier to breathe suddenly, and he wondered if it was because Stevi had given up watching for Tanner or because she was flirting with Duncan.

Seriously? You're worrying about Stevi and Duncan?

Wasn't that a girl thing? Worrying about their friends' or sisters' love lives? He gave himself a mental shake.

"Too much man for you right here." Duncan ducked down

behind the bar now. Stevi cut her eyes to Trace as if to say *can you believe him?*

"Right. You're right." She grinned and winked at Trace. "Leah back yet?"

"Leah's right here." Leah's voice carried from the back of the bar at the same time the driver's door of the bus out front opened and Tanner's driver, Mac Newman, climbed down to street level.

CHAPTER 40

EVEN THOUGH SHE HAD KNOWN—EVEN BEFORE THE HOME test confirmed it—Leah felt different walking into the Queen, seeing Trace with her family, and knowing she was pregnant and due sometime in March. She hadn't heard the heartbeat yet, and there hadn't been an ultrasound yet, but something about talking to her doctor had calmed her fears. Somewhat. The blood test and the pelvic exam were conclusive, and her doctor had listened to her worries about a healthy pregnancy and delivery. Leah hadn't gone into excessive details about her worry over the delivery and Kenzi's experience, but she had mentioned Kenzi and her stroke. Leah knew her fears were irrational, but something about hearing her doctor say so was comforting.

She wasn't sure her feet touched the ground when she left the clinic to head to the Queen. Part of her was so excited now—still scared, but terribly excited—to tell Trace that she had wanted to drop the pedal and speed all the way to the Queen. Gush the words out as soon as she saw him. She couldn't wait to see the look on his face when he heard the words.

You're going to be a daddy.

We're having a baby.

And there was the problem. If Trace were in her position, he would do this with panache. He would make this announcement about the baby something incredibly special. He would either be very sweet and romantic, whisk Leah away for an afternoon picnic in the sun and throw rose petals over a blanket spread out under a shade tree, or he would write a song and strum his guitar and sing to her, just the two of them in their bedroom or down by the river as the sun set behind the bridge.

Or else, he would make it a huge *family* celebration, and he would write a song and play it for them at the Queen. Not for public consumption. Just for the family. He would sing about baby toes and rattles and bottles, and they would all laugh and cry together.

Leah had no idea what to do to make the announcement special the way he would. She couldn't do a gender reveal to let him know, not yet anyway. And she didn't want to wait that long now to tell him. She'd waited far too long, and she only hoped that he would forgive her for keeping it a secret as long as she had. She could make a t-shirt for him or she would make one to wear herself, but again, it would take longer than she was willing to wait now.

She could tell him over dinner tonight. Maybe she would

go out and buy a bottle or something to put at the table with them and wait for him to notice it.

When she stepped inside the back door of the Queen, she saw everyone out front, eyes on the window and the street beyond. Looked like a big silver bullet parked at the curb, but before she could ask what was going on, she heard Stevi ask Trace if she was back yet.

"Leah's right here," she called as she strode deeper into the belly of the bar. Amazing what a little chat with her doctor had done for her confidence about the baby. She was scared, yes, but maybe no more so than any other expectant mother might be at this stage. She realized, too, that her fear would probably triple in size and fade away and grow exponentially before she finally delivered. But at the moment, she felt good, and she couldn't wait to talk to Trace.

In fact, maybe she'd just announce it now. Maybe, she would just throw her arms around him and kiss his neck —the spot below his ear where she would feel his pulse against her lips—and whisper that they were having a baby.

It wouldn't matter to Trace how she did it. It wasn't the fanfare that was a big deal. It was that they had created a baby together, further evidence of their love.

"Hey." Stevi turned to her and grinned. "Put your shades on, woman. The star's about to get out of that bus."

"My star's right here," Leah answered as she stepped up behind Trace. He threw her a crooked grin over his shoulder as she wrapped her arms around him from behind. Covered her hands over his belly. "Mmm." Leah rested her face on his shoulder. Stevi arched her eyebrows in question, and Leah simply nodded.

"Damn."

Leah felt Trace's whole upper body expand on a deep breath. She lifted her head to look over his shoulder just as the front door opened—for a second, she wished it was locked, as if that might stop what was about to happen—and a younger, leaner, cockier version of Trace Dixon stepped inside.

The guy wore a ball cap with the bill pulled low, much the way Trace had the night he had first shown up here at the Queen. But his cap looked brand new, whereas the one Trace had worn, and still did sometimes when he was working, was faded and worn. Leah knew it would take Tanner a few seconds to orient himself inside the Queen, because of the indoor shadows in contrast to the bright sunny day behind him.

"Hey!" Tanner sounded genuinely happy suddenly, and Leah saw the resemblance between the two brothers when a grin split his face. "Trace. Damn, dude. I been chasin' you down for months now."

Again, Leah felt Trace's body expand and then grow tense under her hands and against her chest. She wanted to hold onto him, to shield him from the tension that seeing his brother threaded through his body. But she couldn't. Trace was a grown man, and the last thing he needed was for a woman to think he needed protection.

She squeezed him gently enough that probably no one else noticed, and then she dropped her forehead to rest between his shoulder blades for a moment.

"I love you." She dropped the words and a kiss on the back of his neck and then smoothed her hands over his belly and dropped them to step back and release him.

"Tanner." Trace's voice was lower, tighter, but Leah thought she heard a note of…what? Joy? In his voice. Okay, maybe that was stretching it. But she watched Trace as he and Tanner crossed the old wooden floor. The wood gave up a low groan as the brothers clasped hands and then drew each other in for that shoulder bump men apparently considered a hug. The hint of a smile touched Trace's lips, but it was gone so quickly, Leah almost doubted that she saw it.

"What in blue blazes are you doin' in Adam's What, Illinois, anyway?" Tanner tossed his hands up in question as he looked around the bar again. This time, he realized he and Trace weren't alone, and his eyebrows shot up in happy surprise. "This is a nice place. Bigger and newer than Left Fork, okay. But Illinois? What about the music?"

"Guitars travel pretty easy, Tanner," Trace answered simply. Leah's eyes tracked his arms as he crossed them over his chest. His gray t-shirt molded his shoulders and his biceps and served them up for her to drool over. Before she moved toward him to touch him, to let Tanner know Trace belonged here with her now, she flicked her eyes up over his shoulders and then down over his back and slender hips. Took a moment to appreciate the shorts he wore and the glimpse of his strong, tan legs.

"Mom said you met someone," Tanner announced. "Why am I hearing that from Mom and not you?"

When Trace glanced at her, Leah took a step closer to him again. He held his hand out and slipped his arm around her shoulders. Leah met Tanner's eyes as Trace smoothed his hand over her shoulder and then cupped her upper arm possessively.

"Leah, darlin', this is my brother, Tanner Dixon." He pulled her in a bit closer when he turned his attention to Tanner. "Tanner, this is Leah Hague."

"So you're the Leah who dragged my brother out of Nashville." Tanner sounded a little bit in awe, but Leah wasn't sure if it was about Trace leaving Nashville or her. It wasn't as if she thought she was a great beauty, but from what Trace had inferred, Tanner thought he was a ladies' man. Seemed likely that he would attempt to flirt with her.

"Hi, Tanner." She offered him a smile, reminded herself that the guy might be her brother-in-law one day soon and belatedly stuck her hand out to shake. That good-natured grin made a repeat showing, and Leah felt a pang inside when she saw the resemblance between the brothers again. True, Leah would call that same grin a mix of playful and sexy on Trace's lips, but she could definitely see the family resemblance. Tanner swiped his cap off his head and let it dangle from his fingertips as he shook her hand.

"It's a pleasure to meet you." He sounded sincere. His grip was strong, and he released her hand quickly, making her wonder if Trace was standing at her side, staring daggers at him.

"You guys need a beer?" Duncan called from behind the bar.

"Yeah." Trace kicked into action suddenly, as if he'd stopped breathing for a moment, and Duncan's voice had flipped a switch and set him back into motion. "Yeah. Let's do that."

Tanner nodded.

"Bus okay out there?" He looked from Trace to Duncan and then back to Trace.

Leah started to say it was fine, although she wasn't sure that it was. Technically, there were parking spaces up and down the full block, but they'd never had a tour bus parked there, taking up a good six spots all at once. Not to mention, the bus completely blocked the view.

Trace drew in a breath as if he was going to speak, so when he glanced at her, she nodded. She would go with whatever he told Tanner, unless of course, he suggested his brother climb into the bus and haul his crew back across the bridge. If they hashed out their differences and either called a true or simply decided they couldn't find anything to agree on, Leah would walk Tanner to the door herself. But she desperately wanted Trace to at least give this a shot.

Reconciliation. Forgiveness.

At least a truce.

They were brothers, after all. And despite the hurt that the two of them had shoveled and flung over each other's shoulders, there was something a bit tender in Trace's eyes when he talked about Tanner.

"There's a lot behind the building," Trace told Tanner. "Why don't you move the rig back there?"

Tanner nodded. "Fair enough."

He tugged the cap back on and turned back to the door where two other guys had followed him inside and stopped to wait for further direction. Leah watched Tanner's boots—shiny black and silver, like his bus—thud back over the floor. His jeans looked newer, too, though thankfully the pockets weren't studded or embroidered with fancy clubbing designs.

Not impressed, she took a quick breath and turned to Trace. Surprised to find him watching her, she offered him a soft, private smile. Leaned into him and patted her hand over his chest.

"Talk to him," she said quietly. "Please?"

"You sticking around?"

She arched her eyebrows. "I'm gonna go upstairs and get some work done. You guys catch up for a while. Maybe we can all grab something to eat before we open."

"I'm not gonna leave you for him." He threw the words out like a challenge, but they drew a sharp peal of laughter from her lips.

"Nashville, that's the weirdest thing you've ever said to me."

He folded his arms over his chest and eyed her quietly.

"You have this insane idea that I'm a performer, and that I need that lifestyle. And I don't. Just reminding you I have everything I need right here at the Queen."

"Here ya go." Duncan set two mugs on the bar. Leah looked over her shoulder at the foaming beers and shot a look at Stevi, expecting her to make a comment about Duncan giving good head. Stevi met her eyes, and the unspoken words passed between them. They laughed softly.

"Don't let her fall for him," Trace warned Leah.

"She's not gonna fall for your brother," Leah promised him. "Holler at me in a while."

"I'm gonna check the meal prep for tonight," Stevi announced as she slipped out the back of the bar.

"He's easy on the eyes," Leah told Trace. "But he's not you."

She felt Trace's eyes on her as she moved away from him and climbed the steps to the office.

CHAPTER 41

THEY SAT AT THE BAR FOR A WHILE, HE AND HIS BROTHER, talking about the business. They steered clear of any talk about Shelly, because Trace didn't care if she was currently sitting out there on Tanner's bus waiting for him or if she'd already jumped from Tanner's jeans to someone else's. Duncan came and went as he stocked items behind the bar. Trace introduced him to Tanner, though he knew Duncan didn't give a damn who he was. Trace wasn't sure there was much around here that could pique the guy's interest. Except for Stevi, but that was a story best saved for another time.

Tanner caught Trace up on the latest who's who in Music City and the studios. Trace listened patiently, but it dawned on him about fifteen minutes into the gossip that he didn't care. About any of it. He did sit up and listen closely when Tanner discussed playing the latest song Trace sent him. The Congregation had picked it up quickly—as usual—and they were ready to run with it.

Tanner's eyes were wide and happy as he talked about the guitar licks and the bluesy melody, and Trace found himself nodding along. He wanted to hear it. Damned if he didn't want to hear Tanner and the band play the latest piece.

"You remember when Mama grounded me when I was a sophomore?" Tanner said out of the blue.

"Like I could forget?" Trace snorted. Shoulders hunched now, arms folded over the bar, he rolled his eyes "You and your buddies stole the principal's car, Tanner."

Tanner's laughter was wild and free, and the sound took Trace back to the days when they'd been boys living at home. Before their dad died.

"But Mr. Stanton didn't report it." Tanner shrugged.

"Only because Tug Stanton was in on it." Trace elbowed his brother. "He wasn't gonna have his own son arrested. And anyway, all the parents involved agreed to ground you guys."

"Yeah, well, Mama stuck to that agreement. None of the other moms did."

"Mama's tough," Trace reminded him.

"You're not wrong." Tanner nodded. "Look, Trace."

Tanner's tone suddenly went from proud amusement to hesitant and heavy, and the realization that he was about to start digging about something Trace would rather leave alone goosed him and sat him stiff and uptight in the barstool. Duncan stood at the computerized cash register behind the bar, back to them and head bent over the keyboard. Trace shot him a quick glance, uncomfortable with the idea of having any serious discussion in front of him. Well, that wasn't entirely right.

He was uncomfortable with the idea of having a serious discussion of any sort with Tanner, audience or not.

"Mama read me the riot act."

Heels of his hands shoved into his eyes, as if he could hide from whatever it was Tanner was going to throw down, Trace sighed and groaned. What was Tanner talking about now? He dropped his hands back to the bar and shook his head before sliding a *what-the-hell* look at his brother. Was he still talking about the sophomore class incident?

"What?"

"About Shelly."

Their eyes connected, and Trace almost vibrated with the intensity in his brother's gaze. He groaned out loud, because Shelly was old news. Shelly had never been the true problem; it had always been about how willing Tanner had been to take the women who had used his brother into his life and his arms and his bed and how indignant Tanner had been that the whole thing had pissed Trace off.

"What?" Trace said again. He flicked a glance at the register, but Duncan was gone again. "Tanner, I'm happy here. I'm not leaving—"

"Let me finish." Tanner stared straight ahead, though Trace doubted he was checking himself out in the mirror above the bar. Not this time. Though it pained him, he pressed his mouth closed and watched Tanner twist his lower lip between his thumb and forefinger. The gesture threw Trace back a good twenty years to when Tanner was a skinny, knobby-kneed kid, nervous about stepping into the batter's box and facing Elijah Willer's curveball.

"I was wrong—"

"She's all yours, Tanner."

Tanner shook his head and dropped his hand to the bar. "She's actually long gone, but that's—"

Trace bit back the sarcastic laugh and waited.

"I sent her packing, so no, it's not what you're hoping."

"Tanner." Trace sighed, irritated that his brother had decided to sweep into his life again and taint the Queen just by sitting here with him at the bar. "I haven't been sitting around hoping she would find something bigger and better—"

"Let's leave size out of it." Tanner's lips quirked up in a quick smile, but he turned serious again instantly. "I just. She was a gold digger, and I saw that real fast. And no matter what was between you two or wasn't, it was wrong of me to…"

"Sleep with her?"

Tanner shrugged, clearly uncomfortable.

"Look, I'm just saying." Tanner sucked in a deep breath and then grimaced like he'd swallowed something bad. "The whole situation was my fault, and I apologize."

"Because Mama read you the riot act."

"Yeah." Tanner tipped his head. "No. No. I'm a dick. I get it. But you're my brother. I was wrong."

"'kay." Trace nodded. "We good, then?"

"No, because I want you to know that Mama did let me have it. I know you think she babies me—"

Trace's eyebrows jumped so high, he thought he might have gained an inch of height.

"Okay." Tanner tossed his hands up. "She babies me. But she let me know in plain damned English that I was a jerk—"

"I prefer dick."

"I do, too, but Mama only uses that word when she talks about Dick Arnold at church," Tanner said with a shrug. "You do no wrong, Trace. And she holds me to your high standards."

"Yeah, well, you'll never reach them."

"Don't I know it?" Tanner nodded enthusiastically. "I just. She loves you. And I think she worries you ran outta Nashville just to get away from her and me and the whole damned thing."

"I left Nashville and I ran here, because my whole damned life is right here in this building."

Tanner nodded again. "Fair enough."

"We good?"

"I need you." Tanner huffed out a long sigh. Trace watched his shoulders hitch and then tense up, as if the fear of saying those words had locked them up tight.

Trace shook his head. "I just moved up here. I am in love with that queen you just met."

"Nialls Hennessy's out of commission," Tanner continued. "Permanently."

"Oh, hell no—"

"Hear me out?"

"You hear me, Tanner Dixon." Trace slid off the stool and turned to his brother as he did. "I am not leaving that woman. Ever."

"Zeek Frame is tied up through the end of July." Tanner rubbed his hand over his face and then knuckled the bill of his cap until he knocked it off. Grabbed it and squeezed the bill in his hands as he eyed Trace. "We've got Chicago. Des Moines. Milwaukee. And Indianapolis. I can pick Zeek up in Columbus when we swing south."

"Four shows?"

An apologetic shrug accompanied Tanner's quick nod.

"You want me to walk out on this life and give you what? Three weeks? Are you kidding me?"

"Tops."

"Dammit, Tanner."

"Nialls has severe nerve damage in his hand," Tanner explained. Trace tuned him out. Three weeks. Not even a month, and yet, a day away from Leah was a day wasted, as far as he as concerned. Twenty-one days—at least, and Trace knew somehow it would work out to more—sounded like the end of the world.

"I just got her that ring," Trace told his brother. "It's not an engagement ring. Not exactly. Because I know she's not ready for that. But it might as well be, because I'm damned sure going to ask her to marry me, and I know it, and everyone here at the Queen knows it, and Leah knows it."

"I'm in a bad situation, Trace. Naills is done. And I gotta play the day after tomorrow in Chicago. If I can't replace him until we pick Zeek up, I'm gonna have to start cancelin' shows."

Trace winced. He combed his hair—still on the long side, as he hadn't taken the time to find someone to cut it here yet—and then wrapped his fingers around the back of his neck.

"You heard of Connor Drake?"

Fingers still wrapped around the back of his neck, Trace lifted his gaze to meet Tanner's. Of course, he had heard of Connor Drake. The kid won best new artist last year in the world of country music.

"That guy's crawlin' up my ass, Trace." Tanner's quiet voice took on an edge of desperation. "He won best new artist, and you know damned well, he's gonna be up for song of the year with that damned ballad he just put out last month. He's dating Lily Celeste, and she won best video last year, and the whole damned country loves them."

"And how is this my problem?" Trace ground the words out through clenched teeth.

"Man, I know I owe you. I know you probably think I got the biggest damned balls to come here—"

"You ain't got the biggest damned balls of anyone." Trace pinched the bridge of his nose. "But you are the biggest dick of anyone I know. And you're my—"

"Don't say I'm your dick," Tanner mumbled.

Trace snorted.

"You're my brother."

"Thank you."

"Look." Trace sighed. "I don't know, Tanner. I don't know."

"I'll pay you. I'll—"

"When's Chicago?"

"What?"

"When's the Chicago date?"

"Day after tomorrow."

"Dammit," Trace growled. "I don't want to do this. I never wanted anything to do with the stage. And I damned sure don't want to be on stage with you. On tour with you."

"I thought we were good," Tanner reminded him.

"Maybe we are, maybe we aren't." Trace shrugged. He paced away from the bar and turned his back to Tanner. "Good or not doesn't matter, Tanner. Why would I want to live that life when I have her upstairs? I've been waking up with her for weeks straight. I go to sleep at night with her in my arms. She's all I want."

"I'll pay you. I will fly you back here—"

"It's not about the money." Trace rolled his eyes. "It's about how much I love her, and how I don't want to lose a day with her."

Tanner notched his chin in the air and set his cap back on his head. He tugged it down hard and shrugged.

"Okay."

"What?"

"Okay. You said no. Mama told me she'd tan my hide if I asked this of you. Said you were happy and to leave you and your girl alone." Tanner shrugged. "I'll figure it out."

"You'll figure it out." Trace tilted his head and eyed Tanner suspiciously. "You just said you'd have to cancel shows."

"Then I'll have to cancel shows." Tanner tossed his hands up in defeat. "I guess I can cancel Chicago and see if I can find a studio musician. Hate like hell to do that, because no one out there's as good as Nialls."

Trace's nostrils flared as he scooped up another deep breath. The hint of stain lingered in the air, and something from the kitchen was starting to smell like garlic and heaven. He looked around the shadowed room, wondered what Leah had wanted to talk to him about and wondered what she would say when he hit her with this. Well, he knew what she would say.

If he sent Tanner on his way, if Tanner cancelled shows or hired a studio guitarist to fill in until the Congregation could pick Zeek Frame up in Ohio, Leah would be angry with him. No. He winced and shook his head, though Tanner wasn't privy to his internal dialogue. She wouldn't be angry. She would be disappointed. Family obviously meant everything to Leah Hague. Once upon a time, family meant a lot to Trace.

Here was a chance to bridge the gap in his relationship with his brother. To rescue his damned little brother again. To make things right with Tanner and make his mama happy.

"Let me talk to Leah," he mumbled.

"What?"

"I said let me—"

"I heard what you said. I'm asking you why you need to talk to Leah."

"Because it's not just me anymore, Tanner." Trace turned his hard stare to him, willing his brother to understand what he was asking of him. The sacrifice it was for Trace to walk out of here now. "Everything I do is about me and

Leah. She gets a say in every choice I make from here on out."

Tanner hitched his shoulders and shoved his hands into the hip pockets of his jeans.

"She's beautiful."

"You stay the hell away from Leah." Trace stepped forward and drilled his finger into Tanner's chest. "You hear me? You stay away from her and Stevi and Margo."

"I don't even know who Stevi and Margo are."

"They're my family, kid. And you're not gonna mess with any of them."

"Look. I'll talk to Paul. He's got a line on a guitar player in Memphis. We can get 'em up here for Des Moines—"

Figured. Tanner was here with his dick in his hand—sure as hell wasn't his heart—asking Trace for a favor, claiming he and the band were at rock bottom and desperate for Trace's help. Trouble was, Tanner might still have to cancel a show, and any venue in Chicago was bound to be big. Too big to blow off. And even if he could get someone in for Des Moines, no one knew the music like Trace, since he'd written the majority of the songs that Tanner and his band had taken to the top ten on the billboards.

"Go sit in your tour bus and look pretty. Gimme some time to talk to Leah."

CHAPTER 42

LEAH FIDGETED THE TIME AWAY IN THE OFFICE WHILE TRACE talked to Tanner downstairs. She hated the thought of him leaving, even for a day or two, and yet, if Tanner asked him to lend a hand, she wanted Trace to go and help his brother out. But she wanted it to be Trace's decision. She knew he would come to her; she knew they would discuss it, and Leah would certainly support him, whatever he chose to do. But she prayed that Trace would make the choice to play a show or two, whatever Tanner needed.

Not for Tanner, though she couldn't say she hated the guy at first sight. She didn't feel warm and fuzzy toward him as she did her own family, though it crossed her mind that maybe one day she would care for him as she did her sister and cousin and Duncan. She wasn't attracted to him, either, and that was something she knew wouldn't change. Her desire for Trace, for his heart, his body, his face, consumed her. Those feelings aside, Tanner was too shiny and polished for her tastes. He was too aware of himself and the impact he had on women, and that compared to Trace's affable personality—naturally charming—and his most-beautiful-man status was a turn off.

She had yet to meet the woman who had brought both men into the world, and though she knew she would love the woman, she didn't necessarily want Trace to help Tanner out for her, either. It would be nice for the brothers to bury the hatchet for their mother's sake, sure. But Leah wanted Trace to step up and do the right thing because it was the sort of man he was. And whether he would admit to it or not, Leah knew he loved his brother. Watching Tanner belly flop might give him a small bit of satisfaction, but Leah suspected it would hurt him, too.

Margo joined her in the office, and for a while, they pretended that they were working. Leah sat at the desk and stared at the bank statement and pretended to check off funds transferred for online payments, and Margo paced the floor and wondered aloud if they could possibly get Raj Echo to play at the Queen next fall. It was too soon to feel any fetal movement, but Leah imagined over and over again that she felt the baby move. If it was a boy, they could name him after Trace's father, Thomas Dixon. They could stick her dad's name in as a middle name: Thomas Jacob Dixon. Of course that would lend itself to a nickname. TJ. She wasn't sure about that. She had never loved the use of initials as a nickname. She'd have to ask Trace—

"He's not that cute." Margo's voice tugged her from her thoughts. Leah looked around the office, surprised to find she was still here with Margo. In her head, she had been in the baby's room in their house. With Stevi still living there, they would have to make the room Trace had stayed in when he had first come to Adam's Bay the nursery. Then again, a newborn should—

"I mean. Okay. Sure." Margo grabbed her again and threw her back into the office chair. Leah sighed and rubbed her eyes. She tossed her pencil down when she realized Margo had put her iPad down and admitted defeat. "He's cute. But he's not even in Trace's league."

"You're talking about Tanner?"

"There's a nationally known singer in our bar." Margo leaned over the desk and waved her hands at Leah. A tiny frown of pain danced over Margo's face, gone almost instantly. Leah eyed Margo's hand, still wrapped like a mitten with gauze.

"Do you need a pain pill?" Leah cocked her head and arched her eyebrows.

"What?" Margo's face pinched in a *what-the-heck-are-you-talking-about* frown.

"Your hand. You looked like you were—"

"I'm fine." Margo rolled her eyes. "Focus."

"I don't want to focus on Tanner Dixon," Leah griped. Because even if it was the right thing to do, watching Trace head out on the road for even just a day or two was going to be hard.

"Me neither!" Margo raised her hands over her shoulders in a rah-rah movement, but this time the look of pain on her face moved in and stayed, and she quickly lowered her arms and cradled her injured hand against her stomach. "That's what I'm sayin'. He's cute. Nothing special."

"I agree." Leah rubbed her eyes. "Although Trace carries his third-grade school picture in his wallet. Now, that's cute."

"Why?"

"Um. It was the year Tanner grew out of his...school anxiety or something."

"And that's a big deal? For Trace?"

Leah rolled her lips inward and shrugged. "Remember when I learned to spell hippopotamus?"

"Yeah, I taught you, but I don't carry your picture around with me."

"But we see each other every day," Leah reminded her.

"Mm." Margo's lips twitched. "Why do you look so sad?"

"I'm not."

"You do."

Leah sighed. "Tanner's guitarist is injured, and he needs Trace."

"And you think Trace is gonna go?"

"I do." Leah licked her lips. "And I want him to. But."

"You trust him?"

"Absolutely." Leah didn't hesitate or flinch.

"You trust all the women who're gonna be throwin' themselves at him?" Margo asked quietly. Leah understood that Margo was asking because of how her relationship with Jess had played out. Didn't make it any easier to talk about it, though.

"No."

"He loves you."

"And when he comes back home to me, I'm going to have gained weight. I'm gonna have stretch marks. I'm gonna be exhausted from getting up with a baby—"

"His baby," Margo reminded her. Leah arched her eyebrows and waited for Margo to make her point. "You're having his baby. To a man like Trace Dixon? That's everything, Leah. Every. Thing. Every. Damned. Thing."

Leah's throat tightened. Margo was right. Trace would love her forever, to the moon and back, and he was going to be thrilled about the baby.

Which is why she couldn't tell him. Not now.

STEVI WOULD ARGUE WITH HER TOMORROW. ONCE TRACE was gone—cowboy boots and Loretta headed to Chicago with The Lightning Congregation—and she realized Leah hadn't told him about the baby yet, she would snap. Leah would have to sit on her cell, Stevi's too, because she didn't trust her sister to keep her secret another second. But how could she have told him earlier?

Okay, sure, Trace had come upstairs to find her in the office after he talked to Tanner. Leah had known the second she laid eyes on him the things that had been said between him and his brother. If Trace wore a hat, he'd have sulked into the office, hat in hand, and approached her reluctantly with what he thought he needed to do. As it was, he'd done just that, minus the hat, and he had told Leah he didn't want to leave so soon. But he felt like he had to stand in for Tanner's lead guitarist for a couple of shows. Just long enough for some guy from Memphis to head up and meet them in Ohio.

She hated that he was going to leave. That he had just come back from Tennessee, just moved in with her, and they were just beginning their life together, and he had to pack up and hit the road. Especially now. But, she reminded him, they had a life together now. Adam's Bay was his city; the bungalow where she would be waiting for him was now his home. Another week or two apart wouldn't hurt either of them. In fact, Leah had teased him that absence is supposed to make the heart grow fonder.

Trace had answered with a begrudging smile; he might have made up his mind to man up and help Tanner out, but he wasn't happy about it. Leah had cajoled him with hugs and kisses and promises for later, and she'd shoved her secret down a little further under her heart for safekeeping. She would tell him, of course, but she couldn't tell him before he left for Chicago. Trace was a family man, as Margo and Stevi had both pointed out, and as such, his head and his heart were already at odds over leaving. Telling him the truth about the baby would have planted his boots firmly in Adam's Bay, and Leah knew even then, he would stew over the fact that he hadn't helped his brother.

Why make him choose? Why put that burden of guilt on him, when she could easily keep the baby to herself another couple of weeks?

Making out in the office—though limited to heavy kissing and a few feels copped through clothing—had taken his mind off how angry he was with Tanner for asking for something so big, and eventually, they'd climbed off the couch and righted their clothing and headed back downstairs. Didn't happen often at the Queen, but they ordered pizza and Tanner's guys joined Leah's family, and except for the tension in the lines of Trace's face and the steel set of his shoulders under the soft cotton of his shirt, they all had fun.

Trace had been on edge at first, watching Tanner and his guys like a hawk. Leah figured he was watching them to make sure no one flirted with Stevi or Margo. Leah kind of thought it was chivalrous of him to be so protective, but a little old-fashioned of him, too. If Stevi or Margo wanted to flirt—or Leah supposed, mess around—with Tanner or any of his guys, that was their decision. Wasn't every day that true celebrities breezed in and out of the Queen.

Then again, Leah had her own celebrity, and it wasn't Music City that made him shine in her eyes. So maybe Stevi and Margo weren't that attracted to Tanner and the guys. They drank a few beers while they put away the pizza. Stevi snagged each beer Duncan put in front of Leah and either drank them or slid them into Tanner's camp for his guys to drink. Finally, Leah made a point of getting up and grabbing a bottle of water, which wasn't out of the ordinary.

Most of the guys headed back to the bus, and from there, Leah had no idea where they went or what they did. But Tanner and his driver, Mac, stuck around for the evening crowd. Tanner sang a couple of songs with Trace, and Leah watched several of the women and girls in the bar fall over each other when they realized the guys in the ball caps and jeans, playing acoustic guitars and singing some big country hits, were Trace and Tanner Dixon. She thought a few of them might have wet their pants and even said as much to the guys when they took a break for a drink. Face wearing a big, cocky grin, Tanner's eyes coasted over the small crowd. Trace had only rolled his eyes and dropped his arm around her shoulders.

Leah and Trace took off just before closing, and Leah only felt guilty for it because she knew Stevi assumed that at some point before Trace got on the bus to leave with the band that Leah would tell him about the baby. Instead, they barely made it inside the kitchen before he undressed her and claimed her with his hands and his mouth.

Fingers wrapped around the edge of the table, Trace on the floor with his lips between her legs, Leah had watched him until she couldn't, until she'd flown apart in a million tiny pieces and then she'd had to wait what seemed like forever to pull herself back together and get up the steps to their bedroom for him to do it all over again. Trace slept like the dead, but he usually did. Curled in the safety and comfort of his arms, Leah slept but not long and not peacefully. She dreamt about the baby, and those dreams could run the gamut from sheer perfection to terrifying, and though Trace's chest rose and fell against her, though she heard his heartbeat against her cheek, she dreamt of losing him.

In her dreams, it was Trace who surveyed the crowd with the satisfied, smug grin on his face instead of Tanner, and when she awoke in the morning, the dream lingered, and she felt guilty. The brothers were nothing alike. Tanner liked the fame. Trace loved the music.

And her.

They made love again before he left, and Leah managed to pull herself together and fix him coffee and biscuits. Nothing fancy. She popped open a can of ready-made biscuits and stuck them in the oven, constantly assuring Trace as he threw things in a bag that she would be fine while he was gone. That she would text him and call him, and she asked him to please text or call whenever he wanted to talk. Even at odd hours after a show. She didn't say so to him, but she would much rather he call her at three a.m. and wake her from a deep sleep to talk, to have phone sex, whatever he needed, rather than hook up with anyone on the road for conversation, blowjobs, or a quick hook up in a bar.

He hugged Stevi goodbye when she wandered out of her bedroom for coffee. Gave Leah such a big hug he lifted her feet from the ground and twirled her around. Dropped a kiss on her lips and said goodbye. Ten steps out the door to his truck, he dropped his bag and came back for another goodbye. She held him for a moment, kissed him full and hard on the mouth, brushed her lips over his cheek to his neck, and promised she loved him.

"You'll bring my truck home?" he asked as he walked backwards across the driveway. He'd scooped his bag up, and he jiggled his keys in his other hand, eyes on her.

"Stevi and I will bring your truck home." Leah nodded. "I might drive your truck while you're gone."

"Yeah?" He stopped at the tailgate and tipped his head. "That's kind of sexy."

"Don't you forget it."

"You'll wear your ring?" he asked quietly.

"Never taking it off."

He nodded. Leah watched him turn and head around to the driver's side. He pulled the door open, slung the bag in, and climbed up without looking back. When he backed down the drive and passed the door, she blew him a kiss and then turned on the back step and bumped into a groggy, grouchy-looking Stevi.

"You didn't tell him. Did you?" Stevi hid behind her coffee mug, but Leah saw the scowl on her face.

"When was I gonna tell him, Stevi? Before he said he was going to do the right thing by his brother? Or after? It would have put him in a horrible position. I don't want to make him choose between me or his brother."

"It's not your right to take the choice away from him."

Stevi's words were a sucker punch in the gut. Leah winced and looked away. She believed she was right. Mostly. She didn't want Trace to have to choose between her and the baby and his brother, not so soon in their relationship. She didn't want to be the girlfriend to put demands on him, and she did want Trace to mend fences with Tanner. For his sake. For their mama's sake. And yet, keeping the secret from Trace served her well, too. She could stick this little bit of knowledge on the back burner for a while and go on pretending it wasn't going to happen.

CHAPTER 43

THE MOMENTS ON STAGE WERE THRILLING TO HIM, THOUGH not for the same reasons as they were for Tanner. Trace couldn't have cared less about the crowds gathered at the amphitheaters. Sure, he wanted them to love the music. The songs. Sure, that excitement, that rumble that moved over the crowd, up and over the stage in the darkness, the time between the opening act and the moment the lights went up, and Tanner and the Congregation lit the place up with sound—he loved the hell out of that. He loved that he wrote the songs that fired people up and made them move. And he loved that he wrote the songs that slowed those same people down and made them love and need the ones they loved.

But he had no desire to walk amidst the concertgoers the way Tanner did. Trace was happy to stay on stage and make his guitar sing. He preferred Loretta, and if not Loretta, Lucille. But he could tickle the strings on an electric guitar, and he played bass, and he could play steel guitar, too, though there wasn't much of Tanner's music that called for it. He enjoyed singing backup to Tanner, his voice in harmony with the rest of the band. He liked all that just fine, kind of the way he liked going to church on special days with his mama and loving the people there that day and voicing his praise and thanks for his blessings.

But he didn't love the women in the crowds. He appreciated them as fans, but he didn't angle for hookups or peeks at cleavage or in some cases, all out nudity. He'd never been that guy, and he knew now that he would never find another woman who would call to him on every level. Not the way Leah Hague did.

After Chicago, he was ready to come home. He had his fix of the applause and the electric guitar and the drum solos. He had signed a hundred different CD cases and a hundred t-shirts and posters, and while it had been fun for a while, the only thing his hand wanted to write now was music. Maybe a little something for Leah.

Maybe a little something about a woman strong enough to watch her man leave and trust that he would come back.

If he was tired of the stage after one show, he was ready to burn the tour bus to the ground a hundred miles outside of Chicago, bound for Des Moines. A few of Tanner's guys were young and green and had yet to blow through the drinking and women phase, the one that Trace had tinkered with just a bit way back in the beginning. Trace texted with Leah for a while. Drank a beer but turned down the next six Tim Jones—hell of a drummer, but a little short on social graces—offered him. Did his best not to watch as the guy as good as fingered a girl at the table before finally moving to the back room that apparently the band guys shared when it was necessary.

Like when someone else was sitting at the dinette, maybe.

Trace was pleased to note that Tanner had apparently slowed down his own drinking. Then again, it was possible Tanner was working at tame just to keep peace for the time being. Who knew what hell might break loose when Trace was done and Zeek Frame joined them? Zeek was one of the best guitarists around, as far as Trace was concerned. He was also a recovering addict, and Trace wanted no part in that.

Nope. Even the thrill of making music, bending guitar strings, and shaking the ground with their sound couldn't compare to being at home with Leah.

The thought of her driving his truck around Adam's Bay was his anchor. Each time the distance between them—miles and current lifestyle—threatened to overwhelm him, he pictured her in his truck. Her sexy little bottom in the snug denim shorts, a blouse open over a cami, the hat he brought her—God, he loved her laugh whenever she put it on and straddled his lap to take a ride—and her ring. And that beautiful smile. Singing one of his songs. Because she had admitted—with that grin and that not-gonna-sleep-with-you, Nashville attitude—that she liked his songs and before he'd moved in with her, she listened to them at night when she was alone in bed.

He played cards with a couple of the guys, Tanner included. Dodged questions about Leah and their life together. Texted Leah and felt goofy and syrupy and whooped as hell because everything she said to him made him feel like a cartoon character, big old heart pumping straight out of his body and back over the miles to her.

He talked to her every day the first week. Even if their phone conversation lasted a minute, her voice was the best music he heard while he was gone.

Two shows down and headed from Des Moines to Milwaukee, Tanner approached him where he was sacked out in a captain's chair on the bus. Hat tipped, bill low over his head, he'd talked to Leah earlier and he was savoring the sound of her voice, of her laughter. She'd told him Berkley was walking, although she tended to wobble a few steps and then crash and burn. Margo's stitches had come out, and now Duncan kept trying to read her palm. Apparently, her scar had a curve that made it look a bit like an S so he had taken to calling her Super Margo. Leah hadn't said much about Stevi, and it crossed Trace's mind to wonder why. But then she'd suggested he call back later in the evening if he could find a little bit of alone time. As frustrated as he was with jacking off and listening to Leah get herself off, it beat hearing the same sorts of sounds on the bus when any of the guys had female company.

Then again, Leah was classier than the women the band guys had brought aboard the bus—thankfully only a few times since he'd joined them in the lot outside the Queen —and he'd much rather listen to her soft moans and purrs of pleasure, to her chanting his name, than the screaming and wailing and the squeak of the whole damned bus when someone got it to rocking.

"Got a second?" Tanner smacked his leg with his ball cap and then tugged it back on when Trace put his feet down and nudged his own hat back down on his head.

"You kidding me?" Trace arched his eyebrows. "I'm a damned hostage on your tour bus. I've got nothing but time right now."

"How's Leah?"

"Counting down the days." Trace sat up straight. "Why?"

Tanner blew his cheeks up with a big breath and then slowly let it out. Trace recognized it as a stall tactic. Already angry, he folded his arms over his chest and cocked his head at Tanner.

"Two things."

Trace answered with a quick shake of his head and a small shrug.

"Christina Folgers is having a holiday special," Tanner started.

"Come again?"

"Mid-December. Happy holidays, rah rah rah. She asked us to make an appearance."

"Points to you." Trace cleared his throat. "What's it got to do with me?"

"Zeek can't do the show. Prior commitment."

"Me too." Trace shrugged. "What else?"

"I didn't give you a date."

"Doesn't matter, Tanner." Trace shook his head again. "I said I'd fill in for you on a few tour dates here. Not next Christmas. Not next summer. This isn't a free call-me card. I'm finishing Indy, and then I'm goin' home. To Leah. Got it?"

"It's Christmas, man. C'mon." Tanner pulled his hat off again and rubbed his hand over his hair. "I need this—"

"Then find another guitar player, Tanner," Trace said firmly. "I meant what I said. I'm helping you out here. That's it. No more knockin' on my door and expectin' favors. Not happening."

Tanner groaned and rolled his shoulders.

"What else?" Trace prodded.

"Zeek got hung up. Can't get to Ohio, so I told him we'd pick him up in Kentucky."

"Then you're gonna have to cancel a show."

"You kiddin' me? You're already out with us. You can't add in one more show? You get me to Kentucky, and I will get you back to Leah. I'll let the Christmas thing go. For now. And I'll get—"

"*For now?*" Trace snapped his gaze back to Tanner's. "I'm sorry. Did you say *for now*? Because what I can do, Tanner, is get off this damned bus at the next stop and not look back."

"I got massive debt, Trace. I can't lose out to the new guys. I can't hand over my spot to someone new who had a hit single. I gotta—"

"That's not my problem, Tanner." Trace shrugged his lips. "I didn't advise you to drop a shit ton of cash on this bus. On that damned mansion on the hill you insisted on building, even though you live there alone. I didn't suggest—"

"I can't ask Mama for the money."

Trace cut loose with a wild peal of laughter. "Ask her. Go ahead. She can't give it to you. Because she doesn't have it. She could take out a second mortgage on the house. She could sell her car. She can give you Daddy's life insurance money—"

"I'm twenty grand into Mama." Tanner spoke so quietly, Trace wasn't sure he had heard him right. He stared at Tanner silently, figured his tense shoulders and tight, angry face mirrored his own right about now.

"You hit Mama up for twenty grand? She's loaning you that kind of money? What the hell are you doing, Tanner? I thought you were just a greedy son-of-a-bitch, and now I find out you're stupid, too?"

Tanner sighed and dragged his hand down over his face. He ground out a few choice words, none of which affected Trace one way or another. Bottom line, his brother had screwed their mother out of money she didn't have. And now he was begging Trace for help, when in fact, no matter what Trace did there was no guarantee he would come up with the cash he needed, not even enough to pay their mother back.

Trace felt his phone buzz in his pocket. He figured it was Leah, and he had promised he would answer any call or text she sent, if he wasn't on stage. Not on stage, but so angry, he could pick his brother up and throw him off the damned bus, he wasn't about to talk to Leah right now.

"Help me out?" Tanner tented his hands over his mouth and eyed Trace over his fingertips. His eyebrows arched hopefully, and Trace saw an eleven-year-old Tanner, asking for a ride in his car. "Please?"

"And then what?" Trace leaned forward. Jaw clenched in anger, worry for his mother heavy on his mind now, he jabbed his finger into Tanner's chest. "And then what? You can't pick Zeek up in Kentucky and you need me to play a few shows there? And then maybe we go back to Nashville? You're on the last leg of the tour, right? You get me to fill in in Nashville. You pick me up on some of the specials. You pencil me in for the awards shows. Then what, Tanner?"

"I'm your brother."

Trace dipped his shoulders in a *who-gives-a-damn* shrug. "And she's your mama, and you took twenty grand from her—"

"She offered it."

"Grow the hell up!" Trace snapped. "Of course, she's gonna offer you money. She's gonna bail your ass outta every damned tight spot you get into. She's sick, Tanner. Show some respect."

"Just Kentucky."

Trace huffed out a harsh breath and turned his face away from his brother, sickened at the sight of him.

"Leave me alone."

"Kentucky? I'll find someone. I got Paul on it right now."

"I'm gonna run it by Leah." Trace dropped his head back to rest on the seat. "And I'm gonna tell her just what I think of this little scheme you hit me with. And if…if…I do this, it's the last damned time I do anything for you. Again."

From the corner of his eye, he saw Tanner's curt nod.

"Nope." Trace twitched his mouth and shook his head. "If I do it, I'm sure as hell not doing anything for you. It's for Mama."

Tanner stood up to walk away. Trace heard him grumbling, but he tuned him out. Focused on his breathing, rather than tearing through the bus and punching something. He closed his eyes and thought of Leah.

Driving his truck around Adam's Bay.

CHAPTER 44

WEEKDAY HAPPY HOURS STARTED OUT QUIET, BUT generally tended to pick up—more so the later in the evening, the later in the week, and deeper into summer. Leah had started the afternoon with two tables occupied, two women at each. Three more ladies had wandered in and grabbed a high top by the front window. And now, she had a regular at the bar, working his beer and iPad with equal attention. Tania Morgan—one of the new girls they hired earlier in the summer—had seated three couples for dinner just thirty minutes ago. Stevi was in the kitchen, dealing with a supposed salad crisis. Margo was at home with Berkley, and Duncan was at the other end of the bar, eyes on the window. He was either intrigued by the goings on at the park across the street— looked like a bunch of kids from a school, though it was summer, lining up in choir formation—or by the women who had just claimed the front table.

Leah's phone had buzzed a few minutes ago in her pocket. She had delivered two glasses of Chardonnay and a longneck to the front table before settling back at the bar. With another quick glance around, she palmed her phone and peeked at it.

What're you listening to?

A rush of warmth rolled over her, strong enough to take the oomph out of the discomfort she'd had in her belly most of the day.

Sinatra. I've Got You Under My Skin.

Busy?

Not bad. It's early yet.

Been to Milwaukee?

Nope.

Hop a jet and meet me here. I'll be the one in the boots.

Her sharp, quick laugh drew Duncan's attention. She waved him away and shook her head.

Wish I could. You don't need the boots. I'd know you anywhere.

I miss you.

Me too.

I need to call you tonight. Need to talk to you.

Leah felt a flutter of unease ride high over the discomfort. Rubbed her belly without thinking about it. Wondered if she was showing yet. When she looked in a mirror, she felt like she could see ten pounds more to her body than there had been four weeks ago. But she knew it was possible that was the power of suggestion rather than actual weight gain. Duncan hadn't said anything. Though Duncan wouldn't say anything, even if she suddenly looked like she was packing acorns in her cheeks for winter.

Okay. Calling before close?

Not sure. Need to find a quiet place to talk.

Leah swallowed hard. Her hands shook, and before she tried to tap out a response, she rubbed them—one at a time—over her jeans. She was still wearing the same size, though by the end of a shift, she was miserable. Stuffed into her pants, muffin top to boot. She'd noticed everything she ate these days gave her heartburn, too. And no matter what Stevi did or said, she ended up hammering on her last nerve or making her cry.

Leah could handle anything about being pregnant if Trace was home with her. Missing him, though, was a bottomless ache inside, and trying to hide that need for him, the longing she felt for his presence, was exhausting.

Are you gonna tell me you changed your mind? You like the stage?

Her finger hovered over the send button for a second, but she tapped it. Felt a jolt of nerves and nearly dropped her phone.

"You okay?" Duncan asked as he slipped around her.

"Yeah. Why?"

He dropped his hands on her shoulders and gave her a squeeze.

"You look a little pale."

She swallowed hard. Jumped when her phone started buzzing in her hand and shook her head at Duncan as she looked down to see that Trace was calling.

"I'm fine."

"Okay." He nodded. "Be right back."

As she watched him go, she lifted her phone to her ear. Even though she wanted to hear his voice, she was afraid of his words and afraid of what he needed to say to her and that he'd gone from needing a quiet place to talk to calling now.

"Hey."

"Leah, I'm not gonna change my mind."

"Okay."

"Ever."

"Okay." She nodded and pinched the bridge of her nose. She dragged in what she hoped was a silent breath, because it wouldn't do for him to hear her ragged breathing and think she was crying. Even though she sort of was. Careful not to let her voice quiver, she continued, "I just miss you."

"I know."

"What's going on?" She cleared her throat. "Tell me now."

"Hang on."

She heard his boots scuffling on what sounded like pavement, and she tried to picture him there at the bus or at a bar, surrounded by Tanner's guys. As much as she loved him, and as much as she wanted him to do the right thing, she didn't like this. She didn't like that he was in the spotlight, because she knew damned well what other women were thinking when they looked at him.

With bedroom eyes and a face like a dream and that body made for slow, lazy afternoon sex, how could any woman look at Trace Dixon and not imagine him naked, between her legs?

"You there?"

Again, she smoothed her hand over her stomach. She had half a mind to yell at Stevi, but what would she say? Even if she weren't on the phone with Trace, what would she say? I don't feel good? Really? Complaining like that was for little kids, and she had a job to do tonight, and she liked the bar, and she was fine. And besides, Stevi was still irked at her for not talking to Trace. Things had been a little bit strained between them lately.

"Yeah." She nodded enthusiastically, but she stopped when she remembered Trace couldn't see her anyway.

"Tanner's a pain in my ass," he announced, and Leah relaxed against the bar. She rested her free hand on the edge and ate up the feeling of the nervous energy flowing out of her. Trace could rage about Tanner all he wanted; she would listen until he felt better. Just as long as he got back home by the end of next week.

"I know."

"No, darlin', you don't know."

She squeezed her eyes closed at the jagged sound of Trace's harsh exhale. The nervous vibration came back to her hands, and she fisted her free hand to crush the feeling.

"What's wrong?"

"He's in some money trouble," Trace answered cryptically. And it didn't matter. She didn't give a damn about Tanner Dixon's money trouble. Except that it added up to Leah losing Trace just a little bit longer.

"And?" She braced herself. Pressed her lips together when her stomach sent that little notice again. Not a cramp, exactly, but a twinge. A hint of discomfort.

"Zeek Frame's tied up. Tanner needs me to do Kentucky."

Because she couldn't hide the sob that slipped out, she moved her phone away from her ear and held it over the bar for a second. Her eyes burned with tears, but she refused to give in and cry them right here. Stevi and Duncan's voices preceded them, as they argued over The Stones and The Beatles, and Stevi edge past her at the bar, turning to eye her suspiciously.

"Leah?" Trace said when she put the phone back to her ear. "Leah? Darlin'?"

"I'm here."

"Look, I didn't tell him yes. I told him we would talk about it."

Leah turned her back to Stevi and hunched her shoulders.

"Of course." She marveled at how normal she sounded, how even her voice was. She swiped at her eyes and nodded more to herself than Trace. "We can talk later, yeah. But Trace, it's okay. You gotta do—"

"I wanna do right by you," he cut her off with a firm voice. "But Leah…"

"Babe, it's okay."

"He's…"

The desperate anger in his sigh shot through her backbone like steel. She lifted her head and stared absently at the back door.

"What?"

"Nothing. I'm just worried about Mama," he mumbled. "I gotta go, darlin'. I'll call you later so we can talk. I'll tell you everything."

"Okay." She swallowed hard.

"Leah, I love you."

"I know. I love you, too." She felt eyes on her back, but she tried to ignore Stevi. Rather than sniffle and let Trace know she was upset, she stepped closer to the bar and groped behind her for a napkin. Stevi plopped one in her hands, and Leah swiped it under her nose. "It's okay. We'll figure it out."

When the call ended and she lowered her phone, she felt Stevi hovering behind her.

"He's right."

"What?" She turned her head, barely saw Stevi from the corner of her eye.

"Duncan. He said you don't look good."

"I'm fine."

"Was that Trace?"

"Who else would it be?"

"I don't know!" Stevi snapped. "I couldn't hear you. Was it Trace? Or Joe?"

Guilt stabbed her low in the belly. She shook her head and turned to look at Stevi.

"I'm sorry. It was Trace. He's upset about something."

Gazes locked, Stevi nodded slowly and raised her eyebrows.

"Why don't you go home?"

"What?"

"Go home. You look pale. Tired. Put your feet up. Duncan and I got it."

"I'm pregnant, not feeble."

"Leah."

Leah shook her head. "Stevi, I'm fine. I don't wanna be alone."

Stevi sighed.

"I know you're mad at me." Leah's voice was thick with emotion. "I get it. But I hate this. I hate that he's gone, and you're mad…"

"Okay." Stevi reached forward and touched her hand. "Okay. I'm sorry. It's not my business, but I'm worried about you. He should know."

Because at the moment she agreed with Stevi, because she wished she had told him and that Trace was at home to let Tanner sink or swim on his own, Leah could only nod.

Stevi nodded and whooshed out a deep breath. She broke the eye contact and looked around the room.

"If you stay, would you at least let me do tables? You take the bar? Sit down if you need to?"

"Stevi, I'm preg—"

"I can call Mom and Dad to come and drive you home."

"I have Trace's truck."

Stevi offered her a dramatic shrug.

"Okay. Promise."

LEAH KEPT HER PROMISE. SHE STAYED AT THE BAR AND LET Stevi and Tania handle the tables. She suspected Stevi had put a bug in Duncan's ear to keep an eye on her, though, because he hovered at the bar and handled three or four patrons to her one. Leah had half a mind to argue with him, but as the night wore on, she grew more tired and irritable and rather than make a scene, she let Duncan take over.

She did argue when Duncan flipped the lock on the door, and Stevi and Tania made a few trips back to the kitchen to carry pint glasses and pilsner glasses and all the other drink ware to be loaded in the industrial dishwasher. Not only did they all refuse to let her get up and help them, Stevi insisted she was driving home. Leah reminded her that she had Trace's truck, but Stevi wouldn't budge. So Duncan walked them out, helped Leah up into the passenger side of Trace's truck, and then stood at the other side as Stevi hiked up into the driver's seat. Leah didn't hear their murmured words, but their soft, private laughter grated on her nerves.

Finally, Duncan smacked Stevi playfully on the thigh, reminded her to buckle up, and then leaned in around Stevi to tell Leah goodnight. She offered him a small smile, but by the time she found the energy to say goodnight, he'd swung the truck door closed and headed back over the lot to the door of the Queen.

"So did he call you back?" Stevi asked as she dropped the truck into reverse and backed out of the parking spot Trace had claimed when he had started driving here on a daily basis.

"Not yet."

"What happened? You looked really upset."

Leah rested her head on the truck seat and closed her eyes. "I dunno."

"Did you guys argue? Is he upset about—"

"No," Leah answered quickly. "No. He's angry with Tanner. The guy Tanner said was gonna meet them in Ohio can't. So now Tanner wants Trace in Ohio. Probably wants him to play Kentucky now, too, until he can get that other guy. Or someone else."

"So he'll be gone longer."

A knot of emotion stuck in Leah's throat, so she simply nodded.

"You trust him to come home?"

"I do."

"You don't sound sure, Leah."

Eyes closed, tears streaked her face. She squeezed Stevi's fingers when her sister closed her hand over hers.

"I'm sure about Trace, but that doesn't mean I like that he's out there. That other women think if they had just a minute of his time, they could tempt him away. That I have to sleep alone because his brother needs him more."

"Sweetie, he loves you," Stevi reminded her. "And you wanted him to do the right thing here."

"I know." Leah sighed. "I know. And I do. But I don't like it."

"You don't have to like it," Stevi told her. "For the record, he's twice the man his brother is."

"I know."

When Stevi stopped talking, Leah still held her hand. Thoughts still on Trace, she kept her eyes closed and wished she would sleep well. She was tired, and no small part of that was the baby, of course. But it didn't help that she wasn't sleeping well with Trace being gone. She'd grown used to his warm body next to hers in their bed. Used to the sound of him breathing. The weight of his leg thrown over hers when he moved through the night and took her in his arms.

At home, Stevi nudged her awake, and together, the two of them made their way inside. Stevi shooed her on upstairs and locked the house up. Leah peeled her clothes off, snuggled into one of Trace's soft t-shirts and climbed into bed. Fingers curled around her phone, she fell asleep waiting for him to call.

CHAPTER 45

THE DREAMS WERE GOING TO GET THE BETTER OF HER, which was yet another reason she wanted Trace back home. He hadn't called again last night, and she wished now that he would. She would ask him. No begging. No crying. She would just tell him she needed to share something with him and that it would be better said if they were face to face. And then, as Stevi had said, the choice would be his.

Maybe if she gave him the choice, he would stay. Not that she was afraid he would never come back, but maybe if she told him about the baby, he would stay with her *now*. He'd honored his original bargain with Tanner. Surely, Trace saw that Tanner was going to keep digging in and twisting his grip on him and taking advantage of him. If he didn't walk away now—after honoring that first commitment—Tanner would keep coming back, expecting Trace to bail him out time and again.

If he stayed, maybe the anxiety would loosen its white-knuckle grip around her throat. Maybe she wouldn't dream the bad stuff, and so maybe she would sleep better, and then maybe she wouldn't feel so tired through the days. Might be good for him, too, to come back to a steady schedule and to the quiet time for writing.

But, God, the dreams were so damned real. Whether it was something vague and unsettling about Trace and being on the road, away from her, or Kenzi in the birthing room, every morning Leah awoke tense and sore, like she'd been battered around a boxing ring. Sadness clung to her, and being tired and irritable didn't help the blue mood, and because she wasn't that person, being blue made her more irritable, which made her more tired.

She trusted Trace, but the dreams seemed to suggest she didn't, and so on top of everything else she felt, she struggled with guilt. Kenzi hadn't made any baby steps toward further recovery, but she hadn't regressed, either. Still, the dreams of the emergency scene in the birthing room were so real, there were nights Leah awoke in tears.

Some nights, lately, she awoke with that vague feeling of discomfort and while sometimes, it centered in her belly, mostly it was a general feeling of malaise that swept from head to toe.

Now and then the dreams featured something bizarre like the dead cat behind the Queen or tonight, the blood in Margo's hand. Only in the dream, Leah walked toward Margo instead of turning away. Her stomach roiled and pitched, but she approached Margo on stiff legs and reached out and put her hand in the blood, calling for Trace to help. But in the dream, he wasn't there.

The blood was warm and thick, and Leah felt hot. The floor of the break room tilted up at her, and then she felt a sharp pain low in her belly. Leah dragged her eyes from Margo's to look down at her stomach. The knife Margo had used to cut the pineapple protruded from her stomach, and Leah stared at it in disbelief. She tried to wrap her fingers around the handle, but it was slick with blood.

"Margo?" she whispered. "Margs?"

She drew her hands away from her belly and stood frozen when she felt warmth spread between her legs.

"Margo?" she said again. She blinked her eyes open to the washed out, barely there gray dawn in her bedroom. Dull cramps alternated in her belly with sharp, hard pains. Her hands clutched her stomach, and when she moved, when she flopped over to lie on her back, she felt the same warmth, the same wetness between her legs.

"Stevi." She mouthed her sister's name, and then she tried to say it again. Only Stevi was downstairs, and she wouldn't hear her. Even if she yelled, it wasn't likely that Stevi would hear her. She felt for her phone; she'd fallen asleep with it in her hand last night, hadn't she? Waiting for Trace to call her.

Had he? Had she talked to him? She couldn't remember.

Her hands, the hands she had been holding protectively over her stomach, were empty. Scared. Her heart thumping wildly in her chest and her throat, she turned her face to the nightstand to search for her phone. Not there. If she could find her phone, she could call Stevi.

Another wave of tight, hard pain moved down through her stomach. Leah sat up and swished her hands over the bed sheets. Her fingertips bumped the edge of something hard and sleek, but they also smoothed over something wet.

"Stevi."

Heart pounding in her ears now, she watched her hand—as if it belonged to someone else—push the top sheet and blanket down over her waist. Propped on her elbows, she lay in a pool of blood. Frantic for Trace, for Stevi, she cried out. Sobbed. Yelled for Stevi, certain her sister wouldn't hear her.

Disgusted and crushed, both, by the blood on the sheets, streaked and dried on her thighs, Leah's hands shook as she scooped up her phone to call Stevi. Three missed phone calls. All from Trace. Starting at 1:30. The last time he called was just before three, and it was just after four now.

Tears streaked her face, and she swiped at her nose and then quickly touched the contacts icon on her phone and chose Stevi's name. The damned dreams made sense now, and she was sick with the thought that she'd miscarried his baby, and he didn't even know she was pregnant.

"What's wrong?" Stevi answered, her voice thick and slow with sleep.

"Stevi." The whisper hung up in her throat and came out sideways. Unable to say more, she drew her legs up and rested her forehead on her bent knees. She dropped the phone, and then she heard hell break loose downstairs. Stevi flipping lights on and running through the hall and the spare room. The light over her stairs was on suddenly, throwing an ugly, garish yellow glow over the far side of the room and leaving her in sulky shadows.

"Leah?"

She looked up when Stevi said her name, and then squeezed her eyes closed when Stevi's eyes jumped over her and the bed and the blood.

"Oh, God." A note of panic crept into Stevi's voice, and Leah sobbed again.

"Stevi," she whispered.

"Oh, Leah. Oh, sweetie, I'm so sorry."

"I dreamt through the whole thing. I knew something was wrong—"

"Leah."

Leah opened her eyes when she felt Stevi's weight on the bed. Stevi knelt beside her, and then she leaned in and threw her arms around her and pulled her sweaty, clammy body against hers to rock her.

"Where's your phone?"

"You can't call him."

"No, I know." Stevi smoothed her hand over the back of Leah's head. "I was gonna call your doctor."

"I'm fine."

"You're not fine," Stevi said in a tone that sounded a lot like their mother. "You need to get—"

Resting on Stevi's shoulder, she shook her head vehemently. "No."

"Leah—"

"Not yet. Please?"

"Dammit, Leah." Stevi sighed. But she didn't argue. Instead, she held Leah tight, kept all of those little pieces of her heart stuck together, though Leah knew the second Stevi let go, she would fall apart, and those pieces would scatter. If they were found, they would never fit back together the same way again.

How would she love Trace the way she was supposed to, if her heart didn't fit back together as it should? Still holding her protectively, Stevi moved against her, reaching for something.

"What're you doing?"

"Calling Duncan."

"What?" Leah pushed at Stevi and blinked at her in the gray light. "Why are you calling Duncan?"

"Because you need to get to the hospital, and I'm not sure I can get you down those stairs."

"Don't call Duncan," Leah whispered. "Please?"

"Leah, I call him or an ambulance." Stevi stretched a bit further around Leah and then sat up straight. Leah licked her lips and stared absently at the hollow of her sister's neck as she dialed Duncan's number.

"I don't need an ambulance."

Sitting as close as she was to her sister, Leah heard Duncan's voice when he picked up.

"Stevi? What's wrong?"

"Duncan, we need you."

"Okay." Leah pressed her lips together and turned her head away when Duncan was quiet for a few seconds. She assumed he was moving around, maybe getting out of bed and pulling on whatever clothes he could manage one handed. "Where are you?"

"At the house. Come up to the attic."

"Stevi, what's going on?"

"Just—"

"I'm on my way, but what's going on?"

Leah ducked her head and pressed her lips together, overcome with grief.

"Leah just miscarried." Stevi cleared her throat.

To his credit, he didn't question her. His quiet promise that he was on his way clawed through Leah's throat. Stevi tossed the phone back to the bed and turned her attention to Leah.

"I never told him," Leah whispered.

"Don't." Stevi shook her head.

"I never told Trace we were having a baby, and now—"

Stevi cupped Leah's neck and leaned closer to press her forehead to Leah's.

"Don't do this to yourself right now." She stared at Leah with wide eyes, eyebrows kissing her hairline, as if she was exacting a promise from her. Leah only blinked, because she wouldn't promise not to hate herself for what she had done. "We'll figure it out. Don't do this now. You have to stay strong."

"Strong?" Leah's whisper was sharp and bitter. "Strong? If I weren't such a damned coward, he would be here with me right now. I wouldn't have to just bury all of this and pretend—"

"You're not gonna pretend," Stevi cut her off. "No way in hell I'm gonna let you pretend this didn't happen. You need him, Leah. You love him. You need him here now."

"Yeah?" Leah tipped her head. Fresh, hot tears streaked her face again. "You think he's gonna haul his life right back here when I call him and say I need you. I just had a miscarriage?"

"Yes," Stevi nodded, "I do think that."

"He won't forgive me—"

"Stevi?" Duncan's voice carried up the steps mere minutes after Stevi's phone call.

Stevi held onto Leah as she turned to look toward the stairs. Leah cringed at the sound of Duncan tearing through the lower level of the house. Duncan, who was like a brother, who had come over before dawn to help her. She had kept this secret from everyone who loved her; she hadn't even told Stevi and Margo. They had figured it out on their own.

Funny to think she used to be so in control of her life. Funny to think she had been so shaken by Kenzi's stroke that she packed a bag and ran to Florida to soak up some sun and ocean breezes and find herself. To think she'd found Trace Dixon in Nashville. She had been determined not to get involved, and now here she was wrecked over him and their baby. And she was about to do the same to him.

While taking down everyone around her who cared about her with her dishonesty and her secrets.

"Stevi?" Duncan shouted. "Leah?"

"We're up here!" Stevi called. Leah turned her head away from the stairs when she heard Duncan's footsteps there. She was ashamed. Not of the blood or the fact that she'd made love in this bed with Nashville and created a new life. It wasn't the bloodied sheets and her tear-streaked face that made her want to hide from Duncan.

Just that she'd kept this from him.

"Leah. Oh, babe. I'm so sorry." Duncan lowered himself to sit on the edge of her bed. He leaned around Stevi, one arm around her middle, and reached to slide his other arm over Stevi's back and Leah's shoulders. "Are you okay?"

Overcome with tears, Leah could only press her fist to her mouth and shake her head.

"I'm afraid she'll be too weak to get down the steps." Stevi's words were feather soft over the back of Leah's neck when she ducked her head again. "She needs to get to—"

"Yeah," Duncan cut her off. "Absolutely."

"Are you still bleeding?" Stevi leaned in and pressed her lips to Leah's hair.

"I don't know."

"Give us just a second, okay?" Stevi lifted her head to speak to Duncan.

"Yeah. Yeah. You do…" He squeezed Leah's shoulders and dropped a quick kiss on top of her head. "You do that. Has anyone called Trace? Do I need—"

"NO!" Leah looked up so quickly, she bumped Duncan's chin with her head. "No. Do not call him."

"He would want to be here for you," Duncan argued as he stood. Leah felt a twinge of guilt when he rubbed his chin. "My God, he would never forgive me if I didn't—"

"Trace doesn't know." Stevi drew in a deep breath and met Leah's eyes. "He doesn't know she was pregnant."

CHAPTER 46

FOR ALL THE DAMNED GALLOPING HIS HEART HAD DONE IN the past five hours, it nearly stopped when his foot hit the top step in Leah's bedroom. In all the days and nights he had spent in her bedroom with her, he had never seen the drapes pulled on her tiny window. There had never been a reason, as her bedroom was an attic room, and there was no possibility any peeping Toms were going to sneak up and take a peek inside. He and Leah had slept and laid together talking and laughing and made love by sunlight and gray daylight on a rainy day and moonlight when the days ended.

Today the curtain was closed, and the darkness in the room thundered with unnatural quiet. Was she sleeping? He took a moment for his eyes to adjust to the deep gloom and blinked at her bed. Of course she was up here; he had just stalked by Duncan and Stevi when he had come inside the house. Stevi had been curled up into a tight little ball in the corner of the couch. He had never seen her look so undone; no makeup, limp hair hanging in her tear-streaked face, and her lips pressed so hard together, they might have been sewn shut.

Of course, Leah was lying in their bed right now, but was she sleeping? Or ignoring him? How the hell had this happened? How the hell had he crowded around the damned dinette on the tour bus last night, Tanner crashed out in a captain's chair, and played Poker with the guys while Leah was here at home losing his baby?

No wonder she hadn't answered his calls last night. Hell, maybe she didn't want him to ever know she was pregnant. She'd had at least a month, apparently, to tell him, and she hadn't let on that she was carrying a baby or that he was going to be a father. Sure, she'd told him a couple of times that she needed to talk to him. But shouldn't she have pressed the issue a bit harder?

She stirred, turned to lie on her side. The small mewling sound she made—sounded like it came from her soul— kicked him into action. Quietly, he tugged his boots off one at a time and set them on the floor. He crossed the room in a few big strides, and then he lifted his knee to the side of the bed and stretched out beside her.

"Leah." Lying with his chest pressed to her back, he draped his arm over her waist and buried his face in her hair.

"Trace," she whispered. She covered his hand with hers and squeezed like she was afraid to let go.

"Dammit, darlin', why didn't you call me?" His throat tight

with emotion, he huffed out a shaky sigh and tightened his hold on her.

"Nashville?" She sounded panicked now, and rather than snuggle in close to him, she let go of his hand and scrambled away from him on the bed.

"I'm here," he said quietly. "I'm here."

"Why—?" In the thick gray light, her eyes were bright with tears. "How?"

"Why didn't you call me?" he asked again.

He reached for her, but she pulled away again.

"Leah."

She flopped over to her back and lifted her hands to cover her face. A wave of relief rolled over him when he saw she still wore her ring, but it was quickly followed by a quick stab of anger and guilt. If she loved him, why hadn't she told him about the baby? Why hadn't she called him to tell him she was in the hospital? If she loved him, why had it been Duncan who had called to let him know Leah had miscarried his baby? Did he have the right to be angry with her? When she was hurting? When he should step up and hold her? Love her through the grief?

"Duncan," she whispered. "Duncan called you."

"Well, I'm glad someone decided I should know what was going on—"

"No," she sobbed. "Please don't be angry with me, Trace. Not now."

"Leah," he groaned and dropped his head to bury his face in his pillow. "Dammit. Why didn't you—"

"Please?" She rolled her head on her own pillow and wiped at her eyes. Pushed her hair from her face. "I'm so sorry. But I can't take you being angry with me on top of…this."

"C'mere." He lifted his arm, face still buried in the pillow, and waited for her to scoot in close to him. "I love you so much."

"Me, too." She pushed in so close to him this time, it was like she wanted to occupy the same space he did. He shifted again to lie on his side and dropped his arm around her again. Leah pressed her face against his chest, her tears warm and wet on his t-shirt.

"Does it hurt?"

Her answer was so long in coming, he wondered if she had gone to sleep. Finally, her whole body shuddered against his, and she gave him a slight shrug.

"It did."

"It's okay now?"

Her bitter laugh gave way to a sob.

"I mean…the pain…the…"

Hell, he'd never been so intimately involved with a woman that he had considered having a conversation like this. Sex was one thing, but what he and Leah had shared —what he thought they had together—and now this; this was a whole different level of intimacy. He felt like an extra at the moment. She hadn't needed him. Not for the first several weeks of her pregnancy. Not for the nightmare she woke up to this morning. Maybe not now.

It had been unfair of her to keep this from him; he was angry about that. Damned right he was angry with her. But she'd been terrified about pregnancies and babies, and she had lain here in this bed without him and suffered whatever the hell kind of pain women suffered when they lost a baby. And now she was lying here in his arms, still keeping everything to herself.

How the hell could he love her through anything if she didn't trust him to be here? His whole body vibrated with helplessness, with his frustration.

"It hurts," she whispered. "It's…uncomfortable."

"You know I love you. Right?"

"I do."

"And I would do anything for you."

"I know."

"Then why? Why didn't you tell me, Leah? Why was it Duncan here to rescue you?"

"Stevi called him—"

"Darlin'." Trace cupped her chin in his hand and held her still. "If I had known you were carrying my baby, I would never have left you here to travel with Tanner."

She jerked her chin to get away from him, but he wouldn't let go. Realization dawned on him when she stared at him silently and finally closed her eyes in a last-ditch effort to hide.

"You didn't want me to stay?"

"I didn't want to make you choose," she whispered. "He's your brother. And you can deny it all you want, Nashville, but that means something to you."

"Choose," he repeated. He loosened his grip on her chin. She rolled her lips inward and blinked at him. "Playing a few shows with Tanner's not like choosing to leave you."

"I know that." She nodded. "But I needed you to do what you thought was right."

"If I had known about the baby, I would have stayed right here. With you—"

"I don't want you to feel obligated—"

"I don't feel obligated to do anything. For you. I love you. Don't you get that? I love you. There's nothing more important to me than you. And us."

"I know." She nodded. "I know. I'm sorry. I was going to tell you, but—"

"When?"

"The first time I was going to tell you, you had to take Margo to the ER."

"Was there another time?"

"The day Tanner showed up." She drew in a deep breath and let her eyes meet his for a moment before looking away. "The errand I ran that morning…was an appointment with my ob-gyn."

"An appointment you made because you thought you were pregnant."

She nodded. Cold, hard anger settled in his stomach.

"I should have been with you."

"Nashville."

"If I had known you thought you were pregnant, I would have gone with you. I would have told my brother to get back on his bus and go. And I would have been with you earlier when you…"

"You just told me yesterday that Tanner was in trouble. That he needed you longer. That you were worried about your mama. I wanted to give you that time. I wanted to be tough enough to wait you out. Until you were done saving them, so you could come back to us."

"It wasn't your right to choose them for me."

"I know." She nodded. Her eyes were glassy again. She blinked and scattered more tears over her face. "I'm sorry, Trace. I'm so sorry."

The sadness and the fear painted on her face twisted his lungs so tight he couldn't breathe. Still angry, not sure when he wouldn't feel angry with her over this, he pushed his own emotions away and gathered her in his arms again.

"When were you due?" His voice was tight and low, and his throat ached. He wanted to know everything.

Everything there was to know. When would they have had the baby? When had she first thought she might be pregnant? It hit him, lying there with her in his arms, that she'd been tired, and he'd heard her in the bathroom a time or two and wondered if she had the flu. She must think he was an idiot. Maybe she thought all southern men were slow on the uptake? Maybe she'd planned to keep the secret and take care of it while he was gone.

The thought brought a rush of rage, but when she stirred in his arms, guilt for thinking such a thing ripped through him and left him weak and sickened.

"What?" she whispered. "What's wrong?"

"Nothing."

"You're not gonna forgive me." Her whisper was heavy with sorrow. "Are you?"

"Is that what you want? For me to stay angry? For me to leave again?"

He opened his eyes to find her watching him with sad eyes.

"You love the music," she reminded him.

"I told you once I feel like everything I've ever done was a way to get to you."

"And now you're gonna leave."

"I didn't say that."

"I lied to you."

"Why?" His voice gruff, he smoothed Leah's hair from her face to gentle the anger a bit.

"I denied it for the first several weeks," she mumbled. "Because I didn't want to admit it."

He let her words hang and finally fall. Let silence blanket them again. Tried to push the anger away. Knowing that she hadn't trusted him the way he thought she did hurt him more than anything Tanner could ever have done to him.

"Tanner's got money trouble."

"Did he ask you for money?" She slid her hand under the tail of his shirt. Trace flinched, determined not to moan with pleasure just because she spread her warm fingers over his belly.

"No. But he's taking money from Mama, and I don't like it."

"It's okay." She fiddled with the button of his jeans and then cupped his dick, denim and all, in her hand. "I can't do this for a while, anyway."

"Because that's what we're about?"

"You might get lucky if you're out on the road with the Congregation."

Rather than answer her, he rolled to lie on his back. Blinked at the ceiling.

"And what? You go back to your battery-operated cock for orgasms?"

She sobbed and pressed her face to his chest. "I love you, Nashville."

"But you want me to leave."

"You're not gonna be happy here. Not with Tanner out there doing what he's doing. Not if you're worried about your mother."

"And what about you? I'm just not supposed to worry about you?"

"I'll be okay."

She would. She'd just lost her baby—could he even claim this baby as his, this loss as his, if she had never even told him she was pregnant?—and Stevi and Duncan had handled it. Taken care of her. Cleaned up the aftermath. Tucked her back in bed. Called him. Never mind that he'd rented a car and driven eighty-five miles per hour and faster, desperate to get to her and put his arms around her.

Never mind that he loved her.

She would be okay without him.

CHAPTER 47

IT WAS EASIER TO HURT IN A GRAY ROOM, AND EVEN EASIER just to keep her eyes closed. Leah slept so much she had no idea what day it was when she did open her eyes. Sometimes she awoke curled up in Nashville's arms. Sometimes she woke up alone. Once she woke up to Stevi napping beside her.

Trace was angry with her, and though she knew she deserved it, she hadn't been prepared for how much his anger, his disappointment, would hurt. He wrestled with his responsibilities, and his indecision was a knife slicing clean and slow over her skin. She watched him when he didn't notice. Fisted her hands around her sheets and hung on while she watched the play of emotion on his face. She knew he loved her, but she waited for him to decide he needed to go back to Nashville.

He needed to check on his mom; she got it. But while he was there, he would want to check in with the crew at the

Fork. He would tell Pearl that Leah had kept his baby from him. That she had miscarried, and if it had been up to her, she wouldn't have told him. They would have eventually started their lives together on a pretty big lie of omission that would eventually burst through the foundation and tear them apart.

She wouldn't have done that. She would have told him. She had just asked Duncan to wait, because she wanted to scrape herself together before she called Trace. If she had looked a little more put together before he came for her, it would have been easier to push him away again. Not forever. Just long enough for him to straighten things out with his mother and for her to grieve on her own.

Her phone buzzed on the nightstand. Head buried in her pillow, she closed her eyes and listened to the drone of voices from downstairs. Trace was here, talking to Stevi. But he would go any day now.

Maybe it was Margo on the phone. Or Leah's mom. The vibrating stopped, and Leah breathed a sigh of relief. Maybe it was simply the grief still crushing her, but at the moment, she didn't believe she and Trace would work. Love wasn't always enough, and this clearly was one of those times. Their lives were too different. Trace was responsible for too many people; she didn't want to burden him. Maybe. Maybe he would take care of things and then come back to her. Maybe they could pick up the pieces and go on.

She would pray for that, but maybe that was a lost cause. She'd bargained with God once, and she'd gone back on her word. Maybe instead of taking that out on Kenzi and Joe, God had just exacted revenge on her and Trace.

She didn't believe that, either.

A twinge low in her belly sent her heart to her throat again. Her phone vibrated again on the nightstand. Downstairs, Duncan's voice joined the conversation. They were probably tired of Leah's wallowing. Trace needed to get on the road. Stevi and Duncan needed her to pull herself together to get back to the Queen.

She blinked and reached for her phone. Flopped over to her back when she saw Joe's number on the screen. Pressed the talk button, put the phone to her ear, and cradled her stomach with her free hand.

"You okay?"

She had talked to Joe and Kenzi. No idea when, because time had stopped mattering after waking from that dream. The one where she'd felt the warm, sticky blood on her legs.

"Sure."

"Stevi said you won't get out of bed."

Leah squeezed her eyes closed. "I will."

"When?"

"I don't know, Joe."

"Leah?"

"What?"

"You think I wanted to get out of bed the morning after my wife had a stroke?"

She sniffled and lifted her other hand to dash at her eyes.

"No."

"What about now?" Joe sounded urgent, frustrated. "You think I'm happy to get out of bed every morning? Doing the mom things and the dad things? You think I like the way my kids have already accepted this new life? You think I want to visit my wife in a nursing home every day?'

"No."

"I don't. Leah Hague, there are days I open my eyes, and I hate my life. I hate God for this. I hate cigarette companies. I hate my wife for smoking. I hate my wife's doctor for not stopping this. And most of all…"

Leah swallowed hard when he stopped talking.

"Most of all what?"

"I hate myself most of all."

"It's not your fault."

"Isn't it?"

"How could you have stopped what happened?"

"I could have insisted she stop smoking. I could have told her I would leave. Might not have changed a damned thing, but every day I ask myself why I didn't insist."

"It's not the same, Joe."

"No, Leah, it's not. You're lucky. You're healthy. You can do this again. You can have a baby with the man you love. Or you can not have a baby with the man you love. Doesn't matter. The thing is, you have a choice. You can choose to get up and love him and get on with it. You can grieve with him and draw strength from each other. I can't do that."

Leah covered her eyes with her hand, as if she could hide from Joe, as if he was watching her.

"I don't have any answers about why you miscarried. About why my wife had a stroke. I don't have any wisdom to share." His deep breath, the attempt to rope his emotions under control, was a jolt to Leah's heart. She bit her lip.

"But I can tell you one thing."

"What?" she whispered.

"Life's too damned short to waste even a second of it."

His words hung in the air between them. Leah ground the heel of her right hand into her right eye.

"Remember that."

The line went dead, but Leah didn't move. She wasn't trying to figure out how to reply to Joe. Even if he hadn't hung up, she would have held her silence. Tears crept from her eyes and rolled into her hair. Finally, she lowered the phone to the bed and pushed herself up on her elbows.

Laughter floated up the steps. Stevi's voice. Trace. Stevi again.

Leah sat up and cast a long look around the dark room. Slowly, she scooted to the edge of the bed and swung her legs over to put her feet on the floor. She'd been up to use the bathroom since that nightmare, but she hadn't ventured down the steps.

Now she padded to the bathroom and peered at herself in the mirror. The darkness was thicker in here, and she only saw a dark shape reflected back at her. With a trembling hand, she flipped the light on and stared at her pale, tear-stained face.

Disgusted with herself, she moved slowly but with new determination. Leaned in to the shower to turn the taps. Stripped her clothes off—Stevi had picked out clean pajamas for her when they'd come home from the hospital—and waited a moment to make sure the water was hot before stepping into the shower stall.

THE FIRST THING SHE SAW WHEN SHE LINGERED AT THE kitchen door was the duffle bag tossed down between the table legs and the door. Duncan was talking, and Stevi—at the table—was laughing with her legs drawn up to rest her feet on the edge of the chair. Leah marveled at her sister. She'd taken care of her. She'd been angry with her for keeping the baby from Trace, but Stevi had done everything for her since she'd called her for help.

Suddenly, Stevi turned her head and noticed her. Her eyes grew wide with wonder, and she glanced toward the other side of the kitchen. Leah assumed that meant Trace was over by the pantry or the basement door.

Life's too damned short to waste a second of it.

Joe's voice pumped through her like a second heartbeat. Hand on the door trim, she took a slow, deep breath to steady herself, swallowed hard, and took a step into the kitchen.

"Hey." Duncan grinned. Leah wasn't fooled. He was angry, too, that she had kept Trace in the dark about the baby.

"Hey."

"Sit down." Stevi climbed out of her chair so quickly, she almost sent it crashing into the wall behind her. "Let me get you...what? Do you want some water? Are you hungry?"

Leah cleared her throat and shook her head at Stevi. "No, thank you."

"Leah."

Leah ignored the concern on Stevi's face and turned slowly, stomach at her feet, to look at Trace. He stood by the pantry, left shoulder propped on the wall, arms folded over his chest.

"Can I..." She hesitated. Licked her lips. *Life's too damned short to waste a second.* "Can I talk to you about something?"

Probably, he'd like to throttle her. Rage a little. Yell. Maybe she needed to let him go back to Nashville to do just that. Or maybe the road, Tanner's tour, would better serve him as an outlet for his rage. They'd covered that, though. That he loved his brother and his mom and the music, and that maybe he could find someone else out there to give him things Leah couldn't.

"Sure." He straightened. Guilt bowled her over when she saw the bruised skin under his eyes. "You can walk me out."

Leah's heart slammed in her chest and then crashed down to her stomach, still at her feet. She watched him lean over to snag the handles of the duffle bag and then shoot a look at Duncan and then Stevi.

"You're leaving?" The emotion in her throat skinned her voice to a hoarse whisper.

He shrugged. Wrapped his arms around Stevi, kissed her cheek, and then he and Duncan did the shoulder bump and hand clasp guys did. Stevi's fingers found hers and squeezed before letting go. Leah followed Trace outside and halfway across the driveway on trembling knees.

"Nashville." She stopped. Folded her arms over her chest and pressed her fist to her mouth. He tossed the bag into the backseat of the car. Leah eyed the Indiana plate on the back of the car and then looked at him curiously.

"When Duncan called me to tell me you were in an exam room after miscarrying our baby upstairs in our bedroom, I was desperate to get home to you. So I rented a car."

His words were sharp enough to penetrate her skin and land in her heart and her belly, making it hard to draw a breath, let alone speak.

"But you're leaving me." She tipped her head. She'd pulled her wet hair back into a ponytail after her shower. The humidity out here was enough to make Trace sweat; he ducked his head now to wipe his face on his shirtsleeve. Leah shivered, cold with the knowledge that he was leaving. "Again."

"You told me to go," he reminded her. "You said you would be okay."

"And what if I won't be?"

Trace leaned on the back of the rental. Leah tore her eyes away from him and looked at his truck, parked in front of the garage.

"I gotta check on Mama. I'll be back."

"What about Tanner?"

Trace lifted his hands and pushed his fingers through his hair. He offered up a long, low, frustrated growl and a deep, dramatic shrug.

"I dunno, darlin'."

"Am I still?" She blinked. "Your darlin'?"

"Of course."

"Because this feels like goodbye, Nashville."

"It's not goodbye," he promised her. Too bad he promised from all the way across the driveway. Leah hunched her shoulders and lowered her chin to her chest. Tempted to let it go, she remembered what Joe had just said. *Everything* Joe had just said. He couldn't change anything for his family.

Leah could. Leah could try. And life was too damned short to put it off a second longer.

"There's something I need to tell you."

Even from across the wide expanse of concrete, Leah saw his eyebrows jump.

"What could you possibly have to tell me now?" He propped his hands on his hips and filled his cheeks with air. Let it out slowly, as if he'd needed to count to three to stay calm.

"I'm still pregnant." She took a few steps toward him and then faltered. Afraid that he wouldn't care. That she'd hurt him too badly with her secrets.

"You're what?"

She nodded.

"Stevi and Duncan—"

"Were not in the exam room," she whispered. "I was carrying twins."

"You were—? What?"

"Twins," she whispered. "I lost one baby. It's…there's a thing called vanishing twin syndrome…when…" She stopped talking when he only stared at her, but she was anxious to say the rest of it. "But…I…this was…actually a miscarriage…"

"When did you find this out?"

"The morning…" She breathed deeply and squeezed her eyes closed when she felt dizzy. "I lost the baby. I had no idea…before then. Dr. Hendricks said my HCG…the pregnancy hormone…was really high before, but she never said…"

"Dammit, Leah." He pushed off the car and paced a small circle on the driveway.

"What?" She wailed and threw her arms up in surrender. "What, Trace?"

"You've known this since it happened. You knew when we were lying in bed together just this morning that you were still carrying my baby, and you didn't—"

"I'm telling you now!" The words would have been a shout, but again, the emotion and the tears were so tight in her throat, she could barely get them out. "I'm telling you now. I'm pregnant, Trace. And I love you. And I *need* you with me. I need you *here*. With me. With us."

Trace huffed out a deep, harsh breath. Followed it up with another. Leah took a step toward him when he sank to a squat there in the driveway. He ducked his head and covered his face with his hands.

"I don't want to be that girlfriend. That wife. The wife that makes you choose between me and your family. I don't want to nag you. I don't want to hurt you. I never meant to hurt you. But I don't want to be here, alone, with our baby. I love you. I love you, Nashville. Please?"

"Do they know?" He stood, threw an accusing arm out to gesture at the house. "Stevi? Duncan?"

"No one knows. But you and me."

"We're having a baby."

She nodded.

"Son-of—twins. Twins?"

"I really, really need you to say you love me," she whispered. "I need you to put your arms around me. And tell me this is all gonna be okay."

"Oh, Leah, darlin', my head is spinning. I can't—"

"Nashville," she sobbed. Her knees were weak, and she felt a rush of nausea. What if he didn't come back? What if he had decided he didn't need her drama?

"C'mere." He sidled up to her, boots bracketing her feet, her middle pressed to his, and slipped his arms around her.

"I love you." He dropped a kiss on top of her head. "I loved you from the word go."

"I hurt you."

He nodded his head against hers. "You did."

"I'm sorry." She pressed her whisper to his neck and wrapped her arms around his back. "I'm so sorry. I just wanted to do the right thing."

"The right thing's gotta be something we decide together."

She nodded. Breathed in his scent and let it calm her.

"Just promise me you'll always come back."

"I promise I will always come back home to you."

CHAPTER 48

LEAH RESTED HER HAND OVER HER BELLY. SHE FELT HUGE, and it surprised her each time she caught a glimpse of herself in the mirror to find her stomach only slightly bigger. No one had noticed yet that she was carrying a baby.

Then again, she supposed it was much too early to show.

Trace called most nights, though sometimes he was too busy. And sometimes, she was too busy to answer. He had been gone long enough to make her uneasy. Apparently, Tanner had gambled some big money, and he'd spent big money on the bus and a mansion no one lived in, and suddenly he had found himself close to bankrupt. Add in some new good-looking star encroaching on his heartthrob territory, and he was feeling threatened. Thank God, Trace had told him no. No more touring with him. No holiday shows. No awards shows. Nothing.

But Trace was up to his elbows at his mom's. He had decided to dig into her finances while he was there, to make sure his brother hadn't helped himself to more than the initial twenty grand he'd copped to.

Either that, or Trace was stalling because he wasn't sure about Leah. About their future.

Leah watched a group of guys come in and glance at the stage. They had a new girl—singer, songwriter—setting up to play, but she wouldn't go on for at least another hour.

"Hi, guys. What can I get you?" she asked as the four of them approached the bar. Two kept their eyes on the stage, one studied a drink menu, and the other studied her.

"Can I get a glass of Dykstra cab?" he asked. "And a date with you."

"I can do the cab," she answered with a smile. "Not the date."

"That's a shame."

She laughed and shook her head as she slipped away from him to get his wine. Stevi bumped her hip as she passed her behind the bar. Margo and Tania waited tables. For a Thursday evening, they were busy. Busy meant Leah crawled into bed exhausted—even when Duncan insisted she cut out early—and exhausted meant she didn't dream so much.

Patrons lined the bar two deep. Leah saw four more guys come in now, as she turned to deliver her customer's wine. Looked like college guys. That was somewhat unusual. Their clientele was usually a bit older. She watched them approach the bar. Saw one of them high five a guy, and then say something to a guy at the other end of the bar. Noticed three guys huddled in conversation, one of them with a ball cap pulled low.

Her stomach flip-flopped, but she had just talked to Trace no more than an hour ago. He had been at his mom's house, eating pot roast and mashed potatoes.

"So you don't date customers?"

"I'm seeing someone," she answered simply.

"Seeing someone." The guy shrugged. "Doesn't sound serious."

Leah rested her left hand on her stomach. The guy noticed the ring and looked up to meet her eyes. She arched her eyebrows and nodded. "Pretty serious, actually."

"Well, no wonder you look so happy." He sipped his wine. "Congratulations."

"Thank you."

Her phone buzzed in her pocket. She backed away from the guy—his buddies still weren't ready to order—and pulled it out to look at it.

What're you listening to?

City and Colour. Lover Come Back.

She glanced at the guys huddled at the end of the bar, disappointed when her phone buzzed again and none of them was looking at a phone. She rolled her eyes and huffed out a sigh. As if she wouldn't know her lover if he was standing at the bar.

Besides, he couldn't have covered four hundred miles in an hour.

Me, too.

Heart in her throat, Leah looked up again and swept her gaze around the bar. Nowhere in sight. Her phone buzzed again.

Look up.

She lifted her eyes to the stairs and finally to the mezzanine level of the bar. Trace leaned on the rail and grinned from ear to ear.

"Nashville!"

She nearly tripped over the bar as she hurried to get to him. Edged through people standing around the tables. She reached the bottom of the staircase as his foot hit the bottom step.

"I thought you were at your mom's." She threw her arms around him and tucked her face to his neck.

"You're not the only one who can keep secrets." He gathered her in close to hold her. "I left first thing this morning."

"I am so happy to see you."

"Me, too." He smoothed his hand over her back and patted her butt. "How're you feeling? How's the baby?"

"Good. We see Dr. Hendricks tomorrow."

He nodded. "I know. That's why I'm back."

"You're going with me?" She pulled her head back to grin at him.

"I am going with you to every appointment you have until we have this baby."

"Good."

"Was that guy hitting on you?"

She laughed softly. "He asked me out."

"And what did you say?"

"That I'm seeing someone, of course." Trace rested his chin on her head as she pressed her lips to his neck. "And that it's pretty serious."

***

Thank you for reading Love, Nashville. I hope you loved Leah and Trace as much as I do. If you enjoyed reading their story, please consider leaving a review on Amazon or Goodreads or other book review sites. Your time is very much appreciated!

FOREVER, DUNCAN CHAPTER 1

Yep. She was probably gonna kill him. Guys his age and younger dropped dead from sudden cardiac arrest, right? Jesus. No way was Duncan Marks gonna live through much more of this. If she leaned over one more time, anywhere near him, and treated him to a glimpse of the smooth, tan skin in the deep v of her blouse and the pale pink lace of her bra, he was down. For the count. Knock out. He had tried—Scout's honor times a trillion—not to look. But damn, even keeping his eyes on the long, slender column of her neck and her strong cheekbones, the curve of her full lips when she smiled—her full pink lips and thoughts of what they might taste like, *feel* like, could kill him, too—made his heart race and his dick kick to life in his jeans.

Tried and failed. Given up. Looked as often as he could. Working the bar—hell, *breathing in* the same room—with Stevi Hague was lethal. His blood pressure was in stroke zone; he felt it skyrocket whenever she was around.

And to make matters worse? Didn't help to look away. So save the *save yourself, Marks* thing, thanks anyway. He could give the woman his back—oh, he'd fantasized about that, too, wondered what her skin would feel like pressed up against him, her breasts against his bare back—all night long, but he was still skating on the edge. Just her whiskey thick voice and deep, throaty laugh turned his dick to steel. No getting around it.

If he didn't get his hands on her soon, done. Over. Heart attack.

If he did get his hands on her anytime soon, still done. Dead by shotgun, maybe. Stevi's dad's finger on the trigger. Or even her sister Leah's.

Stevi Hague was Off-Limits. Hands. Off. Do not pass go. Do not collect kisses and definitely no touching. Do not engage.

The strappy shoes she wore tonight were enough to drive a man fucking crazy. Never mind the skin in the v of her blouse—she had six freckles and a faint puckery scar near the hollow of her throat—and her hands—he loved the sight of her long, elegant fingers wrapped around a pint glass or a wine bottle when she poured, the red straps around her ankles and her bare feet brought to mind those same red straps and ankles wrapped around his waist and similar red straps around her wrists—

"I need you."

Back to her in a useless attempt at self-preservation, Duncan clamped his jaws shut and clacked his teeth together hard enough to make them hurt. He ran through a mental list of the spirits he used to mix drinks, called to mind the many times he'd overdone it on said spirits and spent the next day cozied up to the porcelain god, and breathed deeply through his nose. Might've worked, but then there she was, soft curves pressed up against his side. Instead of calming him, the deep breath filled him with the scent of Stevi's shampoo and perfume and a whole damned lot of longing.

"Wondered when you'd come to your senses." He bumped her hip and dropped a wink, even though technically, that should be off-limits, too. She had started flirting back a while ago, and holy hell, if that didn't just make his life more complicated.

Stevi rolled her eyes and shook her head, which only gave him another strong whiff of her shampoo.

"I need Blue Balls," she told him with a sweet grin.

"Yeah? How about that? I got some," he muttered as he looked away from her big green eyes.

"What?"

Duncan wasn't sure what was more painful: her hearty laugh (because he sure as hell wasn't joking) or that she rested her hand on the back of his wrist. Because hello? There were times when skin-on-skin contact with her was like a lit match on a stream of gasoline.

"That all?" He cleared his throat and set the bottle of Merlot he had been pouring down on the back bar.

"Um."

He heard the little giggle and braced himself for whatever she was about to ask for next.

"An Angel's Tit." She offered him a little grin and wriggled her eyebrows at him.

He snorted. "Yeah, not going there," he answered. "Thought I taught you how to make that one."

"You did…"

He turned with the two glasses of Merlot in his hands and set them on the bar. Stevi hovered beside him as he pushed the glasses gently over the polished wood to the guy waiting on them.

"But?" Duncan spared her a quick glance—she was leaning just so again, and this time not only did he get a peek of the skin in the v of her blouse, but also the curve of her right breast twisted just so in the pink lace.

"Um. I was gonna go hit that table in the back. They've been waiting a while."

Already fixing the Blue Balls, the first drink she'd asked for, Duncan shot a look toward the table Stevi mentioned. Four guys, all of them probably in Stevi's wheelhouse, stood around a tall table. One of them was talking with his hands, and from where he stood at the bar, Duncan saw a tattoo peeking out from under the t-shirt straining over his bicep. Definitely something Stevi would go for, no doubt.

Stevi still waited at his side. Duncan swallowed down a snide comment—it was one thing to tease her about her serial dating habits, but he would never take a serious shot at her for it—and gave her a curt nod.

"Go."

"Yeah?"

"Yep. I got this."

He watched her go, mesmerized by the sway of her hips, but he caught himself. Turned his attention back to the Blue Curacao in his hand and let his anger—okay, jealousy—kill the damned raging hard-on. It did kind of frustrate the hell out of him. He'd known Stevi since she was sixteen or seventeen and he was twenty, and suddenly, ten years later, he noticed she was pretty and sexy as hell, and he didn't remember inviting his dick to the party, but here it was, and it had to notice and approve of every damned thing she did.

Determined not to look at her again, because who the hell wanted to watch the woman he wanted flirt with a whole table full of guys, Duncan finished the Blue Balls and started mixing the Angel's Tit.

"Is Leah okay?"

He nodded without looking at Tania. He liked the new girl they had hired to waitress okay—was she still new, he wondered, after a month of working here?— and sure, she was cute to look at, too. But he wasn't going to discuss Stevi's sister or any of her particulars with her just yet. Leah had been fine a half hour ago, but she was tired, and Trace—her boyfriend or fiancé or whatever the hell they were calling it these days—had insisted she sit down for a bit. Duncan had to give the guy credit. If Leah were his girlfriend and carrying his baby—complications or not—he would insist a lot harder and a lot more often that she take it easy.

Of course, Leah would get in his face if he did so. One thing about the Hague women—and even though his stepsister Margo's name wasn't Hague, she was a first cousin, so Margo, too—they were damned stubborn and independent, and a man better be damned sure of himself if he thought he was going to step in front of one of them to catch a bullet for her. He wouldn't put it past any of them to shove that man aside and catch the bullet barehanded. And then mosey home to put dinner on the table or to the Queen to serve up a round of drinks.

Aaannddd, there he went again. Looking over at Stevi. The girls owned the bar; Duncan worked for them. They had talked a time or two about Duncan buying in. He wanted a piece of the place. First of all, it was prime real estate. Second, the bar had wobbled a bit in the beginning and recently baby-stepped to the top five bars in Adam's Bay, Illinois. Having Trace Dixon—country music songwriter and brother of Tanner Dixon country music sensation—here didn't hurt business, either. Tanner Dixon and the Lightnin' Congregation had topped billboard charts on and off for a few years, mostly with hit songs Trace wrote, and Duncan was man enough to admit both Dixon brothers were good-looking guys.

Might not say that if Trace had fallen so stupidly in love with Stevi Hague rather than Leah.

Duncan had tended bar here and there through the years. That he had a degree in business management surprised a lot of people. He hoped it was because he tended to dress in a style best described as 90s grunge and not because people assumed he was dumb or not ambitious. When he started working with the girls, he upgraded from bartender to mixologist, but he helped with everything at the Queen.

Including security.

Not that they ever needed much in the way of muscle.

Still, he sized the guys up at the table where Stevi was just walking away. Two of them were head to head, eyes directed toward a girl at the end of the bar, so Duncan all but dismissed them. As a threat to himself or Stevi, not general safety, because at the moment he was more in tune with Stevi than the safety of anyone in the place. One of them was looking at his phone, but the fourth one—the guy with the bulging biceps and the tattoo—was watching her. Eyes on her ass, actually. Duncan squeezed his hands into fists.

"Easy."

His stepsister's voice at his left shoulder was cool and calm. She eased by him, patted his back as if he were a toddler gearing up to throw a tantrum—Margo would know, as she was the mother of a thirteen-month-old tyrant slash princess—and settled in to stand at his right side.

"She won't go out with any of them." Margo spoke quietly

as she reached over the bar to gather empty glasses. Three girls slid up to the bar even as Margo cleared the spot.

He knew that. Stevi was a flirt, with a capital F, and a serial dater who just loved to be on the go. She rarely dated the same guy twice, and she often told them—Duncan and Leah and Margo—that the goodnight kisses were about all she could bear. Duncan got it; listening to her talk about goodnight kisses or good morning kisses or any other kinds of kisses made him see red. The thought of anything else happening on her dates drove him to the gym more often than not. Not like he could go anywhere else and throw punches and not end up arrested for assault or property damage.

"Tania asked about Leah," he ignored Margo's comment. With a room full of people, Green Day on the sound system, and Stevi making her way back over to him to tell him again what she needed, now wasn't the time to talk about Stevi and how he felt about her.

Duncan nudged the dirty sounding cocktails at Stevi as she approached, heard her ask for four drafts—a Blue Moon and three Buds—and glanced at Margo.

"I was just up there. Trace is rubbing her feet," she told him. "How anyone can make you feel like you're interrupting something wildly intimate when it's a foot rub is beyond me, but they did it."

"Because she moans the same way when they're having sex," Stevi announced as she picked up the drinks and slipped behind them down the bar to deliver them.

"She knows this how?" Duncan narrowed his eyes at Margo.

"She lives there," Margo reminded him with a shrug.

"She's never home!" He tossed his hands up and laughed. Tried to anyway. His brain was still hung up on the guy with the tattooed gun who had kept his eyes on Stevi's ass until she reached the bar to deliver his order.

"You think I should ask her to move in with me?"

"What?"

"To give Leah and Trace some room?"

"Their bedroom is upstairs." He reached for a pint glass, stuck it under the Blue Moon tap, and stared at Margo with wide eyes this time.

"Yeah, well, me and Berkley don't need privacy like they do."

"They'll have a live-in babysitter." He set the first glass on the bar and reached for another, eyes still on Margo.

"I could use a live-in babysitter." Margo tipped her head and arched her eyebrows. Duncan opened his mouth, ready to deliver the line she most likely knew was coming. Trace and Leah might need private time and a babysitter, eventually. Margo didn't. He didn't say it, though, because Margo's ex had been poking around a bit lately, and Margo looked exhausted and sad about it. And Jess suddenly appearing in Margo and Berkley's life again made Duncan angry.

No need to argue about that here.

"Really?" Margo eyed him suspiciously. "You're goin' easy on me? God, it's time to do something a little crazy if you're goin' easy on me."

"No need for crazy," he answered as he draped an arm around her shoulders and gave her a squeeze.

"Remind me," Stevi clutched at Margo's arm as she appeared behind her again. "When Leah and Trace do get engaged, we are not having an asinine drink-fest bachelorette party. 'Kay?"

"Sure we are." Margo shrugged. "Duncan just told me I need to do something crazy. You can babysit Berkley that night if you're not looking for a good time."

Stevi watched Margo duck away from Duncan's arm and slip out the other end of the bar. She blinked and looked up at Duncan.

"Really, it might be a good thing for Margo to do something crazy," she mumbled as she reached for two of the beers he'd just pulled. "I, for one, am done with it. Crazy is so overrated."

"Right." Duncan nodded. For the hell of it—who didn't want to follow Stevi across a room and watch her ass work her sexy little jeans—and also just to get a feel for the guys at the table she was serving, he picked up the remaining two beers and followed her over.

***

Want to read more about Stevi and Duncan? Download Forever, Duncan, The Mississippi Queen book 2 here:

https://amzn.to/3pZuS46

ACKNOWLEDGMENTS

Updated notes: Revelry in my hometown is closed. Still thankful to Paula & Rusty Williams for the good times I had there and for the welcome to hang out as often as I wanted to write the series! Wishing you both well!!

While the Mississippi Queen is an awesome place to be in Adam's Bay, Illinois, it actually all started in my head and in this great wine bar called Revelry. If you follow me on Facebook or Instagram, you know I spend a lot of time at Revelry. You should, too.

I have had planning and strategy sessions there with my very creative and smart editor, who yes, happens to be my daughter. I've had more than a few days at Revelry when I was totally in the zone (writing) and was shocked to look around and see the subtle differences between Revelry and the Mississippi Queen, and remember that the Queen is a fictitious bar. And, of course, my husband and I spend a lot of evenings there with our friends.

So, thank you to Paula and Rusty Williams, who own Revelry. Thank you to your staff, most specifically Amanda, Klancy, and Austin. Thanks for putting up with us hanging out there all the time.

If you'll have me, I'll still be hanging around to write there, even after this series is complete.

And thanks to Dawn Peters and Kate Carley for being the best beta readers ever! You guys rock!

ABOUT THE AUTHOR

As an only child, Tracy Broemmer grew up with a wild imagination. An avid reader from a young age, she spent a lot of time with her nose buried in books and a lot of time making up her own stories. She penned her first book in grade school and hasn't stopped writing since.

Tracy is the author of the Lorelei Bluffs women's fiction series, the women's fiction series the Williams Legacy, and several stand-alone women's fiction novels. She has recently dabbled in contemporary romance as well.

Learn more about Tracy and her books at www.broemmerbooks.com

ALSO BY TRACY BROEMMER

Women's Fiction Novels:
Luther's Cross (Writing as Therese Kinkaide)
Luther's Cross 10th Anniversary Edition (Tracy Broemmer)
Fairytale (Writing as Therese Kinkaide)
Just Like Them
Small Hours
Picket Fences
Two Story Home
Green-Eyed Girl
Say Everything
Come Home For Christmas
Sketching Litchfield Lake
Ever, Again
Safe as Houses
Damsel

Every Little Thing, Lorelei Bluffs, Book 1
Two A.M., Lorelei Bluffs, Book 2
Blind, Lorelei Bluffs, Book 3
Leaving July, Lorelei Bluffs, Book 4
Hesitation Marks, Lorelei Bluffs, Book 5
Four Letter Words, Lorelei Bluffs, Book 6
See Kate, Lorelei Bluffs, Book 7

Loved You More, Lorelei Bluffs, Book 8

A Lorelei Ending, Lorelei Bluffs, Book 9

I Do, Lorelei Bluffs, Book 10

Truth Is, The Williams Legacy, Book 1

Other People's Ugly, The Williams Legacy, Book 2

Omissions, The Williams Legacy, Book 3

Contemporary Romance Novels:

Destiny's Calling: Your Future Is Waiting

Wedding Day Shenanigans

Holiday Fling

The Kiss Off

Something Like Love

Love, Nashville, The Mississippi Queen Trilogy, Book 1

Forever, Duncan, The Mississippi Queen Trilogy, Book 2

Always, Jess, The Mississippi Queen Trilogy, Book 3

Getting' Hitched, The H Books, Book 1

Contemporary Romance Novellas:

Indian Summer, A Novella

Dear Jaclyn Perris, A Novella

French Stuff, A Novella (Previously published in Just Coffee)

Boone's Girl, A Novella (Previously published in Aced)

Holdin' On, A Novella (Previously published in Snowed Inn)

Contemporary Romance Short Stories:

Perfect Pictures, The Wine Tasting Series, Traminette

Coming Home, The Wine Tasting Series, Edelweiss

Save Me Every Dance, The Wine Tasting Series, Rosé

Marry Me, The Wine Tasting Series, Shiraz

Birthday Wishes, The Wine Tasting Series, Muscat

Dad Jeans, The Wine Tasting Series, Vignoles

Novellas:

The Devy Man, A Horror Novella

www.ingramcontent.com/pod-product-compliance
Lightning Source LLC
Chambersburg PA
CBHW030327010826
48973CB00004B/893